Dances & Dreams on Diamond Street

Also by Craig Revel Horwood

All Balls and Glitter

Tales from the Dance Floor

In Strictest Confidence

Dances & Dreams on Diamond Street

CRAIG REVEL HORWOOD

Michael O'Mara Books Limited

First published in Great Britain in 2020 by
Michael O'Mara Books Limited
9 Lion Yard
Tremadoc Road
London SW4 7NQ

A CIP catalogue record for this book is available from the British Library.

Papers used by Michael O'Mara Books Limited are natural, recyclable products made from wood grown in sustainable forests. The manufacturing processes conform to the environmental regulations of the country of origin.

ISBN: 978-1- 78929-238-1 in hardback print format
ISBN: 978-1-78929-249-7 in ebook format

1 2 3 4 5 6 7 8 9 10

Designed and typeset by Claire Cater
Printed and bound by CPI Group (UK) Ltd, Croydon, CR0 4YY

www.mombooks.com

MIX
Paper from
responsible sources
FSC® C020471

Dedication

I dedicate this work of fiction to all the incredible bohemian, nonconformist, unconventional, alternative, eccentric and idiosyncratic *'Heartbreakers'* of 49 Pratt Street, Camden Town NW1, aptly christened 'The Heartbreak Hotel', where residents lived together in peace, harmony and love – sometimes – but always dreaming, creating and living life to its fullest, unashamedly being themselves. They were one of the most loving families I still have the pleasure of loving, some of whom are sadly no longer with us, but still missed and loved all the same.

'The Heartbreak Hotel' ran for twenty glorious years 1992-2012 before it was sold on and eventually turned into modern flats. The souls that graced its rooms will live there for ever and their ghosts will haunt the winding 'rabbit warren' (as Sir Cameron Mackintosh described it once) corridors for eternity.

This is for you darlings! I give you,

Dances and Dreams on Diamond Street

June

1994

One

It was Sunday lunchtime and, to quote one of his most sarcastic former dance teachers, Danny looked as if he was chewing on a wasp that had been pickled in vinegar. There were about a million things he'd rather be doing with his one precious day off than letting complete strangers rifle around his bedroom. His bedroom was his sanctuary, the one place on this earth where he could fully relax and which was guaranteed to be imbecile-free. But not any more.

'So, this wouldn't be my actual bedroom?' Clive from Chelmsford asked, peering at Danny through glasses as thick as milk-bottle bottoms.

'No, this is *my* actual bedroom,' Danny replied through gritted teeth. How many more times did he need to explain this? 'Your bedroom would be the room next door.'

The thought of Clive and his greasy anorak and flaky skin doing God knows what on the other side of the wall sent a shudder through him.

'It's exactly the same shape and size, I just can't show it to you at the moment as it's having some, uh, renovations done.' Danny shuddered again as he thought of what was actually going on next door.

'Would my room have a four-poster bed, too?' Clive asked, going over to Danny's bed and stroking his stubby little fingers over the quilt.

It took every fibre of Danny's being not to lunge at Clive and drag him kicking and screaming from the room.

'No. That's *my* bed,' Danny hissed. He'd bought the bed about a month after moving into 27 Diamond Street, after watching the Kevin Costner movie, *Field of Dreams*. He wasn't really into baseball, but Costner was cute, and Danny really liked the concept of building something in order to help make a dream come true. In Costner's case this had meant building a baseball field to summon the ghosts of baseballing greats. In Danny's case it had been building a fabulous bed. A year later, he was still waiting for the rest of the dream to come true.

'That's good, 'cos heights make me anxious.' Clive sniffed loudly and went over to inspect the fireplace.

Danny frowned. His four-poster was slightly higher than the average bed but only by a matter of inches. It was hardly like scaling a cliff face. It wasn't as if he got altitude sickness every time he went to sleep. He was about to explain this to Clive when he stopped himself. He didn't have to justify his bed of dreams to anyone, least of all to a slimy little slug-man who by the smell of things had never encountered the concept of antiperspirant.

'What's this?' Clive asked, pointing at one of Danny's awards on the mantelpiece. It was Danny's most prized award – the prestigious West End Best Male Dancer – which he had won for his role in *Cats* in 1984.

I swear to God if you touch that I will ... Danny took a deep breath. 'It's an award. *My* award ... and no, your room won't come with one.'

Not that the room next door was ever going to belong to Clive. It would be a cold day in hell before Danny let that happen.

'Right then, I guess you've seen enough,' he said, hurrying over to the bedroom door and flinging it open.

'Why have you got a sewing machine?' Clearly unable to take a hint, Clive moved over to the antique Singer displayed in the bay window.

If you touch it I will crush you, Danny thought. 'It belonged to my mam.' He instantly felt like kicking himself. The sewing machine's backstory was none of this imbecile's business.

The loud trill of the telephone echoed up the stairs, causing both men to jump.

'I'm very sorry,' Danny lied, 'but I'm going to have to get that.'

'OK,' Clive said, moving over to inspect the bookshelves.

'So you're going to have to leave.'

The ringing got shriller, forming a discordant din with the blood now pounding in Danny's ears. On the landing above, a door creaked open.

'Is anyone going to, like, get the phone?' came Pete the Poet's Eeyore-like drone from upstairs. 'I'm trying to write.'

Trying being the operative word, Danny felt like yelling back. Pete had been on the dole forever and spent most of his days composing poems – dire dirges lamenting the misery of his existence. Danny bit his lip. He couldn't afford to piss off any more of his housemates – that's what had got him into this current mess.

'Come on,' he said to Clive, adopting the no-nonsense, teacher-style tone he'd developed since moving into choreography.

Clive shuffled out of the room, picking at a scab on the back of his hand as he went. Danny shut the door firmly behind him and made a mental note to nab a stick of sage from Trippy Lil and give his room a thorough cleansing as soon as this whole hideous experience was over. Overtaking Clive, he ran down the creaky staircase into the hall, and grabbed the receiver from the phone on the wall.

'Hello,' he barked, tucking the receiver into the crook of his neck. The phone cord was long enough to stretch from the wall to the front door. Danny took full advantage of this now, opening the front door and ushering Clive out on to the street.

'But what about …?' Clive stammered.

'I'll call you,' Danny mouthed, making a mental note to burn Clive's number along with Trippy Lil's sage.

'Hello,' a woman's voice said at the other end of the line.

'Hello,' Danny said, closing the front door behind Clive and sighing with relief.

'I'm calling about the room to rent – the double room.' The woman sounded young and her voice had a soft Scottish lilt. 'I saw the advert in

Time Out. Is it still available?'

'It most certainly is.'

One of the doors leading off the hallway opened and Lachlan's tousled head appeared. He was wearing a T-shirt and boxers and his eyes were bleary with sleep.

'Could you keep it down a bit, mate?' he said in his low Australian drawl. 'I've got another night shift this evening.'

'Sorry,' Danny whispered and he pulled the phone cord into the kitchen.

'That's great,' the girl on the other end of the line said. 'Would it be possible to come and view it today?'

Danny sat down at the kitchen table, which for once in its life – or its life at 27 Diamond Street at least – was clear of all detritus. Danny had swept all of the mess – the smeared wine glasses, ringed coffee mugs, overflowing ashtrays and assorted papers and magazines – into one of the cupboards five minutes before the first viewing this morning. He'd also squirted some 'Ocean Spray' cleaner into the downstairs toilet and invested in an 'Arabian Nights' air freshener to put on the cistern. As a result, the downstairs toilet now smelled like some kind of beach-side harem, but it was still a vast improvement on the usual aroma of stale urine and spliff – apparently Pete got his best ideas when he took a crap while stoned. As far as Danny was concerned, this explained *everything* about Pete's poetry.

'I'm not sure if I'm able to fit in any more viewings today,' Danny said.

The truth was, he could fit plenty in but all he wanted to do right now was go straight back to bed and pretend this hellish morning had never happened.

'How about tomorrow morning?' he asked.

'Ah, that's a shame,' the woman sighed. 'We've both got auditions tomorrow so that might be a bit tricky. We really don't want to miss out on the room. Camden's my favourite part of London, it's so quirky and cool and …'

While the woman wittered on about her love of all things Camden, two key words echoed around Danny's head. '*We*' and '*auditions*'. Did this mean she was part of a couple? Couples were good, as they brought down everyone's share of the bills. And auditions were good, too. This implied they worked in the entertainment industry. In Danny's dream houseshare, all of the tenants worked in the entertainment industry and there were no paranoid poets or grumpy Aussie nurses who worked shifts. Not that he had much of a problem with Lachlan. The Aussie kept himself to himself and always paid his rent on time.

'Are you a couple looking to rent the room, then?' Danny cut in, just as the woman was about to tell him her favourite stall in Camden Market.

'Yes, me and my boyfriend, Justin. Would that be OK?'

'Absolutely. Do you mind me asking what you do for a living?' Danny reached into the kitchen cupboard and pulled out an ashtray containing a half-smoked cigarette from last night. He'd managed to resist smoking all through his life as a dancer, but two years ago, when he turned thirty and made the transition into choreography – and had his heart broken – he had decided to embrace the dark side.

'We're dancers – but we're always in work,' the girl quickly added. 'We've been touring on cruise ships for ages so we have quite a bit of money saved.'

Danny couldn't help giving a wry grin. He knew all about the financial roller coaster that came with the dancing life. 'I work in the dance world, too,' he said.

'You do?' the woman exclaimed. 'That's amazing. Clearly this is destiny!'

Danny lit the cigarette and inhaled deeply. While her exuberance was a welcome change from Scabby Clive, it was a bit much for a Sunday lunchtime. He heard the low hum of a male voice at the other end of the line. The boyfriend, he assumed.

'The guy advertising the room works in dance, too,' the woman explained. 'I'm sorry, I didn't catch your name.'

'It's Danny. Danny Hall.' He leaned back in the chair and took another drag on his cigarette.

'Hi, Danny. I'm Catriona. But my friends call me Cat. You can call me Cat. I have a feeling this is all meant to be.'

Two

Cat put the phone back on the receiver and rifled through the newspapers on Justin's parents' coffee table. Justin's parents were so posh they did things like have 'supper' instead of tea and preferred playing bridge to bingo, so the chances of her finding what she was looking for were slim. But to her delight she spied the red top of a tabloid nestled between the broadsheets. She pulled out the colour supplement and flicked to the horoscopes.

'Yes!' she exclaimed as she scanned the forecast for Taurus.

'What?' Justin muttered from where he was standing by the fireplace, checking his hair in the ornate mirror hanging above the mantelpiece.

'My stars say it's a perfect time for new beginnings,' Cat replied, editing out the bit where Mystic Meg predicted that she might find love at a car boot sale, especially if she wore yellow.

'I don't know why you believe in all that nonsense,' Justin said, pulling his mouth into an exaggerated grin and examining his perfect teeth.

That's not what you used to say, Cat thought, remembering how, when she and Justin first got together, they'd spend lazy Sunday mornings in bed, drinking coffee, eating croissants and reading each other's horoscopes in funny voices. Instead she stayed quiet and had a quick read of the forecast for Scorpio, Justin's sign. Instantly, she regretted it, as it was all about Mars bringing tension and conflict.

'Yeah, well, I think it's a good time for new beginnings,' she said firmly, trying to convince herself as much as Justin. 'What are the chances of the man on the phone being a dancer, too?'

Justin shrugged.

'He said we can go round whenever we're ready.'

'What, now?' Justin turned to face her, his mouth curling down. It never ceased to amaze Cat how dramatically Justin's model good looks were ruined the instant he gave one of his sulky frowns.

'Yes. Don't worry, it won't take long. It's only a couple of stops on the Tube. You did say last night that we could spend today room hunting.'

Cat felt a familiar anxiety building inside of her. Ever since Cat and Julian's last cruise ship gig finished a fortnight ago, they'd been staying at Justin's parents' Hampstead home. What with Justin's mum's obsessive cleaning and his dad's constant, 'I'm not a racist but ...' running commentary about all that was wrong with the world, it had been the longest two weeks of Cat's life.

'OK, then.' Justin gave the kind of tortured sigh you'd expect from someone who'd just agreed to eat a plate of raw liver. He'd been sighing like this a lot lately. Cat was spending a great deal of mental energy trying not to think about what this might mean. Maybe once they had a place of their own things would get better again.

'Oh, shit!' Justin exclaimed, looking back at his reflection.

'What?'

'I've got a grey hair in my left eyebrow!'

Cat went over and examined his flawless reflection. 'No, it's just a really blond hair.'

The corners of his mouth turned up again, and it was like the sun appearing from behind a cloud.

Cat and Justin emerged from the depths of Camden Town Underground station on a wave of tourists, shoppers and sightseers.

Blinking at the sudden brightness of the summer sunshine, Cat took her battered *A–Z* from her bag and studied the page for Camden Town. According to the map, Diamond Street was tucked away behind the high street, by the lock. The lock was her favourite part of Camden, and Cat couldn't help thinking that this was another sign that they were destined to have the room. Not that she dared say this to Justin.

The scowl returned to Justin's face as he barged through a gaggle of Japanese tourists who'd stopped in the middle of the pavement by some graffiti on the wall. Their hands all went to the huge cameras hanging around their necks and they started snapping photos of the graffiti.

'It's so annoying when they stop like that,' Justin hissed.

'They're on holiday. They don't understand the Keep Moving at All Costs rule,' Cat said with a chuckle.

She hadn't been aware of this rule, either, when she'd first arrived in London from Scotland. She'd soon learned, though – the day she had the audacity to stand still on the left-hand side of the down escalator at Piccadilly Circus Underground. The glares and tuts she'd received had actually made her fear for her life. But now she was used to it she actually liked London's impatience, and she understood it. There was so much to do and see here that there was no time for dawdling.

Half running to keep up with Justin's stride, Cat felt the tension from the past couple of weeks begin to ebb from her body. It was impossible to feel down in Camden. It fizzed and crackled with so much life, from the basslines pounding through the open shop doorways to the assortment of weird and wonderful hairstyles and outfits streaming along the pavements.

'Can we go and see that film this week?' Cat asked, pointing to a billboard on the other side of the street. The film was a recent release called *Four Weddings and a Funeral*. According to the reviews, it was about a couple who were fated to be together in spite of the odds. It sounded like just the kind of inspiration she and Justin needed.

'What? Oh, OK.' Justin's gaze drifted from the poster to a willowy blonde sashaying towards them. She was clad in a lime-green crop top, lilac cycling shorts and hi-tops.

Cat felt a sudden burst of anger, red and hot, making her cheeks burn. She glanced at the darkened window of the shop they were passing and, as she glimpsed her reflection, the words 'a tad too big' rang through her mind. The words she'd been told at an audition last week. 'I'm sorry, we were looking for someone slightly more petite,' the casting director had said with a dismissive shake of her head. 'You're a tad too big.'

The blonde who'd captured Justin's attention wasn't 'too big', though. Not even a tad, with her concave stomach and jutting ribs. Justin slowed his pace as they drew level with the woman. Cat didn't, though. She marched right into him, clipping the back of his ankle with the toe of her shoe.

'Ow!' he yelped.

'Oh, I'm sorry,' Cat muttered.

Diamond Street wasn't quite as sparkly as the name suggested, but Cat didn't mind. She liked the fact that each of the four-storey townhouses were in vastly differing states of decor and repair. She thought the peeling paintwork, crumbling brickwork and faded net curtains added character, something that was seriously lacking in the pristine crescent where Justin's parents lived. She loved the different aromas lingering on the warm air, too. The wafts of incense and curry and food frying.

'Here we are,' she said cheerily, as they reached number 27.

The front door was painted flamingo pink. Next to it there was a large bay window lined with a greying net curtain. As Cat pressed the doorbell she noticed a handwritten sign above the letterbox saying: NO

LEAFLETS, FREE PAPERS OR JEHOVAH'S BLOODY WITNESSES.

'I'm not sure about this,' Justin said as they waited for someone to answer the door. 'It's a bit … grotty.'

'We haven't seen inside yet,' Cat replied, trying to keep her voice carefree.

They had to like this room. She couldn't stand a second longer at his parents'. She pressed the doorbell again.

'All right, all right,' a deep male voice with an Australian accent boomed from inside the house. The door opened to reveal a man in a T-shirt and boxer shorts. His sandy hair was tousled as if he'd just been asleep.

Cat checked her watch. It was almost two.

'Yes?' the man asked, looking them both up and down.

'We're here about the room,' Cat explained.

'Oh, right. Come in.' The man opened the door wider.

They followed him into a narrow hallway. A bare bulb hung from the ceiling and a huge pile of junk mail and free newspapers teetered in the corner behind the door. Clearly the sign above the letterbox hadn't been that effective.

'Danny!' The Australian man yelled up a narrow flight of stairs at the end of the hall.

'Yeah?' A voice replied from somewhere upstairs.

'There's some people here about the room to rent.'

The man turned back to Cat and Justin. 'Danny will show you around,' he said, before disappearing into a room off the hall.

Cat sighed. He didn't seem very friendly. Hopefully Danny would be more welcoming. A man came running down the stairs, taking them two at a time. He was tall and wiry with broad shoulders and dark, wavy hair.

'Catriona?' he said, looking at her before casting his gaze upon Justin. As so often happened, his gaze lingered. Cat was used to it by now. Justin's beauty seemed to mesmerize both men and women.

'Yes, I'm Cat,' she replied. 'And this is Justin.'

'Good to meet you, I'm Danny.' He shook their hands. 'The room that's for rent is currently being redecorated but I can show you around my own room. It's pretty much identical when it comes to the size and shape.'

'Cool,' Cat replied.

'How many people live here?' Justin asked as they followed Danny up the stairs.

'Four at the moment, but we've got six rooms in total so we're hoping to get a couple more – or three more if you pair are sharing.'

The man had a northern accent. It was quite faint, but it sounded to Cat like Liverpudlian. She smiled; she'd always liked Scousers. This was another good sign.

They followed Danny up to the second floor and he led them into a room at the front of the house. As soon as Cat stepped inside she couldn't help gasping. With its plum-coloured walls, green velvet curtains and four-poster bed, the room was like an illustration from a fairytale.

'This is beautiful,' she whispered, standing in the middle of the room and turning full circle to drink it all in. There were so many interesting antiques and knick-knacks that Cat had to stuff her hands in the pockets of her dungarees to stop herself from touching anything.

'Thank you.' Danny's expression visibly softened.

Cat glanced at Justin to try to see what he was making of it. His gaze came to rest on the mantelpiece.

'Is that a West End Award?' he said, pointing to an award in the shape of a glass dance shoe.

'It certainly is,' Danny nodded.

Justin went over to the fireplace to have a look. Cat noticed Danny tense slightly but thankfully Justin didn't touch it.

'You were in *Cats*?' he asked, turning back to Danny. His earlier reticence was now replaced by a look of awe.

'Yep.' Danny shrugged as if it was no big deal, but Cat could tell he was pleased at the recognition.

'Are you still a dancer?' she asked.

'Oh no, darling. I'm thirty-two, which as you know is about a hundred and five in dance years. I'm a choreographer now, for my sins.' Danny sat down on the edge of the bed.

Cat tried to stop her heart from sinking. She knew all too well about dance years. It wasn't just her weight that had been stressing her out lately.

At twenty-five, her age was also starting to work against her in auditions.

'So, you're both dancers, then?' Danny asked.

Cat nodded.

'Yes. I trained at the Royal Academy,' Justin said.

Danny turned back to Cat. 'And what about you?'

'Me? Oh, nothing so glamorous, I'm afraid. I studied dance back in my hometown, Aberdeen. I came down to London when I was twenty-one. Got a few chorus roles. I've been working on cruise ships for the past couple of years – that's where we met.' She nodded at Justin.

'Yeah, well, I was only doing the cruises because I wanted to see a bit of the world,' Justin said quickly. 'I've come back to London to get some serious roles.'

'We,' Cat muttered.

'What's that?' Justin asked.

'*We've* come back to London to get some more serious roles.' Cat's face flushed.

'Of course, honey,' Justin put his arm round her and pulled her close. 'Well, I think this place is great. I'm in.'

Cat looked at him in surprise.

'Don't you want to see the rest of the house, the kitchen and bathroom?' Danny asked.

'Sure.' Justin treated Danny to one of his boyish grins.

Cat gave a sigh of relief. She wasn't sure what had brought on Justin's sudden change of mood, but if it meant they would be moving out of his parents' house she was truly grateful.

Lachlan went into the kitchen and banged the cold tap three times. This wasn't some kind of obsessive-compulsive ritual – it was the only way you could get the tap to work. One of the many quirks of life at 27 Diamond

Street. He filled the kettle with the water that was now coming from the tap in fits and spurts and fetched the teabags down from the shelf. With all the comings and goings in the house today there was no point trying to get any more sleep. He opened the cupboard to get a cup and was hit on the head by an avalanche of magazines.

'What the hell?' he yelped.

The cupboard was full to the brim with assorted crap and dirty dishes. Lachlan scratched his head, and then the penny dropped. This must have been Danny's idea of cleaning up before the house viewings.

'Strewth!'

Lachlan gingerly took out one of the dirty mugs. Although it was ringed with old tea stains, there wasn't anything growing in the bottom, and in this place that was always a bonus. Lachlan scrubbed the cup clean and plopped two teabags inside. This was definitely shaping up to be an extreme caffeine day.

Once the tea was made he sat down at the table. He wasn't sure he'd ever seen it completely clear of crap before. It was slightly disconcerting. He sighed and shook his head. When he was growing up in Queensland he'd never imagined ending up in a house like this. He'd never imagined ending up in London. But one thing he'd learned at the ripe old age of twenty-seven was that your plans and the plans life has for you can be hugely different things.

When he'd come to view his room at 27 Diamond Street almost a year ago shock was still numbing all of his senses. He couldn't have cared less what state the house was in or who he'd be sharing a kitchen with. All he wanted was a roof over his head and a bed to crash in. The fact that the guy in the room above him was a total party animal didn't bother him in the slightest. Ditto the fact that there was a poet with Morrissey-levels of gloom living in the attic. And as for Lil … her permanently trippy state hadn't even registered with him. But recently the numbness seemed to be fading and Lachlan wasn't sure if this was a good or a bad thing.

He heard footsteps on the stairs and the sound of chatter. It must be the couple who'd come to view the room. He looked down at his faded Pink Floyd T-shirt and boxers. *Shit*, he hoped they weren't going to view the kitchen. He was about to get up and head back to his room when the door opened and Danny and the couple came in.

'And this is the kitchen,' said Danny. ''Scuse the mess.'

What mess? Lachlan thought to himself. *The mess is all in the cupboard.* His skin prickled with indignation. Was Danny referring to him?

'Oh, this is great!' the girl said, coming in and looking around.

She smiled at Lachlan. Her hair was deep auburn and her skin the colour of cream, which made her green eyes even more striking. Lachlan gave her a tense smile and looked down at the table.

'I'm Cat,' she said, holding out a hand. 'And this is Justin.' She pointed at the guy with her. He looked as if he'd stepped straight off the pages of a clothing catalogue, with his chiselled jaw, buttery blond hair and pale-lemon jumper draped over his shoulders. He was the kind of bloke Lachlan's mates back home would say had got tickets on himself. Lachlan took an instant dislike to him.

'G'day.' Lachlan shook Cat's hand and nodded in acknowledgment at Justin.

'We're going to be your new housemates,' Cat continued.

'What, both of you?' Lachlan couldn't help asking.

'Yes, we're going to share the room upstairs, as soon as Danny's finished doing the redecorating.'

'Redecorating?' Lachlan raised his eyebrows at Danny.

'Yes,' Danny replied with a knowing look. 'You know, the wallpapering and stuff.'

'Right.' Danny clearly hadn't told them what had actually happened in the room then, not that Lachlan could blame him.

'When do you think it will be ready?' Cat asked.

'By the end of this week,' Danny replied.

'That's great.'

Lachlan wondered how many times Cat said 'great' in a day. He was willing to bet it reached the hundreds. She was the polar opposite of Pete the Poet.

'So, are you a dancer, too?' Mr Mail Order Man said, sitting down at the table opposite Lachlan.

'No, I'm a nurse,' Lachlan replied.

'A nurse? But you're …' Justin trailed off but Lachlan knew what he was about to say. Some people still couldn't get their head around the concept of male nurses.

'I'm what?' Might as well make him sweat a bit.

'Nothing.' Justin looked away. Lachlan saw Cat shoot him a look.

'That's great,' she said, smiling warmly. 'You nurses do such a brilliant job.'

'Thank you.' Lachlan downed the rest of his tea and took the mug over to the sink.

'Lovely to meet you,' he said, as he left the room.

'Great to meet you, too,' Cat replied.

Lachlan stepped back into the refuge of his bedroom, shutting the door firmly behind him. Then he looked around the room, at the unmade bed, the threadbare carpet and bare white walls, and he felt another uncomfortable stab of reality piercing his numbness. How had it all come to this?

Jewel was having another one of his stress dreams. In this one he was being chased along a dark, windswept street by a Tyrannosaurus rex wearing a bowler hat and a man's suit. To make matters worse, Jewel was wearing a pair of insanely high stiletto boots and a skin-tight pencil skirt, so no matter how fast he tried to run it was as if he was standing still. He felt something prodding his back and turned to see the T-rex stabbing at him with an umbrella.

'Leave me alone!' he yelled.

He sat bolt upright in a cold sweat, breathing heavily. Slowly, the room came into view around him, like a Polaroid photo developing. He wasn't being chased by a suit-wearing dinosaur, he was on his friend Cynthia's sofa-bed. That was why his back was aching. The pesky loose spring had been sticking into his spine, not an umbrella.

He rubbed his back and looked at the clock on the wall. It was two-thirty. Crap. Jewel swung his thin, pale legs off the sofa-bed and rubbed his eyes. Cynthia had made a big point of telling him he could crash at her place for as long as he needed, but there'd been signs recently that he was outstaying his welcome. Yesterday, Cynthia had made a drama about not being able to use the living room to host a Tupperware party, as Jewel's 'stuff would all get in the way'. The fact that all of Jewel's worldly goods could fit into the one battered suitcase he brought with him seemed to completely pass Cynthia by.

Jewel had meant to get up early this morning and go out for the day to get out of Cynthia's way. But once again it had taken him ages to drift off. Daylight had been creeping in beneath the curtains when he had finally succumbed to a fitful sleep.

Jewel grabbed the copy of *Time Out* from the coffee table and turned to the listings in the back. He needed to crack on with finding a place of his own – or at least a room of his own. Now that he'd landed his first proper job since arriving in London, he'd be able to afford something. He scanned the columns of rooms to rent until he found one in his price range. A house in Camden was advertising two rooms for rent. The double room was too expensive, but he could just about manage the rent for the single. He picked up the phone and dialled the number. It rang for so long he was about to hang up when finally there was an answer.

'Hello,' a man's voice barked at the other end.

'Oh, hello, I'm calling about the room to rent,' Jewel said, crossing his fingers that it was still available.

'Which one?' the man replied. 'The double's just gone.'

'The single.'

'Yep, that's still available.'

'Cool. Can I come and see it?'

'Sure. When were you thinking?'

'As soon as possible.'

Jewel thought he heard the man tutting, but it could have been interference on the line.

'All right, how about this afternoon?'

'Yes, I can do that.' Jewel gave a sigh of relief. At least now he'd be able to tell Cynthia he was going to view a room, and that a return to her Tupperware glory days was in sight.

'What's your name?' the man asked.

'Jewel – Jewel Brown,' he stammered. The name still felt weird on his lips.

'Jewel?' He could hear the surprise in the man's voice.

'Yes,' Jewel replied, trying to ignore the insecure chatter now going on in his brain.

'OK, great. My name's Danny and the address is 27 Diamond Street. I'll see you soon.'

Before Jewel could reply there was a click and the line went dead.

'Yes, see you,' he murmured, and put the receiver back in place.

Three

Danny took a deep breath and flung open the door. Even though he'd dowsed himself in aftershave, the stench of putrid fish instantly overwhelmed him. It was so strong now it was more than just a smell, it was as if it had become a being in its own right – some kind of eerie entity. But where the hell was it coming from? Danny scanned the empty room.

After Cat and Justin had said that they wanted to move in as soon as possible, Danny had persuaded Lachlan to help him try to get to the bottom of the mystery once and for all. Actually, he hadn't persuaded Lachlan, he'd had to pay him – in two cases of beer from the offie. Those Aussies drove a hard bargain. They'd spent the rest of Sunday stripping the room of its remaining furniture and pulling up the carpet. Danny had been convinced that the smell was coming from beneath the floorboards. He'd imagined discovering a giant fish corpse rotting away there. But there was nothing.

One thing he did know for certain was that the smell had to be the work of the previous tenant, an act of revenge for what Lachlan was now calling 'The Barbecue Massacre'. But how had he done it?

The previous tenant had been a humourless man named Brendan O'Toole – possibly the only Irishman in existence who didn't understand the concept of the craic – who'd moved into 27 Diamond Street just before Danny. This seemed to make Brendan think that he was the boss of the house, even though Trippy Lil had lived there longer than anyone. He liked to leave passive-aggressive notes all over the place, saying things like 'The handle on the cistern is meant for flushing' on the toilet and 'If it's on the top shelf it doesn't belong to you' on the door of the fridge. And if this wasn't bad enough, he was pretentious to the point of puke-inducing, dressing in cravats and suits made from shiny, two-tone material, so he looked like some sort of pound-shop version of Oscar Wilde. He even walked with a cane, despite there being nothing wrong with his legs. Well, he *used* to walk with a cane.

Danny sighed. It was the cane that had caused all of this. A couple of weekends ago, some of his old dance crew from *Cats* had come over and, after one too many flaming sambucas, they had decided to have a barbecue. It was actually Lachlan's fault. He'd come into the kitchen just as Danny and his friends were talking about cooking up some sausages they'd found on the top shelf of the fridge.

'Why don't you have a barbie?' Lachlan had suggested, before going back to his room.

Danny and his friends were nothing if not enterprising. They'd built an impromptu barbie in the backyard from some old bricks they found in a skip across the road. But the one thing they were lacking was kindling. Danny had cast his eyes around the kitchen and spied Brendan's cane leaning against the wall. Ten minutes later it was chopped up and aflame, and the sausages were grilling away merrily. Danny had been planning on pleading ignorance when Brendan started looking for his cane. What he hadn't considered was the stupid, parrot-head handle made of brass, which Brendan had found in the smouldering remains of the barbie. There had then followed the longest tantrum ever thrown by a fully grown man, culminating in Brendan moving out a week later.

'You'll regret the day you cremated my cane,' was the last thing Brendan hissed at Danny before flouncing from the house.

At the time Danny had shrugged it off with an 'Er, I don't think so!' But then the day after Brendan moved out the smell moved in, and had been getting worse ever since.

'Where are you?' Danny sighed. The room was now completely bare. The only thing that remained were the floor-length velvet curtains, but there was no way they could contain the rotting remains of a fish. Could they? Danny went over to the curtains and gave them a nervous sniff. They smelled musty – and fishy. Very fishy. He lifted them up and the waft grew stronger. He crouched down and brought the bottom of the curtain to his nose.

'Ewww!' he exclaimed. The stench was unbearable.

Keeping the curtain at arm's length this time, he examined the hem. It looked as if it had been freshly stitched. Then he felt the hem. It was bumpy. Like there were little lumps of something inside of it.

'You sick bastard!' Danny exclaimed.

He pulled on the curtain so hard the rail came off the wall. But Danny didn't care. He'd finally discovered the source of the smell, and now he wanted it gone for good. He bundled the curtains up and raced down the stairs, along the narrow passageway to the back of the house and out into the yard, where he dropped the curtains. Then he went to the kitchen and grabbed a pair of scissors from the drawer. Back in the yard, he sliced through the hem's stitching.

'Euuurgh!' The hem was full of little, grey, stinking lumps. Prawn-shaped little, grey, stinking lumps. Danny pictured Brendan hunched over like some 1990s version of Rumpelstiltskin, cackling as he stitched them inside the curtain.

'Unbelievable!' Danny piled the curtains onto the remains of the barbie and set fire to them with his lighter.

'Ooh, are we having another barbecue?'

Danny turned to see Trippy Lil standing in the doorway. She was wearing her long, rainbow-coloured kaftan and bright red clogs, and her silvery hair hung in a loose braid over her shoulder. As always, her eyes were lined with kohl. It didn't matter what time of day or night, Danny had never seen her without her sixties-style cat eye make-up.

'No, we're having a cremation,' Danny replied, turning back to stoke the fire.

Lil came and stood beside him. 'Who died?'

'About a hundred prawns. They were inside the curtains,' Danny added. In anyone else this would have sparked an instant flurry of questions, but not Lil. Lil was entirely unflappable.

'Bummer,' she said, reaching into her robe pocket and pulling out her tin of tobacco. 'Reminds me of the time Keith and I found a crab in Ronnie's guitar case.'

Danny looked at her and raised his eyebrows.

This was the reason Lil was so unfazed by things. Apparently, she'd been a wild child in the Swinging Sixties, and in many ways she was still there, still swinging.

'Ciggie, darling?' she asked, taking a pack of papers from the tin.

'Yeah, go on.' At least the smell of cigarettes might drown out the stink of burning fish now filling the yard.

Danny sniffed his wrist for a waft of aftershave but instead of comforting him it prompted an unwelcome flashback: Paris, the bright red lights of the Moulin Rouge, Gabriel's arm around his shoulders, strong and … Danny snapped himself back to the present. He'd rather smell putrid prawns than be taken on a tour of painful memories.

'Isn't fire marvellous?' Lil said in her husky London drawl, gazing into the flames. 'Don't you just love the way it burns away all of the crap?'

Danny stared into the flames that were now tearing through the curtains. 'I guess so. I've never really thought of it like that before.'

'Maybe that's what you need to do, then.' Lil handed him a rollie. 'Imagine it's not the curtains and the prawns burning. Imagine it's all the crap you need to let go of.'

Danny pictured flinging his memories of Gabriel onto the fire. The walks by the Seine. The apartment in Montmartre. The fucking aftershave Gabriel had given him.

'Are you picturing it?' Lil asked.

Danny nodded.

'Good, isn't it?'

Danny grinned. It did feel strangely liberating.

'Don't let the bastards get you down, as my good friend Kris used to sing to me.' Lil gave one of her throaty laughs. 'Burn them instead.'

Danny nodded and stoked the fire. And they both stood there cackling like a pair of Macbeth's witches.

The audition was in a studio just off the Euston Road. As Cat ran to keep up with Justin's long-legged stride, she started repeating today's affirmation in her head: *I am talented. I am beautiful. I am strong.* She'd read an article about the power of positive affirmations in last month's *Cosmopolitan*. According to a life coach called Destiny Bloom, affirmations had the power to make all of your dreams come true.

But the awkward truth was, Cat wasn't really sure if she wanted to get a part in the show they were about to audition for. It would mean working in Berlin for almost six months and, after two years of working on cruise ships, she really wanted to stay in the UK for a while. Plus, they'd just found the room to rent in Camden.

She followed Justin over a crossing, just as the green man was turning red. A black cab honked at her. 'Get out of the road, you idiot!' the cabbie yelled through his open window.

Cat's face instantly flushed. *You're so stupid, why didn't you look where you were going?* her inner voice started berating her, before she remembered her affirmation. *I am talented. I am beautiful. I am strong.* But the words felt hollow.

'Hurry up,' Justin called over his shoulder. He always got really uptight before an audition. Cat knew this, but sometimes it was hard not to take it personally. Sometimes it would be nice if he actually acknowledged that she got stressed out, too, and if he would offer some kind of moral support.

She followed him down a narrow side street. The studio was halfway down, sandwiched between a greasy spoon café and a pub called the Brewers Arms. Even though it was only just gone eleven, a handful of drinkers were already sitting at the tables outside, their faces raised, soaking up the warm sunshine. They looked so happy and carefree.

Cat's stomach churned. *I am talented. I am beautiful. I am strong.*

As Justin looked for something in his bag, she pushed the studio door, but it wouldn't budge. Then she saw a sign right in front of her saying PULL. *I am stupid. I am thick. I am an idiot.*

Inside, the corridors were bustling with dancers. Instantly, Cat fell victim to a serious case of comparisonitis. She knew she should stay inside her own mental bubble and not pay attention to anyone else, but she just couldn't help it. These people were her competition, and she felt the overwhelming urge to see how she sized up. *I am old. I am huge. I am fat,* her inner voice started taunting as she looked at the other women warming up. All she could see were concave stomachs, jutting ribs and willowy limbs. All she could see was shiny hair and glowing skin.

Once the dancers had been given their numbers, they were ushered into the studio.

Cat closed her eyes, trying to tune into her body. What if Justin got a job and she didn't? She pushed the thought from her mind. They'd already agreed that if one of them didn't get accepted then neither of them would go to Berlin. She took a deep breath. It was all going to be OK. Whatever happened they'd still be together. She opened her eyes and glanced across at Justin. He was doing a hamstring stretch and gazing into the middle distance. Or was he? She followed the direction of his gaze to a willowy brunette who was warming up at the front. She was one of those dancers who brought her own spotlight. *Look at me! Look at me!* her body seemed to scream, as she effortlessly stretched her right leg parallel to her head. *SHE is talented. SHE is beautiful. SHE is strong,* Cat thought.

Cat sighed and looked away. She never used to get like this in auditions. She always used to get a perverse sense of enjoyment from them. Back then, the nerves she felt were way closer to excitement than to dread. She couldn't quite work out what had prompted the change. It was as if she was having some kind of midlife crisis in the middle of her twenties. *Get a grip,* she told herself as a lithe black man wearing a Pineapple Studios top and bright purple leggings strode to the front of the studio.

'Alrighty then, are you guys ready to show me what you've got?' he called.

All around her the dancers whooped and cheered. Cat stayed silent and felt herself begin to shrink.

Afterwards, they spilled out onto the pavement and into the warm afternoon sun.

'That was awesome!' Justin exclaimed. 'I can't believe I've got a callback.'

'Yeah, but …' Cat tailed off.

'What?' Justin looked at her, his eyes shining and his smile wide. 'Shall we do something? I know. How about we get something to eat and then go and see that film you've been going on about. The four funerals one?'

'*Four Weddings and a Funeral,*' Cat corrected him.

'Yep, that one. Let's jump on a bus to Leicester Square, see it there.'

He put his arm round her shoulders. This was the Justin Cat had fallen in love with, all eager and excited and puppyish. He pulled her close. 'Love you, Scottie.'

Cat felt a shiver run up her spine. It had been a long time since he'd used his nickname for her. Come to think of it, it had been a long time since he'd said 'I love you', or at least said it first.

'Love you, too,' she replied. But as they headed off to the bus stop an unsaid question hung over her like the thought bubble from a comic strip. *Why are you so excited about a callback when I didn't get one, too?*

As Jewel pressed the buzzer by the stage door he felt a tingle of excitement course through him.

'Yep?' a woman's voice barked through the intercom.

'Hi, it's Jewel. Jewel Brown. I'm here for work in, in Wardrobe,' he stammered.

'I'm sorry, did you say you're in a wardrobe?' the voice replied.

'No, I work in Wardrobe. I'm Jewel Brown, I'm a dresser,' Jewel replied, his face flushing. When he'd left Cynthia's earlier he'd felt so excited. He'd seen today as an important marker. It was Day One of his new life, the life he was always meant to have been living. But now his newfound confidence was rapidly unravelling. He sounded like a stammering, nervous wreck. He looked down at the outfit he'd chosen to wear for this momentous occasion – a sea-green vest top and black harem pants, the waistband customized with pearl sequins. Did he look ridiculous? He'd really gone to town on his make-up this morning, too, giving himself sea-green cat eyes, ruby lips and a pencilled-on beauty spot. He'd wanted to make a statement, to start as he meant to go on, but was it too much?

Thankfully, before he could spiral too far down, the door buzzed open. Jewel stepped into a narrow passageway, dimly lit by a row of red light bulbs set into the wall. He followed the passageway to the end and down a flight of stairs, coming out into a small reception area. A woman with bright pink dreadlocks was sitting behind the desk, reading a magazine.

'Sorry about that, I can't hear a thing above all the noise out there,' she said, glancing up at Jewel.

'That's OK. It's my first day. I wasn't sure what to say anyway.'

'Sign in here, and I'll buzz someone to come and get you.' The woman pointed to a clipboard on the counter. As Jewel signed it he had to fight the reflex urge to write his old name. He wondered if he'd ever lose this urge. It was bound to take some time. He had to fight eighteen years of programming.

'Hiya, Margot,' the pink-haired woman said into a phone. 'I've got your new dresser here. OK, cheers.' The woman looked back at Jewel. 'She'll be right out to get you.'

'Cool. Thanks.' Jewel looked at the posters on the wall, pretending to read them when really his mind was racing so fast he was incapable of reading anything. This was it. His new life was officially beginning. No more soul-destroying temp office jobs. Now he was finally working in an area that actually interested him. He was a dresser on a West End show!

'Cool harem pants,' the woman said, leaning over her desk to study them.

'Oh, thanks.' Jewel's face flushed.

'Where did you get them from?'

'I, uh, I actually made them.'

'Really?' The woman tilted her head as if trying to decide something, then she stretched a thin arm over to Jewel. 'I'm Alice.'

Jewel shook her hand. 'Pleased to meet you.'

'Yeah, you too. Welcome to the madhouse.' Alice pulled a serious face but her brown eyes were warm.

'Thank you.'

A door at the other end of the reception area burst open and Margot came out. She was wearing a wrap-around dress in a paisley print and huge, turquoise hoop earrings. Just as he had felt in his job interview, Jewel found something strangely comforting about Margot's soft, curvy body, something maternal. Not that Jewel's own mother looked anything like Margot: his mother was all bones and jagged edges.

'Jewel, welcome,' Margot kissed Jewel on both cheeks. 'Not a moment too soon! I'm drowning in last-minute alterations. I hope your sewing's up to speed.'

'He made those harem pants,' Alice said from behind her magazine.

'Really?' Margot gave the harem pants an appraising stare. 'I knew I'd made the right choice hiring you.' She placed her hand on Jewel's shoulder and he got a waft of her rose-scented perfume. 'Come on, let's get you to work.'

Ever since the bizarre prawn-curtain funeral pyre, Danny hadn't been able to get the image of fire out of his head. Anytime something annoying happened he visualized adding it to the flames. The bus conductor who'd split his sides laughing when Danny almost fell down the stairs as they'd gone round a sharp bend. The woman working in the newsagents who'd had the temerity to pick a lump of wax from her ear right before serving him. The bike courier who'd almost mown him down at Piccadilly Circus. And now, as he stood at the side of the studio and watched his arch-nemesis, German choreographer Johannes Schmidt, attempting to motivate a group of dancers with a mixture of passive- and pure aggression, he mentally conjured up the inferno once more.

'That was diabolical,' Johannes spat at the dancers. 'Are you trying to make me look stupid? Are you trying to make this show a total failure?'

Danny pictured in his head pushing Johannes onto the fire. It wasn't the dancers who were making the show look stupid, it was Johannes and his so-called groundbreaking ideas. Danny was all for pushing the boundaries, but interpreting *Romeo and Juliet* through a cast of farmyard animals was taking things a step too far. In a recent interview in *The Times*, Johannes had said he wanted his interpretation of the classic Shakespearean love story to reflect the baseness of humans. 'We are all animals under the skin,' he had said. 'We are all dogs and donkeys and pigs.'

It struck Danny that Johannes' sadistic choreography showed that the man didn't really like people very much.

'And you ...' Johannes pointed an accusing finger at Terri, the dancer playing Juliet – as a cow. 'You should be ashamed of yourself. Call that a pirouette? I've seen more grace in a bowl of lumpy custard.'

'But the udders keep getting in the way,' Terri stammered from inside her latex cow's head.

'A poor workman always blames his tools,' Johannes snapped. 'And a diabolical dancer always blames her udders.'

A snigger rang out from the back of the studio.

'Who was that?' Johannes yelled. 'Who thinks this is funny?' He started stalking amongst the dancers, most of whom recoiled as he passed them.

'I have had enough! Enough!' He marched over to Danny. 'I give up. You try and do something with them.'

Danny watched as Johannes marched out of the studio, and pictured him walking straight onto the fire and burning away to a frazzle. Then he looked back at the dancers, who were all slumped heads and drooping shoulders. Trying to reignite their self-belief was going to take a miracle. Or a good dose of Dr Dance. He marched over to his bag and took out a CD.

'Right, everyone, take off your animal heads, it's time for some freestyle,' he called, putting the CD on the stereo. 'The theme is fire.' He flicked through till he got to the track he was after. 'Fire' by Arthur Brown started to play. He cranked up the volume. 'As you dance I want you to imagine any crap you're dealing with being burned away. Release it from your body and dance it into the flames.' Danny couldn't help grinning. Trippy Lil would be proud of him. He only hoped that it worked.

He watched as one by one the dancers' bodies loosened. 'Go on, let it burn away!' he called.

Terri ripped her plastic udders off with a roar.

'Great work!' Danny called.

The dancers became wilder and freer. Danny wondered how many of them were also picturing burning Johannes to a crisp. He closed his eyes and took a deep breath before joining them in their dance.

Four

Lachlan strode along Diamond Street, his head pounding in time with his aching feet. Today had been one of those shifts where it felt as if all of London had descended upon the Accident and Emergency unit at the Royal Free. Still, at least he'd been on a day shift. He pitied the poor staff who were working tonight. Not only was it a Friday – always one of the busiest nights for A&E – but it was a full moon, too. And, as any A&E nurse knew, a full moon brought out the craziest incidents. Insane drunken brawls, the weirdest kind of injuries, not to mention the bizarre objects stuck in certain orifices. Lachlan wasn't remotely woo-woo, but there was no denying the full moon had some kind of effect on people, and it wasn't a good one.

When he got to number 27 he said a small prayer. He wasn't religious, either, but sometimes he needed whatever assistance he could get. *Please, please, let my housemates be out …* he silently implored. All he wanted to do was grab a tinny from the fridge, sling a frozen pizza in the oven, and hole up in his bedroom. He really wasn't in the mood for one of Pete's morose poems or an impromptu dance party in the kitchen.

'Ah, Lachlan, my darling, you're just in time for the festivities.'

He opened the door to see Trippy Lil wobbling her way down the stairs. She was wearing a Jimi Hendrix T-shirt, leather trousers and a scuffed pair of biker boots. Her silver hair was piled up into a messy bun, held together by what looked like a pair of chopsticks.

'We're having a party,' Lil drawled, taking a puff on her ever-present cigarette.

Lachlan's heart didn't just sink, it plummeted.

'And not just any old party,' Lil continued. 'We're having a dinner party – to welcome the new members of our family.'

'What family?' Lachlan shut the door behind him. He could hear the sound of chatter coming from the kitchen. He could also smell something delicious, something roasting. This caused an immediate conflict within him. His head was urging him to make up some excuse and hide out in his bedroom but his stomach ... They'd been so busy at work he hadn't had time to eat since breakfast. *Take me to the kitchen. Let me eat meat!* his stomach seemed to be yelling. He dropped his bag in the corner of the hallway on top of the mountain of junk mail and followed Lil into the kitchen.

The new couple were sitting at the table. The guy, what was his name, something beginning with J, was studying his fingernails, while the girl, Cat, was flicking through a magazine. Her red hair tumbled in loose curls around her shoulders. Danny was at the cooker, stirring a bubbling saucepan, an uncorked bottle of red on the counter beside him.

'Aha! Lachlan!' Danny exclaimed, picking up the wine and adding a generous slosh to the pan. 'Take a seat. I'm making us all Christmas dinner.'

'Christmas? But it's June.' Lachlan sat down next to J-man.

'I know!' Lil shrieked, collapsing into the chair on the other side of him. 'Isn't it a trip?'

The pounding in Lachlan's head grew louder. This had to be something to do with the full moon. Even in the safety of his own home he couldn't escape its insanity.

'I mean, why should we only get to have Christmas dinner once a year?' Lil continued. 'It's the best bloody meal in existence, it makes no sense to deprive ourselves.'

Cat giggled and looked across the table at Lachlan. 'Hi.'

'G'day. Welcome to the madhouse,' he replied.

'You may mock,' Danny said, taking a swig from his glass of wine. 'But you'll be grateful when you're chowing down on one of my infamous pigs in blankets.' He opened the oven door and the kitchen was flooded with a mixture of the delicious smells of turkey, bacon and potatoes roasting.

Lachlan's stomach gave a loud rumble.

'Ooh, someone sounds hungry,' Lil laughed, nudging him in the ribs.

'Yeah, well, I haven't eaten since seven this morning.'

'Have you been at work?' Cat asked.

'Yeah, for my sins. I work in A&E,' he explained. 'Fridays are always a bit of a nightmare, especially when there's a full moon.' As soon as he said it he regretted it. Now the new couple would think he was a total fruit loop and, what with Lil being trippier than ever, there really wasn't any room at the table for more lunacy.

Sure enough, J-man gave him a sideways smirk. 'What's the moon got to do with it?' he asked.

'It brings out all the werewolves,' Danny joked.

'It's always more hectic than usual,' Lachlan muttered.

'I read an article about that once in *Spirit & Destiny* magazine,' Cat said enthusiastically, but not really helping his cause. If only it could have been in something a little more highbrow, like *National Geographic*. 'I think the writer said it's because humans are made of eighty per cent water.'

'What's that got to do with anything?' The man beginning with J turned to Cat, but he wasn't smirking any more, he was scowling.

'Well, the moon controls the tides, doesn't it,' Cat replied.

'And ...?' J-man's scowl deepened.

'And so the moon probably pulls on the water in our body in the same way.' Cat's voice petered out beneath the weight of his stare.

'Apologies for my girlfriend. She isn't always this bonkers,' J-man said, with a smug laugh that made Lachlan want to punch him.

Cat's face flared red and she turned back to her magazine.

'Nothing bonkers about it, mate.' Lachlan said. 'We get forty per cent more accidents coming in on the night of a full moon. Can't argue with the statistics.'

Actually, you could argue with them, as Lachlan had just made them up on the spot. But dickhead wasn't to know that. Cat shot Lachlan a grateful grin and J-man returned to studying his fingernails.

Thankfully, at that point there was a knock on the door, breaking the awkward silence.

'That'll be our final guest – and new housemate,' Danny exclaimed.

Jewel stood on the pavement outside 27 Diamond Street shifting nervously from foot to foot. When he'd come to view his new room, earlier in the week, he'd only met one of his new housemates, the man called Danny. But there were five other people living there, five completely unknown entities, and any one of them could answer the door. *Hi, I'm Jewel, your new housemate,* he mentally rehearsed. It had been quite a week for new beginnings what with the job, too, and it had all left him feeling exhausted. He was about to knock again when the door burst open.

'Welcome, my darling!' A woman greeted him. She was dressed in a vintage rock tee and leather trousers, and was smoking a cigarette. It was hard to tell exactly what age she was. Her hair was silver and wrinkles fanned from her eyes, but she had the chiselled cheekbones of a model. 'You must be our final guest and housemate.'

'What? Oh, yes. I'm, uh, Jewel.'

'What a wonderful name! So sparkly. Come in, come in. You're just in time for Christmas dinner.'

Jewel followed the woman into the hallway, frowning. Perhaps she was suffering from some form of dementia. The house did smell delicious though, and suspiciously like Christmas dinner.

'I'm Lil, by the way,' the woman said over her shoulder. 'I live up in the attic.'

Jewel bit his lip, fighting the sudden urge to giggle. Lil led him into a large kitchen and living room area which spanned the length of the house. At some point it must have been two rooms, but a large archway had been knocked through the adjoining wall. Jewel hadn't seen the kitchen before. He'd been so relieved to have liked the bedroom that he took it on the spot, and Danny had seemed to be in a rush to get it all over with. It was only when Jewel got back to Cynthia's and she'd asked what kind of oven the house had that he realized he hadn't even looked. Cynthia had shuddered and told him he'd made a massive mistake, that kitchens in shared houses could be 'so, like gross, they cause botulism'. Jewel wasn't entirely sure if this was scientifically possible, but still.

He quickly scanned the room. The walls were canary yellow and the fitted cupboards were mustard-coloured Formica, giving it all a bit of a seventies feel. Danny was standing at a large, sauce-splattered cooker stirring something, and three other people were sitting at a long, wooden table. It was all a little chaotic but bright and cheery. The polar opposite of the sterile, white kitchen Jewel had grown up with at home.

'Come on in, Jewel, take a seat,' Danny said.

Jewel smiled shyly at the people sitting at the table. On one side there were two men. One of them looked as if he'd walked straight off a catwalk. He was all chiselled and tanned, with creamy blond hair. The other man was more rugged, with messy, sandy hair. He looked at Jewel and nodded. Across from them sat a young woman with curly red hair and pale skin. Jewel instantly warmed to her. A feeling that grew as the woman gave him a welcoming smile.

'Hi, I'm Cat, we're new here, too,' she said. 'My boyfriend Justin and I just moved in.' She pointed at the man who looked like a model.

'Hi. Nice to meet you.' Jewel sat down next to her. He noticed Justin staring at him across the table. The kind of stare that felt as thorough as an X-ray. Jewel felt his face start to burn, which wasn't helped by the heat of the room.

'OK, turkey's done,' Danny said, taking a huge roast turkey from the oven.

So Lil hadn't been hallucinating, then. They really were having a Christmas dinner!

'Can I get you a glass of wine, sweetheart?' Lil asked, offering Jewel a choice of white or red.

'A glass of white would be great, thanks,' Jewel nodded.

'Can someone go and fetch Pete from his garret?' Danny asked. 'Tell him I'm about to start carving.'

'Of course.' Lil finished pouring Jewel a huge glass of white and headed back out of the room. Jewel took a large gulp of his drink. Then he took a deep breath and tried to absorb all that had happened in the few minutes he'd been there. One thing was for certain, life at 27 Diamond Street seemed anything but boring.

Five

As she looked around the table, Cat knew she should feel happy. She was finally out of Justin's parents' pristine prison. Her new housemates all seemed lovely, in a host of different ways. They were eating her favourite dinner, Christmas dinner – in June. Danny had cooked the roast potatoes to perfection and, as any true foodie knew, the perfect roastie was a fine art form, with just the right balance of golden, crispy exterior and soft, creamy interior. *And* Danny had seasoned them with fresh rosemary. So why, when Cat had more reasons to be cheerful than Ian Dury and his Blockheads, did she feel so low?

The answer was Justin. Ever since Cat had reminded him about their deal that neither of them would take an overseas job without the other, he'd gone into one of his sulks. He hadn't overtly said that he was angry with her but he'd certainly showed her, with every sullen scowl and disdainful put-down. Part of her felt like saying, 'Just do it then, just take the job and go without me', but then she'd be stuck having to pay for a double room with no job and only limited savings.

She looked longingly at the roast potatoes on her plate. They were still waiting for Lil to return with the mysterious Pete, and an awkward silence had fallen at the table.

'So, where do you work?' she asked, turning to Jewel.

'At the Theatre Royal in Drury Lane.'

'Oh really, doing what?' Justin asked.

'Assistant dresser.' Jewel blushed. With his delicate features, beautiful make-up and closely cropped black hair, he was the definition of androgynous. There was a vulnerability about him that made Cat want to hug him.

'That's great,' she said.

'So what's Jewel short for?' Justin asked.

Cat held her breath. Why was Justin asking this?

There was an awkward silence, during which Jewel flushed even redder. 'It isn't short for anything,' he finally muttered, looking really uncomfortable.

'What, your parents named you that?'

'I think it's a great name,' Cat said, shooting Justin a death stare, but he was too busy looking at Jewel and smiling smugly to notice.

Thankfully, at this point Lil swept back into the room. 'Sorry, we got a bit waylaid by the car chase upstairs. Oh, hurrah, Father Christmas has been!'

Everyone looked at her blankly.

'The dinner,' she explained, stubbing her cigarette out in the sink.

'Father Christmas doesn't make the Christmas dinner, darling,' Danny said, plonking a jug of gravy on the table. 'He fills the stockings. Oh, never mind. What car chase upstairs?'

'The O. J. Simpson car chase,' a man said, entering the room behind Lil. He was dressed all in black, there were dark rings beneath his eyes and his sallow skin was shaded with stubble. He looked as if he hadn't been outside in a very long time. 'He's trying to escape the long arm of the law – at about twenty miles per hour. I've been writing a poem about it.'

Jewel coughed and looked down into his lap. Cat wondered if he, too, was fighting the sudden urge to laugh.

'And it's a work of genius, sweetheart.' Lil took her seat.

'Thank you.' Pete sat down at the table and took a notebook from his pocket.

'Er, hello?' Danny said.

'Hello, Danny,' Pete replied, leafing through the book.

'No, I mean, aren't you going to say hello to our new housemates?'

'What new …' Pete looked around the table distractedly. 'Oh, hello. Welcome. Would you like to hear my poem?'

'No!' Danny exclaimed.

'We don't want them moving out before they've even moved in,' Lachlan muttered. Cat caught his eye and he shrugged and grinned.

'Nonsense,' Lil retorted. 'Pete is a wonderful poet. Camden's very own Hamlet. Isn't that right, sweetheart?'

'Shakespeare,' Pete corrected with a bashful smile. 'Well, if you insist.'

'Oh, we do, don't we?' Lil looked round the table pointedly.

'Yes,' Cat and Jewel said in unison.

'Huh! Well, don't say I didn't warn you,' Danny said, coming to sit down.

Pete cleared his throat.

'The man they named Juice
Is now on the loose.
In a white Bronco
Being driven oh so slow.
But the curse of the guilty
Is that they can never truly flee.'

Pete paused, then added, 'I'm going through a bit of a rhyming couplet phase.'

There was a moment's silence, which Cat could best describe as stunned, then Lil squealed and Jewel started to clap. Justin shot Cat one of his sarcastic stares, but Cat didn't reciprocate and instead began clapping loudly.

'Is O. J. really trying to escape?' she asked. A few days previously, the world had been shocked by the news that the American football star had been accused of the murder of his ex-wife and her friend. This was even more of a shocking twist.

'Yes, but the police are following him in their cars and helicopters,' Pete explained.

'Hardly an effective escape bid, then,' Danny muttered. 'Anyway, enough of all that.' He raised his glass. 'To new housemates and new beginnings.'

'New beginnings,' Cat said, a little too loudly. Had the wine already gone to her head? Justin shot her yet another glare across the table. A small knot of defiance tightened inside of her. He wasn't going to ruin this evening. She was going to have a good time if it killed her. She took a mouthful of potato.

'Oh my God. This roast potato is …' she scanned her mind for a suitably gushing adjective … 'supreme.'

'Why, thank you.' Danny's face broke into a grin. 'I do consider my roasties to be one of my greatest achievements.'

'So you should, they're delicious.'

'Yeah, mate, top job,' Lachlan grinned. It was good to see him looking slightly more relaxed. He'd seemed so off when they first met that Cat had been worried he hadn't wanted her and Justin to move in.

'What's that saying about a moment on the lips?' Justin said, giving her a pointed stare. He was smiling but she could instantly read the subtext. 'A lifetime on the hips,' he continued.

When they'd argued about the Berlin job last night he'd implied that she hadn't been offered a callback because of her weight. 'Maybe if you ate a bit less we wouldn't be in this mess,' was what he'd said. Ever since, it had been ringing around her head like an annoying jingle. The potato in her mouth turned from delicious to ash.

'What a load of crock,' Lachlan said, pouring some gravy on his dinner.

'What is?' Justin asked.

'That saying. Just get it down you, mate.'

Justin's face flushed such a deep shade of red it was practically purple. 'I wasn't talking about me, I was …' he broke off.

Cat held her breath, mortified. Was he about to shame her at the table in front of their new housemates?

'Yeah, well, we don't have to worry about that, do we?' Danny said.

'We'll soon burn it off dancing.' He looked at Cat and smiled.

She nodded, but inside she felt like dying. Had the others worked out that Justin was talking about her? Did they all also think she was overweight?

'Happy Christmas, everyone,' Lil cried. 'It's so lovely to have you all together at last.'

'At last? Some of us have only just met,' Danny said.

'Exactly,' Lil replied enigmatically.

'Pig in blanket?' Lachlan asked Cat, offering her the dish. The little sausages wrapped in bacon looked delicious. Just like the potatoes, they were cooked to perfection.

'If you want to know my trade secret, I baste them in honey before putting them in the oven,' Danny said.

Cat began to drool again.

'Doesn't honey have a super high sugar content?' Justin said in a smug tone that made Cat want to stab him with her fork. She stabbed a couple of the pigs in blankets instead.

'Thank you.'

'You're welcome,' Lachlan replied.

Danny sat back in his chair and surveyed the scene. Apart from dancing, entertaining others – whether through food, wine or song, or all of the above – was his greatest pleasure in life. And he had to admit, the sight of his housemates new and old all sitting around the table, faces flushed and laughing, made even his cynical heart happy.

The meal hadn't been without a couple of tense moments, though. He'd wanted to christen Cat's beautiful but dreary boyfriend with the gravy jug after the way the man had put poor Jewel on the spot about his name, not to mention the 'lifetime on the hips' dig. And it obviously had been a dig. The guy had a line in passive-aggression that triggered some uncomfortable memories of Danny's final months with Gabriel. Good old Lachlan had soon put Justin in his place, though, no doubt still smarting from Justin's jibe about the full moon.

Jewel hadn't said much, but Danny had to admit being intrigued. He couldn't wait to get the young man on his own and find out his story. There was pain beneath that mask of make-up, he could tell.

And, thankfully, Pete and Lil had behaved themselves, so all in all it had been a very successful welcome meal.

'Ooh, I love this song,' Lil exclaimed, as 'Love is All Around' by Wet Wet Wet came on the radio. 'Turn it up, would you, sweetheart.'

Danny leaned over to the radio and turned up the volume. The song had been number one for a couple of weeks now and was really starting to grate on him. But the wine and a belly full of turkey were making him unusually mellow.

'Has anyone else seen the film this song is from?' Cat asked.

'The funeral one?' Lil asked.

Cat nodded. '*Four Weddings and a Funeral.*'

'No, not yet,' Lil replied. 'Is it any good? I do like the look of that new actor in it. Hugh Whatshisname.'

'It's great,' Cat said. 'Justin and I saw it the other day. It's so romantic.'

Justin shrugged. 'If you like that kind of thing.'

There was something about the way he said this that reminded Danny of that excruciating interview Prince Charles gave when announcing his engagement to Lady Di. When asked if he was in love he replied, 'Whatever love means.' Cat was giving a pained look to rival Di's, too.

'I think I'm going to turn in,' Lachlan said, taking his plate over to the sink. 'Leave the dishes, Danny, I'll do them in the morning.'

'Don't go, sweetheart,' Lil said. 'The party's only just getting started.'

'That's what I'm worried about.' Lachlan grinned. 'Seriously, I'm bushwacked. Cheers, Danny. Good night, everyone.'

'I think I might go to bed, too,' Justin said, pushing back his plate, which still contained half his dinner. A mortal sin as far as Danny was concerned. Damn Justin and his snakelike hips.

'Are you coming?' Justin asked Cat.

To Danny's surprise, she shook her head. Maybe she wasn't quite as much under the thumb as he'd imagined.

'But I've got my second audition in the morning,' Justin whined.

'You'd better get an early night, then,' Cat muttered, not looking up from her plate.

'OK, fine.' Justin got up. 'Good night, everyone.'

'Night,' Danny replied, making a mental note of the fact that Justin hadn't thanked him for the dinner. Probably blaming him for all kinds of hip-related weight gain, the ungrateful arsehole. Still, at least now the party-poopers had left maybe they could have some real fun.

'How about we adjourn to the parlour?' he suggested. 'Sadly, I don't have any Christmas pud, but I do have a bottle of brandy, which is surely the crucial ingredient.'

The others laughed and they all made their way through to the living room. The back door was open and a refreshing breeze was blowing in, causing Lil's dreamcatcher wind chimes to sing. For the first time in what seemed like forever, Danny felt something close to content.

'Oh, you have a record player!' Cat exclaimed, spying Lil's vintage portable in the corner.

'I sure do, sweetheart. That record player has seen me through thick and thin – and I'm not just talking about Ronnie and Mick,' Lil chortled.

Danny went over to the vintage drinks cabinet in the corner – it dated back to the 1950s – and poured out some brandies while Lil, Cat and Jewel sat on the floor going through Lil's record collection.

'Neil Diamond!' Jewel exclaimed. 'My gran loves him!'

'How dare you.' Lil gave him an affectionate nudge. 'I can't believe my records are now classed as Grandma Music.'

'This is brilliant!' Cat exclaimed, pulling out the soundtrack from *Saturday Night Fever*.

'Put it on,' Danny grinned. It was one of his favourites, too.

The crackle of the needle on vinyl filled the living room and then the Bee Gees rang out. Cat stood up and started to dance. Danny could tell immediately that she was the kind of dancer who led from her heart rather than her head – his favourite kind of dancer. She caught him watching and immediately started to blush.

'Sorry,' she said with a giggle. 'The second I hear the Bee Gees my hips want to move. It's like the disco version of Pavlov's dog.'

'Never apologize for dancing in this house,' Danny said, handing her a drink.

As Cat and Lil started doing their best John Travolta impressions, Jewel went over to the back door and looked outside. Danny took a drink over to him.

'This backyard is so cool,' Jewel said, gesturing at the array of plant pots and Lil's collection of naughty gnomes in various states of undress. 'I love the bust. Who's it of?' He pointed to the weather-beaten stone bust by the back door.

'It's Lil's. I mean, it's not of Lil, it belongs to her. It's meant to be Yoko Ono – apparently they once had a threesome with John Lennon.' Danny chuckled. He took most of Lil's trippy tales with a huge pinch of salt, but there was no doubt they were entertaining. He took his cigarettes from his pocket and offered one to Jewel. 'Do you smoke?'

Jewel shook his head. 'Thanks so much for the dinner.'

'You're welcome.' Danny lit himself a cigarette. 'So, what's the story with your name?'

Jewel blushed. 'My name?'

'Yes, I take it you weren't christened Jewel.'

Jewel laughed. 'No!' He looked down at his feet. 'I was actually christened Julian.'

Danny nodded. 'Well, I think Jewel is a vast improvement, darling.'

'You do?' Jewel gave him a hopeful smile.

'Absolutely.'

'I only just …' He broke off.

'What?'

'I only just started using this name – when I moved to London.'

'Right. How long have you been here?'

'Just over two months.'

'I see. So you're still getting used to your new identity?'

'Yes.'

Danny thought back to the time he had left home as a teen, and the courage it had taken to come out fully, and he felt a weird, paternal-style instinct to look out for Jewel. 'I think you're doing fabulously.'

'Really?' Jewel's hazel eyes widened and for a moment Danny was able to see the anxious kid beneath the make-up.

Danny nodded. 'Trust me, darling. Now you've moved to London the sky's the limit.'

Jewel took off his clothes and slipped beneath the duvet. His head was racing from the alcohol and the evening's events. He stared up at a crack in the ceiling. When he'd stared at the ceiling in his childhood bedroom, plotting his escape, there'd been no cracks. Like the rest of the house, it was immaculate. His vicar dad and vicar's wife mum had worked so hard to create the perfect Christian home for their perfect Christian family, but they didn't know how to cope with anything that broke the mould – like their child.

When Jewel was younger his parents had viewed him with blinkers, unwilling to acknowledge or accept anything that didn't fit their preconceived notion of how he should be. When he wanted to go to a fancy dress party as a princess, he was made to go as a pirate or a Jedi knight. When he was caught playing with his mum's lipstick, her make-up mysteriously disappeared from view. But when Jewel became a teen it became increasingly hard for his parents to ignore the signs – the Culture Club records and posters, the discovery of eyeliner and Impulse deodorant in the bottom of his school bag.

When Jewel had finally come clean and told them that not only did he consider himself gender-fluid, but he was attracted to other boys as well, all hell had broken loose. His dad had been distraught at his 'sinful behaviour' and begged him to pray for forgiveness, and his mum had been only marginally better. 'I'm sure it's just a phase, dear,' she'd said. 'Remember that summer your cousin Colin became a punk rocker? He soon grew out of it.'

Jewel had known there and then that gaining his parents' understanding was a completely lost cause. But he didn't give up. He collected articles about his heroes – Boy George, Steve Strange, Marilyn, David Bowie – in a shoebox under his bed and he dreamed of the day he'd be able to escape to London, and follow in their footsteps in legendary clubs like Mud Club, the Wag and Blitz.

The night before he left for London – the night after he turned eighteen – Jewel's father had made one last attempt to get him to see the error of his ways and begged him to stay. It was the first time Jewel had ever seen his dad so emotionally exposed, and for a moment he almost weakened. But then he remembered that if he stayed at home he'd forever have to suffer the pain of never fitting in. 'I can't,' Jewel had whispered. His dad's eyes went glassy with tears. 'I'll keep praying for you,' he'd said, before turning to leave.

Jewel rolled on to his side. A cooling breeze was drifting in through the window, bringing with it the late-night London soundtrack of chatter, glass breaking and a distant siren's wail. Jewel smiled. For the first time in his eighteen years, he felt he belonged.

Six

Cat woke with a start and for a moment she was completely disorientated. Where was the hideous floral wallpaper? Where were the framed photos of Justin through the ages? Where was the sound of Justin's mum hoovering?

And then she remembered. They didn't live with his parents in Hampstead anymore. They lived in Camden.

She could hear the clanging and rumble of a dustcart outside and the shouting of what she assumed were the bin-men. She looked around the room at the boxes and suitcases containing her and Justin's belongings. She couldn't wait to get their things unpacked and make it seem more like home. Later today she'd go down to the market and pick up some things to accessorize the room – some ethnic throws and brightly coloured cushions. And some incense to try and get rid of the weird, slightly fishy smell. She felt ridiculously happy at the thought of an afternoon spent browsing around Camden Market, but then she felt Justin stirring beside her and her stomach tightened. He'd been so weird at dinner, hardly making any effort with their new housemates, then going off to bed early.

Although that had been a blessing really, as it had enabled her to relax and have fun. She thought back to how she and the others had ended up dancing the night away. All except Pete, who'd sat curled in an armchair, scribbling away in his notebook.

Justin cleared his throat and stretched.

'Morning,' Cat said cheerily, trying to ignore the apprehension building inside of her. Today Justin had his second audition for the Berlin gig. Would he go? And if so, what would it mean for them?

'Morning,' Justin shifted into a sitting position.

It was impossible to tell from the tone of his voice whether he was still upset with her, so she decided to test the water. 'It's the first morning in our new home,' she said, snuggling up to him. 'Maybe we should … christen it?'

'I don't think so. I need to conserve my energy for the audition.' Justin sniffed loudly. 'Can you smell fish?'

'No,' Cat lied. 'It might be coming from outside. The bin-men have just been.' She sat up. 'So, you're going to the audition, then?'

Justin gave an exaggerated sigh. 'Not this again.'

'What?'

'This emotional blackmail.'

'It's not emotional blackmail, we'd agreed that neither of us would take a job abroad without the other. How would you feel if it was the other way round?'

'I would give you my blessing.'

Yeah, right, Cat thought to herself. She got out of bed and pulled on her robe. She had to get out of the room before she smothered him with a pillow. 'Do you want a cup of tea?'

'Yes, please.'

Cat marched downstairs, oscillating between feeling furious and upset. For the first year they'd been together Justin had treated her like she was the brightest star in his universe. Trying to adjust to his recent indifference was hurtful and confusing. It was like being caught up in a weird game she'd never wanted to play and had no clue about the rules.

As Lachlan filled the sink with hot water he risked putting on the radio. He normally tended to avoid the radio, or music stations at least, to try to steer clear of a musical ambush. He'd never realized that he and Michelle had so many 'our tunes' until after the accident, then it seemed as if every other song brought back a painful memory – of a holiday, a road-trip or a kiss. And even once, bizarrely, of a visit to an orthodontist. As teenagers, Lachlan had accompanied Michelle to get her brace fitted, and 'Legs' by ZZ Top had been playing in the waiting room. They'd ended up air-guitaring along to the song. A memory that had come crashing back from the recesses of his memory when he'd heard the track last year, playing on the radio in a newsagents. Every time he'd heard a song that reminded him of Mich it brought yet another crushing wave of grief. But now it had been almost two years since the accident, and radio music felt a little safer.

He heard the door open and turned to see Cat standing there. Her hair was a wild tumble of red curls and she was wearing a green, silky gown, revealing a triangle of creamy skin pointing the way to her cleavage. Lachlan felt an unfamiliar stirring deep within him and he quickly returned his attention to the congealed gravy on the plate he was cleaning.

'Good morning.'

'Morning,' she replied cheerily. 'Do you need any help?'

'I think I'm all right, ta.'

'Are you sure? It looks as if every dish in the house has been used.' Cat picked up a tea towel. 'How about I dry and you wash?'

Lachlan squirmed. It was way too early and he hadn't had nearly enough caffeine to be capable of small talk. 'Suit yourself,' he shrugged.

But thankfully Cat didn't seem in the mood for small talk, either, and he washed and she dried in what felt dangerously close to companionable silence.

'And coming up next,' the breakfast show DJ said on the radio, *'the smash hit from the smash film, "Love is All Around" by Wet Wet Wet.'*

'Oh God, I hate this song,' Cat muttered.

'Really?' Lachlan stared at her. He'd had her down as one of those romantic chicks. 'I thought you said you liked the movie.'

'I did, but it's all just wishful thinking really, isn't it?'

'What is?' Now Lachlan was genuinely intrigued.

'The soulmate thing. The happy ending.'

Lachlan shook the bubbles from his hand and turned off the radio. 'Better?'

'Yes. Thank you. I'm sorry, I think I got out of bed on the wrong side this morning.'

'No worries. I think it's all a crock of shit, too.'

Cat laughed. It was a nice laugh. Throaty and warm. 'I really enjoyed our Christmas dinner.'

'Yeah, it was surprisingly good – for June.'

Cat laughed again.

'You weren't put off by some of our more colourful characters?' Lachlan began scrubbing at a roasting tin.

'Not at all. I thought they were great. Seriously, compared to where we were living before, this is so much better.'

'Where were you before?'

'At Justin's parents'.'

'Right.' Lachlan tried to imagine the kind of couple that would have produced the entitled, arrogant Justin and concluded that they had to be hell on earth to live with. What Cat was doing in a relationship with Justin was baffling. From what Lachlan could tell, she was what his mates back home would call a top drawer Sheila. He focused back on the roasting tin. He didn't really know her, though.

'I don't mean to be horrible,' Cat said quickly. 'They just weren't really my kind of people.'

'No worries. It's OK to call a spade a spade – or an arsehole an arsehole.'

There was a moment's silence and Lachlan wanted to kick himself for going too far, but then Cat started cracking up laughing. And her laugh was so infectious he couldn't help joining in.

'What's going on?'

They both turned to see Justin standing in the doorway wearing nothing but a pair of shorts, his abs a well-defined washboard.

Poser, Lachlan thought, and turned back to the dishes.

'I was just helping Lachlan,' Cat said.

'So I see. I'll make my own tea then, shall I?'

Jeez! Lachlan glanced at Cat, whose face had flushed deep crimson.

'Sure,' she replied coolly.

Attagirl. For one awful moment he thought she was going to make it for Justin. If Justin had talked to Lachlan like that he'd be wearing the kettle.

Justin clicked the kettle on, then to Lachlan's surprise he came up behind Cat, put his arm around her waist and kissed the top of her head. Cat looked as shocked as Lachlan felt by this sudden display of affection.

'Would you like a cup, darling?' he asked, his whole tone softened.

'Oh, er, yes, please.'

'No problem.' Justin turned her around so she was facing him and planted a kiss on her lips.

Lachlan's stomach churned. Maybe he'd take a break from the dishes and come back when they'd gone.

Then Justin whispered something in Cat's ear.

'But I thought you said you needed to conserve your energy,' Cat replied.

'I've got more than enough.' Justin took her by the hand. 'Come on.'

'But I'm drying the dishes.'

'That's OK. You get on, there's not many left,' Lachlan said hurriedly.

'Are you sure?' For a split second he thought he detected a hint of desperation in her voice, as if she wanted him to save her from Justin and whatever dire fate his limitless energy had in store for her. 'OK, then, see you in a bit.'

'Yep, see you.' Lachlan tore at a stubborn piece of grease on the roasting tin. Then he turned on the radio to drown out the sound of their laughter as they went upstairs.

Seven

On his way into work, Danny stopped off at the rental agents on the high street to break the good news that the new tenants had all moved in and to confirm that 27 Diamond Street was now fully occupied. The agents acted on behalf of the owner of the house, Sir Alexander Huntingdon-Davies. Apparently, Huntingdon-Davies now resided in the Caribbean on the proceeds from his estate. It was all very Princess Margaret.

'Sir Alexander was very happy to hear that the house would be fully occupied,' Denise, the assistant manager at We Let, You Get, told him, batting her false eyelashes at a rate of knots. 'I told his PA how helpful you'd been, interviewing the new tenants and showing them the rooms.' She leaned forward on her desk, revealing a generous expanse of cleavage.

Put 'em away, love, Danny felt like saying. *They're completely wasted on me.* But instead he smiled back. No point pissing off the agents. Keeping them happy meant a quiet life on the home front and he was all for that.

'She asked me to tell you that from now on, you should see yourself as the head of the house,' Denise continued breathlessly. 'Basically, you're the daddy,' she leaned over further and giggled.

Jesus! Danny stood up. 'That's great. Tell her to tell Sir Alexander that I feel very honoured.'

Once he'd returned to the safety of the street outside, Danny couldn't help feeling a tiny bit chuffed. The thought of being the head of 27 Diamond Street did give him a certain sense of accomplishment. And last night had been fun. Especially once the killjoys Justin and Lachlan had gone to bed. It had been great dancing with Cat – she'd fit in brilliantly with his dance friends. And he'd got a strange sense of comfort from talking to Jewel. It had been nice to feel needed. Or at the very least, listened to. He shuddered as he thought of the rehearsal to come. Johannes never listened to him, despite the fact that Danny had achieved a far better rapport with the dancers and right now, he was the only thing stopping at least half of them from quitting. Just hang on in there, he told himself. This assistant choreographer gig was a stepping stone to a far bigger and better dream. As Danny walked along a sun-drenched Camden High Street he really hoped that dream was inching closer to coming true.

As Jewel sat in the Wardrobe department on the top floor of the theatre sewing buttons onto soldiers' coats he daydreamed of the kind of soldiers' coats he'd create if he were actually a costume designer. He pictured broad shoulder pads and tapered waists and silver lightning bolt motifs. Just then the intercom speaker in the corner crackled into life and Alice's voice filled the room.

'Jewel Brown, contact reception, please.'

Jewel went over to the phone and pressed the button for reception.

'What are you doing for lunch?' Alice said before Jewel even had the chance to say hello.

'Oh, I hadn't really planned anything. I brought some sandwiches in.'

'Great. Do you fancy a picnic? We could go to Leicester Square and play Spot the Tourist Most Likely to Get Mugged?'

'Play what?'

'I'll explain when we get there. One p.m.? Are you in?'

'Sure.'

The line clicked dead.

As Cat wove her way through the stalls at Camden Market she felt something dangerously close to joy bubbling up inside of her.

'I love you,' Justin had whispered when they had made love earlier. And it really had been making love, as opposed to the hasty, muffled quickies they'd had to grab at his parents' house. This morning was how it had used to be, when they'd first got together. A heady mix of urgency and intimacy, which left her hollowed out with desire. She could still feel Justin's fingers upon her, hours later, their trails tingling across her skin.

She stopped by a stall selling Day-Glo tops and leggings, drawn from her reverie by the vivid colours.

'All right, love? Can I help you?' the stallholder asked. He was thin and wiry, with ears full of piercings and was wearing a smiley-face acid house T-shirt.

Cat took a vest top from the rack. It had an intricate mandala design on the front, in vibrant shades of hot pink, luminous green and neon blue. It was a little on the bright side, but it perfectly mirrored how she was feeling. And besides she could afford to splash out a bit now she wouldn't have to pay for the double room on her own. Justin wasn't going to take the Berlin job now, she was sure of it. He'd practically said as much, when they'd lain together this morning in a tangle of sweaty limbs.

'I don't think I'm good enough to make it through the final audition,' he'd confided, twisting a curl of her hair around his finger. Seeing this increasingly rare glimpse of his vulnerability was another welcome reminder of how things used to be. When they first got together they'd seemed so perfectly matched in terms of their passion for dance *and* their insecurities.

'You'll do great,' she'd said, relishing the opportunity to be the strong, non-neurotic one for once.

'Yeah, well, as long as I've got you,' he said, pulling her in for a hug.

Cat paid for the luminous vest top then wandered over to a stall selling brightly embroidered cushions and throws from India. She picked out a couple of emerald-green cushions embellished with tiny mirrored discs and a throw woven in rich shades of purple, green and gold. They would be the perfect shades for the bedroom, really restful. As she waited to pay she breathed in the sweet scent of patchouli incense and felt another piece in the jigsaw of her perfect life slotting into place.

'So, how do you play Spot the Tourist Most Likely to be Mugged?' Jewel asked, as he and Alice sat down on the grass in the centre of Leicester Square.

'Easy. Once you know the signs.' Alice took a huge bite of her burrito.

'And the signs are …?' Jewel tried to act all nonchalant but in truth, he still felt a bit like a tourist when it came to London, and being mugged would be his worst nightmare. He was viewing this game as an educational opportunity as well as a spot of lunchtime entertainment.

'OK, there's a major sign.' Alice pointed at an overweight man holding a map. 'Maps scream, "Mug me, please. I have absolutely no idea where I'm going."'

Jewel thought of the pocket *A–Z* in his bag. The book had been indispensable since moving to London. Admittedly, it was more discreet than the huge map the man was holding, but still. Maybe he should try to disguise it inside the covers of a novel, or read it inside his bag. He unwrapped his lunch.

'What's in the sandwich?' Alice asked.

'Turkey and stuffing.' Jewel took a bite.

Alice raised her thin, painted-on eyebrows. 'Very festive.'

'It's leftovers from last night. My housemates and I had a Christmas dinner.'

Alice frowned. 'In June?'

'Yeah, it was kind of a joke, to welcome me and the other couple who've just moved in.'

'Wow, your housemates sound cool. I wish I lived in a shared house.'

'Where do you live?'

'In Surrey. With my parents.' Alice rolled her eyes. 'Trust me, both of those things are a fate worse than death. You're so lucky.'

Jewel wasn't sure that anyone had ever called him lucky before. He certainly hadn't called himself that before. It was a very strange feeling. But one he could definitely get used to.

'OK, there's another one.' Alice pointed at a couple with huge cameras hanging around their necks. 'I mean, only a tourist wanting to be mugged would wear a thousand-pound camera on full display. It's like saying, "Yoo-hoo, come and rob me!"'

Jewel laughed, relieved that this was one thing he'd never been guilty of. The only cameras he'd ever owned were the disposable ones you got from the chemist. Made mainly from cardboard, they definitely weren't worth stealing.

'I love how you've done your eyeliner, by the way.' Alice squinted at him in the sunlight.

'Oh, thank you.' Emboldened by his chat with Danny last night, Jewel had made an extra effort with his make-up this morning, going for a heavy, winged, Cleopatra look in black kohl. He'd extended the Egyptian theme to his outfit, too, teaming a pair of plum-coloured harem pants with a beaded vest top and gladiator sandals.

'I love your whole look. It's very Boy George.'

'Thank you.' This was praise indeed!

Jewel looked at the crowds of people swarming through the square. 'How about that one over there? The woman with the purse sticking out of her pocket?'

'Yes! And you get a bonus point for great observation skills.' Alice held up her hand to high-five him. 'You know, if it doesn't work out in the world of costume assistanting you could always start a new career as a pick-pocket.'

They both laughed. On the other side of the iron railings that fenced off the grass from the rest of the square, a busker began singing 'What a Wonderful World'. As Jewel took a bite of turkey sandwich, he couldn't help agreeing.

Eight

Buoyed up by the positive developments in Diamond Street, Danny had been determined to have a good day at rehearsals and not let Johannes get to him. But, as he headed to the changing rooms at the studio, he heard the sound of sobbing coming from the ladies toilets. He halted in his tracks, his better judgement telling him that he ought to just ignore it and carry on. But he'd only ever listened to his better judgement about once before, so he wasn't going to change the habit of a lifetime. He cautiously poked his head round the toilet door.

'Hello? Are you OK?' Clearly, whoever was producing such gut-wrenching sobs was far from OK, but he didn't really know what else to say.

'Danny, is that you?'

Danny relaxed as he recognized the voice. It was Terri, a.k.a. bovine Juliet. 'Darling, what's wrong?' He took a tentative step inside the ladies. 'Is it OK to come in?'

'Of course.'

He found Terri hunched on the floor next to the sinks, her huge latex cow head beside her.

'What's happened?' He crouched down in front of her.

'That arsehole Johannes just told me that he doesn't quite believe my performance and that if I don't … if I don't improve … he's going to recast … recast my part,' she sobbed.

Danny sighed.

'Doesn't quite believe my performance,' Terri's voice climbed an octave. 'He's turned Shakespeare's greatest play into Old Mac-fucking-Donald. No one's going to believe it.'

Danny couldn't help agreeing with her, but much as he disliked Johannes, he felt troubled. If the critics slated the show it would be a black mark against Danny's name, too, as assistant choreographer. And in the dance world people could be very unforgiving. His new career as a choreographer could be over before it began. He had to do something. He had to save the show, not to mention the dancers' sanity. But how?

'All right, love, I've got an idea.' He got up and fetched a handful of toilet paper from one of the cubicles. 'Sort your face out, then come and meet me in my dressing room.'

He helped Terri to her feet and she gave him a hug. Danny couldn't help cringing. The shirt he was wearing was Dolce & Gabbana. He really hoped she hadn't got snot all over the shoulder.

He went through to his room, put on the kettle, and rooted around in his bag, pulling out a battered deck of tarot cards. He'd been given the cards when he ran away from home to join the circus – a line he never tired of telling. And it was actually true. Coming out as gay to his Neanderthal docker of a dad had not gone well at all, but then Danny had seen a job ad for a member of the dancing troupe in a French contemporary circus company called Cirque de la Lune. Although there were no animals in Cirque de la Lune, there was a tarot-reading gypsy called Colette, complete with crystal ball and hooped earrings. She'd taken eighteen-year-old Danny under her wing, becoming a sort of psychic surrogate mother to him. When he left the circus for a role in a show at the Moulin Rouge, Colette presented Danny with his own deck of cards, with the instruction that he should always let them guide him.

'You have the gift, *mon cher*,' she'd told him. 'And the cards, they will never lie to you.'

Danny wasn't exactly sure what kind of gift he had when it came to the tarot, but he always seemed to get some kind of wisdom and reassurance from the cards. He took the pack from their purple velvet bag and gave them a shuffle. Just the act of shuffling the well-worn cards felt comforting. They were like old friends, always there for him in times of trouble. Never judgemental, always impartial. Always offering him a solution. He really hoped they wouldn't let him down now.

The door opened and, to his horror, Johannes marched in.

'It is a disaster!' Johannes cried. 'These dancers, they are the pits!'

Danny instantly bristled. He might officially be a choreographer now, but he would always be a dancer at heart. And he would always have his dancers' best interests at heart, unlike this egomaniac.

'Perhaps it isn't the dancers that are the problem,' Danny suggested.

Johannes' eyes narrowed and he came closer. As always, he was dressed in black from head to toe, and his breath reeked of the horribly strong cigarettes he smoked. 'What do you mean? Who else could the problem be?'

'Not who, but what,' Danny replied, standing up. He was a good foot taller than Johannes and about a foot broader, too. He wasn't going to let Johannes intimidate him.

'What?' Johannes echoed.

'I think the problem is the farm animals. I just don't think the audience will take it seriously.'

'You don't think they will take me seriously?' Johannes practically shrieked. 'ME?'

'Not you, the animals. I don't think they'll take the animals seriously.'

'So, you have a better solution, do you?' Johannes stared at him. And for a split second Danny was sure he saw something other than indignation in his eyes. He could swear he saw desperation and fear. 'Do you?' Johannes yelled.

Shit. He was actually asking for Danny's advice. But what should Danny tell him? Danny looked down at the tarot cards. If only he was able to do a quick reading. Then he had a light-bulb moment. 'Actually, I think I might,' he replied softly. He knew he had to play this very carefully. Handling Johannes' ego was like handling a piece of extremely delicate bone china. 'Of course, it's only a suggestion and you would need to put your mark on it... to, you know, make it really good.'

'Of course, of course.' Johannes nodded impatiently. 'So what is it?'

'The tarot.' Danny showed him the cards.

'I do not understand.'

'I think the characters from the tarot should be the theme,' Danny said. 'They're so much more powerful than farmyard animals. I mean, if you think they are, of course. Look ...' He flicked through the pack until he found the card for the Lovers. 'Here are Romeo and Juliet. And the Swords could symbolize the Montagues and the Cups, well, they're obviously the Capulets. If you think they are, of course ...'

As Johannes studied the cards, Terri appeared at the door. Seeing Johannes, her face fell. Danny silently gestured at her to leave.

'They do look slightly more in keeping with Shakespeare's original vision,' Johannes muttered. He sighed. 'But I am known for being a maverick – a creative genius.'

'Exactly. And what more genius idea than to link Shakespeare with the tarot? For all you know, the great man himself might have used the cards as inspiration.'

'He might.' Johannes looked at Danny hopefully. 'And I could be the genius who first made that connection.'

'Yes, you could,' Danny replied through gritted teeth.

'OK. Assemble the dancers in the studio,' Johannes barked, all of his earlier despair evaporated. 'Tell them I have made a stunning breakthrough.'

'Will do.'

Danny found Terri waiting for him in the corridor.

'Well?' she said, looking at him hopefully.

'Well, I think I may have just saved the day and you, my dear, owe me a *very* large drink.'

Lachlan woke with a start to the sound of a thumping bass line from a passing car stereo. The room was hot and bright. Too hot and bright. He'd only meant to close his eyes for a couple of minutes. He looked at his alarm clock, which he'd forgotten to set. It was gone five. *Shit.* He'd been asleep for seven hours. Now he'd never sleep tonight. Jeez, he hated working shifts. He stumbled upstairs to the bathroom and stood under a freezing cold shower, trying to get rid of his sluggishness.

Once he was suitably revived he returned downstairs, craving an ice-cold tinny. He found Cat in the kitchen chopping some veggies.

'Hello,' she said, and he could have sworn he saw a blush rise in her cheeks. She was no doubt embarrassed about Justin's earlier gruesome display of affection.

'G'day. You look busy.' He went over to the fridge and took out a beer.

'I'm making a king prawn curry.' Cat tipped some chopped onions into a pan on the stove and they began to sizzle. 'I found this great Indian food store on the high street. I got all the ingredients to make it from scratch.'

'Nice.' He wondered if he ought to offer her a drink. It would probably be rude not to. And anyway, she probably didn't drink beer. She looked like the kind of girl who'd drink that new sickly sweet alcoholic lemonade. 'Beer?' He offered her a can.

'Oh, yes, please. Thank you.' She took the can from him and cracked it open. 'How's your day been?'

'Not bad.' Lachlan coughed. 'I actually spent most of it asleep.'

But instead of looking all judgy, Cat nodded. 'I'm not surprised. You must get so tired working such long shifts in A&E.'

'Yep, sure do.' He hovered by the table again, uncertain of what to do. Would it be rude to go back to his room? Since she'd taken the beer he guessed they were officially having a drink together. He sat down at the table. His stomach rumbled as the smell of frying onions filled the room. 'How about you? How's your day been?' He tried not to think of her and Justin.

'Great, thanks. I spent the afternoon browsing around the market. I love it so much here.'

'Really?' Lachlan knew that Camden was a popular part of London, but so far he'd been immune to its charms. Mind you, ever since he'd got here he'd only really seen the world in black and white or the various shades of grey in between.

'Yeah, it's so full of life. So different to where I grew up.'

'Where was that?'

'Scotland. Just outside of Aberdeen. Don't get me wrong, it's really beautiful up there but …'

'Boring?' Lachlan filled the gap.

'Exactly! How about you? Whereabouts are you from in Australia? I can't imagine anywhere there being boring.'

He laughed. 'Yeah, well, the grass is always greener. I'm from the Gold Coast, in Queensland.'

Cat grinned. 'Well, that definitely doesn't sound boring.'

'It's OK, I guess. If you like surfing. And the rainforest.'

'It sounds amazing! What made you want to come to the UK?'

His throat tightened. 'Just fancied a change of scene.'

Thankfully, at that moment the phone in the hall started to ring. 'I'll just go and get that.' He hurried into the hall and picked up the receiver. 'Hello?'

'Can I speak to Cat, please?' He could tell instantly from the clipped, arrogant tone that it was Justin.

'Sure.' He left the receiver dangling and went back into the kitchen. 'It's for you. It's Justin.'

The way Cat's eyes lit up when he said this made him feel strangely disappointed. She seemed OK in every other way. He couldn't for the life of him figure out what she saw in Justin. Still, their relationship was none of his business. At least he now had the perfect excuse to go back to his room.

'Could you keep an eye on the onions, make sure they don't burn?' Cat asked as she headed into the hall.

Shit. 'Oh, uh, OK.' He went over to the pan and gave the onions a stir. Cooking was another thing he'd abandoned since leaving home. If it couldn't be slung in the oven on a tray or, even better, ordered from a takeaway, he wasn't interested. But as he stirred the onions he felt something softening inside of him. It was probably to do with his gnawing hunger, but the whole thing felt strangely comforting.

After a minute or so Cat came back in the room. Lachlan wasn't the most observant of people, especially when it came to women, but even he could tell something was up.

'Thanks,' she muttered, grabbing the pan back from him.

'Everything OK?'

'Yep. Great.' Her words came out like jabs. She turned the hob off and put the pan on the side.

'Hey, what's up?'

'Justin's not coming home.'

'What, ever?' Lachlan asked hopefully.

'No, for dinner.'

'Oh.'

Cat looked at the pile of vegetables amassed on the counter. 'So this was a complete waste of time, then.'

'What, do you not eat dinner if he's not with you?'

'No, of course I do, but … it just feels like a lot of effort for just one person.'

'What's that, sweetheart?' Lil wafted into the room, a riot of colour in a kimono, headscarf and red patent leather clogs. 'What's a lot of effort for just one person?'

'Making a king prawn curry from scratch,' Cat mumbled.

'Hmm,' Lil surveyed the food on the counter then turned her gaze back to Cat. 'If you loved yourself enough you wouldn't be saying that.'

Lachlan almost choked on his mouthful of beer. Even though he was used to Lil and her eccentric ways, her lack of filter still had the power to surprise him. Clearly it had surprised Cat, too, judging by her open-mouthed stare.

'I, uh, I do love myself,' she spluttered. 'I mean, obviously not too much. Like, I'm not *in love* with myself. I'm not arrogant – I hope.'

'I rest my case,' Lil said. 'So why, if you don't love yourself enough to make a prawn curry from scratch, have you assembled all of the ingredients?' She opened the fridge and took out a half-drunk bottle of white. 'Vino, darlings?'

'I'm good, thanks,' Lachlan replied, raising his beer.

'I was going to make the curry for Justin and me but he just rang and said he's going to be home late. He's out celebrating.'

Lachlan didn't think he'd ever heard the word 'celebrating' said with such bitterness.

'Celebrating what?' Lil poured herself a glass of wine and sat down at the table.

'He's got a part in a show,' Cat muttered.

'I see.' Lil took her tobacco tin from her pocket. 'The tragedy of young women today is that you have it all and yet you still give it away.'

'What do you mean?' Cat sat down opposite Lil.

Lachlan was now the only one still standing. Things were straying dangerously close to girl talk, a topic that always made him feel slightly uncomfortable, having grown up one of five brothers. Perhaps he should make his excuses and leave …

'Sit down, sweetheart, this affects you, too,' Lil commanded, waving her cigarette papers at him.

'It does?' Lachlan sat down at the end of the table closest to the door so he'd be able to beat a hasty retreat if need be.

'What do you mean, we have it all?' Cat asked again.

'You have your education, and your work, and the freedom to follow your passions and explore your sexuality.'

Lachlan cringed.

'But you still throw it all away on a man. No offence, Lachlan, sweetheart.'

'None taken.' Lachlan willed the phone to start ringing again to give him an excuse to leave – not that anyone ever rang him. His workmates had accepted long ago that he lived the life of a hermit outside of his shifts.

'I haven't thrown anything away on Justin,' Cat protested.

'You were about to throw a prawn curry away!' Lil exclaimed.

'Who's throwing a prawn curry away?' Danny asked, striding into the room. 'Don't do it, I'm starving.'

'Cat is,' Lil said.

'I'm not throwing it away, I'm just not cooking it,' Cat said.

Danny shot Lachlan a confused look. Lachlan raised his eyebrows and shook his head, as if to say, *I don't know, mate, Sheilas!*

Danny looked at the fresh herbs and veggies spread all over the counter. 'Why aren't you cooking it?'

'Because her lover is going to be home late,' Lil said, lighting her roll-up.

'Because I bought way too much for just one person,' Cat said.

Lil stared at her pointedly.

'I do love myself,' Cat cried. 'Just not enough to cook for hours to have to eat it all by myself.'

Danny shot Lachlan an even more bemused look. Lachlan had to bite his lip to stop himself laughing.

'Well, I'm very glad to hear that you love yourself, darling.' Danny went over to examine the veggies. 'But as far as I can tell, there's more than one person in this kitchen, so you wouldn't be eating alone and we can all pitch in and help you cook it, am I right?' He looked at Lachlan and Lil.

'Fine by me, mate,' Lachlan replied. He had to admit all this talk of curry and the smell of onions had left him starving.

'Sweetheart, that would be wonderful, I'm absolutely famished!' Lil exclaimed.

Lachlan stared at her. Had she engineered this entire conversation just so she could get a dinner? He wouldn't put it past her.

'Really? You'd all eat it with me?' Cat looked at them hopefully.

'Of course!' Lil exclaimed. 'We're family.'

'Family?' Danny echoed.

'Absolutely,' Lil replied. 'And the family that eats together stays together, don't they?'

She shot Lachlan a menacing stare.

'Er, yes,' he replied quickly. He glanced at Cat. She was smiling at Lil, but her eyes were shiny as if she might be close to tears. For some weird reason this sparked a sudden urge in Lachlan to march over and give her a huge hug. He took a swift swig of beer, trying to wash the feeling away.

'Thank you so much,' Cat said. 'I'd love to cook you all dinner.'

'All right then, let's get this party started.' Danny marched over to the radio and turned it on. 'Love is All Around' by Wet Wet Wet was playing.

'No!' Lachlan and Cat groaned in unison, before looking at each other and cracking up laughing.

Nine

Cat looked along the table at her new housemates – or family as Lil would say – and smiled. Danny had insisted she sit at the head of the table since she had cooked, and looking at them all so happy and animated made her feel warm inside. Of course it could have been the curry. And the wine and the beer. Whatever, at least she was feeling better than she had earlier on.

When Justin had rung and told her he'd got the Berlin gig, and that he was going to take it, she'd felt her entire evening teetering on a knife edge; her entire life, really. He'd gone for a celebratory drink in Soho with his new cast members and although he'd invited her to come and join them, she'd known that would only make things a million times worse. Seeing him with the people he was going to spend the next few months with, seeing them all buzzing with excitement, would have just about finished her off.

When she'd gone back into the kitchen and turned off the hob she'd seen a dire evening ahead of her. Holed up beneath the duvet consuming industrial quantities of chocolate, or ice cream, or both, while listening to eighties power ballads on repeat. The likes of Bonnie Tyler and Foreigner drowning out the sound of her sobbing, the curry ingredients flung in the bin. She never would have imagined her evening turning out to be so much fun. Cooking and dancing around the kitchen with Danny, while Lachlan and Lil and then Jewel and Pete had all congregated around the table. And now the curry ingredients weren't in the bin: they were inside all of them. At this thought, Cat let out a giggle.

'What's so funny?' Lachlan asked.

'Nothing, I'm just happy,' she replied. And somehow, weirdly, in spite of everything, she was.

'Well, cheers to that,' Lachlan said, raising his glass.

She noticed that his muscular forearm was covered in a sheen of golden hair, a sight that gave her a weird, shivering sensation in the pit of her stomach. Clearly, she was getting tipsy. But she didn't care. Anything was better than the horrible emptiness she'd felt earlier. She picked up her glass of wine and drained what was left of it.

'I do love your eyeliner, sweetheart,' Lil said to Jewel. 'It's very Cleopatra.'

'Thank you.' Jewel gave a shy smile. 'You're the second person to say that today.'

'Well, make me the third,' Cat said. 'I think it's great.'

'Did you know that Cleopatra was the product of incest?' Pete said from the other end of the table. It was the first thing he'd said since they'd started eating. There was something about his slow, low voice that reminded Cat of Eeyore from *Winnie-the-Pooh*.

'I did not know that, no,' Jewel replied.

'She married two of her brothers, too,' Pete added, before returning his attention to his ever-present notebook.

Cat glanced at Lachlan, who it turned out, had glanced at her at exactly the same time. Seeing him grin gave Cat the urge to giggle.

'If only the Jerry Springer Show had been around in forty-eight BC,' Danny quipped.

'She also had three of her siblings murdered,' Pete murmured, writing something. Cat wondered if he was writing a poem about Cleopatra's dysfunctional family, and the urge to laugh became overwhelming.

'I'll just go and do the dishes,' she spluttered, getting to her feet.

'Oh no, you don't,' Danny said. 'First rule of 27 Diamond Street – the chef never does the dishes.'

'I thought the first rule was always flush the toilet after taking a shit,' Pete muttered.

'Yeah, that's your first rule,' Danny replied. 'For most other humans it's a natural instinct. Anyway, it's way too early for talk of dishes. The night is young, let's carry on the party.'

Cat looked at the clock on the wall. It was almost ten and Justin still wasn't back. He was clearly bonding really well with his new dance crew. *Well, screw him.*

'Who's up for a nightcap at the Lemon Tree?' Danny asked.

'What's the Lemon Tree?' Cat asked.

'It's this great little Greek taverna just round the corner,' Danny said. 'Stelios, the owner, always stays open after hours. Who's in?'

'I am, their ouzo is to die for,' Lil said.

Cat looked back at the clock on the wall. Surely Justin would be home soon.

'Don't think about him. What would *you* like to do?' Lil said quietly.

Cat stared at her. Was Lil some kind of mind reader? But whether Lil could read her mind or not, the last thing Cat needed was another lecture on self-love and, actually, why should she consider Justin's feelings? He hadn't considered hers.

'I'm in,' she replied.

'Me too,' said Jewel.

'How about you?' Cat asked Lachlan.

'What the hell, I'm not back at work till Monday,' Lachlan replied.

'Nice one, mate,' Danny said. 'How about you, Pete?'

They all looked at Pete, who was still scribbling away in his notebook. 'I think I'm going to have to take a rain check,' he replied. 'The muse has struck.' He looked at Jewel. 'Thanks for the inspiration.'

'Oh, uh, you're welcome.' Jewel grinned.

'OK, let's take a break to freshen up and regroup in the hallway in five,' Danny said, getting to his feet.

Cat hurried up to her room and looked at herself in the wardrobe mirror. She was wearing shorts and an old Pineapple T-shirt, which had been perfect for cooking in but weren't exactly going-out clothes. Then she remembered the top she'd bought from the market earlier. She pulled it from her bag and put it on. Although it was way brighter than anything she'd normally wear, it really seemed to suit her and the vivid colours accentuated the red of her hair. She only hoped she wasn't viewing herself through beer goggles. She did feel pretty light-headed. She put on a pair of leggings and some beaded flip-flops. Then she ran a brush through her hair and applied a quick coat of gloss to her lips. She barely wore make-up any more, not since Justin told her he preferred the natural look on women. She gave herself a quick spritz of White Musk then wrote GONE OUT on the back of a receipt from the market and stuck it on top of Justin's pillow.

Danny looked at his reflection in the mirror and smiled. What with the breakthrough at work and a delicious homemade curry, it hadn't been a bad day at all. And it wasn't even over yet! He could hardly believe his housemates were all up for going out. Well, apart from Pete, but that was par for the course. Things were definitely looking up at Diamond Street.

Cooking and eating together had been a surprisingly fun experience, especially now the ice had broken with the new housemates and everyone was relaxed. And Justin being absent was a blessing, too. He might look fabulous but God, did he put a dampener on things, or more specifically on Cat. It had been fabulous seeing Cat come into her own this evening. And even Lachlan seemed to have relaxed and was up for coming out. Yep, the times they were a-changin'.

And maybe it was time for some other changes. He applied a quick dab of cologne to his face, studiously avoiding the bottle Gabriel had bought him. Perhaps it was finally time for him to move on romantically. But how? Maybe he needed to take affirmative action, like he'd done with the house and finding new housemates. Maybe it was time he looked in the classifieds for a new partner – or placed an ad there himself. Almost immediately the thought made him shudder. Why on earth would he advertise to have his heart broken all over again? Maybe a relationship wasn't an answer. Maybe he just needed to have some no-strings fun. Danny had always been a monogamous kind of guy, but where had that got him? Sobbing into his pillow, while he watched cheesy daytime films, that's where. He looked through his wardrobe and took out his favourite shirt – the one that made his blue eyes pop, or so the salesman had told him. Although he had clearly been desperate to make a sale, in more ways than one. Danny looked back at his reflection. 'It's time to get out there again,' he said, with rather more conviction than he felt.

As Jewel followed the others round the corner to the taverna, he couldn't quite believe what a great day he was having. Feeling the first buds of a friendship forming during his lunch with Alice had been a big enough bonus, but now this. He'd been expecting to come home to a quiet night in with a ready meal. Having a delicious homemade curry and going out on the town with his housemates was surpassing all of his expectations.

'Oh, wow!' he heard Cat gasp ahead of him.

As Jewel followed her inside the taverna he could see why. It was like stepping into Greece itself. Not that Jewel had ever been to Greece, but he'd seen enough of it in his all-time favourite film, *Shirley Valentine*. In the film, the main character, Shirley, had become so frustrated with her life and her marriage that she'd been driven to talking to the kitchen wall. Jewel could relate to this, due to his late-night conversations with his bedroom ceiling. He could also relate to the sense of frustration that was caused by being trapped in the wrong life. For Jewel, Greece had become synonymous with the freedom to be yourself – whether you were a middle-aged woman like Shirley Valentine, or a young man who didn't really feel male or female, like Jewel.

He looked around the taverna, trying to drink in every detail. The stencilled green vines clambering the whitewashed walls. The decorative shelf filled with plates painted in bright shades of red, orange, yellow and blue. The small, round tables, dotted with tealights flickering gold, and the bar at the back, lined with gleaming bottles and glasses. A short, round man with olive skin and jet-black hair came out from behind the bar and greeted Danny like a long-lost friend.

'Stelios!' Danny cried. 'So good to see you.'

'Danny! Where have you been? I miss your face.' Stelios kissed Danny on both cheeks and the men hugged.

'I just started a new job, I've been trying to keep a clear head,' Danny explained. 'But hey, it's the weekend and I need to come out to play.'

'Good for you.' Stelios grinned. 'How they say? All work and no play ...'

'Makes Danny a very dull gay,' Danny replied and they fell around laughing.

'You have some new friends?' Stelios nodded at Cat and Jewel.

'Yes, these are my new housemates.' Danny beckoned Jewel and Cat over.

'Very nice to meet you,' Stelios shook their hands. Then he turned to a tall, heavyset man behind the bar. 'Achilles, some drinks for Danny and his new friends, please.' He grinned at Jewel and Cat. 'These are on me. Welcome to the Lemon Tree.'

'Thank you,' Cat said. 'This place is really lovely.'

Cat had changed into a brightly coloured top, which made her red hair glow like flames. Jewel made a mental note to ask her where she'd got it. He looked around at the tables. About half of them were still occupied with diners finishing their meals. A couple of waiters, dressed in black trousers and crisp white shirts, wove in and out, clearing plates and fetching coffee. The warm air smelled of grilled meat, herbs and olives.

Even though Jewel was full of curry, it still made his mouth water.

Stelios showed them to a table in the corner by the bar, and the barman, Achilles, brought over a tray of thin glasses each containing a couple of ice cubes. He then produced a bottle and poured a generous shot of a clear liqueur in each. As it hit the ice, the drink turned milky white.

'Cheers everybody!' Danny raised one of the glasses.

'Cheers!' Jewel and the others all raised theirs, too.

Jewel smiled. Not only was he in what was essentially a piece of Greece, but he was about to drink the Greek national drink. Could he be any more Shirley Valentine! The silky liquid burned at the back of his throat and his mouth filled with the taste of liquorice. *Don't choke!* he yelled at himself inside his head. The last thing he wanted to do was make a fool of himself in front of his new housemates. It was bad enough being the youngest. He didn't want to advertise his lack of experience. Thankfully, the others were all busy laughing and 'cheers'-ing. Jewel settled back and took another sip. This time he was prepared for the strong taste, and it went down a lot easier. A passing waiter gave him a lingering stare. Instantly, Jewel's skin prickled. But the look wasn't unfriendly. If anything it was the opposite.

'Looks like you've got a fan,' Danny said, giving Jewel a playful nudge.

'Oh! No, I don't think so.'

'Stop being so coy.' Danny took a sip of his drink. 'Just make sure you leave the other one for me.' He nodded to Achilles, who was now back behind the bar.

'OK, you've got a deal.' Jewel laughed. Not that Danny had anything to worry about. Apart from a drunken kiss with a boy in sixth form, which had gone horribly wrong, Jewel was still massively inexperienced on that front. He looked across the table at Cat, who'd already downed her drink and was laughing at something Lil had just said. Cat's cheeks were flushed and her eyes were sparkling. She certainly seemed like a different person when Justin wasn't around, so much more relaxed.

Danny reached across the table for the bottle of ouzo and topped up Cat's glass.

'I think our Cat needs to let off a little steam,' he confided in Jewel.

'Oh, really? How come?'

'She's going out with a total and utter bellend. Although obviously that's just between you and me.'

'Of course,' Jewel agreed, although Danny wasn't exactly telling him something he didn't know already. Jewel was still smarting from the way Justin had quizzed him about his name in front of the other housemates.

'Stelios, could I get a beer?' Lachlan called.

'Oh, me too!' cried Cat, downing her second ouzo. 'This is so much fun.'

'Wait till the dancing starts,' Danny said.

'There's going to be dancing?' Cat's eyes shone even brighter.

'Of course there is. There's always dancing.' Danny grinned.

Lachlan watched as Stelios and the other waiters pushed the tables to the edges of the restaurant. All of the other diners had gone now and the only people left in the taverna were the residents of 27 Diamond Street. Stelios had hung the CLOSED sign on the door and pulled down the blinds, and Greek music was blasting away on the stereo. Lachlan had only been to one of Stelios's infamous lock-ins once before, when he'd first moved to Diamond Street. Danny had brought him down here with a group of dancers he was in a show with. It had all got pretty rowdy and Lachlan wasn't exactly one for dancing, so he'd made his excuses and left early. He was starting to feel the same instinct now. That old, familiar, nagging guilt, tugging away inside of him. He took another swig of beer to try to dilute it, but, if anything, the drink only made it stronger. *What right have you got to be out having fun?* his sense of guilt was saying. *How can you have a good time after what you did?* He watched as Danny shimmied his way to the middle of the impromptu dance floor. There was no denying the bloke knew how to move.

'Come on, Cat, come and join me,' Danny called.

Cat stood up, wobbling slightly. 'Whoops,' she laughed. 'The floor's rocking.' But once she reached Danny and started to dance, her drunkenness seemed to disappear.

'They're great dancers, aren't they?' Jewel said.

'They sure are.' Lachlan didn't seem to be able to drag his gaze away from Cat's hips. There was something hypnotic about the way they were swaying. Lil got up and joined them, her eyes closed, arms flailing, an unlit cigarette pressed between her lips.

'Come on, guys,' Cat called, breaking Lachlan from his trance. 'Come and join us.'

For a brief moment, Lachlan allowed himself to imagine what it would feel like to have his arm around those hips, to pull Cat close and … *What the fuck is wrong with you?* He stood up so quickly the room span. He hadn't realized how drunk he'd got.

'Yay, come on.' Cat danced over, holding out her hands.

'I've got to go, sorry.'

But Cat grabbed hold of his hands and started pulling him towards the dance floor.

Panic rose inside Lachlan, raw and fierce. 'I said no, I've got to go!' He hadn't meant to yell, and to make matters even worse the track came to an end just as he said it, the sudden silence amplifying his voice.

Cat dropped his hands as if they were hot coals.

'I'm sorry,' she said, looking horrified.

'No, I'm sorry. I didn't mean to yell. The music was so loud. I didn't know it was going to stop. I've got to go.' Lachlan stumbled over to the door and fumbled with the lock. Why wouldn't the door open? Why wouldn't the music come back on? After what felt like several lifetimes, Stelios came over and let him out.

Outside, the warm night air smelled of takeaways and car fumes. For the first time since he'd been in London, Lachlan wished he was back on the Gold Coast. How he longed for the space and peace of the ocean. He heard drunken laughter and a fox howling in the distance. He was such an idiot. He never should have gone out tonight. There was a very good reason why he'd lived like a hermit since getting to London, and what had just happened was a cutting reminder. And now he'd made things really awkward with Cat – the last person he would have wanted to hurt. *But that's you all over, isn't it,* his inner voice taunted. *You hurt the nicest people.*

Lachlan half stumbled, half marched round the corner to Diamond Street. He let himself in and went straight to his room. Without getting undressed he crashed face first on his bed – and let out a deep, gut-wrenching sob.

Ten

As Cat followed Danny, Lil and Jewel into the house she got a flashback to herself as a teen, sneaking home drunk in the early hours of the morning. But as she crept through the hallway she realized that, with Pete two floors above, the only people she was likely to wake up were Lachlan and Justin, and right now she didn't give a crap about either of them.

'Night,' said Jewel, heading off along the passageway to his room.

'Night,' the other three chorused, before heading upstairs.

'Thanks for a great night,' Cat said to Danny when they reached the first-floor landing.

'You too, darling.' Danny gave her a hug.

'Sweet dreams,' Lil whispered. Her make-up had smudged, turning her cat eye into more of a panda.

As Lil trooped upstairs and Danny went into his room, Cat took a deep breath and tried to gather her thoughts. But, thanks to the ouzo, wine and beer, her thoughts didn't seem to want to cooperate. They were slipping around inside her brain, just out of grasp.

She opened her bedroom door and stepped into the darkness

– promptly stumbling over something, sending her crashing into the chest of drawers.

'What the hell?' The silhouette of Justin rose up in the bed like Dracula in his coffin, giving Cat a fit of the giggles.

'Cat? Where have you been? My God, it's half-past three.'

She heard a fumble and a click and the room was flooded with the glow from Justin's bedside lamp. Justin was staring at her. Or were there two of him? She squinted and tried to get her balance.

'Are you drunk?'

'A little bit.' She waited for him to start having a go at her. Not that she was bothered. Alcohol-induced numbness wrapped itself around her like a quilt.

'Come here. Have some water.' His voice was surprisingly tender.

She somehow stumbled her way over to the bed. Justin brought a glass of water up to her lips. She took a sip. And another. Then she keeled over sideways and her head hit the pillow.

'I've been out with our new family,' she mumbled.

'What new family?'

'Here at Diamond Street.'

'Oh. Right.'

'So, you're going to Berlin.'

'Yes, but I have some good news.'

'What?' Cat curled up on her side. Her eyelids felt so heavy.

'I want you to come, too.'

'Cat, Cat, wake up.' Justin's voice sounded as if it was coming down a very muffled tunnel.

Cat groaned and rolled over.

'How's the head?'

'Not good.'

She tried to open her eyes, but they were stuck together with the clogged remnants of her mascara. She felt absolutely putrid.

'I'm going for a run along the canal. Do you fancy it?' Justin sprang from the bed with what seemed to Cat like an impossible amount of energy.

'I don't think I'm able to, sorry.'

'No worries.' He put on a T-shirt and shorts and came and sat down next to her. 'Did you have a chance to think about what I said?'

'What you said?' As Cat tried to sit up the room seemed to tilt on its axis.

'About Berlin.'

Justin was going to Berlin. The memory slammed into her, jarring her from her hangover.

'You got the job.'

'Yes. And I want you to come, too.'

'What?'

'I want you to come, too. I did ask you last night but you were so out of it I don't think you heard me.'

Cat blinked hard, trying to make sure that she hadn't slipped Alice-like into some weird wonderland where Justin didn't mind her getting drunk without him and did nice things like invite her to Berlin.

'You want me to come to Berlin?'

'Yes. It'll be so cool. You could get a job waitressing or something.'

'Waitressing?'

'Yes. Or bar work.'

'But what about my dancing? And what about this place?'

'Oh, come on, Cat, do you really aspire to this?' He cast his arm about the room.

Well, yes, actually, I do, Cat wanted to say, but she was feeling way too fragile to provoke an argument.

'The people who live here are all really weird.'

'No, they're not.'

'Seriously?' Justin's blue eyes widened. 'Lil acts like she's on something the whole time and that poet guy is seriously depressing. And the Australian bloke is a total freak.'

'What's wrong with him?' Cat said, before getting a hazy flashback of Lachlan yelling at her.

'When I got home last night I could hear him crying,' Justin said with a weirdly triumphant tone.

'What?' The thought of tough Aussie Lachlan in tears was too much for Cat's befuddled brain to handle.

'I could hear him crying in his room. I'm telling you, Cat, it's a house full of losers. Apart from Danny.'

'But we've only just moved in.'

'Exactly. It'll be easy to move out. We can just say it isn't for us. That my work's taken us away. Danny will understand. He's a dancer. He's worked abroad. He knows the score.'

'But …' Cat trailed off, unable to articulate the growing fear she was experiencing, even to herself. She'd been dreading Justin going to Berlin without her. Now that he was inviting her to go with him, they could still be together. So why did she feel so sick? It had to be her hangover.

'I think I need to take a shower and have a cup of tea. Can we talk about this when you get back from your run?'

'Of course.' He plonked a kiss on top of her head.

After her shower Cat went downstairs to the kitchen. Thankfully, the room was empty, but the kettle was piping hot as if it had just been boiled. No doubt one of her hungover housemates had just visited, also in need of a caffeine fix. She made herself an extra strength coffee with two sugars and sat down at the table, which was still covered in last night's dinner dishes. Feeling a bit sick at the sight of the congealed remains of the curry, she decided to take her coffee into the backyard. It was only when she got there that she saw Lachlan was already sitting on one of the rusty garden chairs, nursing a cup of tea.

'Oh, hello.' Cat's face flushed, which instantly made her angry. Why the hell should she be embarrassed? She wasn't the one who'd acted like a shouty idiot.

'G'day.' Lachlan at least had the good grace to look mortified. His face flushed red and he stubbed at a loose paving slab with his foot.

Cat was about to go back inside, but she stopped herself. He was the one who'd done something wrong. Why should she miss out on coffee in the sun and some precious Vitamin D because he'd acted like an idiot? Lachlan was from the Gold Coast, where they got sunshine on tap. No, not on tap, that was a bad analogy, you would get rain on tap. How would you describe copious amounts of sunshine? she pondered. Sunshine on a loop, maybe. Whatever! Lachlan's stores of Vitamin D were no doubt overflowing. But she was from Scotland. She needed to soak up every ray she could get. *Stop dithering and just sit down,* she told herself.

She moved one of the chairs into the patch of sunshine. This meant that she was now closer to Lachlan than was comfortable given the circumstances, but so what? If he didn't like it he could leave. As if on cue, Lachlan got to his feet.

'I'm sorry about what happened last night,' he mumbled, still looking at the ground. 'I, uh, don't really do dancing.'

'No kidding.' Then Cat remembered what Justin had said about hearing Lachlan cry. Surely he didn't hate dancing so much that it would have brought him to tears. There had to be more to this, more to Lachlan than him just being an idiot.

'I'll, uh, leave you to it.'

'Don't go.' The words popped out before she had time to judge whether they were the right thing to say. 'Please.' She gestured at his chair.

His expression softened. 'Are you sure?'

She nodded.

Lachlan sat back down. 'I'm sorry I yelled. The music was so loud and I ...'

'It's OK,' Cat cut in. 'We'd all had a lot to drink. I don't want it to be awkward between us. I mean, we've only just become housemates. Although we might not be for much longer ...' She trailed off and took a sip of her coffee. The more she woke up, the more the enormity of Justin's proposition was hitting her.

'What do you mean?' Finally, Lachlan made eye contact. 'You're not moving out because of me?'

'Of course not. Don't flatter yourself. I've had far worse rejections.'

Lachlan looked mortified.

'I'm joking! Honestly, it's fine. Justin's got a job in Berlin. He wants me to go with him. Please don't say anything to Danny or the others. I only just found out. I don't know what's going to happen.'

'Oh. Right.'

Cat looked around the yard, at the faded mosaic on the wall and the clusters of plant pots and the stone bust of someone who looked suspiciously like Yoko Ono. Just like the rest of the house, there was a ramshackle beauty to it, a homeliness. She'd been so excited to find this place, to escape Justin's parents, but now it felt as if Justin was calling the shots all over again. But Berlin didn't mean living with his parents in suburban hell. Berlin was exciting. Wasn't it?

'Do you want to go to Berlin?' Lachlan asked softly.

'I don't know. It was always a dream of Justin's to dance there.'

'And what about you?'

'What do you mean?'

'What's your dream?'

'I – I'm not sure.'

Lachlan finished his drink and stood up. 'I'm going to have a shower.'

'OK.'

'We have a saying back home – someone I used to know was always quoting it.' He smiled, but there was a sadness in his eyes, as if he was recalling a poignant memory. '"Those who lose dreaming are lost."'

'Oh.' Cat waited for Lachlan to say something else.

'See you later.' He walked past her into the house.

Well, what was that supposed to mean? *Those who lose dreaming are lost.* Lachlan's words echoed in her head. She wasn't lost. Was she? She'd felt lost at Justin's parents' place. But since finding the house on Diamond Street it was as if she'd rediscovered an important part of herself. The reason why suddenly hit her with light-bulb clarity: it was because living in Camden had always been one of her dreams!

She stared into the house after Lachlan. She really couldn't work him out. Was he some kind of Australian Confucius? With an extreme allergy to dancing? Whatever, he'd somehow managed to point her in the right direction. She needed to figure out if going to Berlin could be her dream, too.

Lachlan sank down on to his bed with his head in his hands. What the hell had he said that to Cat for? After what had happened last night and now this she must think he was a crazy person.

Then he noticed the corner of a photograph sticking out from beneath his pillow, and his stomach lurched. For over a year that photo had stayed hidden away inside the innermost pocket of his backpack. He'd had to bring something with him when he left Australia, some kind of memento. But just knowing it was there was enough for him. He'd never felt the urge to look at it – until last night. Last night it was as if the lid he'd spent so much time and effort pressing shut for the last couple of years had exploded open, and now he didn't know if he'd be able to get it shut again. This was a terrifying prospect. He *had* to get it shut again. He grabbed the photo and took it over to the cupboard where he kept his backpack. But as he opened the door the photo came into his vision and he caught a glimpse of that grin. *Damn it!*

He held the photo up and studied it fully. It was of him and Michelle at Bondi during Mardi Gras. Michelle had painted rainbow streaks across her cheeks and she was holding a banner saying CHOOSE LOVE in matching colours. When he looked at himself in the photo it was like looking at a stranger. He looked so young. So happy. Being with Michelle had softened his hard edges, and this photo acted as some kind of scientific proof of that. She had eased the cynicism out of him, calmed him down when he got hot-headed. She always knew the right thing to say. Like that Aboriginal quote he'd shared with Cat. Michelle had loved that quote so much that she had it as the screensaver on her computer. Lachlan wasn't sure why it had come back to him just now, out in the yard. At that moment it had seemed so glaringly obvious to him that Cat was living in the shadow of Justin's dreams. But what did he really know?

'You would have known, wouldn't you?' he whispered to Michelle in the photo.

Oh great, now he was talking to dead people.

You did the right thing, he imagined Michelle whispering back to him. Jeez, now he was *hearing* dead people! This was no good. He tucked the photo in the pocket of the backpack and zipped it up tightly. He'd been looking forward to having a whole weekend off, but now the prospect of being alone with his thoughts for two whole days was terrifying. There was only one thing for it. He'd have to call the hospital, see if there were any extra shifts going.

Jewel shoved a Pop-Tart into the toaster and stirred his mug of tea. Surprisingly, apart from a slight headache, he seemed to have escaped a full-blown hangover. And even the dull throb in his head felt like some weird kind of badge of honour, evidence of a life being lived to its fullest. He looked around the kitchen and grinned. Even the congealed remains of curry on the dishes looked great in this new life of his. Finally, he was a part of something he actually wanted to belong to. He cleared a space at the end of the table and sat down. Because the show he was working on was still in rehearsals he didn't have to work again till tomorrow. Today he would go exploring the charity shops of Camden Town for some clothes to customize. He wanted a new wardrobe to go with his new life.

The door opened and Lil walked in. She was wearing the remains of last night's make-up, a purple kaftan and a tiger-print scarf wrapped around her head as a turban.

Jewel imagined the reaction someone like Lil would get if they were spotted walking down the high street in the town where he had grown up. Back there, everyone wore the generic 'uniform' deemed appropriate for their class or age group, and the older people got, the more generic the uniform. Someone like Lil would be labelled a freak. But not here. And this was exactly why Jewel had moved to London – it was a home for the mavericks and the so-called freaks.

'Good morning, sweetheart,' Lil gave Jewel's shoulder a squeeze as she walked past to the kettle. 'How's your head? Mine hasn't ached this much since Keith Moon practised a drum solo on my headboard. May his tortured soul rest in peace.' Lil paused to quickly cross herself.

'I'm actually feeling OK, thanks.' Jewel grinned.

'Ah, to be young again and immune to the perils of alcohol!' Lil turned the kettle on and sniffed the air. 'What is that heavenly smell?'

'I've got a Pop-Tart toasting.'

Lil clasped her hands together like an excited kid. 'Oh, aren't they the best thing to have ever happened to the toaster?'

'Oh … yes, I suppose.'

'Toast is so tedious. You always have to spread it with things, but Pop-Tarts. They just pop up and off you go.'

As if on cue, Jewel's Pop-Tart popped up.

'Ta-da!' Lil cried theatrically.

'Would you like one?' Jewel offered.

'Oh, that's so kind of you.' Lil put the Pop-Tart on a plate and brought it over to the table. 'Delicious,' she said, taking a bite.

'Oh, right, OK. I'll just put another one on for me then.' Jewel couldn't help grinning. What might seem annoying or even downright rude in another person somehow seemed endearing in Lil. It was an impressive skill.

'So, what are you going to do today?' Jewel asked as he dropped another two Pop-Tarts in the toaster. He wasn't just asking out of politeness, he was genuinely intrigued as to what someone like Lil would get up to.

'I'll probably go flâneuring,' Lil replied through a mouthful.

'What?'

'Flâneuring. Please don't say you've never heard of it.'

Jewel shook his head. 'Sorry. Is it some kind of dance?'

'No. Well, I suppose it involves the dance of life, but no, it's walking, or rather strolling, with no purpose other than to observe society.'

Jewel nodded but he still felt slightly confused. Why not just say she was going for a walk?

'I bet you're wondering why I didn't just say I was going for a walk,' said Lil.

'Oh, uh, yes.'

'Going for a walk is boring. It's the equivalent of toast. Whereas flâneuring is a delicious Pop-Tart of an experience. A *flâneur* roams free. A *flâneur* sees everything there is to see.' Lil gesticulated wildly, showering the table with crumbs.

'Right,' Jewel replied. Although he really wasn't any clearer.

'I have a wonderful idea!' Lil exclaimed. 'Why don't you come flâneuring with me?'

'Oh, well …'

'We can go to Soho. I can show you my old haunts – and how to flâneur like a pro – and I mean professional, not prostitute,' she added.

Jewel laughed. 'That sounds great. I would love to go flâneuring with you.'

Cat got off the Tube at Covent Garden and let the tide of people carry her into the lift and up to the street. It had turned into one of those humid, overcast days that smelled of imminent rain. She didn't care, though. Ever since her weird chat with Lachlan in the backyard she'd felt the compulsion to go for a wander on her own. She needed some time and space to process her thoughts. At first, Justin had been annoyed when she told him she wanted to go out for a bit. But then she'd made up an excuse about needing to buy a birthday present for her mum in Fortnum & Mason and he'd softened. Justin detested going shopping, unless it was for him.

Cat turned right out of the station and headed towards Covent Garden Market. A man spray-painted silver was standing motionless on a crate, pretending to be a statue. As she approached he waved at her suddenly, causing her to shriek. Her face flushed as she hurried by. Why was she so jumpy? *Because you need to make a major decision, a major, life-changing decision,* her inner voice replied.

She walked around the edge of the market. The cobbled street was crowded with tourists, buskers and shoppers laden with fancy bags from the designer outlets. Her gaze fell upon a poster outside the Royal Opera House, advertising *Swan Lake*. As she looked at the ballerina on the poster she was cast back in time to her eight-year-old self. Back then she hadn't felt lost. Back then she had a clear vision – to one day be dancing here, for the Royal Ballet. She looked at the ballerina's elfin face and delicate limbs. Then she looked at her reflection in the glass, cringing at how sturdy and curvy she looked in comparison. She'd lost her ballet dream when she kept growing taller and curvier and sturdier, but did this mean she was destined to spend the rest of her life lost? On a whim she went into the foyer of the Opera House and over to the ticket desk.

'Do you have any returns for the matinee?' she asked.

'There's one left up in the gods. It's a restricted view, though,' the woman replied, looking at her computer.

'That's fine. I'll take it.' As Cat waited for her ticket to be printed she felt a nervous energy bubbling inside her. She wasn't entirely sure why she was doing this, whether it was a compulsion to say goodbye to her dream for good, or if she was hoping for some kind of divine inspiration. Either way, she hoped it would help bring her clarity.

As Jewel followed Lil through Chinatown he ran through a quick mental checklist to make sure he wasn't fitting any of Alice's Tourist Most Likely to be Mugged criteria. *A-Z* hidden away in bag, check. Wallet also hidden away, check. No expensive camera on display, check.

'Now, the main rule when it comes to flâneuring is that we have no objective and no final destination,' Lil said.

'OK.'

'To aimlessly wander is the only objective.'

Jewel nodded. It sounded like the perfect laid-back way to spend the day.

'Although if we were to at some point aimlessly wander into an establishment that serves alcohol, that would also be very agreeable,' Lil added. 'I'm in urgent need of a little hair of the dog.'

Lil was wearing a charcoal pinstripe man's suit, complete with patent leather brogues and a burgundy fedora. Her black kohl cat eye make-up had been freshly applied and her lips were painted scarlet. She looked awesome.

Jewel hadn't exactly been sure what a flâneuring outfit entailed, so he'd gone for a short-sleeved shirt dress, leggings and patent DMs. It was only the second time he'd worn a dress in public, but he figured that since they were going to Soho it would be pretty low-risk. And so far it was Lil who was drawing all the stares. And they were definitely looks of admiration rather than ridicule.

'Never, ever eat in there,' Lil said ominously as they walked past a Chinese restaurant with a gaudy, red and gold façade. 'I got such a bad case of food poisoning there I thought I was going to expire. It was even worse than the time I OD'ed on mushrooms at Woodstock and nearly choked on my own vomit.' She nodded soberly. 'Yes, I too was almost a member of that tragic group – the Twenty-seven Club. Although strictly speaking I was thirty-one at the time but anyway ...'

'What's the Twenty-seven Club?' Jewel asked.

'It's the collective noun for the singers who all tragically died at the age of twenty-seven. Jim Morrison, Janis Joplin, Marc Bolan, Hendrix. I had soul connections with most of them, although that's got nothing to do with them croaking it. That was far more to do with the drink and drugs and vomit. And in poor Marc's case, an unfortunately placed tree.'

Jewel looked at Lil blankly. As was becoming the norm, he didn't really have a clue what she was talking about, but it was still hugely entertaining.

'This place was so much better in the sixties,' Lil said as they made their way to Wardour Street. 'It was so much grittier.'

They walked past an adult cinema. A neon sign with three flashing *X*s hung on the wall. Across the street, Jewel saw a woman with maximum make-up and minimum clothes standing in a doorway, smoking a cigarette. It was hard to imagine Soho being any grittier, but then they turned a corner and came upon an expensive-looking wine bar that was all tasteful, low lighting and leather seats.

'There was nothing like that back in the day,' Lil said with a haughty sniff. 'Bloody yuppies ruined everything.'

Jewel nodded, but privately he didn't care one bit. Even with its yuppie wine bars, Soho was still way edgier and more exciting than anything that the town he had grown up in had to offer. The closest that had come to edgy was when the American-style diner advertised a special named Chicken Swingers, causing a collective meltdown on the letters page of the local newspaper.

'Ooh, that reminds me, I need to pick up this month's issue of my magazine,' Lil said, heading across the narrow street to a video store with a blacked-out window.

As Jewel followed her into the store it took every muscle in his face to maintain his composure. Judging by the predominance of leather-clad men on the video cases, this clearly wasn't a branch of Blockbusters.

'Duncan, my darling!' Lil cried, greeting the man behind the counter.

He was wearing a tight, white vest top and black leather trousers, and his arms were covered in Navy-style tattoos – a ship's wheel on one forearm and a huge anchor on the other.

'Lil!' he called. 'Lovely to see you, babe. How have you been?'

'I've been wonderful, sweetheart. This is my new friend, Jewel.'

Jewel willed himself not to blush as Duncan gave him the once-over.

'We're out flâneuring,' Lil continued.

Duncan nodded as if this was the most natural thing in the world.

'And as we were just passing, I thought I'd get my magazine.'

'Sure thing.' Duncan took a magazine from beneath the counter and put it into a bag. 'You're going to enjoy this one. It's a Wild West special.'

'Ooh, goodie!' Lil paid and tucked the magazine inside her handbag. Then, after a brief chat with Duncan about how Soho was going to the dogs and yuppies were the scum of the earth, they resumed their flâneuring.

'You might be wondering why I get my kicks from a magazine titled *100 Percent Beef*,' Lil said, as they wove their way along the narrow street.

'Oh, uh, no – well, yes, I suppose ...' Jewel stammered.

'I adore the male form.'

'Right ...'

'And as much as I love and respect the sisterhood, I have no desire to see them naked.'

'OK ...'

'So gay porn is the only way forward.'

A passing woman shot Lil a bemused stare.

'It's the same reason I haven't eaten cabbage since becoming an adult and being free to make my own dietary choices,' Lil continued.

'It is?'

'Yes, why ruin your palate with things that make you squeamish?'

'That's actually a very good point.' Jewel nodded.

'Of course it is. I'm full of them, sweetheart.'

Jewel laughed, and they continued flâneuring their way along the street.

Danny had planned to spend his day nursing his hangover with bacon sandwiches and copious cups of coffee in bed. But no such luck. Johannes had paged him at nine in the morning with the code 999. Danny had staggered to the hall phone, his body aching and his mouth lined with a foul, ouzo-flavoured fur.

'What's the emergency?' he asked as soon as Johannes picked up.

'Everything! Everything is the emergency!' the choreographer barked back. 'I'm calling everyone in for an emergency rehearsal to help explore my new tarot-based interpretation.'

'What, today?' Danny mumbled.

'Of course today!' The line went dead.

And so, instead of enjoying his bacon sandwich and coffee in bed, Danny found himself squashed into the corner of the back seat of a bus, cursing Johannes' existence.

The worst thing about this development was that Danny had gone to bed last night determined that today would be the day he kick-started his love life. He had meant to have a night out at Heaven or the Royal Vauxhall Tavern. He'd been planning on having himself some fun. But now, thanks to Johannes, he'd be way too tired to go out, let alone for anything else. He had a horrible feeling Johannes would keep them rehearsing for hours.

As the bus trundled up a congested Camden High Street, an acute attack of hangover anxiety began to kick in. What if he never met anyone ever again? What if he was destined to grow old alone – or even worse, with cats? What if Gabriel hadn't just broken his heart? What if he'd broken Danny beyond repair?

An old man sitting on the seat in front of Danny started coughing like his lungs were about to explode. Great. Now he'd probably catch some kind of horrific summer plague, making his chances of pulling even more remote. The woman next to him kept expanding further and further into his personal space, swamping him with her rolls of flesh, shopping bags and cloying floral perfume. *Relax!* Danny yelled at himself, his anxiety mounting. *Your life isn't over, you're only thirty-two.* Oh God, he was only thirty-two. If he lived to be eighty-two, or whatever the average life expectancy was these days, he could be facing fifty years of solitude and very possibly cats. That was half a bloody century! What if he ended up dying alone and unloved and, oh God, eaten by his cats? His chest tightened. *Do not have a heart attack!* he internally yelled. *You are not going to die on a bus next to this hideous, ever-expanding woman. When you die it will be in a blaze of glory doing what you love.* Danny wrestled his way free from his seat and past the woman. He pressed the STOP bell, and kept on pressing it.

'All right, mate, I heard you the first time,' the driver yelled.

Danny didn't care, as long as the bus stopped and he could be free from this can of horrors on wheels. The bus door opened and Danny leapt onto the pavement.

One thing was for certain. He had to get laid.

Cat came out of the opera house tingling from her head to her feet. In spite of her seat being practically high enough to cause altitude sickness and her view being partially blocked by a pillar, the ballet had been wonderful. And instead of convincing her that she ought to say goodbye to her dancing dreams, it had reignited her passion. As she'd lost herself in the performance she felt like that same little girl who, at the age of eight, had been taken by her parents to see *The Nutcracker* in Edinburgh and had come home too excited to sleep. Dancing was the only thing that made her feel this alive, this invigorated. Nothing else came close. Lachlan was right. Without her dream she'd been lost.

It was weird, because even though Justin was a dancer and shared the same passion, as soon as she had fallen in love with him it was as if the dreaming girl inside of her had been put to sleep. Their relationship had become her main focus instead. She'd taken the cruise ship jobs so that they could be together. But they had felt more like dancing on autopilot rather than the explosion of creativity she'd just witnessed in *Swan Lake*.

She made her way through the crowds to the Punch & Judy pub, where she bought an ice-cold glass of pinot. Something was happening to her. Something was changing. It felt as if the tectonic plates that formed her life were shifting.

She went out to the balcony of the bar and looked over the edge. The sky had cleared now and the warm air was slightly fresher. Down below a group of young black guys was assembling on the cobblestones around a portable CD player. They were dressed in tracksuit bottoms, vest tops and snowy white trainers. One of them pressed play and a hip-hop beat rang out. The guys fell into a loose formation, moulding their bodies to fit the beat. Cat grinned. She loved street dancers. She loved the fluidity of their movements and the way they tore up the rule book. It was all so different from the rigidity of ballet. One of the guys started doing a shoulder spin and passers-by stopped to watch and cheer. The energy from the dance crew was infectious. Cat felt it drifting up to her on the warm evening air.

They looked so happy. So free. So lost in the music and the moment. She couldn't remember the last time dancing had made her feel like that.

She lifted her gaze and took in the lights of London twinkling in the thickening twilight. And suddenly she was gifted a moment of dazzling clarity. This was where she wanted to be. In London. Pursuing her own dancing dreams. Not in Berlin, watching Justin from the wings.

Eleven

Jewel curled up on the sofa with his sewing box on his lap and a pile of charity shop purchases beside him. After he and Lil had flâneured their way around Soho, they'd stopped off for lunch and the hair of the dog in a pub on Rupert Street, then got the Tube back to Camden. Lil had now retired to her room to 'read her magazine' and Jewel was doing everything in his power not to imagine what this might mean. He picked up a cropped jacket from the pile of clothes and studied it. Then he searched through his scraps box for some military-style patches he'd bought a while ago in Spitalfields Market. They'd look great sewn onto the breast pockets. Jewel had always found sewing soothing, from the moment he'd had his first needlework class in school. But sewing wasn't just a relaxing pastime to Jewel, it had become his main creative outlet. Just as an artist expressed themselves through paint and a writer through words, Jewel expressed himself through fabric and nips and tucks and adornments. And now he was no longer living at home he didn't have to hide his creative flair. The notion that he could sit on a sofa in a living room and create to his heart's content, without fear of his parents staring at him like he was some kind of alien, was yet another thing that made his heart sing.

The kitchen door opened and Danny walked in. He was holding a tower of red and white striped takeaway boxes and he looked exhausted.

'Hey, Danny!' Jewel called.

'Oh, hey.' His voice was drained of its usual spark. 'Have you eaten? I stopped off at the Chicken Shack and I practically bought an entire poultry farm. I'm in urgent need of soul food.'

'Are you sure you've got enough?'

'Trust me, darling, I wouldn't have offered if I wasn't sure.' Danny grabbed a couple of plates from the cupboard and came into the living room, kicking his shoes off as he went. 'What's that you're doing?'

'Oh, uh, I'm just customizing a jacket I bought.' Jewel had a flashback to one of his dad's bemused stares. He really hoped Danny wouldn't think what he was doing was stupid. Danny didn't seem in the best mood.

Danny took the lid off a huge bucket of fried chicken and tipped half the contents onto a plate. 'Do you do a lot of that, then? Making clothes?'

Jewel nodded. 'Yeah, I love it.'

Danny put the chicken on the sofa in between them. 'Help yourself.'

Jewel put down his sewing and took a chicken wing. It looked and smelled delicious. 'Have you been working?'

Danny sighed. 'Yep, for my sins. We got called in for an emergency rehearsal. The choreographer I'm working with has had a bit of a meltdown. It's all very tedious. And not at all how I wanted to spend my day off. How about you? How did you spend your day? Please don't tell me you spent it in bed with a bacon sandwich or I might have to kill you.'

'What? Oh, no. Lil and I went flâneuring, in Soho.'

Danny raised his eyebrows. 'Flan-whating?'

'Flâneuring. It basically means walking.'

'Ha! How very Lil. Where is she now?'

'Oh, uh, upstairs in her room.' Jewel took a bite of chicken and hoped Danny wouldn't ask for any more details.

Danny opened a box full of chips and grabbed a handful. 'So, how are you finding life here at Diamond Street?'

Jewel instantly knew it wasn't cool to be quite so enthusiastic, especially in front of Danny, who was the epitome of cool.

'That's great. Chip?' Danny offered the box to Jewel.

'Thank you. It's really nice to be living with people who don't, you know, judge me.'

'I hear you,' Danny mumbled through a mouthful of fries. 'That's exactly how I felt when I ran away to join the circus.'

Jewel froze, with a chip midway to his mouth. 'What? Is that an actual thing? I thought people only ran away to join the circus in films.'

Danny laughed. 'Yeah, well, there have definitely been moments when my life has felt like a film. Although right now it's hovering a little too close to the horror genre!'

The kitchen door opened and Cat walked in.

'Oh, hey,' she said when she saw them. 'What are you up to? Are you having a picnic?'

'You're welcome to join us, darling,' Danny called. 'I'm eating my feelings so I've got enough to feed half of Camden.'

Cat laughed and came through to join them. Her hair was loose and her face was glowing. 'Oh dear, has it been a bad day?' She sat cross-legged on the floor in front of them.

'You could say that,' Danny replied. 'But nothing a bucket of the Chicken Shack's finest can't fix. How about you? How's your day been?'

'I went to see *Swan Lake*.'

'Oh, wow,' Jewel exclaimed. He'd read an article about *Swan Lake* when the show opened. The costumes looked stunning, the kind of thing he dreamed of designing one day in the future.

'What, at the Opera House?' Danny asked.

'Yes. I got a return ticket for the matinee. It was amazing.' Cat's smile grew.

'You lucky cow. I withdraw my offer of chicken,' Danny grinned, pretending to shield the bucket from her.

'And then I went for a drink in the Punch and Judy and there were these street dancers performing outside and it was just so …' Cat broke off and laughed. 'Sorry, I think I'm a little high on London.'

'That's exactly how I feel!' Jewel said.

'He's been out flanning in Soho with Lil,' Danny explained.

'Flâneuring,' Jewel corrected.

'What's flâneuring?' asked Cat.

'Meandering with no real purpose,' Jewel replied.

'Sounds a bit like my life,' Danny muttered.

'Have either of you seen Justin?' Cat leaned forward and helped herself to a chip.

'Yes, he came in about half an hour ago,' Jewel replied. Justin had come into the kitchen, taken one look at Jewel, and retreated without saying a word. 'I think he's up in your room.'

'OK, wish me luck.' Cat stood up.

'Why?' Danny asked.

'I'll explain later,' Cat replied. 'If I talk about it now I might lose my nerve.'

'OK, darling, good luck. Here, have a chip for courage.' Danny offered her the box.

'Thanks.' Cat took a chip and headed for her room.

'Sounds a bit ominous,' Jewel said, as soon as she'd left.

'Yes. I wonder if she's going to give Beautiful but Basic his marching orders,' Danny mused.

'Beautiful but Basic?'

'Justin.'

'Oh, right.' Jewel giggled and took a chip. He couldn't help hoping that Danny was right. As far as Jewel was concerned, Justin was the one fly in the ointment in Diamond Street.

I am not lost. I have a dream. I am strong. Cat recited a quick affirmation in her head before opening the bedroom door. Justin was sitting up in bed, watching something on their portable TV.

'Where have you been?' he asked, without looking away from the screen.

Cat's heart sank. He sounded tense. This did not bode well for what she was about to tell him.

'I went to see *Swan Lake.*'

'What? Who with?' Now he was looking at her.

'By myself. I popped into the Opera House while I was in Covent Garden and I managed to get a return for the matinee.'

'You went to the ballet by yourself?'

There was something about the way he said this, and the incredulous look he was giving her, that made her feel a weird mixture of embarrassment and anger. Did going to the ballet on her own make her some kind of freak? Why the hell shouldn't she go by herself?

'I thought you were going shopping?'

'I was. I did. It was a spur of the moment thing.' She sat down on the bed.

'Right.'

The sound of cheering on the TV filled the awkward silence.

'What are you watching?'

'Rocky III.'

'Oh. OK. Could we have a chat?'

'What, now?' Justin looked back at the TV. 'Rocky's about to fight Mr T.'

Cat felt a steely determination rising inside of her. 'I'm not going to go to Berlin.'

'What?'

'I'm not going to Berlin with you. I'm going to stay here.'

Justin picked up the remote and muted the TV. 'Why?' He frowned at her like she was insane. Was she insane? Was she about to throw away an amazing opportunity? It's not your amazing opportunity, it's *his,* she reminded herself.

'I need to stay here. Focus on my own dancing.'

'But you didn't get through the first audition. Don't you think ...' his voice softened.

'Don't I think what?'

'Don't you think it might be time for you to call it quits?'

Cat stared at him, horrified.

'You didn't get that other role you went up for, either.'

'I know, but that's the way it goes in this business. It doesn't mean I won't get anything.' *Does it?* she thought to herself.

He smiled at her and took her hand in his. 'Not everyone can make it in this business, hun. Maybe it's time you had a change of direction.'

'No!' she pulled her hand from his. But it was too late. He'd planted a seed of doubt in her mind and it was starting to sprout tendrils. Was he right? Was she just kidding herself? Had she lost what little talent she had? Was it time to call it quits?

'You could always teach.'

Those who can, do. Those who can't, teach. Wasn't that how the saying went? So, effectively, Justin was saying she should give up on her dream because she didn't have what it took to be a dancer.

'I don't want to teach,' she said, as much to try and reassure herself as to respond to him.

'I'm only trying to help.'

'Yeah, well, I don't need your help.'

'What is wrong with you?' The stare was back. The same patronizing stare she'd seen his dad repeatedly give his mum while they were staying with Justin's parents.

'Nothing.' Her firm tone completely belied the doubt she was now feeling. Was there something wrong with her? Was she in complete denial? The only thing she knew for sure was that she had to get away from Justin before she completely capitulated. She picked up her bag and went over to the door.

'Now where are you going?' he asked, muting the TV again.

'Out.'

'I really don't know what's got into you lately.' There was something about the way he said this, a smugness, that made her want to scream.

'Nothing's got into me. I just need to work out what I want to do.'

'Right, fine.' He pressed the remote and the sound of a baying crowd echoed around the room.

'Fine.' Cat left the room. She ran downstairs into the hallway and looked at the front door. Now what was she going to do?

The kitchen door opened and Danny came out.

'Oh, hello.' He looked at her, surprised. 'Are you OK?'

'Yes … no … I don't know.' Infuriatingly, she felt dangerously close to tears.

'Ha, pretty much sums up how I feel. I take it things didn't go too well with whatever it was you had to do.'

'You could say that.'

Danny nodded. 'OK. Dance, Tarot, Drink?'

'Sorry?'

'It's like that game Kiss, Marry, Kill, but you play it when you're facing a dilemma – or I do anyway.'

'How do you play it?'

'You just ask yourself, do I need to dance, tarot or drink my way through this dilemma. Or all three, if you're facing a real head-fuck.'

Cat laughed. 'Well, I think I did enough drinking last night to last me a month and I don't really know anything about tarot, but dancing could be good …'

'Great! Well, Jewel and I are about to head up to Heaven and you're welcome to join us. Although I have to say I am intending to get lucky tonight, so you guys may well have to make your own way home.'

'But isn't Heaven …?'

'A gay club? It's all right, darling, we'll let you in.'

'OK, cool.'

'Excellent.' Danny started heading up the stairs. 'Go and make yourself look fabulous and I'll meet you back down here in fifteen.'

'Oh.' Cat's face fell.

'What?'

'I've just had a bit of a bust up with Justin. I really don't want to have to go back up to my room.'

Just then Jewel appeared from the kitchen, holding an armful of clothes.

'Just in time, we need your help,' Danny said.

'What with?'

'Cat here is going to be joining us tonight but she needs a makeover.

Obviously she can't come to Heaven looking like that.' Danny gave Cat's leggings and over-sized T-shirt a withering look and shook his head. But unlike Justin's withering stare, there was a definite twinkle in his eye. 'Could you be her emergency stylist?'

'Sure.' Jewel's face lit up and he smiled at Cat shyly. 'Do you want to come to my room and have a look through my clothes?'

'If you don't mind?'

'Of course not.'

Cat followed Jewel along the narrow passageway to the back of the house and into his room. Although it was half the size of the room she shared with Justin, it was cosy rather than cramped, and awash with the most beautiful colours, from the patchwork quilt on the bed to the gold voile panels hanging in the window. Clothes were piled on every available space, and three rolls of fabric were propped against the wall. A tailor's dummy stood beside the wardrobe, with a tape measure draped around its neck. The overall effect was half bedroom, half fashion designer's studio. Cat loved it.

'Wow, that's beautiful, did you make it?' Cat asked, pointing to the main wall, which was draped with peacock-blue satin, accessorized with tiny golden flowers made from fabric.

Jewel nodded.

'I love what you've done with the bed, too.' Huge, brightly coloured cushions had been lined up against the wall so that the single bed could double up as a sofa.

'Thank you. Please, take a seat.'

Cat sat down and watched as Jewel added the clothes he was carrying to the pile already on the armchair by the window. The more she saw of Jewel, the more she was intrigued by him.

'Excuse the mess. I went a bit crazy in the charity shop earlier.'

'It doesn't look messy, it looks … Bohemian.'

'Oh, cool.' Jewel grinned, then he lowered his gaze as if he was embarrassed. 'Are you sure you want me to do this? Style you, I mean?'

'Of course. Danny was right. I can't go out looking like this. It'll be fun.'

'OK, then.' Jewel looked at Cat for a moment, then he opened the old oak wardrobe and rooted around. 'How about these?' he said, pulling out a tiny pair of sparkly silver hot pants.

'Oh wow, they're very ... small.'

'Yes, but they're very fabulous, too,' Jewel said with a grin.

'This is true.' Cat laughed. She had the feeling Danny would approve.

'And this top would look great on you.' Jewel pulled out an equally sparkly turquoise crop top. 'What size feet are you?'

'Six.'

'Perfect. Same size as me.' Jewel went over to a suitcase in the corner and pulled out a pair of silver boots. 'I was thinking maybe I could paint a silver lightning bolt on your face. A bit like David Bowie on the *Aladdin Sane* album cover.'

'Really?' An image of Justin's face loomed into Cat's mind: *I don't know what's got into you,* he was saying in that stupid, smug tone. 'Sure, go for it,' she added quickly.

Jewel put on some eighties music and set to work on Cat's hair and make-up. As Jewel brushed her hair, Cat felt the tension in her ease. This was fun. It reminded her of when she and her best friend back home used to get ready to go out when they were teens. They'd drink cider and play their favourite going-out songs and talk about their crushes and do each other's make-up. She sighed. Life was so much simpler then. The huge irony was that, back then, they couldn't wait to leave.

Finally, Jewel put the make-up down and stepped back, studying Cat's face. 'OK, I've finished.'

Cat's stomach fluttered as she went to look at herself in the wardrobe mirror, afraid she'd look ludicrous. But as soon as she saw her reflection she gasped. Jewel had sectioned off one side of her hair into thin, tight braids and swept the rest over to one side, giving her a slightly punky look and showing off the silver lightning bolt on her face to full effect. She looked edgy and cool, and so different from anything she would have come up with by herself! 'I love it!'

'Really?' Jewel looked so relieved it made Cat want to hug him.

'Yes. You've made me look like a superhero.'

Jewel laughed. 'Now all you need is your cape. Or your hot pants.'

Cat quickly got changed. Thankfully the hot pants just about fitted, although they had to be the tiniest shorts she'd ever worn. But instead of making her feel exposed, the outfit made her feel powerful, which was a definite improvement on how she had been feeling earlier on. While she studied her reflection, Jewel got changed into a black crop top, luminous green ra-ra skirt, fishnet tights and black patent DM boots. Then he adorned his thin arms with bangles in Day-Glo pink, yellow and orange, and painted miniature Day-Glo rainbows on his prominent cheekbones. He looked beautiful. Like a pixie about to go raving.

'Do I look OK?' he asked, coming to join Cat in front of the mirror.

'You look amazing.'

'Thank you. I, uh, this is all … dressing like this …' Jewel looked down at his skirt '… it's still quite new to me.'

'Really?'

'Yeah. I could never have worn this kind of thing back home.'

'Right. Not everywhere's quite as open-minded as London.'

'Exactly.'

'That's why I came here, too.' Cat sat down on the bed. 'I love how everyone's free to be themselves.'

There was a knock on the door. 'Are you decent?' Danny called from outside. 'Or rather, are you terribly indecent?'

'Yes, come in,' Jewel giggled.

'Holy cow!' Danny exclaimed as he walked in, bringing with him a crisp, clean waft of aftershave. He was wearing a tight white shirt and black trousers that showed off his toned physique. 'You both look fantastic. Jewel, you're a miracle worker.'

Jewel blushed. 'Thank you.'

'Stand up, darling, give us a twirl,' Danny said to Cat.

She stood up and gave him a pirouette.

'Very Ziggy Stardust meets Barbarella. I love it!'

'Cheers.' Cat grinned.

'OK, you fabulous pair,' Danny exclaimed. 'Let's go dancing!'

Twelve

Danny wove his way into the middle of the dance floor. The beat was pounding and the strobes were flashing. All around him people were losing themselves in the rhythm. He closed his eyes, letting his body find its way into the groove. As he started to lose himself in the dance, anger pulsed through him in hot waves. *To hell with Johannes. To hell with Gabriel. To hell with everyone.* The music got louder. The beat got faster. He shook the anger from him, throwing his body into increasingly frenetic shapes. He wanted to yell. He wanted to scream. He wanted to punch and kick. But instead he danced. And danced. Sweat streamed down the sides of his face. He didn't care. All that mattered now was losing himself in the music. The beat dropped and everyone cheered. Danny kept on dancing. Kept his eyes shut. The anger was fading now and in its place came that sweet, sweet release. He wouldn't be working for Johannes forever. It was just a means to an end. It was just a stepping stone. He imagined himself choreographing his own show – being able to work on his own terms – and his limbs loosened.

The air was humid and smelled of a delicious mix of cigarettes, alcohol and aftershave. On the track a siren wailed. Danny opened his eyes. Pink, green and purple beams swept across the dance floor like searchlights. The crowd moved as one, ebbing and flowing with the rhythm. Danny raised his arms. A feeling of liberation surged through his body. Nothing mattered any more. As long as the music kept playing and he kept dancing, he was free from all the crap. He saw a flash of red hair through a gap in the crowd and spotted Cat. Like him, she appeared completely lost in the music, her body turned from solid to fluid. Danny danced his way over. There was a rawness to her dancing he hadn't seen in her before. It was infectious. The siren wailed again. Cat threw her head back and screamed. Danny laughed. There was a manic energy in the air tonight and he loved it. Sweat trickled into his eyes. He pulled his top off over his head and a man behind him whooped. The beat built again. He swung his shirt above his head like a lasso. Faster and faster and faster, and then he let go, flinging it into the crowd. At exactly that moment Cat opened her eyes and saw him. She threw her head back and laughed.

Danny noticed a guy to his right throwing some impressive moves. He was blond and blue-eyed, and thin and wiry. The polar opposite of Gabriel. *Fuck Gabriel.* The beat slowed, the lights dipped. Danny let his body follow suit, melting into the slower melody. The blond guy looked up. They locked eyes. Danny felt an energy coursing between them, surging in through his eyes and right down to the ends of his feet. The guy danced closer. Danny followed suit. And just like that, he was in a dance of two. In the middle of the crowd of hundreds it was as if a spotlight had fallen just on them. Their bodies wove in and out, closer and closer. And then a drop of sweat fell from the guy's face on to Danny's and it was like a touchpaper being lit, setting off a burning deep inside of him.

Jewel took a sip of Bacardi Breezer and surveyed the dance floor. The music was so loud and the lights were so powerful it was breathtaking.

He'd never been in a club like this before. Of course, he hadn't said that to Danny when Danny had invited him to come along. Instead, Jewel had nodded and said, 'Yeah, sure,' when Danny asked if he'd been to Heaven before. The one night club in the town Jewel had grown up in – Pharaohs, 'Apsley's premier Egyptian-themed dance experience' – was about a quarter of the size of this club and felt more like someone's front room. The lights were arranged around the DJ's desk and looked like a set of traffic lights turned on their side. The only other decorations were a mournful-looking glitter ball that was no longer able to spin, and faded paintings of Egyptian mummies on the walls. It was all very tragic and nothing at all like this. This was ... incredible. But also slightly daunting. It didn't help that Jewel had somehow managed to lose both Danny and Cat. He knew they were dancing somewhere, but trying to spot them on the crowded dance floor was a bit like playing *Where's Wally?*

Jewel felt way too nervous to hit the dance floor by himself. He'd never been the most confident dancer, even alone in his bedroom, so the thought of demonstrating his lack of skill in such a public arena was terrifying. He looked at the seething mass of bodies. This was what he'd wanted for so long, to come to a club like this, but now he was here he felt really out of his depth. He took another sip of his drink. It suddenly seemed too sickly, while the music now seemed too loud and the cigarette smoke too thick. Maybe he should go. But he couldn't leave without telling Danny and Cat, or they might get worried. Then he spied a glimmer of silver on the dance floor. It was Cat. And there was Danny behind her, dancing up close with another man. They both seemed to be having a great time. It wouldn't matter if Jewel left them to it. He decided to go over to Cat, make his excuses and leave.

He necked the rest of his drink, left the bottle on a table, and made his way on to the dance floor. He wove his way through the pulsing bodies over to Cat and reached out to touch her shoulder. Her skin was slick with sweat.

'Oh, hi!' Cat exclaimed. Or at least that's what Jewel lip-read over the music.

'I'm going to go,' Jewel yelled.

'It's great, isn't it?' Cat grinned.

Crap! She hadn't heard. Jewel leaned closer so he could yell right in her ear. But before he could say anything, Cat grabbed hold of his hand and Jewel had no alternative but to dance along. At first he felt awkward and stiff but then he realized that the dance floor was so crowded no one really had the room to look at what anyone else was doing. And they all seemed too lost in the music, anyway. Jewel felt his body relax a fraction. Cat grabbed hold of both his hands and started spinning him around. Jewel's final defences loosened. He threw back his head and lost himself in the rhythm.

'That was bloody brilliant!' Cat exclaimed as, three hours later, she and Jewel spilled out of Heaven onto Villiers Street.

'Best night ever,' Jewel agreed. His pale face was flushed and his luminous face paint was slightly sweat-streaked. Cat dreaded to think what had happened to her lightning bolt. She'd danced non-stop for about four hours. It was the best workout she'd had in years – physically *and* mentally.

'Shall we try and find a shop before we get the night bus,' she suggested. 'I'm so thirsty.'

'Me too!' Jewel replied. 'I could murder a freezing cold 7 Up.'

'Oh, yes! Come on.' Cat linked arms with Jewel. She was so glad he hadn't left early. Especially as Danny had disappeared off with some random blond guy about two hours ago. When Jewel told her he was going home, Cat had pretended not to hear. She had a hunch that Jewel just needed a little help loosening up and letting go. She'd turned out to be right. 'It was really fun dancing with you.'

'You too.'

'And it was so cool not being hassled by any men.' As soon as she said it, Cat wanted to kick herself. She still wasn't entirely sure what Jewel's preferences were in that department and whether or not Jewel would welcome a guy's advances. 'Well, it was a relief for me, anyway,' she quickly added.

'Me too,' Jewel said quietly. 'I mean, I do like men, it's just that …'

'Sometimes they can be a little overwhelming?' Cat said softly.

'Exactly. And …'

'Yes?' Cat stopped walking.

'I'm not … I haven't … I'm not very experienced yet. It was impossible for me to be, you know, who I really am, when I was living at home.'

Cat nodded. 'How long have you been living in London?'

'Only a couple of months.'

'I think you're doing brilliantly. Come here.' Cat opened her arms. ''Scuse the sweat.' She giggled as she hugged Jewel to her.

'Ditto,' Jewel mumbled into her shoulder.

He felt so small, so fragile. Cat couldn't begin to imagine how much courage it must take to come out as a teenager, especially if your family weren't supportive. And then to make a new start on your own in London, like Jewel had done. That took real guts.

'I'm here if you ever need to chat about anything,' she said, stepping back slightly.

'Really?' Jewel's eyes widened.

'Of course. You turned me into a superhero tonight, it's the least I could do.' Jewel looked so grateful it tugged on Cat's heartstrings.

'Thank you so much.'

'You're welcome. Anyway, we're family now, don't forget – according to Lil, at least.'

Jewel giggled and they continued walking up the road. 'Yes, the Diamond Streeters.'

'Hmm, that's a bit of a mouthful.'

'Good point. How about the Diamonders?'

'Sounds a bit like a Neil Diamond fan club.'

Jewel frowned. 'How about the Rough Diamonds?'

'Love it!' Cat grinned. And as they made their way towards Trafalgar Square, with her limbs aching and her heart full of hope, a diamond in the rough was exactly how she felt.

July
1994

Thirteen

'Oh God, please make it end!' Danny exclaimed as he swept into the kitchen.

Cat and Jewel were sitting at the table drinking tea and eating Pop-Tarts while 'Love is All Around' by Wet Wet Wet was droning out of the radio. It was hard enough having to listen to that insufferable song at the best of times but at seven in the morning – there ought to be a law against it.

'Make what end?' Cat asked.

'This godawful dirge.' Danny nodded at the radio. 'How is it still number one? Who the hell is still buying it?'

'It's been about seven weeks now,' Jewel said.

'Seven weeks! Feels more like seven bloody years!' Danny turned the kettle on and started pacing up and down. It was the press night for *Romeo and Juliet* tonight and he'd hardly got a wink of sleep. 'God, it's hot in here. Is anyone else hot?' He grabbed one of the free newspapers from the counter and started fanning himself.

'They said on GMTV that it was going to be twenty-eight degrees in London today,' Jewel said.

'Twenty-eight? That's freezing!' Danny exclaimed.

'I think he's talking Celsius,' Cat laughed.

Danny took a mug from the cupboard. 'I only speak Fahrenheit. Can you please translate?'

'It's over eighty, so basically, really bloody hot,' Cat replied.

'Oh, great!' This was all Danny needed, a heatwave turning London into a giant pressure cooker on his big day. *It's not your big day, it's Johannes'*, he tried to remind himself, but to no avail. The fact was, once Johannes had capitulated and embraced Danny's tarot-inspired vision for the show, he'd also taken far more notice of Danny's advice when it came to the choreography. Of course, Johannes being Johannes, he didn't give Danny any credit for his input. But Danny's ideas were running right through the show like the writing in a stick of rock, and, if the press hated it, it would be a scathing indictment on his talents as a choreographer just as much as it would be on Johannes' abilities.

'Are you OK?' Cat asked as he continued to pace. 'You seem a little … tense.'

'It's press night tonight. It's got me a bit on edge.'

Cat smiled. 'You've got nothing to worry about, the preview was amazing.'

'Yes, it was brilliant!' Jewel agreed.

Danny had got them both comps for the preview a couple of nights ago. And they'd seemed to genuinely rave about it. The audience's reception had been just as effusive. But the preview audience was always full of friends and family of the cast and crew. They were bound to be more positive – unlike the press, who quite frankly, could be evil bastards.

'Thank you. I only hope the critics share your enthusiasm.' Danny put a heaped spoon of coffee granules into his mug.

'Would you like a Pop-Tart?' Jewel asked.

'Ooh, yes, please!' Lil exclaimed, sailing through the door, clad in a leopard-print negligee and her red clogs. A pair of half-moon glasses on a string of beads was perched on the end of her nose.

'I was actually asking Danny,' Jewel said. 'To try and soothe his nerves.'

'Why do your nerves need soothing?' Lil asked, peering over her glasses at him. She looked half brothel madam, half stern headmistress

– which in some brothels, Danny guessed, could be quite a popular look.

'It's the press night tonight, for my show,' he explained. 'And it's OK, you can have my Pop-Tart. I can't eat a thing.' That was one good thing about press-night nerves, it always meant he lost a few pounds, or kilos as that Celsius-fanatic Jewel would probably say.

The front door slammed and Lachlan trudged in. There were huge bags beneath his eyes and his chin was grey with stubble.

'G'day, all,' he muttered.

'Oh, sweetheart, you look ghastly,' Lil cried. 'Would you like a Pop-Tart?'

'Hmm, not quite sure what to make of that greeting,' Lachlan replied.

Cat laughed. 'I think it's what might be described as tough love.'

'I'm worried about you, sweetheart,' Lil said, bustling Lachlan into a chair. 'You're working every hour God sends at that hospital.'

'Yeah, well, it's a dirty job but someone's got to do it.'

'Caffeine?' Danny asked him as the kettle came to the boil.

'Cheers, mate, I could murder a tea. Two bags, please.'

'How was your night shift?' Cat asked.

As Lachlan started telling them all about a fight that had broken out between a couple of drunks in A&E, Danny took a breath and took stock. He didn't like to be dramatic – OK, yes, he did – but for once he didn't think it would be an over-exaggeration to say that his future career as a choreographer was hanging in the balance, and whatever happened tonight had the power to make or break it. Lil came over to him and stood on tiptoes, bringing a waft of her signature scent of tobacco and patchouli.

'I just slipped a little something into your pocket,' she whispered in his ear.

'What? How? When?' He put his hand in his trouser pocket and found what felt like a large roll-up.

'It's one of my special cigarettes,' Lil whispered with a knowing look. 'For medicinal purposes. You look like you could do with a little chilling-out. Maybe I'll roll one for Lachlan, too.'

'I wouldn't if I were you. You know what he's like about smoking.'

'Good point. Maybe I'll bake him one of my special cookies.'

Danny laughed. 'Thanks, Lil.'

'No problem, darling. It's Moroccan hashish, too. Couple of tokes on that and you won't give a hoot what the press vultures say.'

Danny only wished this was true. But he knew that he could smoke all the hash in Morocco, but a negative review wouldn't lose its power to devastate him.

Lachlan opened the fridge door and stared inside for inspiration. He was starving after his thirteen-hour shift, but it was already too hot to think of frying any sausages and bacon. He would have to have cereal, but he didn't have any milk. All of his housemates apart from Cat had left the kitchen now, to get ready for work, or in Lil's case to do whatever she did with her days – it remained a mystery. He glanced at Cat. She was leafing through a copy of the local paper.

'Hey, Cat, can I borrow some milk?'

'Sure,' she replied, without looking up. 'Mine's the skimmed on the bottom shelf.'

'Cheers.' He poured himself a huge bowl of cornflakes and added a token splash of milk. He didn't want to take the piss. He knew only too well that issues like taking a housemate's milk could escalate into a nuclear-style conflict if not handled delicately. And even though it had been over a month since his excruciating experience with Cat in the Lemon Tree, he didn't want to risk any kind of repeat incident.

He sat down at the other end of the table, not wanting to cramp her style. Jeez, he was tired. Every part of his body ached, even his fingernails. Lil was probably right. He probably was overdoing it on the work front, but he didn't want to risk almost unravelling again. At least when he was physically exhausted he didn't have the energy to over-think.

'Anything exciting happening?' he asked, nodding at Cat's paper.

'No, not really. I'm looking through the jobs section.'

'Really? Do they advertise dancing jobs in there?'

Cat shook her head. She looked slightly faded somehow, a paler, less vibrant version of herself. Or maybe Lachlan's tiredness was obscuring his vision.

'I'm not looking for a dancing job. Well, I am, but I'm not having much luck, so I'm looking for something else to do in between. Got to get the rent money somehow, especially now Justin's gone.'

'Right.' Lachlan gave her a sympathetic smile, but inside he couldn't help privately cheering. When Justin had moved out last week Lachlan actually cracked open a tinny to celebrate.

'So, has he moved out permanently, or just while he's working in Berlin?'

Cat shrugged. 'I don't know. I think it's permanent.'

Lachlan bit on his lip to prevent any hint of a grin. 'Hey, I don't know if bar work's your thing but I saw a sign in the Lemon Tree when I walked past just now – they're looking for part-time staff.'

'Really?' Cat's face lit up. 'That could work, especially if it's in the evenings. That way I'd still be free for auditions.'

Lachlan nodded. 'You should pop down there, have a word with Stelios.'

'I will. Thank you!' Cat stood up. She was wearing a vest top and short pyjama bottoms. Very short pyjama bottoms. Lachlan wrenched his gaze away from her seemingly endless legs. Jeez, why was she having this effect on him?

'Wish me luck,' she said.

'Good luck.'

As she left the room Lachlan wolfed down his cereal, trying not to think of Cat's long legs running up the stairs, and tuning in instead to the hum of the fridge.

Cat pulled on a sundress and studied her reflection in the wardrobe mirror. She wasn't sure if it was the right thing to wear on a job hunt, but it was so hot already, and, on balance, less clothing was surely a better look than sweating to death in some kind of corporate business suit. Not that she had anything vaguely resembling a corporate business suit. She pulled her hair up in a loose ponytail and applied a quick coat of mascara and a slick of lip gloss. She wasn't entirely sure how she felt about applying for a job at the Lemon Tree. On the one hand, it felt kind of depressing applying for something that had nothing to do with dancing, but on the other hand, having some money coming in would help pay the rent now Justin had gone.

She looked over at the bed. The night after he'd left she'd arranged a row of cushions in the bed beside her, to try to fill what felt like a gaping hole. But after a couple of days she'd forgotten to assemble her cushion man, and she'd spent the last few nights happily starfishing across the bed. It felt good having all that space to herself for once, and she couldn't help seeing a wider parallel in the rest of her life. Even though it was stressful trying to decide what to do next work-wise, having the space to figure it out on her own, without Justin's disparaging running commentary, felt like a strange kind of freedom. She gave herself a spritz of CK One and headed for the door.

Outside, the heat was even more oppressive, causing Cat's skin to instantly prickle with sweat. Crap! *I am cool. I am unflappable. I am the perfect bar person*, she began affirming to herself. *No, you're not, you're a dancer*, her inner voice annoyingly chirped. *I AM THE PERFECTLY COOL, UNFLAPPABLE BAR PERSON*, she yelled inside her head. *NO, YOU ARE NOT!* her inner voice yelled back. Great. This had to be the worst preparation for a job hunt ever. Getting a bar job was just a means to an end, she reminded herself. It wasn't the be-all and end-all. She turned the corner and the Lemon Tree came into view. The sight of the olive trees in their terracotta pots either side of the door and the brightly coloured cloths on the tables outside was instantly soothing. If she was going to work behind a bar anywhere, this had to be one of the best places. Just as Lachlan had said, there was a handwritten sign on the door, saying PART-TIME BAR STAFF REQUIRED, APPLY WITHIN. She opened the door and stepped inside. It was blissfully cool in contrast to the oven outside, and the air smelled of pastries baking and coffee brewing.

A heavyset, dark-haired man was standing behind the bar, polishing glasses. He looked familiar but for a moment Cat couldn't place him. Then she remembered he'd been working the night Danny brought them here for the first time. He was the barman Danny had a crush on. A crush that remained tragically unrequited.

'Hello,' the man said as she approached. He had a slight accent, which she assumed had to be Greek. 'Can I help you?'

'Yes, I'm here about the job. The part-time bar work.'

'Oh, yes.' He studied her for a moment. 'Do I know you from somewhere?'

She nodded. 'Yes. I was in here a few weeks ago, with my housemate, Danny. We were the ones who were dancing on the tables.' As soon as she said it she regretted it. Reminding a potential employer that she was the type of person who got roaring drunk and danced on tables might not be the best character reference. But thankfully he started to grin.

'Oh, yes, I remember now. When Danny comes in crazy things always happen.'

Cat laughed, relieved that Danny was taking the blame. 'Yep, he's certainly the life and soul of the party.' She looked around, wondering if Stelios was about.

'Would you like a coffee?'

'Oh, uh, OK.' She watched as he went over to the coffee machine and banged the old grounds into the bin.

'I'm Achilles, by the way,' he said, over his shoulder.

'Hi, I'm Cat. So, is Stelios here?'

Achilles shook his head. 'No, he's at the cash and carry.'

'Oh, right.' So why was he making her a coffee? A horrible thought entered Cat's mind. What if he was going to make a pass at her? She knew what these Greek waiters were like. She and Jewel had got *Shirley Valentine* out of the video shop the other night. What if he was about to try to seduce her? What would she say to Danny? She'd never be able to come back in here again, let alone work here.

'Do you take milk?' Achilles asked.

'No,' she replied, a little too forcefully, but she didn't want to give him any encouraging signals. Despite the cool breeze coming from the air-conditioning, a bead of sweat ran down her back.

'Sugar?'

'No.' *Please do not say anything cheesy like I'm sweet enough already.*

'Well, you're nice and easy,' he said with a grin, placing a cup of coffee on the bar in front of her.

What the hell was that supposed to mean? Did he think she was going to sleep with him? She'd only come in about a job, for Christ's sake. Oh no, what if he expected her to sleep with him in exchange for a job? What if this was the Greek taverna equivalent of a casting couch moment? And it was only just gone nine in the morning! Did Greek men have no restraint?

'Please, take a seat,' he said, gesturing at the bar stool beside her.

'No, thanks, I'd rather stand,' she replied. *I'm on to you, buster, and I'm ready to make an emergency exit the second you make a move.*

'Fair enough.' He came out from behind the bar.

Cat gripped her bag, ready to make a run for it.

Achilles sat down on the stool next to her. She could see the contour of his muscles through his white shirt and black trousers. He was undeniably attractive, if swarthy was your thing.

'So, do you have any previous bar work experience?' he asked.

'What?'

'Bar work? Have you done it before?'

'Oh, uh, yes. I worked in the Student Union bar when I was at university.'

'OK, and when was that?'

'All through my first and second year.' She quickly did the maths. 'About five years ago.'

'And what have you been doing since?'

'Working as a dancer.'

'Really? What kind of dancing?'

'I was in the chorus for a couple of London shows and then for the last two years I've worked on cruise ships.' Saying it out loud made her heart sink. When she'd been at uni, she'd dreamed that by the time she was twenty-five she'd be starring in a show, not having come full circle and be applying for bar work.

'And you no longer dance?' Achilles asked.

'No.' It wasn't a lie. The only time she danced at the moment was in her dreams.

'OK. And you say you are a housemate of Danny's?'

'Yes. I live in the same house as him, just round the corner on Diamond Street.'

He nodded. 'OK, then.' He took a sip of his coffee. 'So, are you free this evening?'

'What? No. Why?' Had he just been trying to lull her into a false sense of security with all of his work-related questions?

'I thought you could do a trial shift behind the bar for me.'

'For you?'

'Yes. I'm the bar manager.'

Oh God. Instantly, her face began to burn. She was so stupid. Why was she so stupid? But she also had a trial shift!

'Oh, I see, that's wonderful!' she exclaimed.

He looked at her, confused.

'I mean it's wonderful that you would give me a trial shift. And yes, now I come to think of it, I am free. Very free. So free.' *Oh my God, shut up!*

He gave her an amused grin. 'OK, then. How about you come back at six? You will need to wear a white top and black bottoms. Trousers or skirt, both are fine.'

'OK, great. Thank you! Thank you!' She took a sip of her coffee, then started backing away towards the door. 'Thank you.'

'That's OK,' he laughed. 'You can see if you're still thanking me at the end of the shift.'

'Ha, yes!' she said, still backing away and crashing into a lemon tree. 'Whoops! OK, bye!' she turned and fled, embarrassment and relief flooding her body.

Danny knocked on the dressing-room door.

'Come in,' Terri called.

'Hello, darling,' he said, stepping inside. 'I just came to wish you luck.'

The room smelled of hairspray and roses. Bouquets of flowers filled the counter running along the side of the room. Terri was sitting in front of an oval mirror illuminated by a frame of tiny, gold light bulbs.

'Thank you! My heart feels like it's going to explode.'

Danny went over and placed a hand on her shoulder. 'Deep breaths, darling, and remember, it could be worse. You could be wearing a cow right now.'

Terri threw her head back and laughed. 'Oh, don't remind me! This is so much better.' She stood up and admired her dress in the mirror. 'Thank you again.'

'You're very welcome, and you look stunning.' Danny allowed himself a small feeling of relief. This at least he knew to be true. When he'd discovered Jewel was a whizz at clothes design, he'd given the young man his pack of tarot cards and asked him to sketch out some basic designs for Juliet's dress based on the Queen of Cups. Jewel had surpassed his greatest expectations and Danny had ended up sending his sketches over to a costume maker. He'd also made sure that Jewel got a credit in the programme.

The bell rang, signalling five minutes to curtain call.

'Break a leg, darling,' Danny said, giving Terri a hug. 'And remember to be fabulous.'

'I will.'

As Danny made his way along the corridor to take his seat in the auditorium he saw Johannes striding towards him. As was the norm, Johannes was wearing all black and a tortured expression.

'Richard Blatchington-Smythe is here!' he said, as sombrely as if he was announcing the return of the Black Death, although to be fair, he wasn't far off. Richard Blatchington-Smythe was the harshest critic in the dance world, who for some strange and totally unjust reason was so well respected he had the power to make or break a show. He was one of those very worst of critics: a failed choreographer, and he used his reviews as an opportunity to vent his spleen whenever he could. Danny's empty stomach churned.

'I cannot go out there now,' Johannes continued. 'It is too much for my nerves to bear.'

'Fair enough,' Danny said. Much as he would have loved to hide away in the green room, his dancers needed him. He had to be out front, sending them positive vibes, willing them to put on a show-stopping performance. He slipped into the auditorium just as the lights were dimming and took his seat in the second row. His eyes skimmed the row in front, looking for Blatchington-Smythe's toad-like silhouette, but he couldn't spot him, which was probably for the best. The red velvet curtain swept up and an expectant silence fell.

It was only when the cast were taking their final bows at the end of the show that Danny felt able to breathe again. He didn't want to tempt fate, but it hadn't gone badly at all. No one had messed up, and although Terri had seemed a little inhibited at first, once she'd danced off her nerves she gave a wonderful performance. Romeo had done a fabulous job, too, providing the solidity Terri needed to really come into her own. Any time Danny felt fear kick in he reminded himself that the reviewers could have been watching an ensemble of farmyard animals, so things could have been far, far worse.

Finally, the applause died down and Terri stepped forward with a beaming smile, her face flushed.

'We would like to thank the orchestra for their wonderful job,' she called, gesturing at the pit in front of the stage.

The musicians stood up and everyone cheered.

'And thank you to Daniel Barker for his wonderful conducting,' Terri continued.

The conductor turned to face the audience and gave his baton a twirl.

'And now we would like to thank our choreographer, Johannes Schmidt,' Terri said, looking to the wings.

Johannes came running out, beaming wildly, in marked contrast to his earlier fearful frown.

'Thank you, thank you,' he called to the audience, taking a deep bow. And another. And another. *Egotistical maniac.* Danny grimaced. Finally, Johannes turned back to his dancers, gesturing at them to take another bow. But Terri shook her head and stepped forward once again.

'And last but definitely not least, we want to give a huge thank you to Danny Hall, our assistant choreographer. Danny, where are you?' She shielded her eyes from the spotlights and searched the crowd.

Holy cow! Danny felt a weird mix of excitement and nerves fizz through him as he got to his feet. All around him, people began to cheer.

'Come up here, Danny, take a bow,' Terri called and the rest of the cast all started to clap. All apart from Johannes.

'Thank you for your incredible vision and for being our biggest cheerleader,' Terri said, as Danny ran up the steps on to the stage. He knew she was trying to get a dig in at Johannes as well as thank him, but he didn't mind. As he drank in the applause, he was given a snapshot of his possible future, that one day he'd be standing on a stage basking in the success of his own show. And in that moment he didn't care what Blatchington-Smythe or any of the other critics might say. He wanted that future so badly he wasn't going to let anything deter him.

Fourteen

Jewel slipped out of the stage door and into the street. After the quiet and cool of being underground in the wardrobe department all day, London's heat and bustle slammed into him. Not that he was complaining. He'd been living in the capital for three months now and it still hadn't lost its thrill. The energy still felt like being plugged into the mains. Not that he had the time to drink it in right now – he only had ten minutes before it was time to get the chorus dressed for the evening show. The play had gone up a couple of weeks ago and Jewel was finally beginning to conquer the nerves that had initially overwhelmed him. Getting the costumes onto the cast before the show was fine – apart from the ever-present fear that he was going to tear into someone's skin with a zip. It was during the show that things got scary, with two of the actors needing costume changes at lightning speed. Thankfully, Margot, who he'd been teamed up with, had a sense of humour about it, and they'd started approaching the changes like an athlete striving for a personal best, seeing how many seconds they could shave off each time. The only stumbling block was a pair of boots that needed to be laced. He and Margot took one boot each, but Jewel was always lagging behind. He'd seriously considered buying a pair to practise on at home. He pushed the thought from his mind – at the moment he had other things to worry about.

He wove through the crowds of tourists and flustered commuters towards the Tube station.

'*Evening Standard!*' a burly man yelled from a kiosk by the entrance.

Jewel hurried over and bought a copy. There was meant to be a review of Danny's show in the Entertainment section tonight, and he wasn't just anxious for his friend and fellow housemate. Costumes often got a mention in reviews and even though he'd only played a minor role, doing some rough sketches for Danny inspired by the tarot cards, it had been his first tentative foray into the world of costume design. What if the reviewer hated it? According to Danny, the reviewer concerned was known for being harsh. What was it Danny had called him this morning? 'An odious toad.'

Unable to wait until he got back to the theatre, Jewel stepped into a betting shop doorway and started hurriedly flicking through the news stories, the TV guide and the horoscopes, until he got to the sports section. Wait, where were the reviews? He turned back to the front and went through the pages more slowly this time. Then his gaze fell upon the headline 'SUCCESS ON THE CARDS' above a photo of the actress playing Juliet in the dress that Jewel had helped design. His heart practically stopped beating and the palms of his hands began to sweat. Jewel scanned the text for key words, praying he didn't see anything like 'disaster', 'terrible', or 'awful costumes'. Thankfully, all of the adjectives he saw were positive. He drew a breath and began to read the review properly.

When I heard that legendary choreographer Johannes Schmidt had decided to interpret Romeo and Juliet via the medium of farmyard animals I have to admit I shuddered. Could it be that the great man had finally taken his desire to shock a step too far? I was therefore pleasantly surprised to discover that somewhere along the line he had a change of heart. Romeo and

Juliet seen through the prism of a tarot deck was, to my mind, an inspired decision. The question I am left with though is, was it his decision? At the end of the preview, leading lady Terri Grant made a very telling and impassioned tribute to Danny Hall, the assistant choreographer, thanking him for his support and I quote, 'His incredible vision.' Danny Hall has recently made the transition from acclaimed dancer in hits such as Cats, Hairspray and Les Miserables into the world of choreography. A move many dancers attempt but few succeed in. If my hunch is correct, I would say that Hall is a choreographer to watch. All in all, Romeo and Juliet is a moving and powerful performance and a visual spectacular.

Jewel let his gaze linger on the last two words, his fear turning to joy and relief. Not only had Danny received glowing praise but surely 'visual spectacular' had to include the costumes?

'Freak.' An angry voice pierced his happy bubble.

He looked over the top of the paper to see a couple of flashy looking men in suits walking past. Maybe they hadn't been talking to him. Maybe he'd misheard. But then one of them looked back over his shoulder at him, his face twisted into a sneer. 'Faggot,' he hissed.

Fear caused Jewel's insides to clench, and all the joy drained from him. Tucking the paper under his arm, he hurried off in the opposite direction, even though that meant taking the long route back to the theatre.

Danny looked at the newspaper laid out on the kitchen table in front of him and blinked hard. But no, he had not been seeing things. That odious toad Blatchington-Smythe had given the show a glowing review. And not only that, he'd given Danny a glowing review! For a moment the happiness enveloping Danny felt so overwhelming he wasn't sure what to do with it. There he'd been, worrying that Blatchington-Smythe could have killed off his career before it even began, but the critic had actually done the opposite. A review like this was the best calling card ever. He had to phone Johnny, his agent. He had to go out and buy up as many copies of the *Standard* as he could. As if on cue, the phone in the hall began to ring.

'Hello!' Danny said, grabbing the receiver from the wall.

'Danny, what the hell!' A man's voice boomed down the line.

'Johnny! Have you seen the *Standard*?'

'Have I seen it? I'm currently redecorating my office in copies of it!'

'I can't believe he was so nice,' Danny said. 'He's never that nice.'

'How much did you pay Terri to say what she did?' Johnny chuckled.

'Nothing. I was totally gobsmacked when she called me up on stage.'

'Johannes must be spitting feathers.'

'Oh God.' Danny had been so shocked by the review that he hadn't stopped to think what Johannes would make of it. He heard the sound of footsteps on the stairs and saw Lil meandering her way down. She was clad in what looked like a sari and holding a fan decorated with pictures of geisha girls.

'Hello, sweetheart,' she mouthed as she drifted past into the kitchen.

'Yeah, well, that man is a nightmare,' Johnny continued. 'His ego could do with a bit of a savaging. You deserve this, darling. You worked bloody hard to turn everything around and save that show from being an utter embarrassment.'

As his words sank in Danny felt the sudden and weird urge to cry. It was a bittersweet moment of vindication. He'd felt like this when he'd won his West End Award. Now, just as then, an image of his dad popped into his mind. *See, I am a success. I am capable of achieving something*, Danny imagined saying to his father. He swallowed hard. This was not the time to be morose. This was the time to celebrate.

'How are you set next week?' Johnny asked. 'Let's do lunch at Joe Allen's. Work out your next move.'

'My next move?'

'Yes. It's time to step out of the shadows, darling.'

Danny's skin tingled.

Once they'd arranged a date for lunch, Danny went back to the kitchen.

Lil was sitting at the table, tears streaming down her face.

'Lil, what is it? What's wrong?' He hurried over and sat down beside her.

'Wrong? Nothing's wrong,' she gasped between sobs. 'These are tears of joy.'

'Oh.'

She pointed at the paper. 'I'm so proud of you, sweetheart.'

'Really?' He wondered if Lil had been drinking. He couldn't smell any booze on her breath.

'Of course. This is wonderful.'

He smiled. 'Thank you.'

She clasped hold of his hand. 'I know you think I'm just a daft old bat.'

'No, I don't,' Danny lied.

'Well, you might be justified if you did.' She gave him a teary grin. 'I am daft and I am old, much as I hate to admit it. But I do care. And I do notice things, you know.'

'What do you mean?'

'I knew you were heartbroken – when you first moved in here, last year. I could see the pain. Your aura was as black as a coalminer's nose, sweetheart. The last time I saw one that dark was on poor old Paul after John left the Beatles.'

'Oh.' Danny was momentarily stumped. He'd thought he'd done a good job of hiding his pain when he first moved in, trying to be the life and soul of the party.

'"The tears of a clown when there's no one around", eh?' Lil said, as if reading his mind.

'I guess.' Danny nodded.

'But you didn't let it defeat you,' Lil continued. 'You kept going and that's why you deserve every bit of this.' She pointed at the paper.

For the second time in short succession, Danny felt a lump rising in his throat.

'I'm so proud of you.' Lil squeezed his hand tightly. 'And now we must celebrate.'

'Good plan.' Danny grinned.

Lil stood up. 'Shall I go and get my bong?'

'Your what?'

'My bong. I made one this afternoon while I was watching *The Young Doctors*.'

Danny looked at Lil and started to laugh. And laugh and laugh. And then, before he knew it, tears were streaming down his face. 'Lil, darling,' he gasped. 'I love you.'

As Cat made her way home from the Lemon Tree her feet ached and her head was tight from concentration – who knew remembering drinks orders required so much brainpower? Despite her awkward start with Achilles, her trial shift the night before had gone so well that he'd offered her a job on the spot. A fact that should make her happy instead of the weird lethargy she was feeling. If only her feet were aching from dancing. Still, at least Stelios had given her two bags full of food before she'd left. 'In case you or your housemates are hungry,' he'd said. She didn't know what was in the bags, but they smelled delicious. She hoped some of her fellow Rough Diamonds were still up. Although she was exhausted she was too wired to go to sleep yet.

She opened the front door to be greeted by the sound of laughter and chatter from the kitchen, and 'Sweet Caroline' by Neil Diamond playing. She walked in to find Danny and Jewel standing on the kitchen table singing about good times having never seemed so good. Lachlan was getting something out of the fridge, Pete was hunched over his notebook in the armchair in the corner and Lil was sitting at the table. Cat did a double take. Lil was sitting at the table smoking from what appeared to be a washing-up liquid bottle!

Lachlan clocked her shocked expression and grinned. 'Welcome home,' he called. 'I just got back from work, too. Apparently, they're just having a quiet night in.'

'Darling, join us!' Danny cried from on top of the table, holding out his hands.

Cat laughed. 'I don't think I've got the energy. I have got food, though, if anyone's hungry.' She placed the bags on the table.

Quick as a flash, Danny and Jewel leaped down to investigate.

'Is this courtesy of Stelios?' Danny asked, taking the boxes from the bags.

Cat nodded.

'Very serendipitous timing, sweetheart,' Lil said, through plumes of smoke. 'The munchies are just starting to kick in.'

'So, what's the party in aid of?' Cat asked. She took the lid from one of the boxes to reveal a pile of glistening chicken and pepper kebabs.

'*Romeo and Juliet* got an amazing review,' Jewel said.

'Our *Danny* got an amazing review,' Lil added.

'Really?'

Danny nodded. 'In the *Evening Standard.*'

'But I thought that was the one you were dreading. The odious toad one.' Cat offered him a kebab.

'It was.' Danny laughed. 'But for some weird reason he loved it. So from now on I won't hear a bad word about that odious toad.'

'Here, take a look,' Jewel passed her a copy of the *Standard* from a huge pile on the end of the table.

'I think Lil must have bought every copy in London,' Danny said with an embarrassed grin.

'It made me so proud,' Lil said, her voice huskier than ever from the smoke. 'I told the vendor he had to go and see it. I told him it starred my surrogate son.'

'I don't star in it, Lil, I'm the assistant choreographer,' Danny said.

'Well, you're the star of that review,' Lil said with a shrug.

'Ooh, I think I'm going to like you working at the Lemon Tree,' Danny said to Cat, taking a mouthful of kebab.

Cat grinned, but inside she couldn't help feeling a stab of remorse.

Seeing Danny so happy about his review only reinforced her sense of loss.

'How's the new job going?' Lachlan asked, sitting down beside her.

'Good,' she replied, but a flatness had descended on her that she couldn't shake off. 'Kebab?' She offered Lachlan the box.

'Ooh, this one's got halva in,' Lil shrieked, opening another box.

'But?' Lachlan said quietly.

'But what?'

'Nothing, I just thought I sensed a "but" coming,' he said.

She sighed. 'But it's not dancing,' she murmured.

He nodded. 'For now.'

'Does anyone want to hear my haiku about a streetlamp?' Pete asked suddenly from his armchair in the corner.

'Bloody hell, mate!' Danny exclaimed, clutching his chest in shock. 'I'd forgotten you were there!'

'I'd like to hear it,' said Jewel, taking some halva.

Pete stood up and cleared his throat.

'*Into my darkness*
You cast your sodium light
A dog cocks his leg and pisses on you.'

Silence fell upon the kitchen. Even Neil Diamond stopped singing, as the record came to an end.

'I'm experimenting with the structure of the haiku,' Pete said. 'I've been finding five syllables in the final line quite limiting.'

'I see,' said Cat, because quite frankly, someone had to say something.

'I think it's great,' said Danny. Clearly his post-review glow was obscuring his normal cynicism.

'I think you need to come and have a toke on this, sweetheart,' Lil said, offering Pete the washing-up liquid bottle.

'No, thanks. The muse prefers it if I stay sober.' Pete returned to his armchair.

'Suit yourself.' Lil shrugged and reignited her bong, and Danny and Jewel started talking about costumes.

Cat felt a pang of longing. She thought of Justin in Berlin. He'd be deep into rehearsals by now, bonding with the rest of the cast. Had she made a terrible mistake staying here?

'Don't worry,' Lachlan said, as if he could sense her deepening gloom. 'Something will come up.'

But would it? Exhaustion swept through her. And, annoyingly, her eyes filled with tears. *Shit.*

'Are you OK?'

Seeing the look of concern on Lachlan's face only made her feel worse. Thankfully the others hadn't noticed.

'I just … I'm sorry … it's been a really long day.' She stood up. 'Just going to the loo,' she stammered, her voice artificially high, before racing from the room.

Fifteen

Lachlan glanced around the kitchen. Danny and Jewel were deep in conversation about how to lace boots quickly, Lil was toking on her washing-up liquid bong and Pete was hunched over his notepad in the corner. No one had noticed Cat's teary exit – but he had, and now he didn't know what to do. Crying women were so far out of his comfort zone they were practically in another galaxy. He never knew what to do or say, but he felt he ought to do something. The sight of Cat so unhappy was actually causing him physical discomfort. He tried really hard not to think about what this might mean.

'Just going to my room for a bit,' he muttered, leaving the table. Thankfully, no one seemed to hear or care.

He slipped out into the hallway. Cat had said she was going to the toilet, so maybe he ought to check there first. He went along the narrow passageway to the downstairs toilet. It was empty. He couldn't blame her. The downstairs toilet was a distressing enough prospect on a good day, and it would tip you over the brink if you were feeling in any way vulnerable. He went up to the first floor to check the bathroom there. Since Cat had moved in, the upstairs bathroom had vastly improved, with the addition of a new, mildew-free shower curtain and a bowl of rose-scented potpourri on top of the cistern. But it was empty, too. He stood on the landing and looked at Cat's closed door. Would it be weird if he knocked? Would it be an invasion of her privacy? She probably wanted to be left on her own. Perhaps he could make up some other reason for knocking. Yes, that's what he'd do. He'd ask her if she had any … any … He scratched his head. What could he possibly need from Cat at – he checked his watch – just gone one in the morning? As he was standing there deliberating, the door opened and Cat appeared. Black make-up-streaked tears were trickling down her face.

'Lachlan!' she said, instantly wiping her face with the back of her hand. 'What are you doing?'

'I was just wondering if you – if you had any camomile tea.' It was the best he could do on the spur of the moment. He'd heard her and Jewel talking the other night about how it helped them get off to sleep.

'Camomile tea?' Cat echoed.

'Yes. To help me, you know, sleep.' Jeez. He'd never so much as sniffed a herbal tea before. He thought the whole notion of tea without caffeine completely insane. Surely she'd know he was lying.

'Sure. There's some in my cupboard,' she mumbled.

'OK, cheers.' Now what? He turned to go but then stopped. 'Are you OK?'

'Not really, no,' Cat replied, her voice wobbling.

'Do you – is there anything I can do?'

She shook her head. 'It just really hit me, when the others were talking about Danny's review, that's how my life could have been. That's how I wanted it to be, you know, dancing for a living, but instead I'm having to pour endless pints and try to remember endless drinks orders and know the difference between an aperitif and a digestif. Do you know the difference?'

Lachlan shook his head.

'Well, I do now. But I don't want to know, if you know what I mean?'

'I think so.' Lachlan nodded sympathetically although he wasn't really sure what she was going on about.

'Sorry. I'm probably over-tired. I am really grateful to have a job.'

Lachlan's anti-bullshit detector kicked in before he had time to stop himself. 'Screw that.'

'What?' she looked at him, shocked.

'All that grateful bollocks. It's OK to get pissed off when you need to. And it looks like you need to.'

'Yes, but it doesn't really achieve anything.' Cat sighed. 'I saw this life coach on *Kilroy* this morning and she said that we have to have an attitude of gratitude. If we're not grateful we'll only attract more crap in.'

'Oh, jeez!' Lachlan shook his head.

'What?'

'Well, that just sounds like ...' he wanted to say bollocks again but this time managed to refrain. 'It sounds like emotional blackmail to me. You can't fake happy. Also ...'

'Yes?'

'Don't you think this life coach business is all a crock of shit?'

Cat stared at him like a kid who'd just been told Santa doesn't exist.

'I mean, if they're such experts on life why aren't they just getting on having an awesome time of it instead of making money from telling us where we're all going wrong?' Lachlan paused for breath. Cat had inadvertently triggered one of his current pet peeves. He hoped he hadn't overstepped the mark.

There was a moment of awkward silence then, thankfully, Cat started to laugh. 'So what would you advise, then?'

Lachlan thought for a moment. 'How do you really feel?'

Cat sighed. 'Disappointed – and angry, actually.'

A light bulb went off in his head. 'I've got an idea. Come with me.'

'Where?'

'I know somewhere you can get angry.'

'What, outside?'

'Kind of.'

For a horrible moment he thought she was going to refuse, but then she nodded. 'OK.'

He led her downstairs and popped into his room to get his car keys. When he got back she was standing by the front door, expectantly.

Outside, the heat of the day had finally started to fade and the air had lost its soup-like humidity. As they walked along Diamond Street they fell into a companionable silence. At least, he hoped it was companionable.

'Here we are,' he said awkwardly when they got to his car.

'Where?' She looked at him blankly.

He nodded at the car and opened the passenger door. She continued to look at him blankly. Embarrassment started to rise in him. What had seemed like a good idea back in the house now seemed slightly sinister. 'We're only going around the block.'

She frowned. 'Why?'

Shit, was he coming across as some kind of psycho? 'We don't actually have to go anywhere,' he said. 'We just have to get in.'

But this only made her look even more confused. 'I don't understand.'

Lachlan was going to have to explain and explain quickly.

'A couple of years ago, when I was feeling really angry about something, my brother Bruce took me out in his car and told me to start yelling.'

'Yelling what?'

'Anything. I don't think I actually said any words.' An audio flashback filled his mind. The sound of his yells, animal-like and guttural. 'The point is to get the anger out of you.'

'Right,' she said slowly. 'But why do you have to do it in a car?'

'Because in my experience it causes a lot less upset than yelling your head off in the house or the street.'

To his huge relief, she began to grin. 'Come on, then,' she said. 'Let's do it.'

As she got into the car he got into the driver's side and opened the glove compartment. 'It really helps if you have something loud playing.' He pulled out a Guns N' Roses CD. 'This should do the trick.'

Cat leaned back in the car seat and took a deep breath. Of all the possible outcomes, sitting in a car with Lachlan about to take part in some kind of weird yelling therapy was definitely not how she'd imagined her evening ending. But it was definitely preferable to how it so easily could have ended: sobbing into her pillow along to 'Heaven Knows I'm Miserable Now'.

Lachlan turned the key in the ignition and put the CD into the stereo.

'I can always get out if it would be easier,' he said, looking slightly embarrassed.

'No, it's OK, but maybe you should drive somewhere. I don't want to wake the neighbours.' And at least if he was having to concentrate on driving she wouldn't feel so self-conscious.

Lachlan pulled out and headed in the direction of the high street. It was still humming with revellers making their way out of the pubs and into the clubs. It all felt too exposed to just start randomly yelling. They might not be able to hear her but they would be able to see her.

Lachlan turned down a side street. It was quieter here and there were no pedestrians. He cranked up the volume on the stereo. 'Welcome to the Jungle' by Guns N' Roses was playing. As the guitar wailed, Lachlan tipped his head back and let out a yell.

Cat gave a startled yelp. 'You made me jump!'

'Sorry. I had to deal with one too many drunken arseholes at work today. Need to get it off my chest.' He let out another yell, and another. The music started building to a crescendo.

Cat thought about her own night at work and she gave a tentative cry.

'Sorry, did you say something?' Lachlan grinned. 'I couldn't quite hear you.'

She laughed, then yelled properly this time. And this time she didn't feel quite so self-conscious. She thought of Danny basking in the glory of his review. She thought of Justin rehearsing for his show in Berlin. She thought of herself pouring endless glasses of wine and beer. This time when she yelled it came out more like a tortured scream.

'Now you're talking!' Lachlan exclaimed.

Cat thought of all the things Justin had said to her before he left, all of the subtle and not so subtle digs about her dancing and her weight.

'Fuck you!' she yelled at the top of her voice. 'Sorry, not you,' she quickly said, glancing at Lachlan.

'No worries.' He took a right and let out a roar.

Cat thought about all the times she'd let Justin get to her. All the times she'd let him lead in their relationship. And now her anger was at herself. How could she have been so weak? How could she have been so stupid? She let out a shout from the depths of her being. And this time she didn't stop. She kept yelling and yelling as the music built. They were on a main road now and Lachlan was driving faster and faster. He pressed the button to lower their windows, and a welcome breeze filled the car, whipping her hair around her face. She kept on yelling. He kept on yelling. Louder and louder. Driving faster and faster. Months and months of pent-up frustration were transmuting into rage and pouring out of her. And then something really weird happened. She no longer felt pathetic or weak. She no longer felt like a victim. The sound of her roar was making her feel powerful, like some kind of lioness. She stopped yelling and drew a breath. She glanced at Lachlan. He'd also fallen silent. He glanced at her.

'Better?'

'Much.' She looked out of the window at the lights of London glimmering all around them. There were hardly any other cars about and for a moment it felt as if they had the city all to themselves. It was a magical feeling.

Lachlan turned the music down.

'That was so good,' she said.

'Yeah.' He smiled, but it was tempered by sadness. She wondered what had prompted his brother to teach him this yelling trick, what had made him so angry. Maybe she should ask him. She looked at his strong arms grasping the steering wheel, the golden hairs glistening on the ridges of muscle. There was a weird contrast between his physical strength and the flickers of vulnerability she kept noticing about him. The way he'd been that night in the Lemon Tree, then Justin hearing him crying. She decided against asking anything. She didn't want to risk upsetting him.

'Do you fancy going somewhere for a cup of tea?' Lachlan asked.

'Will anywhere be open now?'

'Of course. This is London, the city that never sleeps.'

'I thought that was New York?'

'Whatever.' He grinned. 'OK, London is the city that *rarely* sleeps and I know a greasy spoon that's always open.'

She looked at him quizzically.

'I do a lot of night-time driving when I'm not able to sleep,' he said with a shrug.

'I see. Well, in that case, I'd love a cup of tea.'

'They don't do any of your hippy herbal tea there, though,' he said, taking the exit off the main road.

'Don't mock the herbal tea,' she replied with a grin. 'It has tons of health benefits.'

'I don't know how you can drink the stuff.'

'Hang on a minute, you asked if you could have some of my camomile tea earlier.'

'Oh … yeah.'

It was hard to tell in the flickering orange glow from the streetlights outside, but it seemed as if he was blushing.

Cat looked back out of the window and grinned.

Lachlan parked up in a side street next to Smithfield Market. As they got out of the car he glanced across at Cat. She looked great. Her hair had been blown about all over the place and her face was glowing. It seemed as if the yelling had done the trick. He led her into the café. Daisy, a barrel-shaped woman from Stepney who worked most of the night shifts, was standing behind the counter. She was wiping the surface with an ancient-looking cloth that would probably automatically fail any hygiene standards test.

'All right, love?' she said when she saw him.

'G'day, Daisy.'

'Usual, is it?'

'Please.'

Daisy looked at Cat and gave him a knowing grin. 'And what about your friend?'

'Can I have a tea, please?' Cat said.

They sat down at one of the small, Formica-topped tables. A squeezy ketchup bottle shaped like a tomato sat in the middle of the table, next to a chipped china bowl full of sugar cubes. When Lachlan had discovered the café a few months ago on one of his late-night drives around the city he'd found the lack of frills comforting. But now, seeing it through the lens of

Cat, he wasn't so sure everyone would get its subtle charms.

'What kind of market is this?' Cat asked, peering out into the darkness.

'Meat, mainly. Apparently, it's been here for hundreds of years.'

'Really?' She sat back in her chair and smiled. 'God, I love London.'

He breathed a sigh of relief. 'How come?'

'It's so full of character and history.'

Daisy brought over two mugs of builders' tea. 'I put two bags in, love,' she said, placing a chubby hand on Lachlan's shoulder.

'Ta.'

Cat looked at his tea then at him. 'Did you really want some camomile tea earlier?'

He felt his face start to flush. He'd been hoping she wouldn't bring this up again.

'Not exactly.'

'So why …?' She broke off, looking puzzled.

'I wanted to check you were OK but I didn't know what to say.'

Thankfully, she started to laugh. 'You didn't strike me as the camomile tea kind of guy.'

He grinned. 'Thanks. I'll take that as a huge compliment.'

'Shut up.' She gave his arm a playful nudge and it sparked a weird chain reaction tingling up to his shoulder and down to the tips of his fingers.

'That yelling thing was so cool,' she said quietly.

'Yeah?'

'I feel so much better.'

'Good.' And it did feel good – so good – to see her happy. An alert started going off in his head, but for once he chose to ignore it. 'Any time you need a good yell, just let me know.'

She nodded and grinned. 'You're like an alternative life coach. Very alternative,' she added quickly, no doubt noticing his frown.

'I'm just glad to help,' he said. And in that moment, he wanted nothing more than to help Cat smile. She placed her hand on top of his. This time the tingling sensation travelled deep into the pit of his stomach.

'You've really helped.' She gave his hand a squeeze then let go.

But the imprint of her skin on his lingered.

Sixteen

As soon as Jewel stepped into the reception area at the theatre Alice's jaw dropped open.

'What happened?' she asked.

'What do you mean?' Jewel asked, on the off-chance she wasn't talking about what he thought, although he dreaded that she was.

'Is it bring your drab to work day? Did I not get the memo?' she stared pointedly at his nondescript T-shirt and jeans, and then at his face, which was totally make-up free.

'I overslept. I didn't have much time to get ready.' The truth was, Jewel had barely slept at all. The incident with the two men outside the station had really shaken him. The happy bubble he'd been living in since coming to work in the theatre and moving into Diamond Street had been well and truly burst. And now he felt so naive. How could he have imagined that London would be any different to back home? There were going to be hateful idiots everywhere, and if anything, somewhere the size of London would have even more of them.

'You OK?' Alice raised one of her narrow eyebrows.

Jewel nodded. He didn't want to tell her what had happened. He didn't want to tell anyone. If he said it out loud it would make it official somehow, instead of it being his own private nightmare inside his head.

As Danny came round from sleep he had the strangest sensation he was being watched. He opened one eye a crack. His intuition had been right. Neil was gazing at him across the pillow. And it was definitely a gaze, rather than a casual glance. *Shit.* Danny quickly closed his eyes again. He needed to buy himself a little time to process developments. How had he ended up here again? Slowly, the events of the night before began to materialize through the fog of his hangover. The incredible review in the *Standard.* Partying with his Diamond Street housemates. Neil ringing at some ungodly hour, just as he and Lil were about to have a Barry Manilow dance-off. Neil asking if he could come over. Danny thinking that it seemed like a good idea at the time – damn Lil and her bong. Him and Neil crashing into bed, a tangle of limbs and a meeting of lips and now …

'Good morning, gorgeous,' Neil purred.

Shit.

'Morning,' Danny grunted, keeping his eyes closed. When he'd met Neil in Heaven last month he'd been looking for some fun – a fling – but somehow he'd ended up seeing Neil every week since. It had been a welcome distraction in the run-up to the show, but now the show was up and running and –

'Do you fancy doing something today?' Neil had this annoying habit of talking to him in the kind of cooey, gooey voice you'd use to talk to a toddler. Danny guessed it was his attempt at being affectionate, but in reality it was just intensely annoying. And now he was suggesting they did something together – on a Saturday – this was straying dangerously close to relationship territory.

'I can't, I'm busy,' came his automatic response. How could he extricate himself from this exercise in awkwardness as painlessly as possible?

He felt Neil's hand stroking his face and instinctively he shuddered. *This is all your doing. You invited him over,* he berated himself.

'You're always such a busy little bee,' Neil cooed before planting a kiss on his forehead.

Jesus! Why didn't people come with health warnings, like the kind you got on packs of cigarettes? Danny pictured such a warning stamped on Neil's forehead: 'WARNING: This man's voice may cause extreme nausea and shuddering.' Then he thought of the warning Gabriel should have come with. 'WARNING: This man can cause chronic heartbreak.' Danny sat up abruptly.

'Yeah, well, what's that thing they say? No rest for the wicked.'

'And you, my dear, are truly wicked,' Neil simpered.

Oh God.

'Do you want a cup of tea?' At least getting a drink would give him an excuse to get out of bed.

'OK.' Neil withdrew his hand, clearly hurt.

And now Danny felt like a bastard. Since when did having some light-hearted, no-strings fun become so difficult? He slipped on a T-shirt and a pair of shorts. Neil stayed lying in bed.

'I'll see you down in the kitchen, then,' Danny said.

'Oh … right … OK.' Now Neil was less simpering and more sullen teenager.

Danny left the room and ran down the stairs. He knew he should feel grateful. He knew he should feel flattered that someone wanted to spend a Saturday with him. He knew this was all a vital part of moving on – so why did it feel like such a colossal step backwards? He thought of the first Saturday he'd ever spent with Gabriel, and how they'd passed the day trawling Parisian museums and galleries and boutiques, before holing up in a bistro in Montmartre drinking kir royales and eating cheese – so much cheese – and talking about their hopes and dreams. Danny hadn't wanted the day to end. He'd wanted to draw out every second. When Gabriel touched him he shivered rather than shuddered. Every cell in his body had ignited with longing.

He went into the kitchen expecting to find it empty, with all of his housemates still sleeping off their hangovers, but Lil was standing in the centre of the room, smoking a cigarette and wearing a huge pair of sunglasses.

'Morning, darling, everything OK?' Danny headed straight for the kettle.

'We need to paint the kitchen purple.'

'What?' Danny looked at her and laughed. 'Could we at least have a cup of coffee first?'

'I'm being serious, sweetheart. All this yellow is way too bright first thing, especially if one is feeling ...' she paused and inhaled on her cigarette, 'slightly delicate.'

'So, you're suggesting we make the kitchen hangover-friendly?'

'Exactly! I knew you'd understand.' Lil beamed at him. 'Shall we do it today?'

'Whoa, hold your horses. Firstly, don't we need to get permission from the landlord? And secondly ...' Danny broke off. He was about to say that he was busy, but the truth was he didn't have anything on – but he did need an excuse to tell Neil.

'See, there is no secondly,' Lil said triumphantly. 'And in response to your firstly, I'm sure the landlord won't object to us increasing the value of their property.'

'By painting the kitchen purple?'

'Exactly.' Lil picked up a magazine from the table. 'Did you know that purple has many healing properties?'

'Er, no.' Danny took a couple of mugs from the cupboard.

Lil began to read from the magazine. 'According to *Spirit & Destiny*, it uplifts the mood and calms the mind, and increases creativity, sensitivity and our link to spirit.' She looked at him excitedly. 'Just think, if we had a purple kitchen I could start holding seances again and we could contact the dead.'

At exactly this moment Neil walked in. He looked from Lil to Danny and back again.

Danny pursed his lips to try and stop himself from laughing. 'Neil, this is my housemate, Lil. Lil, this is my friend Neil.'

'Aha, your *partner,* as you youngsters like to call it.' Lil took her sunglasses off and gave them a knowing wink. 'Personally, I prefer the term lover. Partner sounds so dull and dreary. So business-like.'

Danny began to cringe, although Neil seeing Lil in all of her trippy glory might hopefully act as some kind of deterrent. Sure enough, Neil shifted awkwardly from foot to foot.

'So, are you in? Are we painting this kitchen purple?' Lil asked Danny.

'Yes, absolutely,' he replied with utter conviction. Anything to avoid prolonging the agony with Neil.

'Excellent! I'll go and ask Lachlan if he'll give us a lift to the DIY shop.' Lil swept from the room, leaving Danny and Neil and a very awkward silence.

Lachlan was dreaming that he was in his brother Bruce's car, but Bruce was nowhere to be seen. Instead, Cat was at the steering wheel and they were both singing. But then he heard another woman's voice from behind him whispering, 'Don't leave me, Lachlan.' He turned to see Michelle in the back seat. Her face was as white as chalk and her hair was strewn with seaweed. 'Don't leave me, Lachlan.' Her voice grew louder and louder.

'Lachlan!'

He woke with a start. Now the voice didn't belong to Michelle, it belonged to Lil. Lil was yelling at him. What the hell? He sat up in bed and rubbed his eyes. For one horrible moment he thought she was in bed with him.

'Lachlan,' she called again, and he breathed a sigh of relief as he realized her voice was coming from the other side of the door.

'Yes?'

'We need your urgent assistance.'

He looked at the clock. It was eleven. Six hours since he and Cat had finally got home and gone to bed. In spite of the lack of sleep, he couldn't help smiling.

'What's the problem?' he said, bounding out of bed and opening the door.

'We're painting the kitchen purple and need your help getting the paint,' Lil said nonchalantly, like painting the kitchen purple was what everyone did on a Saturday.

For a second Lachlan contemplated asking why, but he'd learned long ago that asking Lil to explain herself usually only led to more confusion.

'Would you be able to give us a lift to the DIY shop, sweetheart?'

Lachlan nodded. 'Sure.' It sounded a simple enough task. He glanced up the stairs, wondering if Cat was awake yet.

'Wonderful! I'll go and ask Cat if she'd like to join us.'

'Great,' Lachlan replied with a shrug, but for some weird reason, the prospect of Cat being involved made this bizarre purple paint mission seem way more appealing.

'Let's regroup in the kitchen in half an hour,' Lil said, making her way up the stairs.

Lachlan went back into his room and closed the door.

Don't leave me … Michelle's voice from his dream echoed in his head. He glanced at the cupboard where he kept his backpack with the photo of her stashed inside.

'I'm not leaving you, you left me,' he whispered, feeling an instant stab of guilt. This was the first time he'd shifted the blame for what happened away from himself, and it didn't feel good. He pushed the thought from his mind and headed to the bathroom to take a shower.

Cat lay in bed staring at the shaft of sunlight streaming in through a gap in the curtains. Dust particles danced in the light, sparkling like glitter. Somehow they seemed to perfectly capture how she was feeling. Lachlan was clearly on to something with his yelling therapy. Even though nothing had changed externally – she was still working behind a bar, she still had no dancing job, or guarantee that she would ever dance professionally again, her romantic life was still a disaster – all the same she felt a strange lightness. It wasn't just the yelling that had helped, either. She'd really loved talking to Lachlan. They'd spent more than two hours in the café in the end. Lachlan was such a good listener. He didn't use the time when she was talking to think of what he was going to say next, like so many people seemed to, he genuinely took it all in, and then asked great follow-up questions. She bet he was a great nurse. The kind who made every patient feel heard and seen, instead of just a number. He'd said very little about himself, though. Cat had tried to find out more, but he seemed to very quickly steer the conversation back to her, especially if she asked about his life back in Australia.

She sat up and hugged her legs to her chest. Today she was going to be proactive, make the most of her new-found positive outlook and have a look through *The Stage* for dancing jobs. She might ask Danny if he knew of anything, too. Just as she was about to get up, there was a knock on the door.

'Cat, sweetheart, are you awake?' Lil hollered.

She couldn't help laughing. If she had been asleep Lil's bellowing would definitely have woken her.

'Yes, I am,' she called, getting up and going over to open the door.

'Oh, don't you just love it when everything comes together!' Lil exclaimed.

'Uh, yes.'

'We're redecorating the kitchen,' Lil said. 'We're painting it purple. Meet us down in the kitchen in half an hour. Lachlan is driving us.'

'What? But …' Cat watched as Lil headed up the stairs to her own room. She grinned. Although she had no clue what Lil was going on about, it sounded like fun. And Lachlan was involved. Her grin grew even bigger.

Seventeen

As Danny made his way along the aisle of the shop he had a bizarre realization – the thought of spending a Saturday in a DIY store had always been his idea of hell – the kind of thing his father liked to do. Danny could never understand why people spent so much time and energy and money trying to improve the boxes they lived in, when there was a whole world out there waiting to be explored. To his mind, the recent spate of home makeover shows on the TV had been the very definition of the opiate of the masses, brainwashing people into thinking that their lives would be complete if only they put up a floral border in the bedroom or rag-rolled the living room. But, weirdly, he was quite enjoying the Diamond Street outing to Homebase. Maybe it was his relief at having found a way to escape Neil's advances.

'Danny, sweetheart,' Lil called to him across the aisle, 'I can't decide between Provence Lavender or Purple Reign. I adore the romance of Provence, obviously, but Purple Reign is a very clever play on words.'

'I don't think you're meant to base your decision on the name of the paint, Lil. It's the colour that matters.' Danny glanced at Lachlan and Cat, who were clearly trying not to laugh.

'Nonsense. Names are everything,' Lil replied. 'How do you think I made my fortune on the dogs? I always back the greyhound with the most compelling name.'

Now it was Danny's turn to try not to laugh.

'I think I'll go for Purple Reign,' Lil continued. 'It's not just clever, it reminds me of Prince. And that man is sex on legs. Very short legs, mind you, but nothing that a pair of purple stilettos can't fix.'

Danny saw a couple throwing Lil a mocking look and instantly he felt a fierce, protective tug inside of him. He wondered if this was what it was like when men felt protective over their mothers. His mam had died when he was so young he'd never had the chance to find out. 'OK, then, darling, let's get the trolley loaded.'

Lachlan brought the trolley over and he and Danny started loading it with tins of paint.

'How many do you think we'll need?' Danny asked.

'About four, I reckon,' Lachlan replied. 'It's a pretty big room.'

'And we'll need some roller brushes,' Cat said. 'And some of that tape to stop the paint from getting on the skirting boards.'

'And some tequila,' Lil said.

They all turned to look at her.

'What? Tequila is *the* drink to decorate to,' Lil replied defiantly. 'Don't you kids know anything?'

'I'm not sure we're going to find any here,' Lachlan said, looking around the store. 'White spirit, maybe?'

Cat started laughing.

Danny looked at her and Lachlan. He could be imagining things but there seemed to be a new thaw between them. This was definitely a good thing. After Lachlan's weird outburst last month in the Lemon Tree things had been slightly awkward.

'That's all right, I'm sure Lachlan won't mind stopping at the offie on the way home, will you, sweetheart.' Lil gave Lachlan one of her most twinkly grins.

'No problem,' he smiled.

Danny felt himself relax even more. His personal life might still be perfect fodder for a tabloid problem page but, in every other area of his life, things were falling into place. *Long may it continue*, he thought as he pushed the trolley along the aisle.

'I've finished!' Cat cried four hours later as she put the finishing touches to the wall above the sink.

'Shot! Shot! Shot!' Danny, Lachlan and Lil called from their respective walls.

Cat got down from the counter and went over to the table where two bottles of tequila and some shot glasses were lined up.

Due to the paint fumes and the fact that they'd turned decorating the kitchen into a drinking game – with shots required every time they swore, coughed, or 'Love is All Around' came on the radio – she was already feeling a little light-headed.

'I've done mine, too,' Lachlan said triumphantly from the wall leading into the living room. He put down his paintbrush and joined Cat at the table.

As she handed him the bottle of tequila her fingers brushed his, and it sparked a weird jolt of excitement inside of her. Their eyes met and he smiled. Had he felt it, too?

'Cheers,' he said softly, taking the bottle.

Lil gave an exaggerated cough. 'Oh dear, coughed again. Looks like I need to take another shot.'

'Lil, you can't cough on purpose just so you can have a drink,' Danny said, now the only one still painting.

'*And coming up next, currently enjoying its ninth week at number one, will it be ten on the new Top Forty tomorrow?*' the DJ on the radio announced as the opening strains of 'Love is All Around' filled the room.

'No!' everyone chorused.

'Oh, well, at least I can get a drink,' Danny said, joining the others at the table.

Cat cast her eyes around the room. She'd been slightly apprehensive about painting the kitchen purple, but actually it didn't look that bad. It was definitely more soothing than the bright yellow that it had been before. But was Lil happy with it? Cat turned to look at her.

Lil downed her shot and slammed her glass on the table. Her silver hair and thin arms were dotted with flecks of purple.

'So, what do you think?' Cat asked her.

'I think it's majestic!' Lil exclaimed.

The door opened and Pete trudged in. He'd been out at a poetry event all evening and was blissfully unaware of the kitchen makeover. Cat hoped he wouldn't mind what they'd done. It was quite a drastic change.

'Evening,' Pete mumbled, going over to the fridge.

They all watched, waiting for a reaction.

Pete took a pack of Dairylea cheese triangles from the fridge and trudged back to the door. 'See you later,' he mumbled before leaving.

'How did he not notice?' Danny asked, shaking his head.

'It's the muse, sweetheart,' Lil said, refilling everyone's shot glasses. 'Once it gets a hold of him he doesn't notice a thing. He walked in on me one evening when I was practising mindful tightrope walking in the living room and he didn't bat an eyelid. Just stepped over the rope and sat down in his armchair and started writing a poem.'

'What's mindful tightrope walking?' Cat asked, praying she wouldn't start laughing.

Lil looked at her as if she was insane. 'It's where you walk a tightrope mindfully, obviously.'

'Oh.' Cat glanced at Lachlan, who turned away quickly.

'I think it looks bonzer but that brown Formica's going to have to go.' He nodded to the cupboards.

'Yeah, it looks even more hideous next to purple,' Danny agreed. 'Maybe we could spray paint the cupboard doors silver?'

'That's a wonderful idea!' Lil clasped her hands together. Despite the wrinkles fanning her eyes and her grey hair she looked just like an excited kid. She was always so effusive. Cat wished she could have a fraction of Lil's lust for life, although it probably required copious amounts of illegal substances.

The door opened again and for a moment Cat thought it would be Pete returning, having had an extremely delayed reaction to the paint, but instead Jewel walked in. He was the most dressed down she'd ever seen him and he was not wearing a scrap of make-up.

'Wow!' Jewel's mouth fell open as he looked around the room.

'Surprise!' Lil cried. 'We decided to give the kitchen a makeover. What do you think?'

'It's great. Very different.' Jewel nodded approvingly.

'We're going to paint the cupboards silver,' Lil added.

'Cool.' Jewel looked at Cat and smiled. He looked tired and there were faint patches of stubble on his chin.

'How was work?' Cat asked.

'OK.'

'Drink?' Danny offered Jewel one of the bottles of tequila.

He shook his head. 'I think I'm going to go straight to bed. I'm really tired.'

'Are you sure you don't even want a nightcap?' Lil said.

'No, thanks. I'll see you all tomorrow.' Jewel turned and left the room.

'Do you think he's OK?' Danny asked, echoing Cat's thoughts.

Lil shook her head. 'There's a sadness about him. His aura's all off. A lot darker than usual.'

'Are you sure that isn't just the paint making the room darker?' Lachlan grinned.

'Of course it isn't the paint,' Lil replied. 'I know the difference between paint and a person's aura field, sweetheart. Yours is looking a lot brighter these days, by the way.'

Lachlan turned away, looking embarrassed.

'Thank you all so much for making my vision a reality,' Lil said, gazing around the room.

'You're welcome,' Cat smiled at her.

'I'll get some silver paint tomorrow and we'll get it finished,' Danny said.

'Sure. I don't mind giving you a lift back to the paint shop,' Lachlan offered.

'Thank you, sweetheart.' Lil yawned. 'Ooh, I'm feeling quite bushwhacked, as you Antipodeans would say. I think I might turn in.'

Danny nodded. 'Yep, I'm feeling the same.'

'Night, you two.' Lil gave Cat and Lachlan hugs.

'Night,' Danny said, following her out of the room.

Cat stood there for a moment unsure what to do. Should she go upstairs too? If Lachlan went to bed now she'd be left standing there on her own. But Lachlan took his paintbrush over to the sink and started rinsing it under the tap. Cat felt oddly relieved at the prospect of prolonging her time with him. She went and fetched her own brush and brought it over to the sink.

Lachlan finished rinsing off his brush and turned to smile at Cat. 'Well, I never thought I'd be spending my Saturday night painting the kitchen purple.'

'Same. But it was strangely fun,' she replied.

Lachlan nodded. Everything seemed to be strangely fun when Cat was around and he was sick of fighting it. 'Fancy another drink?' he said, nodding towards the tequila. To his disappointment she shook her head.

'I'm going to a dance class in the morning. I will have a cup of tea, though.' His disappointment lifted. Cat banged the tap three times and filled the kettle. 'Do you want one?' she asked.

'Yeah, go on.' He watched as she opened the cupboard, took her box of camomile tea out and put teabags into two mugs. 'What are you doing?' he asked, horrified.

'Making us tea.'

'But that's not proper tea.'

She laughed. 'Maybe it's time you tried something new, broadened your horizons.'

For some weird reason her statement seemed loaded with a deeper meaning. 'Yeah, maybe.'

'It might help you sleep.'

Right now, sleep was the last thing he wanted. All he wanted was to sit with Cat for hours like he'd done last night, talking and talking. Letting her slowly and gently pull him out of the shell he'd been hiding in. 'OK, I'm prepared to be persuaded.'

'That's very good of you.' She laughed. 'It's really good with a spoonful of honey.'

'Whatever.' He shrugged and watched as she added generous spoonfuls of honey to the mugs. The honey shone amber like her hair, which was piled up on top of her head, revealing the nape of her neck. He imagined tracing his finger down to where her neck met her shoulder. Jeez, get a grip! He cleared his throat and looked away.

'Shall we drink it out in the yard?' Cat asked, holding a steaming mug out to him. 'Get away from the paint fumes?'

'Sure.' He took his drink and followed her through the living room to the open back door, trying to ignore the single curl of her hair that had come loose and was coiling its way down the top of her back. Her skin was so creamy. It looked so soft. He imagined tracing a fingertip along the curve of her spine and –

'Oh, look at the moon,' Cat gasped as she walked outside. A bright, almost full moon hung in the small patch of night sky between the rooftops above them. They sat down on the rusty garden chairs and gazed up at it.

'I miss seeing the stars,' Lachlan said. 'There's too much light pollution in London.'

'Me too,' Cat agreed. 'I used to love looking up at the stars when I was a kid, trying to find the Plough and the Great Bear.'

'Same here. My old man used to love telling us the stories behind the constellations.'

'Really?'

Lachlan nodded. He had a sudden memory of the night of his seventh birthday, when his family had had a celebratory barbie on the beach. As night had fallen, they sat around a fire and his dad told him and his brothers all about the legend of the Great Bear and how hunters would chase it across the sky. Lachlan had lain on his back on the warm sand, feeling drunk with joy and tiredness. He'd eventually drifted off and in the haze of his dream he felt his dad's strong arms scooping him up and carrying him home. What he'd give to feel that safe and warm and protected again. He sighed.

'Is your dad – is he still alive?' Cat asked.

Lachlan nodded.

'You must miss him.'

'I sure do.' Suddenly he missed his old man with a longing that pierced right through him. He took a sip of his tea. It was so sweet and floral his first response was to cringe. But there was something comforting about it, too. The taste of honey was bringing back more childhood memories. His mum laughing and joking as she piled heaps of warm toast on the table for him and his brothers when they got back starving from footie practice. Honey dripping from the bread on to his fingers.

'Well?' Cat said, looking at him questioningly.

'What?'

'What do you think of the tea?'

'It's not so bad.'

'Ha! Praise indeed.'

'I mean, it still contravenes the basic principle of tea …'

'Which is?'

'Which is that it should contain caffeine.'

'Yeah, well, you'll be thanking me later when you're sleeping like a baby.' Cat's face flushed. 'I mean, you won't be thanking me while you're asleep. I mean we won't be in the same bed or anything. Obviously.'

'Obviously,' he said, unable to hide a grin. Why was she so embarrassed?

'You'll thank me in the morning. Or whenever we next see each other.'

'We'll see …'

'So, what was your favourite story about the stars?' she asked, looking back at the sky and clearly eager to change the subject.

'I loved the story of Unurgunite. It's an indigenous Australian legend.'

'Can you tell it to me?'

'Sure.' He looked up at the sky. 'Unurgunite is a star that has two other bright stars either side of it. The story goes that the other two stars are Unurgunite's wives.'

'Lucky Unurgunite,' Cat giggled.

'Yes, but one day Mityan fell in love with one of Unurgunite's wives and tried to lure her away.'

'Is Mityan another star?'

Lachlan shook his head. 'No, he's the moon.' They both looked up just as wisps of cloud scudded across the moon's face. 'When Unurgunite found out what was going on he was pretty pissed off, so he launched a mighty battle with Mityan.'

'Who won?' Cat asked, looking genuinely gripped.

'Unurgunite, and Mityan was doomed to wander the skies forever alone, with battle scars all over his face. If you look closely, you can still see the scars today.'

Cat looked up at the moon, her eyes wide with wonder. She reminded Lachlan of how he'd felt as a kid the first time his dad had told him the tale. 'I can see them!' she cried. 'I always thought those darker bits were craters.'

Lachlan laughed and shook his head. 'Nope. Battle scars.'

'And all in the name of a love that could never be,' Cat sighed. 'How tragic.'

'Uh-huh.'

'I'll never look at the moon in the same way again.'

'Yep, that's how I felt when I first heard the story.'

'Isn't it great the way people came up with stories to explain things?' Cat took a sip of her tea. 'I sometimes wish science had never happened.'

'How do you mean?'

'Well, I know science is more accurate and everything, but it's so much less magical.'

Lachlan nodded. He'd felt the same, until his life was robbed of all magic. A shiver ran through him. How could he sit here, enjoying the mystery of the moon, talking about the magic of life, when it was something he'd denied to another human being?

'Thank you,' Cat said softly.

'What for?'

'Sharing the story with me.'

'No worries.' For a horrible moment he thought she was going to ask him to tell her another tale. He didn't think he'd be able to, thanks to the lump now forming in his throat. But instead she sipped her tea and gazed up at the moon. This was another thing he liked about Cat: the way she seemed happy to let him be. The lump in his throat shrank a little.

They continued drinking and sitting in silence. Then, finally, Cat got to her feet. 'I'm going to head up to bed.' She stopped by him. 'I hope the tea helps you sleep.'

'Thanks.'

She bent down and kissed the top of his head. 'I think you're really lovely.'

And then she was gone. And Lachlan was left with the battle-scarred Mityan shining down on him.

Eighteen

Danny walked into Joe Allen's and scanned the room for Johnny. His agent was six foot six with a shock of jet-black hair, so he was always easy to spot. And today was no exception. Danny spied him sitting at a table by the brick wall, flicking through his Filofax. He hurried over.

'Well, if it isn't the man of the moment,' Johnny said with a grin. He stood up and they hugged. 'Well done, darling. I've already had a couple of very interesting calls since the review.'

'Really?' Danny's heartbeat quickened.

'Yes. Doug McKenzie's people have asked if you'd be interested in the assistant choreographer gig on their production of *The Rocky Horror Picture Show*.'

Danny sat down, his excitement tinged slightly with disappointment. Doug McKenzie was one of the West End's top impresarios. Getting a gig for him would definitely be good for his CV but ... 'Assistant choreographer?'

Johnny nodded.

'I thought you said it was time I stepped out of the shadows.'

'It is. It is.' Johnny picked up the jug of water on the table and filled them both a glass. 'But you know this business. It's pigeon steps in the very beginning. And *The Rocky Horror Show* isn't some off the wall, arthouse version of *Romeo and Juliet*, it's mainstream. It's Shaftesbury Avenue, darling.'

'I know, but …' Danny gazed at the framed posters from West End shows covering the walls. He knew what Johnny was saying made sense, but he was just so desperate to have full creative control, to really put his choreographer's stamp on things.

Johnny handed him a menu. 'It's exactly like your dance career. You're going to have to work your way up to the limelight.'

'I know.' But it wasn't about the limelight to Danny, it was about expression. He was tired of having to mould himself to someone else's vision – or even worse, have another choreographer take the credit for his vision.

'So what do you say? Shall I tell them you're interested and set up a meeting?'

Danny nodded. He knew he couldn't afford to be precious about this. Being a choreographer was a whole different ball game to being a dancer. He was a one-man band now – a one-man business – and he needed to be business-minded.

'Excellent.' Johnny waved a waiter over. 'I'm telling you, darling, one more assistant choreographer role and then you'll be ready.'

Three hours later, Danny made his way out of the Underground and up to Camden High Street. Two bottles of wine and a pep talk from Johnny had softened his mood considerably. Even the crowd of imbeciles who had decided to come to a complete standstill right outside the station couldn't dim the glow he was now feeling. He expertly dodged the baseball-capped drug dealer hovering by a bin and thought he finally had a clear run of the pavement when a young girl stepped right in front of him, shoving a leaflet in his face.

'No, thanks,' he said instinctively, stepping to the side to swerve round her. But she stepped the same way, as if they were now in a dance. Danny felt his post-lunch buzz start to fade. Damn these people and their leaflets. It was bad enough that they kept shoving them through his door, but shoving them in his face? Well, that was downright rude.

'Help us fight the closure of the White Lion,' the girl said.

'No, thanks,' Danny said again, stepping the other way. Then he froze. 'Hold on, what did you say?'

The girl's face broke into a relieved smile. He was probably the first person to have engaged with her. 'The council are trying to close the White Lion,' she said. 'It's a pub and community theatre, just down the road from here.'

'Yes, I know what it is.' Danny had got his first ever London dancing gig at the White Lion, in a very weird, very dark production of *Dr Faustus*. In spite of all the stage blood and gore it had been a wonderful experience. The director had treated the cast with encouragement and respect, allowing them to have their own input. It had been a wonderful bonding experience and the venue itself had added to it. The pub was hundreds of years old and rumour had it there'd been some kind of theatre on the site ever since Shakespeare's days. It was so rich in history it even had a ghost – of an actress who'd supposedly died of a broken heart when her leading man spurned her advances.

'I don't understand,' Danny said. 'Why are they trying to close it?'

'They've had their government funding cut. If they don't find the funding elsewhere they'll have to shut down at Christmas. Can I give you a leaflet?'

'Of course.'

'We're having a meeting in the pub tomorrow night to try and come up with some fundraising ideas. The info's all on there.'

'Great. Thanks.' Danny tucked the leaflet in his pocket.

'Hopefully see you there,' she called after him.

'Yes, yes you will,' Danny replied, as he continued walking down the street.

Jewel wondered if it was possible to ever truly be happy with everything. His job was going well. He'd finally cracked the record time of lacing a boot in less than six seconds. He really liked everyone he worked with and lived with, and yet ...

'Penny for your thoughts,' Alice said from the other end of the battered sofa in the theatre's green room.

'I was just wondering if it was dangerous to dream.'

'Whoa, heavy!'

'You did ask.'

Alice put down her kebab. 'OK. What is going on with you?'

'What do you mean?'

'I mean, you seem to have lost your sparkle, and with a name like Jewel that's very unfortunate.'

Jewel sighed. He'd even started to question his choice of name lately. He'd meant it to be symbolic and empowering, but did it just seem ludicrous? Had he just created yet another reason to doubt himself?

'Seriously, what's up, mate? And don't say nothing. You've been rocking that drab look all week now. And don't tell me that you've overslept again. It only takes a few seconds to put on a bit of lippy.'

Jewel glanced around the room. A couple of the other dressers were huddled in the corner, deep in conversation. Maybe he should tell Alice the reason for his inner crisis. If nothing else, it might stop her nagging him.

'I had a bit of a bad experience,' he said quietly.

'What happened?' The fact that she looked so concerned was slightly comforting.

'The other night I popped out on my break and a couple of guys ... hassled me.'

'Right ...' she looked at him expectantly.

'Well, that's it.'

'Hassled you about what?'

'About the way I look,' Jewel muttered.

'Ah ...' Alice nodded. 'There are some real idiots out there.'

'Yes.'

'But ...'

'What?'

'Has it never happened before? I'm not being funny or anything, but in my experience, the second you decide to look a little different from the norm every idiot in the vicinity seems to crawl out from under their rock.'

'Does it happen to you, too?'

'Of course. I've got pink dreadlocks and I like wearing bondage boots. On my days off,' she added, noticing Jewel's puzzled expression. 'It's not so bad up here in London but back home, oh my God! Surely you've been hassled before now, too?'

Jewel nodded. 'But not since I've been in London. I know this sounds really stupid, but I thought it would be different here.'

'It is. It's so much better, but let's face it, there are always going to be people who are threatened by anyone who dares to be different.'

'I suppose.'

'Don't let them get to you. Seriously.'

Jewel nodded. Maybe Alice was right. Maybe he was being stupid and weak for letting those men get to him, but he didn't want to spend his whole life feeling scared and permanently looking over his shoulder in case an idiot was about to crawl out from under their rock.

The bell rang for the end of break. Alice gathered up the remains of her kebab. Then she took Jewel's hand and gave it a squeeze. 'The world needs people like me and you. Otherwise we'd all die of boredom.'

Alice's words were still ringing through Jewel's head when he got home from work hours later. He popped into the kitchen to make himself a snack and found Danny sitting at the table.

'Hello, darling,' Danny said, glancing up from a notebook he was writing in. For a horrible moment Jewel thought he'd caught the poetry bug from Pete.

'What are you doing?' he asked tentatively.

'Brainstorming,' Danny replied. 'The kettle's just boiled if you fancy a cuppa.'

'Cool.' Jewel made himself a camomile tea and joined Danny at the table. 'What are you brainstorming?'

'Ideas for a show.' Danny put down his pen and looked at Jewel. 'Are you OK, darling?'

'Yes, I'm fine.'

'Are you sure?'

Jewel's face began to blush beneath the scrutiny. 'Yeah.'

'So what's all this about, then?' Danny gestured at him.

'All what?'

'Darling, you look like the hideous "before" picture from a makeover.'

'Thanks!'

'Are you depressed?'

'No!'

'Taking part in some kind of bet?'

'No!'

'Then why have you unfabuloused yourself?'

'Unfabuloused myself?' Jewel frowned.

'It is a thing,' Danny retorted.

Jewel sighed. 'I had a run-in with a couple of idiots the other day.' He looked down at the table, feeling ashamed. Danny was always so effortlessly confident, he'd probably think he was pathetic for giving in to the bullies.

'What kind of idiots?'

'Homophobic.'

'Oh.'

Jewel glanced at Danny and to his relief saw that he looked genuinely concerned.

'Did they hurt you?'

'What, physically? No.'

'OK. But their words did?'

Jewel nodded, suddenly annoyingly close to tears.

'I've been there, darling. It's shit.'

Jewel felt overwhelmed with relief. 'I know I shouldn't let them win ...'

Danny nodded. 'But you want to feel safe, too, right?'

'Right.'

'The trouble is, if you feel safe you'll never be free.'

Jewel thought back to how he'd felt back in the town where he'd grown up. The suffocating sense of not belonging. The growing urge to be free. This was why he'd been feeling so down for the last few days – he was stuck between a rock and a hard place, or a trapped and a scary place.

'I got my head kicked in when I was fourteen,' Danny said softly. 'After I'd come out to a couple of my schoolmates.'

'Your friends beat you up?' Jewel looked at him, horrified.

'No. But when word got round the school playground, the bullies were quick to pay me a visit.'

'I'm sorry.' The worst Jewel had ever suffered physically was a couple of shoves. Being beaten up was his worst nightmare.

'Yeah, and the worst thing about it was that when I got home my old man laughed.'

'What? Why?'

'What was it he said, again?' Danny frowned. 'Ah yes, "You got what was coming to you."'

'Your dad said that to you?' Jewel stared at him open-mouthed in horror. Suddenly his own dad's lectures on sin didn't seem quite so extreme.

'Yeah. Let's just say my dad is a bit of a throwback to Neanderthal Man.'

'I'm sorry.'

'Yeah, well. I didn't let that stop me. And neither should you.' Danny smiled at him, but it was a smile tinged with sadness. 'I know it's tough

– and scary – but if we ever want to see equality we've got to be brave. We're the trailblazers. We're the ones future generations will thank for paving their way.

Jewel nodded. Thinking of it like this was definitely helpful. It gave overcoming his fear a greater purpose.

'You need to keep blazing that trail, darling.'

'I will.'

'And speaking of which, how do you fancy helping me on a project?'

Jewel looked at him hopefully. 'What kind of project?'

Danny smiled at him. 'A fabulous, theatre-saving project.'

August
1994

Nineteen

C at looked at her *A–Z*, then surveyed the barren industrial wasteland in front of her. She'd been back on the audition circuit for almost a month now and in that time she'd certainly got to see all sides of London. Today she was up for a role in a music video, and the audition was taking place in a studio on an industrial estate in deepest, darkest East London. In a way, it was good having to come somewhere so scary she told herself as she took in the old, abandoned warehouses and the wreckage of a burned-out car. It put the fear of not getting the role into sharp perspective. As far as she was concerned, making it out alive or without being mugged was now her biggest priority.

Finally, she saw a signpost for the street the studio was supposed to be on. OK, 'street' was something of an over-statement. Alleyway would be more accurate. The kind of alleyway you saw in films right before the hero got set upon by a psychopathic killer. *I am brave. I am strong. I am fearless*, she said in her head, hugging her bag tighter to her body.

At the other end of the alley she heard someone laughing and she saw a group of young people in sportswear walking past. She felt a surge of relief. They looked like dancers, which meant she was heading in the right direction. But her relief was soon tainted by a feeling of apprehension. They were also her competition. Over the past month she'd been to six auditions, fitting them in around her evening shifts at the Lemon Tree. So far, she hadn't been offered a job and her newfound confidence was beginning to ebb.

To make matters worse, Justin had called the house last night. It had been six weeks since he'd left, and she hadn't known if she was going to hear from him again. So it was a huge surprise to not only hear his voice but to hear the happy and full-of-life Justin she'd first met and fallen in love with. The show he was in had begun and had been receiving incredible reviews. But he hadn't just called to show-off, he'd seemed genuinely interested in how she was doing, although part of her had wished that he hadn't. She'd ended up telling a small white lie, saying that the audition she was going to today was a callback. She couldn't bear having no good news to share.

Cat reached the end of the alleyway and followed the cluster of people up ahead. It was only just before ten in the morning, but the August sun was already punishing now that she was out of the shade, and sweat started erupting on her skin.

The studio was in a huge, old warehouse that still had the faded lettering TAYLOR'S SOAPS on the brickwork outside. Inside, the building had been stripped clean. It was like stepping inside an aircraft hangar. When Cat saw how many dancers were there she almost did an about-turn and walked straight out again. And if the thought of wandering back through the industrial estate on her own hadn't seemed quite so terrifying, she would have done.

Every audition is an opportunity, she reminded herself, as she went over to register. *Yes, an opportunity for humiliation*, her inner voice sniped as she took in the lithe body of the girl next to her. And she had to be a girl: she looked barely more than sixteen. *You're too old. You're too fat*, her inner voice of doom chirped up.

Trying to ignore the voices in her head, Cat went over to a corner at the back of the studio to warm up. She knew she shouldn't be hiding away at the back. She knew the prime position was at the front. For some weird reason, Lachlan popped into her head. *What the hell have you got to be so afraid of?* his gruff Aussie voice echoed through her mind. *This is your dream, isn't it? Go for it.* Cat couldn't help smiling. She knew it was her fear driving her almost crazy, but if Lachlan knew that he had now taken on the status of unlikely guru he'd probably find it hilarious. She took a deep breath and moved into the centre of the space.

Once the dancers were ready, a blue-haired American choreographer called Janelle came striding out to the front. She was muscular and strong, and was miked-up with a headpiece. 'OK, let's see what you've got,' she said, and a dance track began to play. It was one of the tracks that had been playing in Heaven the night Cat went there with Danny and Jewel. Cat couldn't help smiling at the memory. And as she began to dance it was as if that night had created some weird kind of muscle memory in her body. As she remembered how empowered she'd felt, in those crazy hot pants and with that silver lightning bolt, that same power surged through her and, for a brief moment, she totally forgot she was in an audition with so much riding on her performance. She was wild and fearless and unstoppable.

'Awesome,' a voice said, right by her ear.

She turned and saw Janelle grinning and nodding.

Danny sat at the kitchen table surveying the very large and very blank sheet of paper in front of him. He was supposed to be having a brainstorm, which would imply a surge of ideas pouring onto the page, but so far it couldn't even be deemed a brain trickle. The last month had passed by in a blur. He'd got the *Rocky Horror* gig and rehearsals had just started, but he'd also somehow managed to land his first choreographer/director role for the pantomime *Cinderella*. When he'd first made the move from dancer to choreographer he'd always dreamed that his first choreography role would be in a West End production. But then he'd gone to the public meeting about saving the White Lion and he'd been so outraged at the prospect of such a great venue closing, he'd got whirled up into a vortex in which a simple suggestion that maybe they put on some kind of fundraising show somehow led to him offering his services for free and being appointed creative director and choreographer.

They'd decided on a panto as the thing most likely to get the most bums on seats. Everyone had got really fired up about the idea in subsequent meetings, but now it was just him and a blindingly blank page, the enormity of what Danny had undertaken was starting to hit him.

Desperate to do something, he wrote CINDERELLA in bright pink highlighter at the centre of the page.

The door opened and Lil breezed in. She was wearing an outsized FRANKIE SAY RELAX T-shirt as a dress and her favourite red clogs.

'Very eighties, darling,' Danny remarked, looking at the T-shirt.

'Thank you. I sent Holly some distance healing this morning when I was communing with my spirit guide, White Eagle. Fucking HIV. 'Scuse my French, sweetheart, but I'm so sick of that fucking disease. It's taking far too many beautiful people.'

Danny nodded, experiencing the customary shudder he felt every time he thought of the AIDs epidemic.

'*Cinderella?*' Lil asked, looking at the sheet of paper on the table.

'Yes, turns out I'm going to be directing it in panto.'

'Oh no!'

Danny looked at her, shocked. With her passion for theatrics he'd assumed this news would be right up Lil's street. 'What's wrong?'

'I hate that god-awful story.'

'Why?'

'It's so regressive. Poor old Cinders waiting around for a man to save her. And was there ever a man more insipid than Prince Charming?' Lil sighed. 'Dammit, I forgot to bring my baccy downstairs.' She started foraging in one of the overflowing ashtrays on the table and pulled out one of her old butts, taking it over to the oven and lighting it on the hob.

'If you ask me, that story needs to be completely re-written.'

'Oh yeah?' Curiosity sparked into life inside Danny.

'Yeah.' Lil sat down across from him. 'Not the pumpkin bit. I like that. And the bit where the mice get turned into horses – reminds me of a trip I took back in seventy-six ...' She gazed dreamily into the distance.

'Oh yeah? Where to?'

Lil frowned at him. 'To the wildest recesses of my mind, sweetheart, aided by my good friends *L, S* and *D*.'

'Ah, right.'

'But the rest of it – the glass slipper and the ball and Prince Pathetic – that all needs to go.'

'Hmm ...' Danny stared down at the page. What if he came up with an alternative version of *Cinderella*? Something edgier, funnier, more relevant? Not only would it be more entertaining, but it might also help the White Lion get more publicity for their fundraising appeal. An image of a punkish Cinderella appeared in his mind, kind of like the way Jewel made Cat look the night they went to Heaven. Maybe he could ask Jewel to help him with the costumes.

'If you ask me, Cinderella should wear clogs, not glass slippers.'

'What?' Danny was wrenched from his daydream by the sight of Lil brandishing one of her clogs.

'Glass slippers are a symbol of the patriarchy, designed to stop us fleeing from attackers and to cripple us with bunions.'

Danny stared at her blankly. What on earth was she going on about?

'You can't run in high heels at the best of times, but if they're made of glass, forget it. I'm telling you, clogs are the way forward.'

'Do you know what I love most about living in this house?' Lachlan asked, coming into the room. 'The way you're guaranteed to hear sentences that have never, ever been uttered before. G'day all.'

'Hello, sweetheart,' Lil said, putting her clog back on. 'I'm just schooling Danny in the evils of *Cinderella* and how it's a weapon of the patriarchy, designed to oppress women.'

Lachlan chuckled and took a beer from the fridge. 'Dare I ask why you're getting this lecture?' He grinned at Danny.

'I've offered to direct a production of *Cinders* at the White Lion Theatre.'

'What? I thought that was closing down.'

'It might be. We're putting on a panto to try and raise funds to stop it from being shut.'

'Cool.' Lachlan sat down at the table.

'If I was rewriting *Cinderella* I'd have her going to a Women's Empowerment Conference instead of a ball,' Lil muttered.

Lachlan raised his eyebrows at Danny.

'Yeah, well, that might not be quite the show-stopping climax I was imagining,' Danny replied. Another image popped into his head. Cinderella at a rave: dance music pumping, all Day-Glo and strobes.

'And I'd bin the ugly sisters,' Lil said, taking a long draw on her cigarette butt before grinding it out.

'Why? The ugly sisters are great,' Lachlan said.

'Oh, sweetheart.' Lil shook her head as if there was no hope for him.

'What?' Lachlan grinned.

'They just help propagate the myth that ugly is bad and beauty is good. If I was directing this show I'd make the sisters beautiful and Cinderella a hideous brute.'

Danny pictured the final scene of Lil's version of Cinderella – a hideous brute of a woman turning up in her clogs and pumpkin coach at a Bra-Burning Conference. Somehow he didn't think it would have the crowds going crazy. But she did have a point. If he could figure out a way to make Cinders fresh and exciting he could be on to a winner.

The sound of the front door shutting caused them all to look up. Cat walked into the room and dumped her bag on the floor. Her eyes were shining and her face was glowing.

'I've got a job!' she exclaimed. 'A dancing job.'

Twenty

Lachlan shifted up so that Cat could sit down. She looked amazing. And so happy. In the past few weeks she'd gone for a few auditions, and he'd tried his best to keep her buoyed up whenever their paths crossed in the house, but he'd been beginning to worry she'd give up.

'And you all helped me to get it,' Cat said, looking around the table. 'And Jewel. Where's Jewel? I need to thank Jewel, too.'

'Still at work, darling,' Danny replied.

'Of course.' Cat grinned.

'So, how did we help you?' Lachlan asked.

'Was it that talk I gave you about Kali through the bathroom door the other night?' Lil asked. 'She is one kick-ass goddess.'

'What?' Cat looked blank for a moment. 'Oh, uh, yes, that was very helpful.' She turned to Danny. 'And I need to thank you for taking me to Heaven that night.'

'You're welcome.' Danny frowned. 'Although I can't really see how it would have helped.'

'They played a track in the audition that I danced to that night and it made me feel the way I did back then – all fierce and empowered.'

Cat turned to Lachlan. 'And I need to thank you for being my very alternative life coach. I actually heard your voice in my head today, just before I started to dance.'

'You did?' Lachlan grinned, unsure what to make of this.

Cat's face flushed. 'Yes, I mean, not literally. I'm not hearing voices or anything. I haven't gone crazy. I just imagined what you might say to me in that situation and it was really helpful.'

'What did you imagine me saying?' Now Lachlan was really intrigued.

'Yes, what did he say?' Lil asked, looking equally fascinated.

Cat's face flushed even brighter red. 'You told me not to be so scared,' she muttered. 'And you were quite sweary about it.'

Lachlan laughed. 'Yep, sounds about right.' He didn't really know what to make of the fact that Cat was imagining his voice in her head, but it made him feel good – warm inside.

'What's going on?' Cat asked, pointing to the piece of paper with Cinderella written on it.

'I'm going to be directing a production of *Cinderella* this Christmas,' Danny replied.

'And I'm trying to get him to re-write it,' Lil said.

'She wants Cinderella to have a glass clog,' Lachlan muttered.

'No, I do not!' Lil exclaimed. 'I want her to have a rubber-soled, vegetarian clog. Rubber soles are essential if you're trying to run away from an attacker in the rain,' she added.

'But why … ?' Cat began.

'Don't ask!' Danny interrupted. 'Tell us more about this dancing job.'

Lachlan held his breath. What if it was a job like Justin's? What if meant Cat leaving Diamond Street, too?

'It's for a music video,' Cat replied.

'Oh, how exciting!' Lil clasped her hands together.

'That's awesome,' Lachlan smiled at Cat, as much from relief as happiness.

'That's fabulous, darling!' Danny gave Cat a hug.

'I'm so relieved. I was – I was beginning to give up hope.' Cat looked down at the table. Lachlan fought the urge to throw his arms around her.

'You must never give up on your dreams,' Lil said firmly. 'As I said to David when he felt like giving up – the world needs your special gift, sweetheart. You need to keep daring to dream. And look what happened next …'

Everyone looked at her blankly.

'Ziggy Stardust!' Lil exclaimed.

'You knew David Bowie?' Lachlan asked, incredulous.

'I don't like to betray confidences, sweetheart,' Lil said, suddenly uncharacteristically coy.

Lachlan bit his lip. Danny had a theory that Lil had taken way too much acid back in the day and it had left her on a permanent trip, one where she imagined she'd known a whole bunch of famous people. Lachlan was inclined to agree with him. After all, if Lil was so well-connected, what the hell was she doing renting an attic room in a house share in Camden? Why wasn't she living it up with Bowie, Keith or Mick, or the remaining members of the Beatles?

'Who's the music video for?' Danny asked.

'Some American band. They're trying to break into the UK so they're shooting their next video in London, in all the landmark places. Apparently, I'll be dancing outside Buckingham Palace!'

'Who's the choreographer?'

'An American woman called Janelle something.'

Danny shrugged like he didn't know her.

'I'm so happy,' Cat said again, grinning like a loon.

So am I, Lachlan thought to himself.

'You watch, I bet the jobs will come rolling in now,' Danny said. 'Speaking of which, I don't suppose you fancy auditioning for Cinders? There won't be any money in it, I'm afraid, we're doing it to raise funds to try and save the White Lion.'

'I'd love to!' Cat exclaimed. She leaned back in her chair, revealing an inch of creamy skin between her top and her leggings. Lachlan hastily looked away. 'This has been the best day. And the funniest thing is, I thought it was going to be the worst day because I was sure I was going to get mugged or murdered or worse.'

'What's worse than being murdered?' Lachlan asked.

'Being accused of molesting a mannequin in Harrods,' Lil said with a dramatic sigh. 'That's definitely a fate worse than death.'

Once again, everyone turned to stare at her.

'What? It is.' Lil shook her head. 'And I didn't molest it. I was protesting against animal cruelty.'

They all continued to stare at her.

'It was wearing a fur coat!' Lil exclaimed. 'I just smeared some blood on its face to symbolize the blood shed by the poor mink they'd murdered to make it.'

'I take it you mean red paint?' Danny said.

Lil shook her head. 'Of course not. That's a poor substitute.'

'Whose blood did you use?' Cat asked, her eyes wide.

'My own, of course. It wasn't my fault I wasn't able to stem the bleeding.'

'Bloody hell, darling!' Danny exclaimed.

''Scuse the pun,' Lachlan muttered.

Cat started giggling. 'God, I love living here.'

Once again Lachlan had no choice but to agree with her.

As Jewel let himself into the house he heard the tinkle of Cat's laughter coming from the kitchen. This was a good sign. He knew she had had an audition today. He knew how much was resting on it. Surely she wouldn't be laughing like that if it had gone badly. He went into the kitchen. All of his housemates apart from Pete were sitting around the table. There was a large sheet of paper in the centre of the table, covered in random words in little bubbles, like one of those mind map things.

'Hey,' he said, coming over to sit down. 'What's going on?'

'We're helping Danny brainstorm his next creative extravaganza,' Lil replied.

'*The Rocky Horror Picture Show*?' Jewel asked.

Danny shook his head. 'I've been asked to direct a production of *Cinderella* to try and save the White Lion from closing.'

'No way! That's amazing!'

'I was wondering if you'd be interested in helping?' Danny asked.

'Of course.' Jewel unlaced his pink patent leather DMs. They were brand new and so stiff his feet were killing him.

'I need a costume designer slash maker slash wardrobe master,' Danny said.

'Cool. Do you want me to ask my boss at work if she'd be interested, or if she knows anyone?'

Danny shook his head. 'No, I want you to do it.'

'Me?'

'Isn't this the best day ever?' Cat said.

'Uh, yes ...' Jewel stared at Danny. 'You want me to be the costume designer and wardrobe manager?'

'If you have the time. I know you're busy with work and – '

'I'll make the time,' Jewel cut in. He didn't care if he was up all night long making costumes, this sounded like his dream gig.

'Brilliant,' Danny smiled at him. 'And this isn't going to be any old Cinderella, either.'

'She's going to be wearing vegetarian clogs,' Lachlan grinned.

'Vegetarian clogs?' Jewel echoed.

'No!' Danny exclaimed. 'I was thinking something more along the lines of the look you did on Cat that night we went to Heaven.'

'The silver hot pants and the lightning bolt?' Jewel said.

Lachlan coughed. 'That sounds like some look!'

'It was great,' Cat said. 'Jewel made me feel like a superhero. And you made me feel like that all over again today.' She smiled at him.

'I did?'

Cat nodded. 'They played one of the tracks we danced to at Heaven at my audition. It made me think of how good I felt that night. I'm sure that's how I got the gig.' She giggled. 'I tapped back into my superhero energy.'

'You got the job?'

Cat nodded.

Jewel threw his arms round her. 'That's fantastic.'

Danny yawned. 'OK, I think I'm going to call it a night.' He looked at Jewel. 'Maybe you and I could get our heads together on Sunday? Make a mood board for the costumes?'

'Of course.' Jewel couldn't think of a way he'd rather spend his day off.

'Excellent.' Danny stood up. 'Night everyone.' As he walked past Jewel he stopped. 'Good to see you back to your fabulous self.'

Jewel smiled and blushed. Over the past few weeks his confidence had gradually crept back and he'd started dressing how he wanted to again. Today on his break at work he'd let Alice do his make-up, and he hadn't washed it off before leaving the theatre and coming home.

'I think I'm going to turn in, too,' Lil said. 'Sweet dreams, sweethearts.' She swept out after Danny.

'You missed a great brainstorm,' Cat said.

'So I see.' Jewel looked down at the mind map. 'What the hell?' he pointed to the words FUCK THE PATRIARCHY written in red next to PRINCE CHARMING.

'I think Lil wanted the Fairy Godmother to turn Prince Charming into a pumpkin,' Lachlan said.

Cat laughed. 'Yeah, it definitely made her ragey. Maybe you should introduce her to your yelling therapy.'

'I only introduce very special people to my yelling therapy,' Lachlan replied.

'Well, in that case, I feel very honoured.' Cat giggled.

Jewel studied her face. Was she blushing? He looked at Lachlan. The gruff Aussie was looking equally coy. Was something going on between them? And more to the point, if there was something going on, was Jewel now being a big, fat gooseberry, stuck in between them?

'I think I'm going to go to bed, too,' he said, standing up.

'Oh, OK.' Cat stood up and gave him a hug. 'Thank you again for helping me today.'

'No problem.' Jewel laughed. 'I'm always happy to help without even realizing it.'

'Danny's asked me to audition for *Cinderella*. Won't it be fun, if I get a part, all working on something together?'

Jewel nodded. It was funny to think that a few weeks ago he'd felt so down and helpless. Now everything seemed hopeful again. Maybe life wasn't about finding happiness and keeping it, he mused to himself as he left the kitchen. Maybe it was more of a seasonal thing that came and went, but always came back again.

Cat went over to the sink to get a glass of water and gave another happy sigh.

'Great news about the dancing job,' Lachlan said.

'Thank you.' She wondered if he thought she was a total freak for saying she'd heard his voice in her head, but from the way he was smiling at her, he didn't appear to. He had such a lovely smile. Why hadn't she noticed that before? Maybe because he didn't smile all that often. It was such a warm smile. It made him look so much younger. She thought back to what he'd told her about the moon and the stars, and for a moment she could picture him as a kid, wide-eyed and grinning as he listened to his dad's tales of wonder.

'What are you smiling about?' he asked.

'I'm just thinking.'

'What about?' he got up and brought his cup over to the sink.

'You.'

'Me?' He turned to look at her. They were only about a foot apart now and his close proximity was making every nerve ending in her body stand to attention.

She nodded.

'Why are you thinking about me?' His voice was so quiet now it was practically a whisper.

She looked at his mouth. 'I'm thinking that you have a really lovely smile.'

'Yeah?'

'Yes.'

'Well, that might have something to do with you.'

'Me?'

He nodded and looked down at his feet. 'You make me smile.'

'Why?' Now she was the one whispering.

'Because you're you.' He looked at her and there was such vulnerability in his gaze, such openness, it made her catch her breath.

'I ...'

'Cat ...' he whispered. And then his strong hands were either side of her face, holding it so gently, as if it was the most precious and delicate thing he'd ever touched. 'Cat,' he whispered again, this time with real urgency.

She heard herself gasp and then she felt his lips on hers. So gently at first that she thought she might be dreaming. But then she felt them pressing harder, and her own body responding. She'd never felt such longing. It was as if some weird osmosis was making their lips become one – their bodies become one. His arms wrapped around her and it felt even better than she'd imagined. As she melted into him she could hear his breath hot and fast in her ear. She wrapped her arms around him, tighter and tighter, and she felt him relaxing into her. She traced the contour of his lip with her tongue and he started to moan.

'Oh God, oh Michelle ...'

'What?' Cat broke away. She felt so stunned it was as if he'd poured a bucket of icy water over her. 'Who's Michelle?'

Lachlan gulped. 'I didn't ... I ...'

The door crashed open and Pete walked in. 'Evening,' he mumbled without looking at either of them, making a beeline for the fridge.

Cat watched numbly as he took out a pork pie and a jar of mayonnaise, then turned and left.

'I'm sorry,' Lachlan mumbled, 'I'm really sorry.' Then he hurried from the room.

Cat stood motionless, numb with confusion, the only sound the dripping of the tap into the sink.

Twenty-one

Danny looked at Jewel across the mountain of fabric swatches and magazine cuttings on the kitchen table. He'd got so lost in ideas and images and creations he'd forgotten to eat, and suddenly he felt hollowed out by hunger.

'Do you fancy something to eat?' He got up and went over to the fridge.

Jewel nodded without looking up from his sketch pad. 'Yeah, I'm starving.'

Danny opened the fridge door and stared inside mournfully. 'Well, I don't know about you but all I have left is a tub of I Can't Believe It's Not Butter.'

'Ooh, very Cinderella.' Jewel laughed.

'Actually, scrap that,' Danny said, opening the margarine. 'All I have is an *empty* tub of I Can't Believe It's Not Butter.'

'Shame we don't have a Fairy Godmother to turn it into a roast chicken.'

Danny binned the empty tub and shut the fridge. 'How about we pop down to the Lemon Tree, my treat?'

'Seriously?' Jewel's eyes lit up.

'Of course. It's the least I can do given how hard you've worked today on the costume designs. And Cat's working there tonight. We can go and make her life hell, ordering aperitifs and digestifs.'

Jewel nodded. 'Sounds great.'

'Although maybe we should go easy on her,' Danny added. 'She seemed a little tense when I saw her earlier.'

'How come?'

'I think she and Lachlan might have fallen out again.'

'What? Why?' Jewel put down his sketch pad.

Danny paused. He knew gossip was wrong, especially gossip about housemates, but like most 'wrong' things, it always felt so deliciously good. 'Well, I came in here this morning to make a cuppa and Cat was doing the dishes and her eyes were all red like she'd been crying and then ...' Danny lowered his voice and checked the door to make sure no one was coming, 'then Lachlan walked in, took one look at Cat and walked straight back out again.'

Jewel frowned. 'That's weird. Last night they seemed like ...'

'Like what?' Danny's hunger for gossip was now almost as strong as his hunger for food.

'Like there was something going on between them. They were really flirting.'

'No way!' Danny pursed his lips. 'Right, let's get down to the Lemon Tree. We need to interrogate Cat – I mean, support her emotionally.'

Much as Danny loved a good gossip, as he entered the Lemon Tree with Jewel, he really hoped nothing bad had happened between Lachlan and Cat. With a show to direct and half the housemates involved, he could do without the delicate ecosystem of 27 Diamond Street being knocked off balance. But had Lachlan and Cat become lovers? He felt a frisson of excitement, which was only magnified when he caught sight of the broad-shouldered frame of Achilles behind the bar.

Don't waste your energy; he's straight, he told himself sternly. Much as he'd tried over the past months, his gaydar hadn't picked up the faintest trace of a signal from the handsome bar manager. He scanned the restaurant for Cat. She was over at a far table, pouring glasses of wine for an elderly couple. Even beneath the golden glow of the taverna lighting he could see she looked a lot paler than usual.

'Danny!' Stelios cried, coming out from the kitchen. 'So lovely to see you, and your very colourful friend.' He smiled at Jewel, who was wearing a hot-pink top and neon blue cargo pants.

Danny had been very relieved to see the return of Jewel's sparkle over the past couple of weeks. His heart had really gone out to Jewel when he heard how he'd been hassled by those men. Not least because it had brought back a host of bad memories of his own. He hadn't told Jewel about the beating he'd received at the hands of his dad the night he'd told him he was gay. He didn't want to traumatize the poor kid, but the memory had come back to haunt Danny in his dreams most nights ever since it had happened. His dad's flushed face, his beery breath. The punches raining down on Danny's arms and face. He pushed the memory from his mind and went over to greet Stelios.

'Could we have a table for two and a bottle of your finest cabernet sauvignon, please?'

'Of course, of course.' Stelios ushered them over to a table by the bar, right in front of Achilles. Danny studiously avoided looking anywhere in his direction.

'Cat!' Jewel called as she wove her way back through the tables towards them.

'Jewel! Danny!' she replied, sounding hugely relieved to see them. She tucked a loose curl behind her ear. She looked really tired and the whites of her eyes were streaked pink. 'Have you come to eat?'

Danny nodded.

'Oh, I wish I could join you.'

'It's OK,' Stelios said. 'We aren't too busy. You take a break, have something to eat.'

'Are you sure?' Cat asked.

'Of course.' Stelios pulled out a chair for her at the table.

Cat sat down and gave a loud sigh.

'You OK, darling?' Danny asked.

'Yes, why wouldn't I be?' Cat replied defensively. 'Sorry, I'm just a bit tired, that's all.'

Jewel passed her a menu.

'This is on me,' Danny said, hoping this might cheer her up a bit.

'Really?' Cat gave him a weak smile. 'That's so lovely, thank you.'

Then to Danny's horror, her eyes filled with tears.

'What's wrong, darling?'

'I'm so sorry,' Cat sobbed. 'This is so embarrassing.'

'Here,' Jewel handed her a napkin.

'Thank you.' Cat dabbed at her eyes.

Danny noticed Achilles looking over and frowning. Great. Now he'd probably think Danny had made her cry. Not that it mattered what Achilles thought of him, he reminded himself.

'What's happened?' Jewel asked.

'Something truly terrible.'

Danny's appetite for gossip reached epic proportions. 'Do you want to tell us about it?' he asked softly. *Please, please, let her tell us about it.*

'Do you promise you won't judge me?' Cat sniffed.

'Of course not!' Jewel yelped. Clearly he was as eager as Danny to learn what had happened.

'Last night, Lachlan and I ... we kissed.'

'Ah,' Danny said. 'Was he no good? Did he have a lizard tongue?'

'What?' Cat stared at him blankly.

'You know, that really gross thing some people do with their tongues when they're kissing. When they make it dart about so much you practically retch.'

Now Cat and Jewel were both looking at him blankly. They'd clearly been fortunate enough to have avoided the horror of the lizard tongue.

'No. He was actually a good kisser. Really good …' Cat looked dreamy for a moment. 'Until …'

'Until?' Danny and Jewel chorused.

'Until he called me Michelle.' Cat groaned and dropped her head down on to the table

'What?' Jewel stared at her open-mouthed. 'Why would he call you Michelle?'

'I don't know,' Cat raised her head slightly to look at them. 'Well, I do. He was obviously thinking about someone else while he was kissing me.' Her voice began to quiver. 'Someone called Michelle.'

'Wow.' Danny frowned. In all the time he'd been living with Lachlan there'd been no hint of a woman. He'd never brought anyone back to the house and no one ever rang for him, apart from his boss at the hospital asking if he'd work an extra shift. Maybe Michelle was someone he knew at work.

'That's horrible,' Jewel said. 'And really weird. I thought he was really into you.'

'You did?' Cat looked at him hopefully.

'Yeah. The things he was saying to you last night, about you being special.' Jewel blushed. 'Sorry, I wasn't being nosy. I couldn't help overhearing.'

'It's OK.' Cat wiped her face with the napkin. 'Clearly he's not as into me as he is this Michelle woman.'

'When did he actually say it?' Danny asked, unable to contain his curiosity.

'Last night.'

'No, I mean, what was the context? Was it while you were actually kissing or just after?'

'While. He literally moaned and said, "Oh God, oh Michelle".'

'Oh no.' Danny pulled a pained expression.

'Exactly. It was so horrible.'

'What happened after he said it?' Jewel asked.

'He practically ran out of the room.'

'Shit.' Danny shook his head. This was really shoddy behaviour from Lachlan.

'Maybe there's some explanation,' Jewel said tentatively.

'Yeah, he's an arsehole,' Cat replied.

'Your wine.' Achilles announced, arriving at the table with a bottle of cabernet tucked into the crook of his muscular arm. 'You like to have a taste?' he asked Danny.

Danny tried not to think of the obvious double entendre and nodded. The table fell silent as Danny took a sip of the wine.

'Everything OK, Cat?' Achilles asked.

She gave him a tearful nod.

'The wine's great,' Danny said quickly. 'It's OK, we can pour it ourselves.' The last thing he needed was Achilles hovering about, ruining what was an intriguing conversation – no matter how much his muscular physique improved the view.

'I don't know what I was thinking,' Cat said. 'I never should have kissed a housemate. I promise I won't make it awkward for you. I'm going to try and have a word with him tonight, and get things sorted.'

'That sounds like a good plan,' Jewel nodded.

'Yes, I'm sure it will all be fine, darling,' Danny said, a lot more affirmatively than he felt. As far as he was concerned, Lachlan had a lot of explaining to do.

Lachlan paced up and down in front of the bathroom mirror. 'I'm so sorry,' he said to his reflection. He shook his head. That was no good. It was too weak. He needed to be more assertive. 'I need to explain ...' That was better, but how? How would he explain to Cat why he'd said 'Michelle' while they were kissing? Even though it was practically twenty-four hours since the dreadful incident, the memory still had the power to make him blush with shame to the roots of his hair. He stared at himself in the mirror, flushed and unshaven, with huge bags beneath his eyes. It was not a good look. 'I need to explain,' he said again, squirting a ball of shaving foam into the palm of his hand. 'When I said what I did it wasn't because I wasn't thinking of you.' And it wasn't. He'd been so absorbed in the moment, in the kiss, in *Cat*, he wasn't sure he'd ever felt anything quite so intensely.

He hadn't intentionally thought of Michelle. It had to have been his guilty conscience, trying to sabotage his happiness yet again. 'It was my guilty conscience,' he said, rubbing the foam on to his chin. No, he couldn't say that, that sounded terrible, like he'd done something terrible. *You have*, his guilty conscience reminded him. Lachlan sighed. If he told Cat why he'd been feeling guilty she'd never want anything more to do with him. It was pointless. He swept his razor across his jaw and a sharp sting of pain jolted through him as he nicked his skin. *Great*. But he had to do something. 'You have to do something,' he told his reflection.

He finished shaving and splashed his face with cold water. He would wait in the kitchen for Cat to come home from work. Then he would tell her the truth – every last terrible bit of it. Even if she was horrified, even if she never spoke to him again, it would be better than her thinking that he'd said 'Michelle' because he didn't like Cat.

Lachlan sat at the kitchen table, freshly shaven and heart pounding. Even though the newly purple walls were meant to have calming properties – according to Lil, anyway – they were doing nothing for his soaring pulse rate.

'I need to explain,' he muttered under his breath. 'I was in a relationship before I came to the UK. It ended in very traumatic circumstances.' He nodded. That was definitely correct. 'My girlfriend ...'

His heart skipped a beat as he heard the front door slam. What if she didn't come into the kitchen? What if she went straight to her room? But

Cat always had a cup of that gross camomile tea before going to bed. Sure enough, the kitchen door opened. Lachlan cleared his throat, then froze in shock as Justin strode into the room.

Cat followed Danny and Jewel into the house. Having dinner with them had really helped lift her spirits, but now she was back at Diamond Street all she could think of was Lachlan, or more to the point, Lachlan's voice saying 'Michelle' over and over again. She'd always liked the name Michelle before. She'd always thought it sounded pretty and French, but now she hated it with a vengeance. Now it provoked the same kind of shudder in her as the words 'slug' and 'vomit'.

'Fancy a camomile tea?' Jewel asked.

Cat nodded. Hopefully it would calm the anger sparking back to life inside of her. As she followed the others into the kitchen she almost went crashing into Danny's back as he suddenly stopped in his tracks.

'Oh, hello,' he said.

Cat peered around him. *Oh God. Oh God. Oh God.* Lachlan was standing by the table – and Justin was standing by the fridge!

'Wh-what …?' she stammered.

'Hello, babe,' Justin said, grinning broadly. 'Surprise!'

Cat glanced from him to Lachlan, who was looking ashen-faced.

'Well, it's all happening this evening,' Danny muttered.

'What are you doing here?' Cat asked, turning back to Justin.

'Do I need a reason to come and see my girlfriend?' he said. 'I missed you.'

'But …' Cat fell silent, the words, *I didn't think I was your girlfriend anymore*, left unspoken.

'I'm going to bed,' Lachlan muttered. As he reached the door he went to go past Cat but she went the same way and they ended up doing an awkward shuffle. Cat felt a weird tingling in the pit of her stomach at his close proximity. God, why was her body such a traitor?

'I missed you, too,' she said loudly, going over to the table. She would show Lachlan. He wasn't the only one who could have more than one person on his mind. But saying it didn't make her feel any better. If anything, it made her feel like a fraud.

'Actually, I think I'll go to bed, too,' Jewel said, looking pointedly at Danny.

For a moment it seemed as if Danny was going to stay rooted to the spot, and Cat really wanted him to. Anything to buy herself a bit more time to try to process these latest developments. But to her disappointment he nodded. 'Yeah, I guess it's getting on a bit. Good night, then.' He gave Cat a quick hug.

'Night.'

And then it was just her and Justin.

She sat down at the table, feeling suddenly light-headed from tiredness and shock. 'I don't understand … why didn't you tell me you were coming?'

'I didn't want to ruin the surprise.' He sat down next to her and put his arm round her shoulders. She felt no internal response at all. It was as if her body had turned to stone. Justin's smile faded. 'Is something wrong? Aren't you pleased to see me?'

'No. I mean yes, of course I'm pleased, it was just a bit of a shock, and I'm really tired from work.' As soon as she said this she bit her lip. Justin didn't know about her job at the Lemon Tree and she wasn't sure she wanted him to. It wasn't that she was embarrassed about working in a bar, it was more of a pride thing – not wanting him to know that she wasn't able to make a living from dancing.

'What work?'

'Oh, I've just been doing a few shifts at a Greek taverna down the road – in between auditions.'

'Ah, OK.'

'And speaking of auditions, I've got a dancing job.'

'Oh, yeah?'

She thought he'd be happy at this development but if anything, he looked slightly dejected.

'What kind of job?'

'Dancing in a music video. The choreographer's great. And I've got an audition for a show Danny's directing, too.'

Justin's eyes widened. 'Danny's directing a show?'

'Yeah. A pantomime. A very alternative *Cinderella*.'

'When are the auditions?'

'In a couple of weeks. Why?' She got a sudden, uneasy feeling. Why did Justin want to know?

'I was just wondering if maybe I could try out for it, too.'

'But what about Berlin?'

'Yeah, well, Berlin isn't going so well.' He sighed and folded his arms.

'But when you rang the other week you said it was going brilliantly.'

'Well, I wasn't exactly being truthful.'

Cat frowned, her brain felt stretched to full capacity trying to process all of these sudden, shocking twists. 'What's been happening?'

He sighed. 'I've been so miserable there without you.'

'What?'

'I mean it, Cat, being so far away from you, it's really helped to get things into perspective.' He took hold of her hands. 'I love you, Scottie. I don't want us to be apart, and if you won't come to Berlin then I guess I'll have to come back to London.'

'You're coming back to London?'

He nodded.

Cat frowned. She wasn't sure if it was because she was so tired from work or so traumatized from what had happened with Lachlan, but something didn't feel quite right about all of this. *She* didn't feel quite right for a start. These were the kinds of things that, just a couple of months ago, she'd longed for Justin to say. So why, now he was finally saying them, did she feel so numb? Maybe it was shock.

'That's if you'll have me?' He gave her one of his most boyish smiles and she felt her numbness fading slightly. In spite of the smile, he looked so tired and sad. It was hugely ironic to think that she'd been assuming he'd been having a brilliant time without her. It was so weird how the tables of life could turn like this. Now she was the one with the exciting dance job, the one who was feeling happy and strong. Or at least, she had been until she'd kissed Lachlan. Oh God, she'd kissed Lachlan! And now Justin wanted to move back in. This was going to make things all kinds of awkward. But why should she care how it made Lachlan feel? He hadn't cared about her feelings when he'd started moaning about bloody Michelle.

'Of course I'll have you,' she said.

'Thanks, babe.' He leaned towards her and planted a kiss on her lips.

Her body turned back to stone.

Twenty-two

'Can I ask your advice about something?' Jewel said to Danny as he finished hemming one of the ugly sister's dresses. It was now two weeks since Danny had asked him to help with the panto, and the living room at 27 Diamond Street had been turned into a fully functioning wardrobe department. Danny had loaned Jewel a beautiful old Singer sewing machine that had belonged to his mum, and despite it looking like an antique, it worked like a dream.

'Of course, darling,' Danny replied, checking the stitching on Cinderella's gold sequinned hot pants.

'If I wanted to – uh – meet someone but I didn't want to meet them in a club, how would I do it?'

'Meet them outside the club,' Danny suggested absent-mindedly.

'Outside?'

'Yes, outside by the door. That way it will be so much easier to find them.'

'No, I didn't mean meet, I meant *meet*,' Jewel replied, his cheeks burning. He was already regretting asking the question.

'Meat?' Danny stared at him. 'I'm sorry, darling, I don't understand. How do you meat someone?'

'That's what I'm asking.' Jewel looked at him, confused.

Danny came over to the sewing machine. 'Are you talking about meat, as in a pork chop or meet, as in to rendezvous?'

'To rendezvous, but … romantically.' Jewel pretended to study the hem to try and hide his blushes. He must sound so pathetic. But the truth was, lately Jewel had been feeling a weird kind of craving for a closeness with someone that extended beyond friendship. Maybe it was the fact that winter was coming, but the thought of having someone to get physically cosy with was becoming more and more appealing.

'Aha!' Danny's eyes lit up. 'About bloody time! But why don't you want to meet someone in a club?'

'I don't know – I, uh, I haven't really …' Jewel tailed off. How could he tell someone as worldly as Danny that he'd had so little experience?

Danny stared at him. 'Are you …? Have you never …?'

Jewel shook his head.

'I see.' Danny nodded knowingly. Jewel really hoped he didn't think him too pathetic. 'What you need is a coming-out party.'

'But I'm already out.'

'No, I mean like they used to have in the good old days, when women were formally introduced to society. A debutante's ball.'

'I think we've got enough on our hands with Cinderella's ball – or rave,' Jewel replied, panicking. The last thing he wanted was Danny organizing some kind of massive party in his honour, or even worse, in honour of his romantic life. That would feel just as intimidating as a club.

'I could organize a small soirée,' Danny said, looking thoughtful. 'We could have it here on Sunday. I could invite my single friends. Obviously I wouldn't tell them the reason, but you could see if there was anyone you clicked with.'

'OK,' Jewel replied. 'As long as you don't tell them the reason.'

'Of course. You just leave it to me, Cinderella,' Danny said with grin. 'I'll find you your Prince Charming.'

'I can't believe you're throwing a party to help Jewel lose his virginity!' Lil exclaimed. 'That's so romantic, sweetheart!'

'Shhh!' Danny glanced at the kitchen door, making sure Jewel wasn't about. 'I'm not supposed to tell anyone the reason.'

'Well, I'm honoured you told me. And it's a good job you did because now I can get the room ready.'

'What do you mean?' For one horrible moment Danny pictured Lil filling the room with heart-shaped balloons embossed with HELP JEWEL GET LAID.

'I can get my rose quartz out and cleanse the room with sage. And light some jasmine candles. Jasmine is a great aphrodisiac, you know. As I discovered to my cost that summer I spent in Thailand, back in seventy-nine.'

'Well, as long as whatever you do is subtle, darling. We don't want our guests thinking they've been invited to some kind of Bangkok bordello.'

'Why on earth not?' Lil asked, looking genuinely bewildered.

'Never mind.' Danny looked at the clock on the kitchen wall. There were only a few hours before his soirée was due to begin. 'I'm going to nip down to the offie and get some booze. Do you want me to get you anything?' To his surprise, Lil shook her head.

'I think I'll come with you. I need to get the ingredients for my kismet punch.'

'Are you sure I can't get them for you? You could write me a list.'

Lil shook her head. 'It's kismet punch, sweetheart.'

Danny looked at her blankly. 'What's kismet? Is it a liqueur?'

'No! It means destiny. The recipe changes every time I make it, depending on what's destined to be in it, obviously. That's why I have to choose. It will help everyone who drinks it find their destiny, too.' She gave him a wink. 'So hopefully it will help Jewel find his one true love.'

Danny grinned. 'Yeah, well, a first date would be a good start.'

And so Danny found himself standing by the counter of his local off licence trying not to die of embarrassment while Lil stood in the middle of the shop, eyes closed and chanting some kind of Sanskrit mantra.

'What are you doing?' he hissed, trying to ignore the bemused stare of Rav, the store owner.

'Tuning into kismet,' Lil replied. She suddenly opened her eyes and grabbed a bottle of Merrydown cider. Then, gliding as if she were in a trance, Lil moved around the shop, loading their basket with Babycham, Southern Comfort and a six-pack of Moscow mules. Danny sighed. As far as he could make out, the only thing that was destined to happen to his guests this afternoon was a raging hangover.

Cat looked at Justin asleep in the bed, his tanned arm splayed out across the pillow. She'd always liked his arms before. But now she couldn't help comparing them to Lachlan's, and they seemed too smooth, too perfect, too thin. Since Justin had made his surprise reappearance she'd managed to avoid having sex with him, thanks to a period she'd pretended had lasted almost two weeks. Thankfully Justin hadn't noticed. Ever since he'd got back he'd seemed distracted. Cat assumed he was worried about work. She'd suggested he apply for a job at the Lemon Tree but had been quite relieved when Justin pooh-poohed the idea. It was nice having something that was just hers, especially now she'd got used to the busyness and the drinks orders. These past couple of weeks the sense of space she'd been feeling after Justin left had been rapidly shrinking. As if to prove this point Justin yawned and stretched right across her side of the bed. His eyes flickered open. *Shit*, it was Sunday morning. What if he wanted sex? He always used to want sex on a Sunday morning.

'Do you want a cup of tea?' she asked.

'Sure.'

Before he could make any kind of advance she slipped from the bed and put on her dressing gown.

'Back soon.'

Cat came downstairs to find the kitchen empty and the heady aroma of burning sage wafting through from the living room. There was no sign of Diamond Street's resident sage-burner-in-chief, Lil, though. Thankfully, there was no sign of Lachlan, either. He never seemed to use the communal rooms any more. She'd caught a glimpse of him a couple of nights previously, returning from work with an armful of takeaway boxes and going straight to his room. It was his fault things were so awkward, though, she reminded herself.

She banged the tap three times and filled the kettle. The door opened and Jewel walked in. He was wearing his ironic Care Bears pyjamas and his hair was rumpled from sleep.

'Oh, Cat, good,' he said. 'Are you going to be around this afternoon?'

She shook her head. 'Justin's parents have invited us over for Sunday lunch and a walk on the Heath. Why?'

Jewel's face fell. 'Danny's having some friends over and I was wondering if you'd be my moral support.'

'Why? What's up with his friends?'

'Nothing. At least, I hope not.' Jewel sighed. 'He's inviting them over to meet me.'

'That sounds really nice.'

'No, you don't understand. I told Danny that I wanted to meet someone, you know, *date* someone, so he said he'd invite some of his single friends over and now I'm freaking out just thinking about it.'

'Oh, wow. So they're all coming over to check you out?'

'No! Well, I hope not. Danny promised me he wouldn't tell anyone the real reason. It was more for me to check them out.'

'Oh, right.'

'I just need someone to be there to stop me from hyperventilating.'

Cat nodded. 'OK, I'll stay.'

'Really? But what about Justin?'

'He'll be fine going to see his parents on his own. It's not as if they want to see me, anyway.' And she most definitely did not want to see them, she thought to herself, relieved she now had an excuse not to go.

Just as the kettle came to the boil, Lachlan walked into the room. But instead of doing his usual about-turn when he saw her, he marched over to the fridge and took out his milk.

'All right?' he muttered, looking pointedly at Jewel.

Great, so Lachlan was blanking her. Well, two could play that game. Cat plonked teabags into two mugs, sloshed in some water and headed to the door. 'I'll see you later,' she said pointedly to Jewel, before leaving.

Jewel watched Lachlan watching Cat flouncing out of the kitchen. Ever since Cat had told him about Michelle-gate, as he and Danny now referred to it, he'd had Lachlan down as the bad guy in the incident, but the sorrowful expression on Lachlan's face was now challenging that theory.

'Are you OK?' Jewel asked, fetching his Pop-Tarts from the cupboard.

'Yeah, of course,' Lachlan answered defensively. But he didn't look OK. Not at all. His stubble was so long it was practically a beard, and he looked thinner, and so tired. Cat seemed sadder, too, in spite of Justin being back – or maybe it was because of. Jewel pondered this thought. What if Michelle-gate had been some weird accident? What if Lachlan did really like Cat, and he just had some kind of affliction that made him call out the wrong woman's name in the middle of kissing; like a romantic version of Tourette syndrome? And what if Cat actually liked Lachlan, too? Surely she wouldn't have been so affected by Michelle-gate if she didn't like him, if their kiss had meant nothing. Jewel took a deep breath. What if Lachlan and Cat were in love and it had all been some horrible misunderstanding? This would be a tragedy on a par with Romeo and Juliet. But maybe there was something Jewel could do to fix it.

'Are you busy this afternoon?' he asked Lachlan breezily.

Lachlan shook his head.

'Oh, great, I was wondering if I could ask you a favour?'

'Sure.' Lachlan put two teabags into a mug and added hot water.

'Danny's having a little get-together here at the house, so that I can meet some of his friends and I was wondering if …' Jewel paused, trying to work out a way of phrasing it that would appeal to the rugged Australian. 'I was wondering if you'd be my wingman?'

'Oh?' Lachlan looked really surprised. 'Why do you need a wingman?'

Jewel took a deep breath. If his hunch was right he really hoped Cat would appreciate the embarrassment he was willing to endure to help reunite her with her true love. 'I told Danny that I'd like to meet someone, you know, as in, romantically, so he said he'd invite some of his friends over – his single friends – and now I'm starting to get a bit nervous and it would be really great if you were here as, you know, moral support.' He held his breath, hardly daring to look at Lachlan.

'I don't know why you're bothering, mate. All that romantic stuff, it's more trouble than it's worth.'

Oh, crap. Jewel cringed. Was Lachlan talking about Cat? Was he saying that she was more trouble than she was worth? Had Jewel got it all horribly wrong?

'But yeah, I'd be happy to be your wingman.'

'Oh, OK, that's great.'

'Are any of the others coming?' Lachlan asked. His tone was nonchalant but the intense way he was staring at Jewel definitely wasn't.

Jewel shook his head. He'd cross the bridge of explaining Cat's presence when he came to it. 'Just Danny and maybe Lil. I can't see her wanting to miss a party.'

Lachlan nodded. 'Yeah. OK, mate, what time do you need me?'

'Around two.'

'All right, will do.'

As Lachlan left the room Jewel's nerves grew. The potential for disaster in his cunning plan to reunite Cat and Lachlan was huge. So now, instead of increasing his sources of moral support, he'd ended up increasing the chances of the afternoon being a complete and utter disaster. Great!

Twenty-three

Lachlan lay on his bed with his headphones on, blasting 'Shakermaker' by Oasis at full volume. This new band had instantly become one of his favourites since they'd stormed into the charts earlier in the year with their first single. Their debut album wasn't disappointing either. Its anthemic rock tracks were the perfect way to psych himself up for his unlikely role as Jewel's wingman. He'd met some of Danny's friends at previous house parties and they were a colourful bunch.

The track 'Live Forever' began to play, and Lachlan squirmed. For some really annoying reason the lyrics made him think of Cat. He stopped the CD and got up and looked at himself in the mirror on the wardrobe door. He probably should have a shave, but he really couldn't be bothered. And anyway, it wasn't as if he was the one hoping to get lucky. As Jewel's wingman it would probably help that he looked a bit like a caveman, in case he was needed to fend off any advances.

He put on an old U2 T-shirt and a pair of jeans. Outside in the hallway he heard guests arriving and Danny greeting them. The jarring sound of laughter and chatter hurt Lachlan's ears. Being sociable with a bunch of strangers was the very last thing he felt like doing. All he wanted to do was stay cocooned away in his room. That was all he'd wanted to do since the night that arsehole Justin had reappeared and things had gone so badly wrong with Cat. As he cringed at the memory his urge for a beer overcame his urge for solitude and he ventured out into the hall.

Danny glanced around the living room and smiled. Everywhere he looked he could see members of his dance family laughing and chatting and having a good time. This was always a sight that gladdened his heart. He'd sent invites for his soirée far and wide, assuming that not everyone would be able to make it at such short notice, but pretty much everyone had said yes – and some had even brought plus ones. This soirée now had all the potential of becoming an epic party, a prospect that filled Danny with even more good cheer. Lachlan and Pete had been despatched to the offie to get more supplies, and Lil was busy in the kitchen baking some of her 'special cookies'.

Danny's excitement grew. He'd been so focused on throwing this shindig for Jewel he hadn't realized how badly he needed to let off steam, too. Starting his new job on *The Rocky Horror Picture Show* plus organizing the panto was an intense workload. It would be great to forget about it all for just one day and let his hair down. He looked around for Jewel and spied him out in the backyard talking to a guy called Darius, with whom Danny had danced in *Starlight Express*. Jewel had certainly dressed for the occasion, looking fabulous in a red and gold geisha-style dress over black leggings. He was so pretty, there was no way he'd be without a love interest for long. He just had to overcome his shyness.

'Hey.'

Danny felt a tap on his shoulder and turned to see Cat. Her hair was curled into long ringlets and she was wearing a turquoise satin slip dress, black fishnets and DM boots.

'Wow, darling, you look amazing! Danny said. 'Very punk mermaid.'

'Thank you. I asked Jewel to give me one of his makeovers,' Cat replied with a grin. 'So, where is the party boy?' she asked, scanning the room.

'In the garden, fending off suitors,' Danny replied.

'Oh, I'd better get out there then,' Cat said. 'See if he needs any moral support.'

'Sure.' Danny made his way over to Terri and some of the chorus members from *Romeo and Juliet*. Terri wasn't single and she obviously didn't fit the criteria for a potential love interest for Jewel, but she was always cracking value at a party, so Danny had invited her anyway.

'Hey, Danny, have you heard the latest about Johannes?' she asked, adjusting the strap on her denim dungarees.

He shook his head.

'Apparently, he wants to do a production of *The Nutcracker* using actual mice on the stage.'

'Bloody hell!' Danny gave silent thanks once again that he was free from the nightmare of Johannes' constant desire to shock. Noticing that Terri's glass was empty, he took it from her. 'Refill, darling?'

'Yes, please. Can I have another glass of the kismet punch?'

He frowned at her. 'Are you sure?'

'Yes, it's delicious!'

'OK, then.' Danny hadn't dared go near the punch having seen what had gone in it – and how the mixture of the cider and Moscow mules had given it the appearance of murky pond water. Maybe he should reconsider.

When he got to the kitchen Lil was placing two trays of cookies onto plates. She was clad in a bright scarlet jumpsuit, with matching red hearts threaded through her long, silver hair. The kitchen smelt deliciously chocolatey.

'Hello, sweetheart,' she grinned. 'My cookies are ready.'

'Great. Your punch is going down a storm.' Danny poured a ladle full of punch into Terri's glass.

'Of course it is, it's destiny.' Lil picked up a cookie and took a bite.

Just then Lachlan and Pete came through the door, laden with cases of wine, cider and beer.

'They smell good,' Lachlan said, nodding at the cookies. 'I'm starving.' He put the beer down and grabbed one, shoving it into his mouth whole.

'Oh, uh, they …' Danny stammered.

'Cheers,' Lachlan said, cracking open a beer and wolfing down another cookie.

Danny looked at Lil and she raised her thin, painted-on eyebrows and grinned. Danny decided it was probably best not to tell Lachlan about Lil's 'special' ingredient. He'd find out for himself soon enough.

'And that was the moment I knew I had to share my dancing gift with the world,' the dancer named Darius said.

Cat glanced at Jewel. Darius had been delivering a monologue about his dancing talents ever since she'd joined them in the backyard, and she'd been there for what felt like an hour, although in reality it had been more like ten minutes. She wondered if Jewel was as bored as she was. It was hard to gauge. Jewel was staring at Darius intently and nodding politely, but Jewel was so lovely, he'd never show it if he really didn't like someone. She decided to offer him the option of an emergency exit.

'I'm going to go and get a drink,' she said. 'Would anyone like to come with me?'

'Yes!' Jewel exclaimed.

So her hunch had been right. Cat linked her arm through his. 'Come on.'

'When you get back remind me to tell you about the time I made Andrew Lloyd Webber cry,' Darius called out after them.

'Was it because you didn't stop talking,' Jewel muttered, causing Cat to giggle.

'They were tears of joy, obviously,' Darius called after them.

'Of course they were,' Cat whispered. But as they got to the back door she saw a sight that wiped the smile from her face – Lachlan heading straight towards them, holding two glasses of a murky brown drink.

'Oh,' was all she could manage to say.

'Oh – hello.' Lachlan looked from her to Jewel and back again. His gaze flicked down to her slip dress and she suddenly felt horribly underdressed. 'I didn't know you were going to be here,' he said.

What was that supposed to mean? Was he trying to say that he wouldn't have come if he had known?

'I didn't know you were going to be here, either,' she said. They both looked at Jewel, whose face had suddenly turned bright pink.

'I, I'm so grateful to you both for coming,' Jewel stammered. 'Can you do me a favour? Can you both wait here for me? I just need to pop to the loo.' He took one of the drinks Lachlan was holding and passed it to Cat. 'You have this. I'll get another one on my way back. Stay here. I'll be back soon.'

Great. Cat watched helplessly as Jewel disappeared into the crowded living room, leaving her stranded with the one person she'd been doing everything she could to avoid for the past two weeks.

Lachlan cleared his throat and Cat glanced around the yard. Darius had cornered another of Danny's dancing friends, practically pinning him to the wall with his endless stream of words. Cat was starting to wish she was back over there listening to him. Even his never-ending monologue didn't seem quite as bad as the awful silence currently thickening between her and Lachlan.

'So, where's your boyfriend?' Lachlan finally said.

Cat felt the instinctive urge to yell, *He's not my boyfriend!* What the hell? Why did she not want Lachlan to think that Justin was her boyfriend? Why did *she* not want to think that Justin was her boyfriend? She switched her attention back to Lachlan. He had no right to have a dig at her after what he did. 'Justin is at his mum and dad's for lunch,' she replied.

'Right.'

On seeing Lachlan's hurt expression, Cat felt a pang of guilt, which was swiftly replaced by anger. Why should she be the one to feel bad about what had happened?

'How's Michelle?' she asked, all of the hurt and anger she'd been harbouring for the past fortnight channelled into two words.

Lachlan physically recoiled as if she'd hit him. She wasn't prepared for that reaction. She thought he'd be way more belligerent.

'Michelle is dead,' he said softly.

Lachlan took a swig from the glass of kismet punch Lil had insisted on giving him. It tasted like nothing he'd ever tasted before, and he had no idea what was in it. Not that he cared right at this minute. All he wanted right now was for a sinkhole to appear in the backyard of 27 Diamond Street and swallow him whole.

'She's dead?' Cat asked, looking horrified.

Lachlan nodded.

'But I don't …'

He glanced at Cat. It really wasn't helping that she looked absolutely stunning, in what appeared to be a negligee and a pair of DM boots. He took another swig of his drink. The taste was weirdly starting to grow on him. Maybe this was what Lil had meant when she'd mysteriously said, 'Welcome to your destiny, sweetheart,' as she'd handed it to him.

'Who was she?' Cat asked.

Lachlan sighed. He was feeling really tired and light-headed. 'Could we sit down?' he asked, pointing at a couple of the rusty garden chairs in the far corner of the yard.

'Of course.'

At least she was being a bit warmer now, but for how long, if he told her the full story?

They sat down and Lachlan took another swig from his drink. 'She was my girlfriend. My first ever girlfriend. My only girlfriend before I came to England.'

Cat nodded like she understood, but he could tell from the frown on her face that she was confused.

'I'm so sorry,' she said softly. And she did look genuinely sorry. As long as she didn't ask how Michelle died, things might still be all right.

'How did – how did she pass away? Sorry, do you mind me asking?'

Lachlan sighed. Yes, he did mind. He minded very much because he didn't feel nearly ready to tell anyone how Michelle died, least of all Cat.

'In an accident,' he said, hoping that would be enough for her.

'That must have been horrendous,' she said.

He nodded.

'Were you still a couple when she died?'

He nodded again, feeling suddenly and massively inconveniently close to tears.

They both fell silent. In the other corner of the yard a tall man with a droning voice was telling someone about how he once did an interpretive dance for Andrew Lloyd Webber inspired by a cabbage.

'I'm so, so sorry,' Cat said.

'It's OK.'

'No, it's not. I've been so horrible to you since, since we, you know, kissed.'

A lump was building in his throat now, hot and raw, and he didn't dare look at her, let alone say anything.

'I just didn't realize,' Cat continued. 'I thought you were seeing someone else, or you liked someone else, someone who was …' she broke off. 'I'm so sorry.'

He swallowed hard. All of his normal defences felt as if they were dissolving into nothing. It was a terrifying feeling. If he wasn't feeling so spaced out he would have tried to leave, but his body felt weighted to the chair.

'I'm sorry, too,' he muttered. 'I wasn't thinking about her when we, when we kissed. I mean, I really wanted it, wanted you …' *Strewth, this was excruciating.* 'I think it was my conscience. You're the first person I've … done anything like that with since …' He glanced at Cat. She'd clamped her hand to her mouth as if in shock.

'I really wanted you, too,' she whispered.

His view started swimming as his eyes completely involuntarily filled with tears.

'Oh, Lachlan, are you OK?'

He closed his eyes tight to try and make the tears go away and felt them spilling down his face. Then he felt her hands, cool and small, on his.

'Are you OK?' she said again.

'Yes. No. I don't know.' Why did he feel so light-headed?

She clasped his hands tighter. 'Do you want to go somewhere else? Somewhere we can talk properly?'

He blinked hard again, trying to get himself together, but the light-headedness was getting worse. Maybe he needed to eat something. He'd only had a couple of Lil's cookies since breakfast.

'Please?' Cat implored. 'Could we go to your room?'

He nodded, too numb to argue, and got to his feet.

Twenty-four

Jewel peered cautiously out of the back door into the yard. Would Cat and Lachlan still be there, or would one of them have stormed off in a huff? He breathed a sigh of relief. Not only were they both still there, but they were sitting down together. This was a fantastic development. But, oh no, Cat was standing up. Jewel sighed. How could he have thought that forcing them together like this would be a good thing? But then he saw Lachlan standing up, too. Were they both storming off in a huff, or were they going somewhere together? Jewel's skin prickled with excitement. *Please, let them be going somewhere together,* he silently willed. Not wanting to be spotted, he slipped off to the side of the living room, where a group of Danny's dancers from *Romeo and Juliet* were huddled together looking through Lil's records. Moving round to the back of the group, he kept his eyes on the back door.

Cat entered the living room, followed by Lachlan. Jewel studied their faces, trying to work out what was going on. Cat looked pretty relaxed. Lachlan was completely expressionless. Jewel watched as they went through the archway into the kitchen. Hopefully, they were going to get another drink together. He strained to look through the crowd of people and saw them go straight past the table laden with drinks and out into the hallway. Jewel was about to try and work out if this was a good or bad thing when Terri, the woman who was Juliet, tapped him on the arm.

'Hey, Jewel, have you met Pablo?' She gestured at a young guy standing beside her. A long fringe of glossy black hair hung across his face. He was wearing black jeans and a tight black T-shirt.

'Hey,' he said, smiling at Jewel from beneath his fringe. His eyes were piercing green against his olive skin, emphasized by a thick fringe of dark eyelashes.

The overall effect caused Jewel's face to flush and his stomach to flip. 'Hey.' And, apparently, his voice to squeak.

Pablo continued to smile at him and Jewel had a terrible thought. What if Danny had told Terri the reason for the party, and she had told Pablo? His paranoia grew. What if everybody knew?

'Jewel is the person you need to thank for your awesome costume,' Terri said to Pablo. 'He designed them for Danny.' She turned back to Jewel. 'Pablo is in the chorus in *Romeo and Juliet*. He's one of the Capulets.'

'Thank you!' Pablo exclaimed. He had a European accent. 'If it weren't for you I would have to dress as a lamb!'

Jewel laughed. 'You're welcome.'

'Pablo is from Spain,' Terri said.

'Catalonia,' Pablo corrected. He grinned at Jewel. 'These things are important.'

'Jewel is new to London, too,' Terri continued, giving Jewel a knowing grin.

Jewel's face flushed even redder. He could tell that Terri definitely knew the intention behind the party. But judging from the surprised expression on Pablo's face the dancer was unaware of her attempts to play Cupid.

'Where did you live before?' Pablo asked.

'Apsley,' Jewel replied.

Pablo looked at him blankly and shrugged.

'It's OK, no one's heard of it,' Jewel grinned. 'Catalonia sounds cool, though.'

Pablo nodded. 'It is the best place in the world. London's pretty cool too, though.'

'For sure.' Jewel racked his brain, trying to think of something to say, but his mind seemed to have turned into a blank white page. *SAY SOMETHING, YOU FOOL!* he yelled at himself inside his head.

'I was just trying to convince Pablo to treat us to some of his flamenco dancing,' Terri said, thankfully filling the awkward silence.

'Oh, I don't know …' Pablo's face flushed and he dipped his face so that his fringe fell lower. Jewel liked the way he seemed so shy. It made the whole thing feel slightly less intimidating.

'Come on, we have a Gypsy Kings album. What more do you need?' Terri showed Pablo the record she was holding. 'I'll go and ask Danny to put it on.'

Terri headed over to the record player, where Danny was chatting to a couple of friends.

'Seems like I have no choice,' Pablo said with a shrug. 'Do you like to dance?'

Jewel instinctively shook his head. 'Well, I like it but I'm not very good at it.'

Pablo grinned. 'We are all good at it if we know how to – how do you say – let the music get inside of us, in here.' He put his hand over his heart.

Jewel felt a wobbly sensation in his legs. Was this what it was like to swoon? Was he officially swooning? Oh, if only Cat was here to share this moment. Although if she was actually here it would be quite awkward and inconvenient. He took a deep breath and tried to get a grip on his wobbly legs and runaway thoughts. The Blondie track that was playing came to an abrupt halt as the needle was ripped from the record, and everyone stopped chatting, turning to see what had happened.

'Don't worry, folks, we're just having a flamenco break,' Danny called into the silence.

Several people whooped and cheered and Lil came racing in from the kitchen. 'Did someone say flamenco?'

'Yes, darling,' Danny replied. 'We're lucky enough to have a professional flamenco dancer in our midst.'

'Oh, you are kind, sweetheart,' Lil said. 'I wouldn't class myself as a professional, but I certainly picked up a few moves the year I spent with a bullfighter in Barcelona. I'll just go and get my castanets.' Another silence fell as she left the room.

'Who was that?' Pablo murmured, staring after Lil.

'One of my housemates,' Jewel replied, feeling suddenly defensive. He hoped Pablo wasn't going to make fun of Lil.

'You live in a very cool house,' Pablo said, thankfully with a smile of admiration rather than ridicule.

'I do,' Jewel agreed. And as the lively opening beats of a Gypsy Kings track rang around the room and people started to cheer, he felt overwhelmed with joy. The fact that he now lived in a house that someone as awesome as Pablo would deem cool, made him feel luckier than he'd ever felt in his life before. And the fact that one of his housemates had thrown a party and filled the house with other cool people just so that he, Jewel, might be able to meet someone, made him feel luckier still. He didn't care if the euphoria he was experiencing was due in part to Lil's cookie kicking in. He was going to enjoy every last second of it.

'Come on, Pablo, show them how dancing's really done,' Danny cried, beckoning him over.

Pablo raised his eyebrows at Jewel, as if to say, *What can you do?* then made his way to the centre of the room. Everyone shuffled back to form an impromptu dance floor around him. Pablo closed his eyes for a second, as if he was tuning into the rhythm, and then he opened them, staring straight ahead with an intensity that practically caused Jewel to stop breathing. Then he brought his hands up, crossing his wrists in front of his face, and he stamped both his feet in quick succession, as if bringing his body to attention. The whole room watched, rapt. Pablo had barely moved and yet already he seemed to have them all under some weird kind of spell, especially Jewel, who watched mesmerized as Pablo flung his arms to one side of his body and then the other, stamping his feet again. He reminded Jewel of a bullfighter, brandishing an invisible cloak.

Pablo's feet moved faster and faster, while his upper body remained rigid, his stare straight ahead.

Danny started clapping in time and soon the whole room had joined in. Again, Jewel felt a wave of happiness rush through him. How had he ended up here? How had he become a part of something so joyful and wild, even if he was just watching from the sidelines?

The music built and Pablo danced faster and faster, his hands and legs a blur. His long fringe flicked back and forth, his face now slick with sweat.

Lil reappeared holding a pair of castanets. 'Excuse me, senorita coming through,' she cried, making her way on to the makeshift dance floor. She clicked her castanets at Pablo. He threw his head back and laughed and gestured at her to join him.

Jewel felt like a kid watching a horror film, and fought the overwhelming urge to grab a cushion to hide behind. He couldn't bear the thought of Lil making a fool of herself in front of so many people, which she was bound to do dancing next to someone as accomplished as Pablo. But, to his utter amazement, Lil seemed to know exactly what to do. She thrust her chin out, back ruler-straight, adopting a haughty pose similar to Pablo's, and then she began to dance. Really, properly, flamenco dance!

'Bloody hell!' Danny called, perfectly voicing Jewel's thoughts.

Pablo stood back, clapping as Lil danced faster and faster, her silver hair streaming out behind her. People whistled and cheered and then, one by one, they all started dancing. Jewel was so happy he didn't care if he looked stupid. He closed his eyes and joined in. No matter what happened, today was already going to go down as one of the best days of his life. He felt people moving around him and opened his eyes, Pablo was now right in front of him. As their eyes locked, Jewel felt a shiver of excitement erupt on his skin.

Danny had never imagined that he'd end up dancing to the Gypsy Kings in the living room this Sunday afternoon, and he'd certainly never imagined that Lil would reveal herself to be an expert flamenco dancer, but he was loving the randomness of these latest developments. He also loved the fact that Jewel had loosened up and was dancing – and with Pablo, too. He looked at Terri and they exchanged a knowing grin. Of all the people Danny had invited to this shindig, Pablo had been his highest hope for Jewel. Most of his other single friends were older or players – or Darius! But when he'd told Terri of his plan they'd both agreed that Pablo could be the perfect person to bring Jewel out of his shell. Danny gave a contented sigh. He loved it when a plan came together. Now he could relax and let his hair down.

He danced his way into the kitchen and helped himself to another glass of kismet punch and one of Lil's cookies. He wondered how Lachlan was doing. He seemed to have vanished. Come to think of it, so had Cat. Danny's heart sank. It had been a nice idea of Jewel's to try to bring them together at the party, but Danny knew the plan was ripe for potential disaster. Weren't all affairs of the heart ultimately ripe for disaster?

He looked through the archway at the sea of swaying bodies in the living room. This scenario was the achievement of one of his biggest life goals. He'd transformed 27 Diamond Street into the party house of his dreams, so why did he feel a sudden emptiness gnawing at him? He downed his punch and refilled his glass. There was only one thing for it. He'd have to get shit-faced. He wolfed down another cookie and rejoined the party.

Twenty-five

Cat perched on the edge of Lachlan's bed and tried to glance around his room without it appearing that she was glancing around his room. This was a lot harder than it sounded. Until now, what lay behind Lachlan's door had remained an unsolved mystery, a bit like the staffroom door at school. Apart from Pete's, Lachlan's was the only room she hadn't already been into at 27 Diamond Street, but she had no desire to see Pete's. As she took in the brown and beige carpet, the plain walls, the oak wardrobe, and the mismatching white chest of drawers, she tried to make sense of what had just happened out in the backyard. Michelle was Lachlan's ex-girlfriend, but she was dead. She had died in an accident. And she, Cat, was the first person he'd kissed since. And he'd wanted to do it. Cat sighed. All this time when she'd been thinking that Lachlan hadn't been into her, that he'd been thinking of or even seeing someone else, she'd actually been looking at things through a completely distorted lens.

'Are you OK?' she asked as Lachlan crashed down heavily on the bed. He looked really spaced out.

'Yeah, I think so.' He ran his hand through his hair. 'Welcome to my humble abode.' He grinned sheepishly. 'Sorry, I'm not really one for ornaments and stuff.'

'That's OK. I didn't really think you would be.' Cat wasn't exactly sure how she'd pictured Lachlan's room to be, but she hadn't anticipated it being quite so minimalist. She'd imagined him at least having a couple of pictures on the wall. She took a quick glance at the bedside cabinet for any sign of a photo of Michelle, but there was just an alarm clock and a copy of the *Standard*, turned to the page advertising rooms to rent. A couple of the ads were circled in red.

'You're not – are you moving out?' she stammered.

He sighed. 'I thought it might be for the best.'

'Oh.' Cat was shocked at how upset this made her feel. She wished with all her might that she could turn back time, back to that night in the kitchen, to that kiss, to the moment he murmured 'Michelle' and tell herself, *Don't get mad, stay calm. Ask him to explain himself.* She shifted on the bed slightly so that she could look straight at him. Lachlan was slumped against the wall, staring into space.

'Do you want to move out?' she asked softly.

'Things had got too awkward,' he replied.

'Too painful,' he added in a mutter.

'It's OK. It's not too painful,' she said quickly.

'Not for you, maybe.' He looked down.

'Oh.' She wasn't quite sure what to make of this. 'What do you mean?'

'I mean, seeing you with that … that … Justin.' His face flushed.

'Oh,' she said again, quickly trying to compute what he was saying.

'Do you realize that you look just like a mermaid,' Lachlan said, swaying slightly and staring at her dress.

'What?'

'With your hair and that colour and …' he petered out, grinning.

'Are you OK?'

'Yeah. I've always liked mermaids.' He nodded thoughtfully. 'Even though they lure men to their deaths.' His smile faded.

'I promise I won't lure you to your death,' she said, trying to lighten the mood.

'No, that's my job,' he said, laughing. And then, to her horror, he started crying.

Cat sat frozen for a moment, unsure what to do. Was Lachlan having some kind of breakdown? Maybe he'd never properly processed his grief over Michelle's death. Maybe he was having some kind of weird, delayed reaction.

'Lachlan, do you … shall I get you something?'

'I'm sorry,' he gasped. 'I don't know what's up with me.'

'It's OK.' She stood up. 'Shall I get you a cup of tea or something?'

'Whoa, don't rock the boat,' he said, putting his hands up in front of his face.

'What?'

'Why are you swaying?'

'I'm not.' She quickly checked herself. But she'd only had half a glass of punch and, even though it was strong, it would take a lot more than that to make her lose her balance.

He looked at her and burst out laughing again.

'How much have you had to drink?' she asked.

'Only a couple. But I haven't had anything to eat – apart from one of Lil's cookies.'

'You had one of Lil's cookies?'

'Yeah. Or maybe I had two.'

'OK, I'm going to go and get you some water. Stay here.'

'Aye aye, captain!' He saluted her, then keeled over sideways.

When Cat got back, holding a pint glass of water, she found Lachlan lying face down on his bedroom floor staring at the carpet.

'This is amazing,' he said.

'What is?'

'This pattern. It's like looking down a stethoscope. No, not a stethoscope. What's that other scope thing – the one with all the trippy patterns?'

'A kaleidoscope?'

'Yes!' he yelled, almost causing her to drop his water.

She crouched down beside him. 'Here, sit up for a moment and drink this.'

He lurched up and they almost clashed heads.

'Whoops! Sorry.' He laughed. She raised the glass to his mouth and he took a few gulps. 'Sorry,' he said again, 'sorry I said her name.'

'It's OK.'

'Bloody hell, I feel wrecked.'

'You've had two of Lil's hash cakes and they're starting to kick in,' Cat explained.

His mouth fell open. 'The cookies?'

Cat nodded.

'Oh, strewth!'

'Yep.' She bit her bottom lip to stop herself from laughing.

'So I'm high?'

'As a kite.'

He shook his head then started to grin. 'I'm gonna kill her. She didn't say a word. She just let me eat one – she let me eat two. Where is she?' he struggled to get up, careering into Cat. 'Whoops, sorry!'

'Right now, she's flamenco dancing,' Cat replied with a giggle.

'Of course she is.'

'Actually, the whole house is.'

Lachlan laughed and shook his head. 'So I'm guessing this – me, I mean – is going to get worse before it gets better.'

Cat grinned. 'Depends how you look at it. I'm quite enjoying it, to be honest.'

'That's not very supportive.'

'What? I brought you water, didn't I?' Cat had a sudden idea. 'I don't suppose you feel up to going out, do you?'

'Out?' He looked at her like she was crazy. 'Like this?'

She nodded. 'It just seems a waste of a very good buzz to be stuck in here. I was thinking maybe we could go to Primrose Hill. It's such a nice afternoon.'

'Hmm.' He frowned. 'Will you be my responsible adult?'

'Yes. I'll be your responsible adult,' she replied with a grin. Somehow, and in the most surreal way imaginable, she and Lachlan appeared to be building a bridge between each other, and it was a really lovely feeling.

'OK, then, let's do it. Whoa!' He grabbed her shoulder to steady himself as he got to his feet.

Her skin felt electric beneath his palm.

Lachlan followed Cat along the footpath leading up Primrose Hill. It was late afternoon and the sun was dipping in the deep blue sky, tinting the clouds above the cityscape amber and pink. Now he knew what was up with him – that Lil's seemingly harmless afternoon treats had in fact been spiked – he felt a lot more relaxed about the extremely chilled-out way he was feeling. He was glad Cat had got them a cab here though, as he wasn't sure he was quite up for negotiating public transport.

'Bonzer idea, coming up here,' he said, drinking in the green of the grass and the clusters of trees. 'Is it me, or do those trees over there look like they're dancing?'

'It's you, or rather, it's Lil's cookies,' Cat laughed. 'How about here?' she said, pointing to a spot on the grass. The hill was dotted with other groups of people soaking up the last of the autumn sunshine.

They sat down, and, as if by magic, Cat produced a bag from somewhere and took out some sausage rolls, bags of crisps and a flask. 'I helped myself to some party food. I thought we could have a picnic.'

'Oh, you beaut!' At the mention of food Lachlan suddenly felt absolutely starving. He grabbed a sausage roll, then froze with it halfway to his mouth. 'Hold on, Lil didn't have anything to do with the making of these, did she?'

'No. They're the Co-op's finest,' Cat replied. 'So the only thing we have to worry about is mad cow disease.'

'Hmm, that's a risk I'm prepared to take. I'm starving!' Lachlan wolfed down the sausage roll, then another. 'Great call,' he said, in between mouthfuls. 'Coming here.'

But Cat didn't respond. She just stared at him. 'I don't want you to move out,' she said finally.

'Are you sure?' Lachlan's buzz was momentarily interrupted by the thought of Cat and Justin, and how excruciating life in Diamond Street had been since his arch-nemesis had moved back in.

Cat nodded. 'I feel like I …'

'What?'

'Like I've messed everything up.' She looked so sad all of a sudden, and so beautiful with her mermaid's hair and dress. All of the feelings he'd stuffed back down inside of him since the night of the kiss started hollering to be let out.

'Your hair looks like it's on fire,' he murmured, watching as the setting sun's rays caught in her curls.

'What?' She patted at her hair, looking alarmed.

'Not literally. Metabolically.'

'Do you mean metaphorically?'

'Yep, that's the one.'

She laughed and shook her head.

'I really like your hair,' he said. He was aware he now sounded like a lovestruck ten-year-old, but his entire body was so relaxed he apparently had no way of censoring himself.

'Thank you. I really like your hair, too.'

'You do?' For some reason, Lachlan found this revelation hysterical and he started cracking up laughing. A little toddler who was playing with a toy car nearby looked over and started laughing, too.

'What's so funny?' Cat frowned, which only made him laugh harder.

'My hair,' he spluttered.

'Well, I don't really see why that's so funny. I mean, it's very nice hair,' she said indignantly.

'Stop!' he cried, holding his side.

'I like the way it's the colour of sand,' she continued, 'and I really like the hair on your arms.'

'You like my arm hair?' He stared at her, momentarily too shocked to laugh.

'Yes. It's so golden.' She stared at his arms dreamily.

What the hell was happening here? Was he stoned or was Cat being really weird?

'Can I touch it?' she asked.

OK, now he had to be dreaming. Or tripping? What exactly had Lil put in those cookies? But the thought of Cat touching his arm wasn't exactly an unpleasant one, so he nodded.

She ran her fingertips down his forearm so lightly it felt like being tickled with a feather. Her light touch sent a shiver of pleasure through him.

'That tickles,' he gasped. Now she was giggling, too.

'I may or may not have had one of Lil's cookies before we left,' she said, stroking his arm again.

'What? But you're meant to be my responsible adult,' he said, pretending to be outraged.

'Oh well! Looks like we'll both have to be irresponsible kids,' she said softly. Lachlan wasn't sure if he'd ever heard anything quite so sexy.

'Fine by me,' he replied, edging closer to her hair, her face, her mermaid dress. 'Would it be really irresponsible if I ...' he broke off.

'What?' she whispered.

He took her face in his hands and kissed her on the lips.

Danny wasn't exactly sure how he'd ended up in a bath of Merrydown cider. Well, he knew it had started with a conversation with Pete in which Pete had informed him that Cleopatra had needed 700 donkeys to provide enough milk for one of her infamous baths. Then, if he remembered rightly, he'd opened the fridge and made a joke about only having half a pint of semi-skimmed. Then Darius had pointed to the cases of cider on the table and suggested he bathe in them instead. One thing had led to another and Danny, not ever wanting to be a party pooper, had announced to the entire house that he was about to bathe in cider.

'Ooh-arr, just like a West Country Cleopatra,' Lil had cried in a fake Somerset accent. Then half the party had formed some kind of ant colony, conveying cases of cider up the stairs and into the bathroom and into the bath that Danny was now sitting in, stark naked, his skin sticky and reeking of apples.

'This is the best party ever!' Terri exclaimed, cracking open another can and pouring it over his back.

'Hmm, maybe if I didn't have to bathe alone it might be more fun,' Danny muttered.

'Do you want me to see if I can find you a companion?' Terri asked with a grin. 'Your house is full of eligible gay men, thanks to your matchmaking.'

'That is a very good point, although obviously I would have hooked up with them already if they were up to my standards.'

Terri giggled and shook her head. 'Danny, you are terrible! Let me go and get some more cider. I'll be right back. And hopefully I'll find someone up to your standards, too!'

Danny leaned back in the bath wondering, if the worst came to the very worst, he could bring himself to snog Darius. It would at least get Darius to shut up for a bit. He heard footsteps on the landing outside and then a knock on the door.

'Come in!' he called, turning to see who it was. His blood froze in his veins. 'What the hell are you doing here?'

'I'm here for the party,' Achilles replied, grinning at him from the bathroom door.

'Oh no!' Cat gasped, pulling away from Lachlan's embrace.

'What? What is it? Did I do something wrong?'

'No, not at all. It's me.'

'Uh-oh, not the old, "It's not you, it's me," chestnut.' Lachlan reached for the flask of tea and took a swig.

'It is me. I just remembered that I invited Achilles and Stelios from the Lemon Tree to the party. They were going to pop in before their evening shift and I'm not there.'

'It's all right. Danny's there. They know him. I'm sure he'll make them welcome.'

'I hope so.' Cat smiled as her cookie buzz returned, wrapping her in a warm glow. 'So, it would appear that we kissed again.'

He grinned. 'Yeah, well, what do you expect? All that talk of arm hair.'

'Oh God!' Cat cringed. 'I'm sorry, it must have been the cookie talking.'

Lachlan pulled a hurt face.

'Although they are very nice arm hairs.'

'Armchairs?'

'No, arm hairs!'

They both cracked up laughing. Cat wished they could stay like that, in the golden glow of the setting sun, with nothing to worry about, but in spite of her stoned state, tentacles of reality were starting to worm their way into her brain. At some point, they would have to go home. At some point, Justin would be arriving home. A terrible thought occurred to her. What if he was already back at Diamond Street, wondering where Cat and Lachlan had got to? He wouldn't know that they'd gone anywhere together, though, she reminded herself.

'Are you OK?' Lachlan asked.

She nodded.

A little kid toddled past them holding a toy car and waving to his mum and dad, who were sitting just down the hill from them.

'I'd do anything to be that age again.' Lachlan said softly. 'To have no worries, you know?'

She nodded. 'It must have been so horrible – losing your girlfriend ...' She stopped, hoping she hadn't overstepped some invisible mark.

But Lachlan nodded. 'It was like everything ended the day she drowned.'

'She drowned?'

He nodded. 'We'd gone surfing. She died in a hold-down.'

'What's a hold-down?'

'It's when a wave drives you down to the seabed and pins you there.' His expression had gone blank and his voice was monotone, as if he were reading a shopping list rather than revealing an event of such magnitude and horror.

Cat shuddered, wishing she hadn't asked. It must have been bad enough for Lachlan to have lost his first love, but to have lost her in such traumatic circumstances had to be unbearable. The sun dipped behind the London skyline stretched out below them, causing the horizon to burn gold and red. 'I'm so sorry you had to go through that.'

Lachlan gave a tight little laugh. 'What I've been through is nothing compared to what she did.'

'Yes but …' Cat broke off, unable to find the right words.

'Don't feel sorry for me.'

'Why not?'

'Because it was my fault.'

Cat felt a sudden chill breeze sweep up the hill.

'What do you mean?'

'I mean, it's because of me that she's dead.'

Twenty-six

Jewel followed Pablo into the backyard, nervously scanning it for any sign of Darius. Thankfully, he'd disappeared. The only person in the yard was Pete, hunched over on a chair in the corner, writing in his notebook.

'That's my housemate, Pete,' Jewel whispered. 'He's a poet.'

Pablo smiled. 'Your housemates are so interesting. Not like mine.'

'Who do you live with?' Jewel asked, leading Pablo over to the opposite corner of the yard from Pete.

'I'm not really sure.'

Jewel looked at him questioningly.

'No one really talks to each other. I hardly see them anyway, as I'm always working nights and sleeping during the day. They all work in offices.'

Jewel nodded. He was trying really hard not to let his thoughts run away with themselves, but the fact that he and Pablo both worked theatre hours was a definite tick in the box, relationship-wise. He instantly kicked himself for daring to imagine the possibility of a relationship with Pablo.

'Yes, I'm lucky here. Most of us work in the evenings, too.'

'So, where are you working right now?' Pablo brushed back his long fringe and Jewel was treated to another dazzling display of emerald-green eyes and lashes to die for.

'I'm a dresser for the wardrobe department at the Theatre Royal.' As Jewel heard himself say the words out loud he felt another fizz of joy at the dream life he was now, miraculously, living.

'I know the one.' Pablo smiled at him, causing a dimple to appear in his cheek. Jewel wasn't sure if he could cope with this cuteness overload. 'I really enjoyed dancing with you,' Pablo said softly.

'I really enjoyed it, too. You're amazing.' Jewel's face burned. 'I mean your dancing is amazing.'

'Thank you.'

Much to Jewel's relief he noticed that Pablo's cheeks had flushed, too. Peals of laughter rang out from inside the house. No doubt more people discovering Danny in his bath of cider. Jewel fought the inappropriate urge to giggle.

'I really like this,' Pablo said, running his finger along the scarlet silk sleeve of Jewel's kimono.

'Thanks,' Jewel managed to squeak. He'd never experienced the feeling he was feeling right now. It was simultaneously exhilarating and terrifying. 'I really like you.' The words popped out before he had time to stop them. What was wrong with him? He was doing everything the magazine articles said he shouldn't – acting too eager, too needy. But instead of being repelled, Pablo leaned closer.

'I really like you, too,' he whispered. 'And I would really like to kiss you.'

Jewel's heart began pounding like a flamenco beat.

'Would you like that, too?' Pablo asked.

Jewel nodded, having seemingly lost the ability to speak – or even squeak. All of his fears about his lack of experience were temporarily forgotten. He was completely and utterly lost in the moment, in the presence of Pablo and his beautiful lips, drawing closer and closer, until they were on his. At first Jewel was motionless but then he felt himself responding. His lack of experience didn't seem to matter at all, it was as if his body knew exactly what to do, as if Pablo had triggered some kind of ancient wiring deep inside of him. The kiss became more intense, and Jewel felt as if his limbs were turning from solid to liquid. He felt Pablo's arm move around his lower back. It was surprisingly strong given Pablo's wiry physique. And now their bodies were connecting from lips to chests to hips. They finally came up for air and Pablo smiled at him.

'That was amazing,' he whispered.

'Could we do it again?' Jewel whispered back. Now he'd started he never wanted the kissing to stop. This was so much better than all the practising he'd done on his pillow.

'Oh, yes,' Pablo replied.

Jewel put his arms around Pablo's neck and pulled him closer. As their lips came together once again, he felt Pablo's tongue brushing his bottom lip. He remembered what Danny had said about the lizard kisser. Thankfully, Pablo seemed the complete opposite.

Over on the other side of the yard Pete cleared his throat. 'Would anyone like to hear my sonnet to a Rubik's Cube?'

'What are you doing?' Danny snapped, cupping his hands over his crotch and shooting Achilles what he hoped was his most deadly of death stares.

'Ha, I think I could ask you just the same,' Achilles grinned, looking pointedly at Danny's cupped hands.

'I am bathing in cider,' Danny declared, deciding that it was probably best to try and style it out.

'You should have said, I would have brought a case of champagne.' Achilles chuckled. 'Much more rock and roll.'

'Yeah, well, I was improvising,' Danny muttered.

'Danny, we've run out of cider, but Lil's very kindly offered up some of her Babycham.' Terri entered the room breathless and flushed, carrying a pack of the drinks.

'Oh, hello,' she said, noticing Achilles. 'Have you found yourself a bathing companion?'

'No, I have not!' Danny snapped. What had seemed like a fun idea was rapidly degenerating into an exercise in sheer humiliation. It was bad enough that Achilles had been his unrequited crush for months and months, but never in his wildest dreams had he imagined things reaching quite such a crushing climax, or rather anti-climax.

'What are you doing here, anyway?' he asked, as Terri began opening bottles of Babycham and pouring them into the bath.

'Cat invited me,' Achilles replied, seemingly unable to wipe the grin from his face. 'Do you know where she is?'

'No, I haven't seen her for ages.' Now he came to think of it, Danny hadn't seen Lachlan for ages either. Jewel's plan to patch things up between them at the party had obviously gone horribly wrong. Just as this bath was going horribly wrong. The cloying aroma of Babycham mingling with the cider was making him want to retch. And to make matters even worse, he was now stuck here, with his literal Achilles heel grinning at him from the doorway. Well, sod that. He wasn't going to let Achilles have the last laugh. He was going to do what he did best and brazen things out. He stood up in all his naked glory, his hands on his hips, and stared Achilles straight in the eye. 'Could you pass me a towel, please?'

Lachlan shivered and hugged his knees to his body. The warm buzz he'd been experiencing had drained away, leaving him feeling empty and anxious. He'd done it. He'd said it. Now Cat knew his terrible secret. But she hadn't fled. Not yet anyway. He glanced at her sitting beside him. She was staring down the hill at the London skyline, now a darkening silhouette.

'What do you mean, she died because of you?' she said quietly. 'You said she drowned, that the sea held her down.'

'Yes, but that wouldn't have happened if I hadn't …'

'What?' She turned to look at him and her gaze was so full of concern he could hardly bear it. But it was too late now. There could be no backing out. He might as well tell her the whole sorry saga.

'We'd gone surfing that day, the day it happened, but we realized pretty much straightaway that there was a really strong undercurrent. So we'd come back up to the beach and sat down, and then we got into an argument. A stupid, pointless argument. I said something I shouldn't have. She got really upset and she took her board and went back into the water.'

'Right …'

'And I just let her.' Lachlan's stomach churned and his palms felt clammy.

'But that doesn't mean that … it wasn't your fault.'

'Yes, it was!' His words came out way more forcefully than he'd intended. 'I'm sorry. But it was my fault. It was my fault we argued and it was my fault that I was too pigheaded to stop her going back into the sea when I knew it was dangerous.'

'But she knew it was dangerous too, right?'

'Yes, but …'

'Oh, Lachlan.' She placed her hand on his knee. But for once her touch didn't have any effect. He was too numb. He'd never told anyone about the argument, not even his folks or his best friends. He'd carried it around inside of him for almost two years like a tumour, eating away at the inside of him.

'It wasn't your fault,' Cat said again.

He felt a jolt of anger. 'You don't know. You weren't there. You don't know anything about what it was like.'

She removed her hand from his knee as quickly as if it had been burned.

He felt horrible. But he deserved to feel horrible. He was a horrible person. Better Cat know this now rather than later, rather than too late.

In the trees around them, the birds began their dusk chorus. It was far too beautiful for how he was feeling, the completely wrong soundtrack for this moment. This moment required a deathly silence.

'Would it help you to talk about it?' Cat asked, staring straight ahead of her.

'Not really.'

'Can I just say something, then?'

'OK.'

'I know that I don't know you all that well. And I know that I don't know what happened that day – that I wasn't there. But what I do know is how you've been to me, since we met.'

He stared down into his lap. Why was she doing this? Why was she being so nice?

'And you've been so lovely. Seriously. When I was feeling really down about work you were so supportive. Especially that night when you took me out for yelling therapy.'

He fought the urge to tell her to stop. How could he keep up the barrier that had protected him for so long if she kept being so kind?

'That was the most helpful thing I've ever tried, and believe me, I am the queen of self-help!'

He forced the smallest smile but couldn't bring himself to look at her.

'You helped me so much you even helped me when you weren't there, at that audition.'

He swallowed hard.

'So for what it's worth, I think you're bloody brilliant.'

Now he couldn't swallow, he couldn't speak, he couldn't breathe. It was as if his grief was fighting against Cat's hope, in an epic battle inside of him. Was she just saying all this to make him feel better, or did she really mean it? He glanced at her. She was looking at him, her eyes wide and deadly serious, tendrils of her hair framing her heart-shaped face. How had this punk mermaid chipped her way through his walls? He'd tried so hard to keep people out, to keep to himself, but somehow she'd worked her way in.

'Can I make a suggestion?' Cat's voice blended with the birdsong, sounding as if it was coming to him from deep within a dream.

He nodded.

'Can we lie down?'

This didn't seem too much of a stretch, so he allowed his body to sink down onto the grass. He felt it prickling into the backs of his arms. What was it she'd said about his arm hairs? Had that really been part of this same conversation? Had they really kissed again? What was happening?

'Can I make another suggestion?' she whispered. She was so close he could feel the whisper of her breath on his ear.

He nodded.

'Can I hold you?'

He felt his body sink further into the ground. He nodded again and he felt her arm make its way around his waist. Lightly at first, and then tighter. And then he felt her head nestle into the crook of his shoulder and he could smell her shampoo. Coconut. He closed his eyes and took a deep breath. And another. And another. *'It's not your fault. She knew it was dangerous, too.'* Cat's earlier words whispered to him inside his brain. But could they be true?

Twenty-seven

Danny cast an eye over the devastation in the kitchen and living room with the scrutiny of a forensic scientist examining a crime scene. Everywhere he looked there was evidence of a good time having been had by all, from the dregs of drink in the glasses, to the overflowing ashtrays and the remains of pizzas, sausage rolls and crisps on the table, counters and floor. It was close to midnight and most of the revellers had gone – apart from Darius, who was in the living room doing an interpretive dance to one of Pete's poems, cheered on by Lil. Pablo and Jewel had disappeared upstairs about an hour ago.

Danny sighed. He should be feeling happy. Normally, the carnage created by a good party had the same life-affirming effect upon him as a beautiful sunset, and he always loved it when his attempts to play Cupid paid off. So why, then, did he feel so flat? It didn't help that his skin reeked of cider – a constant reminder of his earlier humiliation in front of Achilles. Danny might have been able to style it out publicly, but privately he was still smarting. What if he was doomed to have disaster after disaster when it came to men? What if he never met anyone he liked again? Or more specifically, what if he never met anyone he liked who liked him back and wasn't seemingly intent on breaking his heart into a million little pieces? Danny frowned. His hangover anxiety seemed to be kicking in way too early. Maybe the best solution would be to go to bed and sleep it off. Tomorrow would be a brand new day, with two new shows to work on. He felt a slight glimmer of hope at this prospect.

Just as he turned to leave the kitchen, Justin walked in. As always, he was a vision of loveliness, with his tanned skin and blond hair. It was such a shame about his hideous carbuncle of a personality.

'What the hell's happened?' Justin asked, staring at the detritus littering the counters, table and floor.

'We had a small soirée,' Danny replied.

'Wow. I'd hate to see what happened if you had a large one,' Justin grinned. 'Are the auditions still on tomorrow evening?'

Danny nodded. When Justin had asked him if he could try out for the panto, Danny's heart had sunk. He had a strong hunch that Justin wasn't the kind of team player he was looking for, but if he didn't cast him as something it was bound to make life in the house awkward.

'Cool. Have you seen Cat?' Justin peered round him into the living room. 'She's not up in our room.'

Danny shook his head. If Cat wasn't in her room, where was she? He hadn't seen her for hours now. He felt a shiver of excitement. What if Jewel's cunning plan had actually worked? What if she was in Lachlan's room?

'That's weird.' Justin frowned. 'She told me she was staying in bed all day as she wasn't feeling well. You know, women's problems.'

'Oh, right.' Danny wasn't entirely sure how to respond to this, but thankfully the silence was interrupted by the sound of the front door opening and closing. Danny heard the low murmur of Cat's voice, but who was she talking to? He followed Justin over to the kitchen door. Cat was standing in the hallway, with Lachlan.

'What's going on?' Justin asked.

Danny decided to postpone going to bed and started collecting some dirty dishes instead, staying well within earshot of the hall.

'Nothing,' Cat replied.

'Where have you been?' Justin asked.

'Out.'

'What, with him?'

Danny took the dishes to the sink and glanced over his shoulder. Lachlan was standing right behind Cat, looking down at the floor with an expression on his face that could only be described as shifty.

'Yes.' Cat sounded remarkably defiant.

'I wasn't feeling too good,' Lachlan said. 'She took me out to get some fresh air.'

'Oh, really? I thought you had stomach cramps,' Justin turned back to Cat.

'I did, but then I felt better.'

'It's almost midnight,' Justin said. 'Where have you been getting fresh air until almost midnight?'

Good question, Danny thought to himself. Where *had* they been?

'We went for a cup of tea after,' Cat said.

Danny glanced at Justin. His mouth was hanging open, clearly too shocked to know what to say to this.

'I'm going to go to bed,' Lachlan muttered.

'Good night,' Cat said.

Danny continued piling dishes in the sink as silently as he could, not wanting to interrupt the unfolding drama.

'How could you do this to me?' He heard Justin hiss.

'Do what?'

'Humiliate me.'

'How have I humiliated you? I'm too tired for this, can we please just go to bed?'

To Danny's disappointment he heard their footsteps creak on the stairs.

'How can you not see how you've humiliated me?' He heard Justin's voice fading off and then the slamming of their bedroom door.

Danny continued piling dishes in the sink, his head filling with unanswered questions. Had Cat and Lachlan really been getting some fresh air? And had they really gone for a tea after? They'd been gone for hours. And where would you go to get a cup of tea in London on a Sunday night? What the hell was going on?

Cat lay in bed staring at the ceiling. Justin was lying awake beside her. She knew he was awake because every so often he'd give a pointed sigh and make a big drama about turning over or plumping up his pillow. But she couldn't think about Justin right now – she didn't want to. Every pathway in her brain was leading to Lachlan.

After they'd lain on the hill watching the sunset in silence she'd suggested they go and get a tea at the café at Smithfields. She'd been hoping that some caffeine would help them both to sober up a bit, so that she could make sense of what had happened and help Lachlan to make sense of it, too. Something about his revelation had deeply unsettled Cat. It had rammed home just how fragile life was, and how you never knew when it might be the last time you saw someone, or the last thing you said to someone. She shivered at the thought. That's why she'd asked Lachlan if she could hold him. She'd suddenly felt adrift and in need of something to hold on to, to ground her. He'd obviously needed it, too, from the way he'd put his arm around her and buried his face in her hair. She thought of him now, lying in his room downstairs all alone, and every fibre in her ached to be down there with him and feel his arm around her.

Justin rolled over so that he was facing her and gave another tortured sigh. Cat wanted to shake him from his self-pity. He had no idea what real hardship was. He always seemed to get the jobs he went up for. And if he didn't, Mummy and Daddy were always there with their chequebooks open ready to bail him out. She gave a sigh of her own.

'I just don't understand why you would want to hang out with someone like him,' Justin said suddenly into the silence.

'What do you mean, "someone like him"?'

'Well, he's not exactly our kind of person, is he?'

'What's that supposed to mean? Who are our kind of people?'

'Dancers, creatives. He's pretty Neanderthal, in spite of being a nurse.'

'Oh, for God's sake.'

'What?'

'Men can be nurses too, you know, just like women can be doctors. We *are* almost in the twenty-first century.'

Justin gave another sigh *and* plumped up his pillow, in a double whammy of passive-aggression. 'I don't want to argue with you, Cat.'

'Well don't, then.'

There was a long silence. So long she was starting to hope he'd given up and had actually fallen asleep, when he put his arm around her waist.

'I'm sorry,' he whispered. 'I've just got a lot on my mind at the moment.'

'Like what?'

'My mum's had a health scare. She might – she might have cancer.'

'What?' Cat shifted into a more upright position and stared down at him.

'She's had some tests and stuff, and it doesn't look good.'

'Shit. I'm sorry. When did you find out?'

'Today, at lunch. That's why I got back so late – she wanted me to stay.'

'Of course. I'm so sorry.'

'That's OK. It's just been a really tough day, and then when I saw you coming in with him …'

Cat felt horrible. What had she been thinking, going out with Lachlan while she was still meant to be in a relationship with Justin? What had she been thinking, kissing Lachlan? Shame crept through her, making her stomach churn. 'I'm really sorry. I thought he needed some fresh air. I was just trying to help.'

'Yeah, well, maybe I need your help.'

'Of course. So what, where do they think she has cancer?'

'In her breast.'

The sickening feeling in the pit of Cat's stomach grew. She and Justin's mum might not have a lot in common, but right now Cat felt nothing but empathy for her. Every time she checked her own breasts in the shower she dreaded the prospect of finding something hard, something unfamiliar. It was horrible thinking of his mum going through that trauma.

'Does she have to have surgery?'

'Yes, she's booked in to have the lump removed in a couple of weeks' time.'

'Ah, OK.' Cat lay back down again.

'At least I've got the audition for Danny tomorrow to take my mind off it.' Justin said, snuggling closer to her. 'I mean, I know it's for charity or whatever, but he's bound to give me one of the lead roles and if I can get casting agents to come along ...'

Cat had a sudden horrible thought. What if Justin got a role in the panto and she didn't? She'd really been looking forward to auditioning for Danny, but now it felt as if Justin was crowding her out again, making it all about him. When he'd got the job in Berlin it had felt as if her world was shrinking away to nothing, but actually his leaving had broadened her life in ways she'd never imagined – bringing her closer to her housemates, getting the job at the Lemon Tree and on the music video.

'Can I have a hug, Scottie?' Justin whispered.

As if on autopilot, she laid her arm across his stomach. Stop being so selfish, she scolded herself. He's just found out his mum might have cancer. But, try as she might, she couldn't shake her growing feelings of dread. She couldn't shrink herself back down to fit in with Justin and his dreams. She closed her eyes and thought back to the night in Heaven, when she'd felt like a superhero. She needed to hold on to that feeling, to that version of herself.

'Love you, Scottie,' Justin murmured, his voice now thick with sleep.

As he tightened his grip around her waist it felt as if he was a leech, sucking the hope and life from her. This couldn't happen again. She couldn't allow it. If she'd learned one thing today it was that life was way too precious to waste a single second. And she couldn't waste another second in Justin's shadow. She needed to find her own spotlight.

Lachlan lay on his bed staring up at the ceiling. Thanks to Cat taking him to the greasy spoon and filling him with egg and chips as well as tea, he was finally back in control of his senses, not that that was such a good thing given the circumstances. Being confronted by Justin as soon as they'd got home had been the ultimate buzzkill. Every time he saw that guy his hatred for him grew. And the more he got to know Cat, the more he couldn't understand what the hell someone like her was doing with someone like Justin. A vision of Cat filled his mind. It was of her on the hill earlier that evening, her hair ablaze in the setting sun. He thought of the gentle way she'd held him, without saying anything. As if she'd known that he couldn't take any more words – that all he needed more than anything was just to be held.

He took a moment to let the enormity of what had happened sink in. He'd told Cat the whole truth about what had happened and she hadn't run, she'd held him. Then he remembered all the things she'd said, about how much she liked him. His thoughts started tying themselves in knots of confusion. Could Cat have been right? Could he have been wrong all this time in blaming himself for what had happened?

'Are you there?' he whispered into the darkness. A distant siren wailed from outside. He didn't know if he was still slightly stoned, but he felt a sudden slight chill in the room. 'Michelle?' he whispered. Silence enveloped him. 'I don't know if you're able to hear me but if you are …' He sighed. What was he doing? But now he'd started he couldn't stop. 'I'm so, so sorry. I'm so sorry that I started that fight. I'm so sorry I didn't try and stop you going into the sea. I'm so sorry you left me.' He felt a huge shiver course through him, leaving in its wake a feeling of complete and utter peace. He rolled on to his side and fell into a dreamless sleep.

Twenty-eight

Jewel stepped into the kitchen and gasped. He knew that the phrase something 'looked like a bomb had hit it' was usually an exaggeration, but in this case it was totally justified. Every inch of table and counter surface – and most of the floor – was covered in wreckage from the party. There were smeared wine glasses and beer glasses, saucers overflowing with cigarette butts and empty bottles everywhere. The floor was covered in spillages and Lil's castanets were dangling from the light fitting. As he took it all in Jewel started to wish he'd never offered to make Pablo breakfast, but at the thought of Pablo waiting upstairs for him his heart raced. This was definitely a good predicament to be in, he concluded. This was the kind of predicament men of the world had to face. Men who had parties and zany housemates and lovers. Jewel felt a shiver of excitement at his brave new reality – one in which he was no longer a virgin.

Gingerly, he made his way over to the cupboard, the floor sticky beneath his bare feet. Thankfully, he managed to locate one clean cup at the back of the cupboard. It bore the logo LESBIANS AGAINST TRIDENT, but it would have to do. At least it didn't have mould growing in it, or contain a cigarette butt. Jewel banged the cold tap and filled the kettle. He supposed he ought to make a start on clearing up while he waited for it to boil, but there was so much that needed doing that he didn't have the first clue where to start. It didn't help that someone had filled the sink with a mountain of dirty dishes.

He was about to start removing them when there was a loud knock on the front door. Jewel contemplated ignoring it, but he didn't think Lachlan would appreciate being woken up if he was working a night shift. Besides, it was probably only the postman. He made his way into the hall, which was covered in limp strands of spray party streamers. Someone had also written CASTRATE THE PATRIARCHY in red lipstick on the hall mirror. Jewel grinned. No prizes for guessing who.

He flung the front door open, but instead of being greeted by the postman's cheery grin, a heavily made-up woman in a bright red business suit was standing on the doorstep.

'Hiya! I'm Denise from We Let, You Get,' she said, like this was supposed to mean something.

'Not today, thanks,' Jewel replied, assuming that she was some kind of saleswoman.

'I'm sorry, but I have an appointment,' she said, looking slightly affronted.

'An appointment with who?'

'An appointment to do the routine inspection of the property on behalf of the landlord. I'm from the letting agents,' she explained.

'Does … does anyone in the house know about this?' Jewel stammered, moving sideways to try to block her view of the hallway.

'I sent a letter a couple of weeks ago, informing you all that I was coming.'

Jewel glanced at the pile of unopened junk mail in the corner. Could her letter have ended up there? Surely if any of the other housemates had seen it they would have said something.

'So, can I come in?' Denise asked.

'Oh … uh …' Jewel stood motionless as he tried to figure out what to do. If he slammed the door in her face – which was his favourite option by far right now – it would look as if they had something to hide. But they did have something to hide. The house looked like a bomb had hit it – literally!

Denise took a camera from her bag. 'I'll need to take some photos to send to the landlord, just to let them know that everything's OK or if anything needs fixing. This visit's just as much for your benefit as it is for them,' she said with a grin.

I really don't think so, Jewel thought to himself, hot waves of panic pulsing through his body.

'OK, let's begin,' Denise said, pushing past him into the hall. 'Oh,' she said, taking in the spray streamers and the writing on the mirror.

'We, uh, had a little party yesterday,' Jewel stammered. 'I haven't had a chance to clean up yet but I was just about to do it.' He held his breath as she went into the kitchen.

'What on earth …?' she gasped. 'It looks like a bomb's hit it.'

'Yes, I know, but it isn't normally like this, honestly,' he said, following her into the kitchen.

'Have you painted the kitchen purple?' Denise looked around shaking her head.

'Oh, uh, yes.' Jewel watched helplessly as Denise started taking photos of the stained floor, the ashtray saucers and the overflowing sink.

'I don't think you need to take photos of the mess,' Jewel said as Denise went through the archway into the living room. 'It's normally spotless in here.'

'Oh, really?' Denise crouched down and took a photo of the carpet. As Jewel joined her he saw not just one but a whole cluster of cigarette burns scarring the faded paisley print.

'And what is this?' she asked, pointing to Lil's washing-up liquid bong, which had been positioned in pride of place on the mantelpiece.

'I don't know,' Jewel said lamely. Damn it. Why did he have to be the one to let her in? Danny would have been so much better in this situation. He would have known exactly what to say. Although even his powers of persuasion might have been found wanting in this situation.

'Has there been illegal drug use on the premises?' Denise asked, writing something down on her clipboard.

'No! Absolutely not.'

'Hmm.' Denise picked her way through the discarded record sleeves littering the floor and made her way over to the back door.

'Oh my God!' she shrieked, clutching her chest.

'Wh-what is it?' Jewel hardly dared ask.

'There's a dead body in the back yard.' She turned and stared at him accusingly.

Jewel's stomach lurched. Could someone have OD'ed on Lil's kismet punch? It was pretty strong. Or what about her cookies? Then a terrible thought occurred to him: what if Lil had died from too much partying?

He hurried over and, to his relief, saw Darius lying on the ground with a coat draped over him. But was he dead or was he just asleep? He was very, very still. Jewel's imagination went into overdrive. What if one of the party guests had murdered Darius for being chronically boring? It would be like one of those Agatha Christie films where everyone had a motive for killing him. Darius jerked suddenly, causing Jewel and Denise to jump.

'It's OK, he was one of the party guests,' Jewel said as breezily as he could muster. 'I guess he's just out there having a nap.'

'But why would he take a nap out there?' Denise asked.

Jewel shrugged.

Denise opened the door and then to Jewel's horror she took a photo of Darius, causing the dancer to shield his half-open eyes from the dazzling camera flash.

'No paparazzi,' Darius mumbled, before closing his eyes again.

Denise shook her head and wrote something else on her clipboard.

'Hey, sexy, where did you go?' Pablo's voice rang out from the kitchen, causing Jewel's heart to race, for all the wrong reasons.

'I'll be right there, go back upstairs,' Jewel yelled. But it was too late. Pablo appeared at the back door wearing a pair of very small, very skin-tight boxers. It was a sight that normally would have been the stuff of Jewel's dreams, but seen through the prism of Denise it took on a nightmarish quality.

'I was lonely in bed without you,' Pablo said, before spotting Denise and Darius. 'Oh, hello,' he said, flicking his fringe back and grinning. 'What is going on?'

'That is exactly what I'd like to know,' Denise replied, her bright red lips pursed tightly.

Danny woke to the sound of pounding on his door - or was it in his head? He couldn't exactly be sure. He opened one eye and tried to focus on his alarm clock, but his vision was so blurred the numbers were just a glowing red haze. The pounding continued. Then he heard Jewel calling his name. It sounded urgent. But then so was sleep. Sleep was very, very urgent indeed. He groaned and burrowed beneath the duvet.

'Danny, wake up, it's an emergency!' Jewel's voice cut through the fog.

Danny lurched upright. How could there be an emergency at – he squinted at the clock – nine twenty-seven on Monday morning. Crap. There was an emergency – he was going to be late for the *Rocky Horror* rehearsals if he didn't get a move on. He leapt out of bed and hurried over to the door.

Jewel was standing on the landing, in his green satin dressing gown, ashen-faced. Danny's first thought was that something must have gone wrong between him and Pablo. But, much as he enjoyed playing Agony Uncle, now wasn't the time.

'Can it wait? I need to have a shower and get to work.'

'No, it can't, it …' Jewel tapered off at the sound of footsteps on the stairs. A blonde woman in a bright red suit and too much make-up appeared, holding a clipboard and a camera, and behind her Pablo emerged grinning, clad only in an indecently tight pair of pants. What the hell was going on?

'Hello, Danny,' the woman said, with a condescending smile and a shake of her hair. Who was she? How did she know him? She did look vaguely familiar, but his brain was way too caffeine-deprived to be able to recollect why. 'I've come to do the house inspection.'

As she barged past him into the bathroom two terrible thoughts collided in Danny's brain: the woman was Denise from the letting agents, and the bathroom was where he had taken his cider bath – but had he let it out? He heard a gasp from the bathroom and followed Denise in. The bath was still full of cider and it stank like a scrumpy brewery.

'What is going on in here?' Denise asked, raising her camera. The room was filled with a blinding flash as she took a picture. 'Are you making some kind of home-brew in the bath?'

Now was the time for some very quick thinking, but Danny's brain appeared to be idling in neutral. 'We were having a party,' was all he could manage.

'Oh yes, I'm very aware of that,' she replied.

Crap. So that meant she'd already seen downstairs. He glanced at Jewel, who was even paler than before.

'Did we … did we know that you were coming?' Danny asked.

'Yes. I wrote a letter a couple of weeks ago to notify you.' Denise took a photo of the mountain of empty cider cans and Babycham bottles next to the bath.

Danny made a silent vow right there and then that if any of his fellow housemates had seen Denise's letter and not thought to tell him, then he was going to drown them in the cider bath.

'Make way, party people, I'm in dire need of a slash,' Darius's drone boomed from the landing. *Shit!* What was he doing still here? Danny watched, horrified, as Darius marched into the bathroom, unbuttoning his 501s.

'I'm doing an inspection,' Denise spluttered, holding her clipboard to her chest as if it were a shield.

'Cool.' Darius continued unbuttoning his jeans.

'Of the house, not your genitals, imbecile!' Danny barked.

'Whoops! Sorry. My bad.' Darius scanned the room. 'Loving the cider bath, dude. Great party trick. Is there anywhere I can take a leak? I'm desperate.' As if to prove the point he started hopping from foot to foot.

'Go ahead,' Denise said, heading to the door. 'I've seen all I need to see.'

'Great, shall I show you out?' Danny hurriedly offered. To his dismay, Denise shook her head.

'I haven't inspected any of the bedrooms yet.'

Oh God! 'Why don't you check mine first,' Danny offered, ushering her into his bedroom. Behind her back he mouthed to Jewel, 'Go and warn the others!'

For the first time possibly ever, Danny was thankful that he hadn't got lucky at a party and that his room was completely free from carnage or stray lovers. It even elicited an approving nod from Denise.

'Ooh, I do love a four-poster bed,' she cooed, looking at him provocatively.

Danny felt a sudden dizziness coupled with nausea. Surely she wasn't about to make a pass at him? And if she was, what should he do? If he responded he'd be able to buy his housemates some time to sort out their rooms, but surely this went way above and beyond the definition of being a good housemate? And why, oh why, was he being expected to grapple with a conundrum like this without having consumed any caffeine?

'I've always thought you can tell a lot about a man from the state of his bedroom,' Denise continued, running a pointed scarlet fingernail along one of the bedposts.

Danny felt his body temperature begin to climb in panic and he caught a waft of stale cider evaporating from his skin. This was officially the most nightmarish start to a week he had ever had. He glanced at the alarm clock. He was now almost certainly going to be late for rehearsals.

'I'm sorry about the mess. This place is normally pristine ... We're a bunch of neat freaks, really ... We...' It was no good. His brain just wasn't going to cooperate.

'Hmm, well maybe I could be persuaded to turn a blind eye if ...' she advanced on him, glossy red lips puckered.

Danny took a step back. The stench of stale cider was now mingling with her floral perfume, creating a horrible, sickly aroma. His stomach churned.

'Maybe we could go for a drink sometime.' She was now so close he could feel her breath on his skin. He could smell it, too: stale cigarettes with a hint of garlic.

The contents of his stomach lurched upwards, causing an acid burn in the back of his throat.

'I'm sorry, I ...' Danny started to retch.

'Ew!' Denise exclaimed, taking a step back.

Danny clamped his hand to his mouth and fled to the bathroom, making it just in time to throw up in the sink.

'What's going on?' he heard Cat ask from out on the landing.

'I'm from We Let, You Get,' Denise replied. 'I'm here to do the property inspection.'

'Oh, cool,' he heard Cat reply breezily. 'Could you let the landlord know that the cold tap in the kitchen needs fixing?'

'Trust me, love, a broken tap is the very least of your problems,' Denise snapped.

Danny groaned as he leaned over the sink and listened to her footsteps fading away down the stairs.

Twenty-nine

Lachlan took a step into the kitchen then recoiled in shock. But, instead of feeling pissed off at the mess that greeted him, he found himself laughing. Maybe it was all the sleep he'd had that was putting him in such a charitable mood. It was almost midday and he'd slept for eleven hours straight – a personal best, in recent times at least.

He cleared the sink of dishes and filled it with hot, soapy water. Michelle always had a system for washing up whenever they had a party: do all of the cutlery first, then the glasses, then the plates and larger items. He'd never questioned the logic of this system, it just seemed to make sense. As Lachlan gathered up all the cutlery he could find dotted around the kitchen, another memory came flooding back to him. It was of the night of their housewarming party, after they'd moved into their first and only place together, an apartment overlooking Main Beach. After the guests had gone, he and Michelle had been too happy and excited to go to bed, so they'd stood at the sink, her washing, him drying, singing along to a Duran Duran album, laughing and flicking washing-up liquid bubbles at each other like a cheesy scene from a romcom film. He'd felt so certain at that moment that they were right at the start of their story, rather than pages away from its ending. He shivered at the thought and turned on the radio to try to distract himself.

'And coming up next, "Girls on Film" by Duran Duran,' the DJ said.

Lachlan stood rooted to the spot, his hands in the sink.

The logical part of his brain was telling him that it had to be a coincidence, but another part was telling him that it had to be some kind of sign. But a sign of what, exactly? He got ready to turn the radio off, afraid of the avalanche of pain the song would unleash, but something stopped him. As the song started playing it was as if he was stepping right back into that night in the kitchen at Main Beach. He could feel Michelle's presence, he could smell her perfume and the wine on her breath.

'You make me so happy,' she had told him as he hooked his tea towel round her waist and pulled her close.

Lachlan closed his eyes and inhaled, as if trying to hold on to what she'd said and the joy it had made him feel. He had made Michelle happy. For almost two years now he'd remained stuck in the memory of their final argument on the beach, trapped by the fact that he hadn't stopped her going into the sea. But that was just one memory from hundreds of thousands. What about all the others? What about all the times he had been there for her and he hadn't let her down?

Then he remembered what Cat had said to him when they'd been on Primrose Hill, about how he'd helped her, how she thought he was 'bloody brilliant'. Even when he'd told her what had happened with Michelle it hadn't changed her perception of him.

'We're such a great team,' he remembered Michelle saying, as they finished doing the dishes that night in their apartment.

'I'll always be the dryer to your washer,' he'd joked.

Lachlan opened his eyes and started gathering up the dirty glasses. 'Slide Away' by Oasis came on the radio. A song that had only just been released. A song that Michelle would never get to hear. A song that would only ever be his, not theirs. She would have loved it, too. He paused for a moment. Discovering new bands together had been one of the things they loved to do, either in the Gold Coast clubs and pubs or on the radio.

Lachlan hadn't been to a gig since Michelle had died. He'd deliberately deprived himself of anything she'd loved, operating on the principle that if she could no longer experience it, why the hell should he? But would she really have wanted him to live like this? Would he have wanted her to live like this if the roles had been reversed? Instantly, he knew the answer was no. He would have wanted her to live her life to the fullest. And he bet she would have wanted the same for him. As he started cleaning lipstick from a wine glass he wondered if he'd got the whole thing wrong. Instead of living in some kind of purgatory as a reminder of Michelle, he should actually be living life to its fullest in tribute to her.

He washed glass after glass, mulling over this strange new concept. All this time he'd been so scared of telling anyone the terrible secret he'd been carrying around inside of him. He had feared that bringing it out into the open would consume him, but telling Cat had been like lancing a boil, allowing his shame and fear to drain away.

He picked up a tea towel and set to work drying the glasses. Then he moved on to washing the plates. A strange feeling was coming over him, one that he'd become so unaccustomed to that at first he wasn't sure what it was. The memories he had of Michelle were becoming poignant rather than painful. Loving rather than fearful. He was able to breathe when he thought about her, instead of choking up with tears.

He turned to look for more dishes and saw to his surprise that they were all done. He banged the tap, filled the kettle and went to the fridge to get his milk. It was only at that point that he noticed a note written in Danny's writing pinned to the door:

EMERGENCY HOUSE MEETING TOMORROW 9 A.M.

Cat raced into the house and up the stairs. Today's filming for the music video had overrun because there'd been a problem with the lighting. As a result, she'd had to hang around in Trafalgar Square for hours on end and the chill autumn breeze had left her frozen to the bone. She didn't have time to warm up with a bath or shower, though, as she had to get straight to the audition for Danny. She raced into the bedroom and found Justin inspecting his hair in the mirror.

'Where have you been?' he asked. 'I was about to leave without you.'

'We overran. Technical issues.' She hurried over to her chest of drawers and pulled out a leopard-print crop top and a fresh pair of leggings. She gave herself a generous spritz of antiperspirant and got changed.

'Is that what you're wearing?' Justin said, frowning at her reflection in the mirror.

'Yes, why? What's wrong with it?'

'I'm not sure about that top, babe. Are you sure you want to draw attention to your stomach?'

'What's wrong with my stomach?' She turned sideways to examine her reflection. She'd lost some weight since working at the Lemon Tree and although her stomach still curved outwards rather than in, there was no way it could be construed as fat – could it?

'Nothing. I think it's cute. It's cuddly.' He gave her stomach a rub, the way you'd pet a dog. 'I'm just not sure if it's the look Danny will be after. Not for Cinderella, anyway.'

What was that supposed to mean? Was he implying that she'd be more suited to be one of the ugly sisters? Doubts started multiplying inside Cat's brain. Why, oh, why could she never get her stomach to curve in? The more she examined it in the mirror, the bigger it seemed.

Justin pulled up his T-shirt, revealing a perfect set of abs, which he patted proudly. 'Right, shall we go?'

'Yeah. I'll just be a sec, I'm just going to get changed.' Cat rummaged through her drawer and pulled out her baggiest T-shirt.

Danny took a seat in the front row at the White Lion Theatre and inhaled deeply. What with the nightmare house inspection followed by a full-on day in a hot and dusty rehearsal room, he'd barely been able to catch a breath all day. He looked at his clipboard that held the list of people auditioning. He was excited to see what Cat would do. If she danced like she'd done that night at Heaven he could see her bagging the lead role. But only if she was better than the others. There were going to be no special privileges for the Diamond Street residents. Too much was resting on this and, besides, Danny was too much of a professional. The quality of the performances had to take priority over personal favours.

Once everyone had arrived, Danny did a couple of ice-breaker exercises to help them get loosened up and into their bodies. Then he asked the men to take to the stage and told them to freestyle to 'Beat It' by Michael Jackson. He noticed Justin shove himself up to the front, practically elbowing one of the other guys in the face. It seemed his hunch was correct – Justin was no team player. But what was he like at dancing? Danny watched while Justin performed a series of body pops and waves. While he looked great physically, his dancing lacked that special something. He was too self-aware, too polished. In contrast, a young black guy called Leon dancing behind him was showing real raw talent and great energy.

Once the track finished, Danny decided to get each of the guys to dance solo to 'Bohemian Rhapsody'. He wanted to see how they'd handle changes in tempo and melody. Leon went first, and the other guys all clapped along from the side of the stage. All apart from Justin, who wasn't even watching; he was too busy doing elaborate stretches, instead. This was another black mark as far as Danny was concerned. He liked dancers who celebrated each other, not tried to steal the spotlight.

When it was Justin's turn to dance he started in an arabesque followed by a fairly basic ballet routine before launching into some body pops as the tempo increased. He was clearly trying to pull out all of the stops, but something about his performance left Danny cold. Justin was far too much in his own head – probably thinking about how awesome he looked. It was a shame because with his chiselled jaw and film-star looks, he looked like the archetypal Prince Charming – but Danny wasn't after the traditional, he reminded himself. He wanted this panto to be different.

'OK, thank you,' he said, once all the guys had taken their turn. 'Can I have all the ladies on the stage, please?'

He looked at Cat, hanging towards the back of the group. Unlike the other dancers, who were clad from top to toe in skintight Lycra, she was wearing a top with all the shape of a potato sack over her leggings. Maybe she was going for the whole poverty-stricken, pre-ball Cinders look. As long as her dancing shone, Danny didn't really mind.

But as soon as the track started he could tell something was wrong. Cat seemed distracted. Like Justin, she seemed too much in her head, but in a more insecure and self-conscious way. Danny felt a mixture of frustration and disappointment. He'd so hoped she'd be good enough to play the lead role – it would have been a great boost to her confidence, not to mention her career, as he was planning on inviting all of his choreographer and casting director friends to come to the dress rehearsal. He glanced at Justin, who was sitting at the end of the front row. But instead of watching Cat, he was busy fiddling with the laces on his trainers.

The track came to an end and Danny asked the women to line up either side of the stage. Hopefully, Cat would do better in her solo dance. He called one of the other women first, a strikingly beautiful nineteen-year-old called Sophie. With her wavy blonde hair and hourglass figure she certainly fitted the traditional Cinderella mould. As she started dancing he noticed Justin clapping along, now fully attentive. But Danny wasn't sure. There was no denying Sophie was good, with all the poise and grace that came from a ballet training. But he hadn't pictured his Cinders being so poised and regal. He wanted her to ooze warmth and authenticity, and a generous pinch of sass.

He called Cat next, willing her to tap into that same wild energy she'd shown at Heaven. She was slightly better this time than she had been in the group freestyle, but she was nothing special. Nothing that screamed lead-role potential. Damn it! It was as if she didn't really care. Danny felt so disappointed. And angry. He hated it when dancers didn't give their all. When she left the stage he couldn't bring himself to look at her, and just called, 'Next, please.'

Cat trudged home from the White Lion with Justin and Danny in complete silence. Thankfully, her silence wasn't noticeable as Justin was talking more than enough for both of them.

'I hope you liked my little jazz-tap fusion at the end,' he said to Danny as they turned into Diamond Street.

'It was great,' Danny replied. But he didn't sound all that effusive.

Cat didn't dare ask what he'd thought of her performance. She knew she'd blown it. Doubt had wormed its way from her mind right down into her feet. She caught a waft of meat and onions from the kebab shop on the corner and her stomach growled with hunger. She hadn't eaten since lunch and now she was starving. But she'd be better off going straight to bed when she got in. Maybe if she started skipping dinner it might make her stomach shrink. Wasn't that what they said? Breakfast like a king, lunch like a prince and dine like a pauper? Maybe if she stopped eating dinner all together she'd look more like that Barbie doll of a dancer, Sophie, who Justin hadn't been able to peel his eyes from.

'So, when will we find out what parts we've got?' Justin asked as they reached number 27.

Cat cringed at his arrogance, even though it was probably well placed. As always, Justin had exuded confidence at the audition. He was bound to be offered a role.

'In the next couple of days,' Danny replied.

As Cat watched him unlock the front door, she had a terrible thought. With her blonde curls and wonderful figure, Sophie would make the perfect Cinderella. And with his chiselled jaw and film-star looks, Justin would make the perfect Prince Charming. What if they were cast in the lead roles? The thought made her feel sick. But this time it wasn't out of jealousy at the thought of him working so closely with another woman. It was more from a sense of injustice. Why was it always the beautiful people who rose to the top? Why did beauty trump talent? *But you didn't exactly give a talented performance*, she reminded herself. She felt empty from hunger and disappointment. All of her new-found confidence seemed to have deserted her completely.

'Cat, can I have a word?' Danny asked, as they stepped into the darkened hallway.

'Sure.' She followed him into the kitchen. 'Wow, someone's been busy.' All of the carnage from the party had been cleared away and the room was spotless.

'Yeah, well, it's probably too little, too late,' Danny muttered. 'After this morning, I'm expecting an eviction notice any time now.'

'That's all right, we can go back to my parents',' Justin said to Cat.

Cat shuddered, and not just at his insensitivity but at the thought of having to move back to Hampstead. She felt herself shrinking even smaller.

Danny gave Justin a pointed stare. 'Could I have a word with Cat on her own, please?'

'Oh, uh, sure. I'll see you upstairs.' Justin planted a kiss on top of Cat's head and left the room.

'So, what the hell was all that about?' Danny turned his glare on her.

Cat flinched and looked down at the floor. 'What do you mean?'

'Your performance in the audition. Or rather your lack of performance.'

Cat felt horrible. She'd been hoping that Danny wouldn't have minded that she'd danced so poorly. There had been plenty of other good dancers after all. And Sophie was the perfect Cinderella; it was a no-brainer.

'I was tired,' she mumbled lamely. 'Shooting for the music video overran and ...'

'You were tired?' Danny's normally twinkling eyes glared with anger.

'I hadn't had the chance to eat, I ...' She broke off, aware that she sounded pathetic.

Danny clearly agreed, from the way he was staring at her. A horrible silence fell, broken only by the slow drip of the tap. Finally, Danny pulled out a chair and sat down at the table. 'How about you tell me what's really going on.'

She sat down opposite him, unsure what to say.

'I'm not stupid, Cat. I can tell when a dancer's distracted and holding back. I can tell when they're not giving me their all.'

Cat squirmed. How could she tell him what had really been on her mind? She'd sound even more pitiful. 'I'm really sorry I let you down.'

'You didn't let me down, darling, you let yourself down.'

And there it was – the cold, hard, horrible truth. She'd let herself down. Yet again. Hot tears began burning at the corners of her eyes. But she wasn't going to cry in front of Danny on top of everything else. She had to get a grip. 'I'm really sorry.'

'Don't apologize to me. I'll be fine.'

'Yes, there were some great dancers there tonight, weren't there? And Sophie would make the perfect Cinderella. She looks like she stepped right out of a Disney film.'

'I'm not interested in Disney!' Danny sighed. 'I want to know what happened to you.'

'I just don't think I've got what it takes.'

'What it takes to do what?'

'To be Cinderella, to be a successful dancer, to be a successful anything.' She hoped that, on hearing this, Danny might give up on her and go to bed, but he stayed put, and his frown deepened.

'For God's sake!' He sighed and shook his head.

'What?'

'How old are you?'

'Twenty-five.'

'Right. So, in dancer years that's about fifty.'

Great. He clearly wasn't on a mission to make her feel any better.

'Exactly. I'm too old and I'm too big and …'

'Wait? What did you just say?'

'I'm too old and I'm too big.'

'Firstly, you're not too old, but if you don't stop feeling sorry for yourself you soon will be. And secondly, how the hell are you too big?'

'Oh, come on, Danny! You see the type of dancers who get cast in shows. They're all long limbs and stomachs that curve in.'

Danny continued to frown. 'So how come you got cast for the music video?'

She shrugged.

'I'm being serious. How did you get that role?'

'I auditioned.' She frowned, unsure where he was going with this line of questioning.

'And when you auditioned did you dance for them the way you danced for me?'

'No ... I ...'

'So what changed between now and then?'

The answer hung in the silence between them, as obvious as a neon sign: JUSTIN.

Cat felt pitiful. How had she let Justin get under her skin again? How had she let him infect her with doubt and fear?

'I lost my confidence,' she muttered.

'Good,' Danny replied.

'What? How is that good?'

'It's good because you're not bullshitting me any more with all that talk of being tired and hungry. And it's good because now I know what we're looking for, I can help you find it.'

A wave of gratitude rushed through her, causing a fresh onset of tears. She quickly blinked them away.

Danny went over to the fridge and pulled out a pack of cheese. 'Toastie?' he asked, fetching a loaf of bread from his cupboard.

Cat felt a pang of hunger mingled with guilt. *Don't do it, you need to lose weight*, one voice was saying in her head. *Do it, you're starving, eat all the cheese!* another voice chimed in. She nodded and tried to ignore the subsequent hot flush of shame that coursed through her.

'I get it, you know,' Danny said, as he began buttering the bread. His tone was a lot softer now, and Cat's body unclenched. 'I get all the pressure. I've had exactly the same insecurities.'

'You have?' Cat stared at him in surprise. Danny always seemed so calm and confident. She couldn't imagine him feeling insecure about anything.

'Of course. I had a massive hang-up about my body shape when I was first starting out.'

The relief that Cat felt grew stronger. Maybe he didn't think she was pitiful, after all.

'And it's so frustrating because actually how you look has very little to do with your talent as a dancer. I mean, seriously, does it really matter if your stomach curves out or in?'

She sighed. 'Well, it shouldn't.'

'It doesn't,' he said firmly, putting the sandwiches in the sandwich toaster with the bread buttered-side out. 'At least not in my book, or on my watch, or whatever.'

'I just wish everyone saw it like you.'

He nodded. 'Yeah, well, hopefully, if I get anywhere as a choreographer I'll be able to shake things up a bit. And I'm going to start with *Cinderella*.'

Cat sighed. She'd had the chance to audition for someone who didn't give a crap whether her stomach curved in or out, and she'd blown it.

'I told you before, I don't want this production to be like all the rest. I want it to turn everything on its head. I don't want a Disney princess. I want a fucking warrior princess.'

'Seriously?'

'Yes. So I'll tell you what we're going to do. We're going to stuff our faces with cheese toasties, and then tomorrow night we're going to workshop Cinders the warrior princess, and I'm going to see if I can get you to find the warrior princess inside of you. Deal?'

Excitement and joy bubbled up inside of her. 'Deal!'

She was about to get up and give him a hug when a cough rang out from the darkness of the living room.

'What the hell?' Cat put her hands to her chest in shock and peered through the archway into the darkness. Someone was lying on the sofa. And now they were rising up like some kind of zombie.

'Who is it?' Danny whispered, brandishing the bread knife.

She shrugged.

'Hey, guys.' Darius's dulcet tones rang out. 'Any chance of one of those toasties? I'm Hank Marvin!'

Thirty

'**M**orning, everyone, welcome to the emergency house meeting.' Danny looked around the table, his eyes coming to rest on Darius, who, annoyingly, was helping himself to Lil's emergency-house-meeting croissants as if he owned the place.

'Great to be a part of it,' Darius replied through a mouthful of pastry, showering the table with crumbs.

'Hang on, who are you?' Justin asked. His usually immaculate hair was still ruffled from sleep and he was wearing shorts and a vest. Danny sighed. It was such a shame Justin was such a knob. It was a terrible waste of beauty.

'Wotcha, I'm Darius, your new housemate.'

Danny's irritation grew. Firstly, he had only agreed that Darius could sleep on the sofa for a week. That hardly made him a housemate. And secondly, who the hell still said 'wotcha'? It was bad enough the first time round in the seventies.

'You're not our new housemate, Darius. He's just crashing on the sofa for a week,' Danny told the others quickly, 'while he finds somewhere else to live.'

'My landlady kicked me out because of her varicose veins,' Darius said without any further explanation, before shovelling another croissant into his mouth.

Danny took a deep breath. It appeared he was going to require industrial quantities of inner grit and strong coffee to get through this meeting.

'Poor thing,' Lil said, nodding sympathetically. 'Landladies with varicose veins can be the worst.'

'OK,' Danny said loudly, before Lil regaled them with the tale of some sixties icon she knew who had varicose veins and the whole meeting descended into farce. 'The reason I've called this meeting is because, as you all know, we had a surprise house inspection yesterday morning.'

'I actually did not know that,' Pete said, looking puzzled. 'Who inspected it?'

'The letting agent, on behalf of the landlord,' Danny explained. Sometimes he wondered how Pete had managed to negotiate adulthood unaided. 'They had written to us to let us know but for some strange reason the letter ended up in the pile of junk mail in the hall. And as you all know, the house wasn't exactly in the best condition when it was inspected.'

Jewel shuddered. 'It looked like a bomb had hit it.'

'Quite. The letting agent was distinctly unimpressed, and she took pictures to send to the landlord.'

'Strewth,' Lachlan sighed.

'Exactly. So I think we need to prepare ourselves for the possible threat of eviction.'

'I'm sure it will all be fine,' Lil said.

Easy for you to say, Danny thought to himself. Lil was probably high already. He had little doubt she was a graduate of the 'wake and bake' school of stoners.

'Isn't there anything we can do?' Cat asked. 'I'd hate to have to move out of here and away from all of you.' Danny noticed her glance at Lachlan as she said this.

'Me too,' said Jewel.

'Well, as it happens, I do have a cunning plan,' Danny said, taking a sip of his coffee.

'Oh, excellent, I do love a cunning plan!' Lil exclaimed.

'What is it?' Lachlan asked.

'I think we should give the house a makeover and then ask Denise from the letting agents to come back and re-inspect the place.' Danny actually hated this plan as it meant more work on top of everything else, but if it also meant they kept the tenancy of 27 Diamond Street, it would be worth it.

'I love makeovers!' Jewel exclaimed.

'Me too,' Cat agreed.

Danny scanned the table for the others' reactions. Justin looked distinctly underwhelmed, studying his fingernails. Pete was staring into space; Lil was grinning like a Cheshire cat.

'I'm in,' Lachlan said, nodding and smiling. He seemed remarkably happy, Danny noted.

Just then the hall phone started to ring.

'Oh no! What if it's the letting agent?' Jewel exclaimed.

'What if she's ringing to say we have to move out?' Cat said, looking equally panic-stricken.

'Don't answer it, mate,' Darius said, as if he was the boss of him.

Purely to spite Darius, Danny got to his feet. 'It's OK, I'll take care of it.' He went out into the hallway and picked up the receiver. 'Hello?' he muttered, crossing his fingers.

'Danny, is that you?'

He breathed a sigh of relief at the sound of his manager, Johnny's voice.

'Hey Johnny, what's up?'

'I, er, have a visitor here for you.'

'What? Where? At your office?'

'Yep.'

'Who is it?'

'Your dad.'

Danny gripped the receiver to stop it falling from his hand. 'But ...' he broke off, the rest of the sentence remaining unsaid. *But my dad lives in*

Liverpool. But my dad and I aren't speaking. But my dad and I haven't seen each other for fifteen years.

All the way to work on the Tube, Jewel's anxiety grew. Thankfully, the phone call to the house this morning hadn't been from the letting agents – when Danny had returned to the kitchen ashen-faced, Jewel had been certain they were all about to be evicted. It turned out it was a false alarm and something else had spooked Danny, but surely it was only a matter of time before the letting agent got back in touch with them.

The train pulled in to Leicester Square station and Jewel joined the tide of people flowing out onto the platform and up the escalators. Somewhere in the depths of the station a busker was playing 'Lovely Day' by Bill Withers. Was it going to be a lovely day, though? If Jewel lost his room at 27 Diamond Street he didn't know what he'd do. It all felt so unfair. Just when he'd finally found a group of people he thought of as family, just when he'd found somewhere he could call home, it could all come tumbling down. And all because Danny had gone to the trouble of trying to find him a partner.

As Jewel rode up the escalator, sandwiched between an overweight business man in a straining pinstriped suit and a mum holding a crying toddler, he thought of Pablo. What if he never saw or heard from him again? What if Pablo had just seen it as a one-night thing? What if Jewel and his friends were all made homeless for no good reason? Pablo had been lovely when they'd woken up together on Monday morning, and he'd found the whole thing with Denise hugely entertaining, but Jewel hadn't heard anything from him since. Admittedly, it had only been twenty-four hours, but still. Jewel had given him the house phone number, written on the back of an old Tube ticket, which Pablo had carefully tucked inside his wallet. But he was hardly going to bin it in front of Jewel, was he? He probably waited until he got home, or maybe he even binned it on the way home.

Jewel felt overwhelmed with despair. For all the years he'd dreamed of meeting someone, he'd assumed that the minute you fell in love, or lust, or whatever this was, all of your problems, all of your angst would be over. He had no idea that it just prompted a brand new set of agonies. If he'd known then how desperate he'd feel now, he wouldn't have said anything to Danny. But then he'd never have had That Kiss. He'd never have felt Pablo's skin on his. He'd never have … He breathed in a lungful of musty London Underground air. He needed to get a grip.

By the time Jewel arrived at work he was completely convinced he was about to become officially homeless and horribly dumped.

'Blimey, what happened?' Alice asked from behind a huge bouquet of white lilies on the reception desk. 'You look like you just found out that Father Christmas doesn't exist.'

'It's not what's happened, it's what's *about* to happen,' Jewel replied glumly.

'OK, what's about to happen?'

'I'm about to be evicted, and dumped. Not that I was in a relationship to be dumped from. I'm about to be dumped from a one-night stand.'

Alice raised her thin eyebrows. 'The Spanish guy?'

'Pablo, yeah.' Jewel really wished he hadn't regaled her with all the details yesterday. Now he would have to endure double the humiliation.

'Hmm, what gives you that idea?' Alice asked, coming out from behind the reception desk

'I haven't heard from him since Sunday. And I know it's only been one day since I last saw him, but I've got a bad feeling about this. Everything seems to be –'

'All right, cool your jets,' Alice interrupted. 'This Pablo guy, is he about your height, dark brown hair, long fringe, insane eyelashes?'

'Yes, why?'

'He called by earlier. Left these for you.' She pointed to the bouquet of lilies.

'What? Are you serious?'

Alice nodded. 'So can you please stop freaking out and read the card. You have no idea how hard it's been for me not to steam that little envelope open.'

Jewel took the envelope from the bouquet and took out the tiny card inside. 'Thank you for a wonderful night. Cannot wait to sea you again,' it read. His pulse raced at the thought of Pablo writing those words to him.

'What does "sea" you mean?' Alice asked, reading over his shoulder. 'Does he want to dip you in the ocean or something?'

'It's a spelling mistake. English isn't his first language.'

'I'd say love is his first language.' Alice chortled, giving Jewel a playful nudge. 'Why were you stressing he was going to dump you? He's clearly into you. I've never had a guy buy me flowers before.'

'Really?' Jewel's elation grew. He was so used to feeling the massively inexperienced one in just about every social situation, it felt weird, but oh-so wonderful, to be the one being envied. 'Can I ask you a question?'

'Of course.' Alice breathed in the scent of the flowers.

'Is falling for someone … is it always so stressful?'

Alice laughed. 'It's definitely very extreme.'

Jewel nodded.

'But hey, that means extreme highs, too, you know. And they make all the stressy bits so worth it.'

Jewel smiled and picked up the flowers. Right now it felt very worth it indeed.

Cat moved the armchairs back as far as they would go and cleared the records from the living-room floor. Justin had gone back to bed, Darius was having a bath, and all of her other housemates had gone to work or their rooms, so she had the downstairs to herself. Her pep talk from Danny last night had left her all inspired, and she wanted to practise before her second audition with him this evening. She was acutely aware of how lucky she was to get another chance, and she didn't want to blow it. Cat had thought about what Danny had said last night and she wanted to pick something suitably empowering to dance to. She flicked through Lil's records and came to rest on an Aretha Franklin album. She put the record on the turntable and moved the needle to the track 'Sisters Are Doin' It for Themselves'.

As she began to dance she pictured shaking all of her doubts and fears from her body. First from her arms, then her legs and hips. She imagined them being shed onto the floor like old skin. Then she stomped all over them. She loved dancing like this, unseen and unguarded. As she sank deeper and deeper into her body she felt a weird sense of shame that she should have ever felt such resentment towards her body, that she should have wanted to starve it. But as she listened to the lyrics of the song the feelings of shame passed and a feeling of strength grew. It burned inside of her, primal and wild. She thought of the storyline of *Cinderella* – the story that had been told a million times in a million different guises. The message was always the same though – that a woman's main aim in life should be to wait for a man to save her. Well, as Aretha was belting out, she didn't need a man to save her. She needed to save herself.

The track came to an end and she leaned over to catch her breath, jumping as she heard someone clapping from the kitchen. She turned to see Lachlan sitting at the table.

'That was awesome,' he said, nodding in appreciation.

Her face flushed. 'How long were you there?'

'Pretty much from the beginning. I didn't want to interrupt you but I didn't want to stop watching, either.' He looked embarrassed. 'I'm sorry. I should have left.'

'No, no, it's OK. It's just that it wasn't exactly a polished performance.'

'I like you unpolished,' he said quietly. 'Do you fancy a cuppa?'

Part of her wanted nothing more than to sit down and drink tea with Lachlan, but the part that had just been unleashed by the dance wasn't ready to get back in its cage.

'I'd love one, but I'd better carry on practising. I have an audition with Danny tonight, for the panto.'

'I thought that was last night.'

'It was, but I messed up, so he's giving me another shot this evening.'

'Ah, I see.' Lachlan stood up. 'Well, if you dance like that you're gonna blow his mind.'

'Really?'

'For sure.' He grinned. 'Now I'll leave you in peace.'

'Lachlan,' she called after him as he turned to go.

'Yep?'

'How are you doing? Since Sunday night, I mean?'

'I've been great, really great.' His smile was warm and genuine.

'That's brilliant.' As she returned to the record player her body glowed with a warm wave of contentment.

Thirty-one

Danny stepped into the foyer of Zoom Talent, his agency, his stomach churning and his palms clammy. He hated the fact that, even after all these years, his dad still had the power to make him feel afraid. He cast a nervous glance around. Thankfully, all of the plush, leather-bound seats were empty. He wondered if his dad was still here, or if Johnny had asked him to wait elsewhere.

'I'm here to see Johnny, he's expecting me,' he told the receptionist, a shiny-haired, super-smiley lady named Becky. Normally he'd make small talk with Becky, but not today. Today, all of his energy was required to keep his anxiety at bay. He paced anxiously while he waited, the bouncy muzak being piped through the speakers in the ceiling doing little to calm him. The lift doors pinged open and Johnny appeared, bringing with him the rich scent of his aftershave.

'Danny!' Johnny greeted him with the usual hug and air kisses. 'Well, that was a bolt from the blue, your old man turning up here.'

'I know, I'm sorry. I have no idea how he found you. We're estranged. I haven't seen him for years.'

'Ah.' Johnny gave a sheepish grin. 'That might be down to me, I'm afraid.'

'What? How?'

'I sent a press release to the *Liverpool Echo* about your gig on *The Rocky Horror Picture Show*, you know, "Local Boy Done Good" kind of thing. They ran the story on Friday, and mentioned that I was your manager. I'm so sorry, I was meaning to tell you this week and send you the clipping.'

'I see. So where is he now?' A horrible thought occurred to Danny. 'You didn't tell him where I live, did you?'

'No, of course not. He said he'd wait for you in the pub on the corner.'

I bet he did, Danny thought, wryly. 'OK, thanks. Sorry you got caught up in this. I hope he wasn't rude.'

Johnny looked surprised. 'No, he was great. Very friendly and really interested in all of your achievements. He was very impressed with the review from the *Standard*. He saw the framed copy on my wall.'

'Seriously?' Danny felt a spark of something dangerously close to hope. He quickly quashed it. 'I'd better get going.'

'Sure. Have fun.'

Fun was the very last thing he was expecting to have, Danny thought to himself as he made his way back out to the street. At least his dad had been pleasant to Johnny, though. Maybe he'd mellowed with age. Maybe he'd turned over a new leaf. *Stop it!* he told himself. He'd spent the first eighteen years of his life hoping desperately for his dad to turn over a new leaf. He wasn't going to make that mistake again.

He pushed open the pub door and scanned the bar. A woman with a frazzled blonde perm was serving a couple of young guys in tracksuits, and an old man was sitting on a stool next to them. Danny looked around at the tables then did a double take. Was the old man his dad? Just at that moment, the man turned to look at him. The cropped hair was white now instead of jet black and the once broad shoulders were stooped, but there was no mistaking those pale blue eyes and that thin-lipped grin. Danny took a deep breath and made his way over.

'All right, Danny, lad.' His dad got down from the stool and held out his hand. 'Jesus, have I shrunk or have you grown?'

'Maybe a bit of both.' Danny shook his hand. His dad's grip felt weak, and Danny was in the weird position of looking down at him. In all of his memories of his dad, the man was looming over Danny. But not anymore. Danny relaxed a fraction.

'Can I get you a drink?' His dad's Scouse accent was as strong as ever.

'I'll just have a lime and soda. I've got to go to work shortly.' Danny waited for his dad to rib him for not having a beer, but to his surprise his father just nodded and got out his wallet.

'Good job, too. Price of beer down here ought to include shares in the pub.' He laughed his wheezy smoker's laugh. 'It's good to see you.'

Danny studied his face for any hint that he was lying, that there was some kind of sinister motive for this impromptu visit, but he couldn't see any. The grin seemed genuine.

They took their drinks over to a small table by the window and his dad took off his old leather jacket. The tattoos on his arms were faded and the once taut muscles on his arms had slackened. 'So, I saw the piece about you in the *Echo*.'

'Yes, Johnny told me.'

'You've come a long way, son.' He paused. 'Your mam would have been dead proud of you.'

But you're not? Danny felt like saying, but he knew better than to ask for trouble. 'Thank you.'

'So, this is what you do now, is it, this choreography business?'

'Yes. I've been doing it since my dance career ended.' Danny emphasized the words 'dance career' to make sure they registered. One of the more polite things his dad had said before he left home was that he'd never amount to anything as a 'faggot dancer'. Danny felt the sudden urge to yell, 'See, I did amount to something!' But he leaned back in his chair instead, reassuring himself that his dad had already got the message.

'Yer man in the agency place told me about the awards you've won.'

'Oh, right.' Danny couldn't help feeling pleased at Johnny's need to boast on his behalf. He wasn't sure if it was pitiful that a thirty-two-year-old man should still need to prove himself to his father, but he didn't care. He hadn't asked his dad to show up on his doorstep. 'So, what brings you down here?'

'Do I need a reason to come and see me own lad?'

Well, yes, in our case, you do, Danny thought. 'I suppose not,' he said through gritted teeth.

'I'd have come to see you much sooner if you hadn't done a disappearing act.' He picked up his pint and drained about a third of it in one go.

Danny felt a tightening in his throat. Had his dad conveniently forgotten the circumstances leading up to his departure? It was less a disappearing act and more an act of self-preservation.

His dad cleared his throat. 'Look, I'm sorry if I was a little heavy-handed when you were growing up. But you have to understand, it wasn't easy after your mam died, bringing up a kid on me own. She was my everything. I was lost without her.'

But you didn't bring me up, Danny wanted to say. *You were always out working on the docks or drinking yourself into a stupor in the pub. I brought myself up.*

'Anyway, you didn't turn out so badly, eh? I mean, look at you now with your fancy job and your fancy agent.'

And there it was, the sour undertone that had always been present in his dad's voice when talking to Danny. Danny's skin prickled with indignation. His dad had better not be implying that his brutal style of parenting was in any way to do with Danny's success. As far as Danny was concerned, he'd achieved his success *in spite* of his upbringing, not because of it. He looked at his watch. 'I'm sorry but I'm going to have to get off to work.'

'But you only just got here.'

Yes, well, I didn't invite you to come here, Danny wanted to say but once again he censored himself.

'OK, then, I'll cut to the chase.' His dad took another swig from his drink. 'I was wondering if you could lend me some money, seeing as you're doing so well for yourself.'

'What?' Danny stared at him.

'Could you lend me some cash?'

'Why?'

'I've got into a bit of bother. On the horses, like.'

'You want me to pay off your gambling debt?'

'I wouldn't ask if I wasn't desperate.' He put his pint down and stared at Danny. Feeling those cold, blue eyes boring into his caused Danny's mouth to go dry. He looked away. 'I've never asked you for anything. And I'll never ask again. Just a couple of grand's all I need.'

'No,' Danny said quietly.

'What?'

'I said, no.' Danny got to his feet. His knees were trembling but he knew he mustn't show fear.

'You're not going to help your own father?' His dad raised his voice, causing the woman behind the bar to look over.

'No, I'm not.'

'After all I did for you?'

Danny's fear was replaced with a red-hot fury. 'And what, exactly, did you do for me? Batter me black and blue all through my childhood. Put me down at every opportunity.'

'Now listen, son ...' His dad stood up.

'No, you listen.' Danny stood tall and stared back, unflinching. 'As far as I'm concerned, I don't have a father, and I don't owe you anything.'

He turned and marched back out of the pub and down the street. It was only when he was running down the stairs into the Underground that his eyes filled with tears.

Lachlan looked at the large pot bubbling away on the oven and gave a contented sigh. It might have been almost two years since he'd made one of his legendary chillies but, like riding a bike, it was clearly impossible to forget. He'd even remembered to add his secret ingredient to the mix, a generous slosh of beer. He closed his eyes and breathed in the spicy aroma. He'd made a huge pot in case any of his housemates were hungry. If not, he'd batch up a load to see him through the week.

Ha! Get you, batching up food, he imagined Michelle playfully teasing and he grinned.

'Wow, something smells delicious,' a voice called through from the living room, causing Lachlan to jump. He peered through the archway to see Darius reclined on the sofa beneath a duvet.

'Strewth, mate! You made me jump.'

'Sorry, I was just having a snooze. Don't suppose you've got any grub going spare, have you? I'm starving.'

'Maybe.' Lachlan returned to the stove shaking his head. He wasn't sure why Danny had let this bludger crash on their sofa, it wasn't as if the residents didn't have enough to worry about. There'd been no sign of an eviction notice in the mail today, but surely it was only a matter of time. He wasn't entirely sure what good a house makeover would do, either – it seemed like a case of shutting the stable door after the horse had bolted. He took a taste of the chilli and added a sprinkle of nutmeg.

The kitchen door opened and Cat walked in. Lachlan's heart skipped a beat. Then Justin came in. Lachlan's heart sank.

'Do you really think it's fair, though?' Justin said.

'What do you mean?' Cat nodded at Lachlan and turned on the kettle.

'Well, why should you get a chance to have a second audition with Danny when the rest of us can't?'

'He knew I didn't give my best performance.' Cat took a couple of mugs from the cupboard.

'Yeah, but one of the other dancers mightn't have given their best performance, either. I definitely didn't exactly give the performance of my career but I wouldn't have dreamed of asking Danny for another go.'

Lachlan turned back to stir the chilli. Jeez, he hated that whiny bastard.

'You looked fine to me,' Cat said.

'Yeah, well, that's because I don't like making a big drama of things.'

Yeah, right, thought Lachlan.

'Yeah, right,' Cat muttered, in an uncanny echo of Lachlan's thought. Lachlan shot her a sideways glance. Her face looked like thunder.

'I just didn't think you'd be that desperate,' Justin said, taking a banana from the fruit bowl. One of *Lachlan's* bananas.

'Hey, mate, those are my bananas,' Lachlan said, with what was meant to be a friendly grin but felt more like a grimace.

'Yeah, well, I'm sure you won't miss one.'

To Lachlan's fury, Justin peeled the banana and took a bite.

'Actually, I do mind.'

'Justin!' Cat hissed.

'What?'

'You can't just take other people's food.'

'It's a banana, for God's sake.' Justin shoved the half-eaten banana back in the bowl. 'Happy?' he scowled at Lachlan.

'No, as it happens, I'm not happy at all.' Lachlan clenched his fists. He was going to wipe the smirk off that arrogant idiot's face if it was the last thing he did.

The door opened and Danny swept in.

'Hi,' he said curtly, not making eye contact with anyone and heading straight to the fridge.

'Hey, Danny,' Justin replied. 'Any word on the casting.'

'What?' Danny gave him a withering look.

Good, Lachlan thought. He was glad he wasn't the only one who thought Justin was a cretin.

'I was just wondering if I'd got a role in the panto.'

'Oh.' Danny took a can of coke from the fridge. 'Yes, you have.'

'Yes!' Justin punched the air with delight. Then he hugged Cat. Lachlan was relieved to see she remained as unresponsive as a statue. 'You won't regret it, mate. I'll do you proud.'

'You're one of the footmen,' Danny replied.

Judging from Justin's frown this clearly wasn't what he'd wanted to hear.

'One of the footmen?' he echoed.

'Yes.' Danny headed back over to the door.

'But that's only a minor role.'

'I know.'

'But you saw me dance yesterday. You know what I'm capable of.'

Justin was pouting like a spoiled child. This was getting painful – and Lachlan was loving every second of it. He turned back to the saucepan to hide his smirk.

'Oh, I know what you're capable of,' Danny said. 'I messaged your director in Berlin the other day to get a reference. He got back to me today, told me the real reason you left the show. So if I were you I'd be grateful you've been cast at all.' Danny turned to Cat. 'I'll meet you down here in half an hour to go to the White Lion.'

'Sure.'

Danny left the room and an awkward silence fell.

'What did he mean, the real reason you left the show?' Cat asked.

Justin's face flushed a deep shade of red. 'It was nothing. The director and I had a difference of opinion. Can we talk about this upstairs?'

'No, I want to know now. What kind of difference of opinion?'

'OK, if you must know, he was a total dictator. He couldn't accept that I had better ideas than him. And now he's ruined things for me all over again.'

'So you didn't come back because you were missing me?' Cat said softly.

'Oh, for God's sake, why does everything always have to be about you?'

'Don't talk to her like that,' Lachlan said.

'It's none of your business how I talk to her.'

'I think you'll find that it is.'

'Stop it,' Cat said.

'Oh, yeah, and why is that?' Justin stared at him.

Lachlan put down his spoon. 'Because I care about her.'

'Oh, really?' Justin sneered.

'Please!' Cat said, louder this time.

'Yes, really.' Lachlan took a step closer to Justin.

'Well, you're wasting your time, mate. She only gives you the time of day because she feels sorry for you.'

'Shut up!' Cat snapped.

'Is that so?' All of the anger Lachlan had been brewing towards Justin came bubbling to the brim. 'That's not how it felt when I was kissing her the other day!' As soon as he said it, Lachlan knew he'd made a mistake.

Not because he was worried about Justin, but because he'd hurt Cat.

'Unbelievable!' Cat looked from him to Justin and back again, fury etched into her face. 'Do you know what? You can both go to hell.' And with that, she stormed from the room.

'Wow. Never a dull moment,' Darius said, trudging into the kitchen with his duvet draped round him like a cape.

Thirty-two

As Cat made her way down Camden High Street she wasn't just angry. She was livid. She was incandescent. She was fuming – she needed a thesaurus to capture all the multitude ways in which she was sick of men.

'Are you OK?' Danny asked as she kicked an empty beer can from her path.

'Yes. No, not really. Are you?'

Danny hadn't said a word since they'd left the house, either, and from the pace at which he was walking he clearly didn't seem chilled.

'Let's just say I've had a very trying day.'

'I'm sorry. I hope this isn't a pain – having to give me a second audition.'

'It will only be a pain if you mess it up again.'

Right, no pressure then. Cat dodged one of the dealers hanging around outside the station, his baseball cap pulled low, muttering about his wares. 'Coke, whizz, E?' After what had just happened with Justin and Lachlan, Cat was hardly in the best frame of mind for dancing. Or maybe she was in the perfect frame of mind – if she could just channel constructively the rage she was feeling. Danny wanted a kick-ass Cinderella, didn't he?

Maybe that's exactly what she could give him.

'Can I ask you something? What made you get in touch with Justin's director in Berlin?' she asked, as they made their way down the side street leading to the theatre.

'I had a hunch,' Danny replied, taking a bunch of keys from his pocket.

'A hunch about what?'

He stopped and looked at her. 'There are two types of dancer in this world – those who work for the good of the show and those who work for the good of themselves. I'm not interested in directing the latter – I had enough of that bullshit back when I was a dancer. And I definitely need team players for this project.'

'And you had a hunch that Justin wasn't a team player.'

He nodded.

Cat thought back to the cruise ship shows she'd worked on with Justin. At first she'd been attracted to what she'd perceived as his confidence, but was it really just arrogance? He'd always wanted to be the star of the show back then. He'd never really been interested in helping the others. When he'd shone his attention on her she'd felt flattered. Now this made her feel slightly stupid.

Danny unlocked the door on the side of the pub leading to the theatre upstairs. 'I've worked with Sven, the guy directing the show in Berlin. He's a good guy. I trust his judgement. He sacked Justin because of his bad attitude. To be honest, I'm only casting him at all because you guys are a couple and I didn't want to cause any friction in the house.'

'We're not a couple,' Cat blurted out.

'What?' He turned and stared at her.

'It's over, or at least it will be as soon as I get home this evening.'

They went upstairs and Danny turned on the lights. 'I'm not being funny, darling, but are you sure?' Danny asked.

'About what?'

'About it being over with Justin. I'm getting *déjà vu*.'

'I'm certain. I never should have got back with him when he came home from Berlin. It's just that he told me he'd come home for me, because he was missing me, and Michelle-gate had just happened and I was feeling all confused – Jewel told me that's what you've been calling it, by the way.'

Danny grinned. 'It did feel on a par with Watergate.'

'Well, let's just say that Berlin-gate is the final straw.'

'Or the final gate,' Danny said.

Cat laughed. 'Yep. No more gates for me!'

She took a CD from her bag. She'd nipped down to the market earlier to get the Aretha Franklin album. 'I have a track I'd like to dance to for you.'

Danny nodded and took a seat in the front row. Cat went up on the stage and put the CD in the stereo. She gazed out at the rows of empty seats behind Danny. She thought of all the shows that had gone on in the theatre over the years, all of the laughter and surprise and applause, all of the joy this place had brought to people. The thought of playing a part in keeping it open felt like such a privilege. And she wanted more than ever to do Danny proud.

She lined up the track and pressed play. As the opening notes rang out she pictured herself as Cinderella – a very alternative Cinderella – full of wildness and courage, not needing a Prince Charming or a glass slipper. She fell into the routine she'd worked out in the living room that afternoon. A fusion of gentle ballet building to explosive street moves – depicting Cinderella's journey from downtrodden stepsister to powerful woman. And finally – *finally* – she was able to tap into the primal energy she'd experienced that night in Heaven. She was a superhero, a sister doing it for herself, just like Aretha and Annie Lennox. She didn't need Justin and she didn't need Lachlan. All she needed in that moment was to pour everything she had into her dance.

By the time the track came to an end she was covered in sweat. But it felt good – cleansing, as if she'd purged her system of Justin and all the myriad ways he made her doubt herself. She stood at the edge of the stage gasping for breath, looking at Danny. He sat completely motionless and expressionless and for a horrible moment she thought she'd got it all wrong. But then, finally, he spoke.

'Darling, that was fabulous!' He stood up. 'Why the hell couldn't you have done that last night? It was like watching a different person. You were on fire.'

'Sorry if it was a bit much.' She made her way down from the stage. 'I can tone it down a bit if you want, I ...'

Danny shook his head. 'Stop apologizing, it was great. Great song choice, too. All that singing about sisters really got me thinking ...'

'Oh, yeah?' Cat fetched her towel from her bag and wiped the sweat from her face.

'What if we turn everything on its head? What if Cinders gets the ugly sisters to see the error of their ways and they end the panto united? I could choreograph a routine to that song for all three of you.'

A shiver of excitement ran up Cat's spine. 'All three of us? Does that mean I've got the part?'

Danny nodded. 'On condition that you only dance like that from now on. No more doubting yourself, do you hear?'

'Yes, yes, of course! Oh, Danny, thank you! You won't regret this, I promise!' Cat threw her arms round him.

'Steady on, darling, this shirt cost me a fortune, I don't want it covered in sweat!'

'Sorry.' Cat backed away, grinning. 'This is going to be so great. You're going to do such a great job. And Lil's going to love the new sisterhood storyline.'

Danny laughed. 'I was actually thinking of asking her to be one of the ugly sisters – well, trying out for the part at least. Apparently she spent the winter of seventy-nine learning to method act from Bob Hoskins.'

Cat giggled. 'Do you think any of her stories are true?'

Danny shook his head. 'The only story of hers that I believe is that she did a shedload of acid back in the sixties – and she's still tripping. But there's no denying she's a total drama queen and I feel like she could probably rock an ugly sister role.'

'Me too.' Cat hugged herself to try and contain her excitement. She had another dancing job. And not only that, she had a lead role!

Danny switched off the theatre lights and locked the door. He and Cat had spent almost three hours workshopping ideas for *Cinderella* and, as always, he was emerging from his dance cocoon feeling born again. Seeing his dad in the morning had left him wrung out – years of traumatic memories he'd worked so hard to forget flooding into his consciousness, making him realize that they'd never been truly forgotten, only stuffed away. But being able to throw himself into the joy of creation and building a story through dance had enabled him to return to himself. It had helped that Cat had clearly undergone some kind of transformation, too. Her dance to 'Sisters Are Doin' It for Themselves' had blown his socks off. Seeing her up on that stage so raw and untamed had given him just the spark of inspiration he needed.

As they made their way out onto the street he looked up at the night sky, stained amber from the London light pollution, and he smiled. Seeing his dad might have thrown him straight back into his childhood – but that was the past. Here, in the present, he was a million miles away from the days when he'd been at the mercy of his dad's cruel tongue, foul temper and drunken rants. He was the strong one now, the one who was able to walk away. Seeing his dad so shrunken and faded had placed a new filter on his memories. Danny was no longer the victim. He was the hero of his story.

'Are you OK?' Cat asked as they headed back towards the high street.

'Yeah, yeah, I'm great. Thanks for all of your hard work tonight.'

Cat laughed. 'It didn't feel like hard work at all, it felt …' she broke off and smiled at him. 'I haven't felt so alive in ages.'

Danny nodded. Again he thought of his dad, stumbling through his days from bookies to boozer and back again, merely existing rather than living. He, Danny, was the lucky one. He wasn't just living, he was living his dream.

They walked on in companionable silence, accompanied by the usual Camden soundtrack of car horns and sirens and the occasional burst of music and laughter drifting from the pubs. When they got back to Diamond Street Cat smiled at him nervously.

'Right, I guess it's time for me to sort out Justin-gate.'

Danny laughed. 'Good luck, darling.' He gave her a hug and went up to his room. He threw his bag down on the floor and looked at the faded photo of his mother on his bedside table. He sat down on the bed and picked up the picture. *'Your mam would have been proud of you.'* His dad's words from earlier echoed through his head. It was a surprising thing for him to have said. And then a thought occurred to Danny. Was that his dad's clumsy way of saying that he was proud of Danny, too? Did his stubborn pride mean he could only say it indirectly? Danny sighed. He looked at the photo of his mum and he wondered all over again how things might have turned out if she hadn't died. He only had a handful of clear memories from before her death. But in all of them his dad was sober and happy. He thought back to his dad in the pub earlier. How his eyes had turned glassy when he talked about Danny's mam, when he'd said, 'She was my everything. I was lost without her.'

Now Danny's eyes filled with tears. 'Why did you have to leave us,' he whispered to the picture. Then he put it back and went over to the antique bureau by the window. He opened it up and took out his chequebook, and wrote a cheque to his dad for two thousand pounds.

Cat crept past the sleeping form of Darius on the sofa and out into the backyard. She sat down on one of the chairs and took a sip of her camomile tea. She needed a moment to gather herself, compose her thoughts. When she'd first found out that Justin had lied to her about his reasons for leaving Berlin she'd felt hurt and humiliated, but not anymore. Something had happened tonight on the darkened stage in the White Lion. A metamorphosis that had begun that night on the dance floor in Heaven had been completed. After months of doubt and confusion, she felt clarity. Dancing for and with Danny tonight had reminded her of how she'd felt when she'd first started dancing as a kid. That sense of freedom and possibility, before her mind had been poisoned with thoughts of age and body image.

She looked up and could vaguely make out a star in the sky, which instantly made her think of Lachlan. When he'd told Justin that they'd kissed she'd felt so disappointed. The two men squaring up to each other, using her to score some kind of point against the other man, had been irritating as hell. She'd expected more from Lachlan. But it didn't matter. Like Danny's version of Cinderella, she didn't need a Prince Charming to save her. She could see now that this was where she'd gone wrong with Justin, falling into his shadow. From now on, this sister was doing it for herself.

She finished her tea and made her way upstairs. Part of her had hoped that Justin had been so outraged at the kiss revelation that he would have stormed off to his parents', but she came into the room to find him sat on the bed watching TV. He picked up the remote and turned it off.

'I've been doing a lot of thinking,' he said, 'and I'm willing to forgive you.'

Cat stared at him incredulously.

'But we'll have to move out of here. I've had a word with my parents and they're fine about us moving back in. They've said we can come back in the morning. Obviously we can't stay here – with him.'

'No,' Cat said, coming to stand at the end of the bed.

'Great. I'll ask my dad to come and pick us up first thing.'

'No, I won't be going back there with you.'

'What?'

'It's over, Justin. We're over.'

'Hang on, wait, you're finishing with me?'

'Yes.'

He shook his head. 'Oh my God, are you dumping me for that – that Neanderthal freak downstairs?'

'No, I'm not.' To Cat's surprise it felt strangely liberating to say this.

'Then what the hell is this about?'

'It's about me.'

He looked at her blankly.

'I don't want to be with anyone right now, I want to focus on my dancing.'

Justin gave a sarcastic snort of laughter.

'What's so funny?'

'You think that because your housemate has given you a part in a crappy panto that isn't even paid work you've hit the big time?'

'No, I …'

'You only got the chance to audition again because he's your housemate,' Justin interrupted. 'If you had what it takes, you'd have made it by now, Cat, but you're twenty-five.'

'Yeah, well, at least I'm not an arrogant arsehole.'

'What?'

'You heard me. And has it ever occurred to you that the reason you might have more luck getting jobs is because you're a man so there's a lot less competition?'

'What are you talking about?'

'There are always twice as many women as men at any audition.' She opened the door. 'Now can you please go?'

'What? But it's the middle of the night.'

'It's eleven o'clock. The Tube is still running. Or get your parents to come and pick you up. I don't care how you go, I just want you gone.'

'Shh! You'll wake everyone.' He got up from the bed. 'Can't we just be reasonable, figure things out?'

'I've figured things out and I want you to go!' Cat was yelling now but she didn't care. It felt great to finally unleash all of her pent-up anger at him. For all the times he had belittled her and made her doubt herself, and so often without her even realizing.

'Cat, for goodness' sake. You're acting like someone from a council estate!'

Cat stared at him, horrified. It was as if Justin had morphed into some weird hybrid of his parents. She had a sudden flash forward into his future. Justin middle-aged and sporting a paunch, setting off for a day at the golf club. It was a future she would thankfully not be playing any part in.

'Get out!' she said again.

'But what about my things? How do you expect me to carry them all?'

Cat marched over to Justin's chest of drawers. 'I'll give you a hand.' She scooped up an armful of his T-shirts, marched over to the landing and threw them down the stairs.

'What the hell has got into you? OK, OK, I'm going.' He grabbed his suitcase and filled it with the rest of his clothes. 'You'll regret this you know,' he hissed as he started going downstairs. 'You'll never get anyone like me again.'

Cat felt high on anger and adrenalin. 'I really hope so,' she yelled after him.

A light came on in the hallway and Darius appeared like some kind of spectre, his duvet draped around his shoulders. 'What's all the noise about?' He looked at the pile of clothes on the floor and Justin shoving them into his case. 'Blimey, this place has got more plot twists than *EastEnders*,' he said, as Justin stormed out of the house.

Cat went into her room and shut the door behind her, leaning against it to support her trembling legs. She'd done it. She was a free woman. She was a sister doing it for herself. Tears of relief slid down her face.

November 1994

Thirty-three

Jewel looked across the restaurant table at Pablo and raised his glass. 'Happy birthday!'

'It is the happiest birthday in my life ever, ever!' Pablo replied with a grin. One thing Jewel had learned in the two months they'd been together was that Pablo was a master in the art of dramatic proclamations – made all the more dramatic by his Spanish accent. 'And it is my favourite birthday ever because I am spending it with my favourite person and my favourite onion bhajis!'

Jewel giggled. He and Pablo had eaten at the Seven Spices Tandoori when they'd come to Brick Lane on their first official date. It was hard to believe that was two months ago. Two months that had flown by in a haze of costume-making for Danny, work and late-night drinks in West End bars with Pablo after work, then catching the night bus home to Diamond Street for hardly any sleep with Pablo. Jewel still had to pinch himself every day that he had been this lucky; that the first person he'd fallen for had fallen for him, too. Cat said she thought Pablo was Jewel's penguin – his mate for life. Jewel didn't dare entertain such a bold hope, but with every day that passed, he felt his anxiety fade as his closeness to Pablo grew.

To make things even better, there'd been no word from the letting agents since the dreadful house inspection, so he'd begun to relax on that front, too. And now that Justin had left, tensions in the house had gone. Even the fact that Darius was still sleeping on the sofa wasn't fazing Jewel.

'You look amazing tonight,' Pablo said, leaning across the table and lowering his voice. 'I love white on you.'

'Thank you.' As well as being Pablo's birthday it was the first night of Danny's panto later, so Jewel had wanted to make a special effort. He'd gone to Camden Market earlier and bought a pair of white Guess dungarees, which he was wearing with one strap down, over a glittery silver polo top.

'You look very sexy.' Pablo placed his hand on top of Jewel's on the table.

A raucous bellow of laughter rang out from the table behind them, causing Jewel to jump.

'Oi, can we get some more beers over 'ere!' a man yelled. His voice was gruff with a strong East London twang. The kind of voice that instantly conjured the image of a shaven head and tattoos in Jewel's mind. As one of the waiters hurried over to the man's table, Jewel instinctively drew his hand away from Pablo's.

'Would you like your birthday present?' he asked, trying to feign another, more positive reason for his withdrawal.

'Of course.' Pablo grinned.

Jewel reached into his pocket and took out the gift. He'd wrapped it in gold paper, complete with a scarlet bow. He hoped it didn't seem too much. It was hard to gauge what to get someone you'd been going out with for two months. It was a long enough time to warrant a gift but not long enough for anything that could be deemed too intense. Pablo's face lit up like an excited kid's as he took the present.

'Oi, mate, these poppadoms are soggy!' the man behind them yelled.

'Yeah, sort it out,' another voice said. It was the kind of voice that was ripe with pent-up aggression, and it caused a shiver to run down Jewel's spine.

'Oh, this is beautiful,' Pablo gasped as he unwrapped the present.

'It's a mood ring,' Jewel explained. He'd found the ring at the market earlier that day. The stone was oval-shaped, set in silver. He knew that buying someone a ring could definitely be construed as a little intense, but he was hoping that the mood element added just the right amount of levity.

Pablo put the ring on his finger. 'It is turning red, what does that mean?'

Jewel took the piece of paper that had come with the ring from his pocket. 'It means you are passionate,' he said with a grin.

'This place is shit,' the gruff voice behind them barked.

Again, Jewel felt a wave of dread, but Pablo appeared unfazed.

'I certainly am passionate,' he said with a grin, before standing up, leaning over, and kissing Jewel on top of his head.

'Fucking poof,' the man with the pent-up voice said, causing Jewel's blood to freeze. The aroma of onions and spices that permeated the restaurant and had been making him drool now made him feel sick. He glanced to the back of the restaurant for any sign of the waiter bringing their food. The sooner they were out of there and back in Camden for the first night of Danny's panto, the better.

'Where the hell is Jewel?' Danny asked, pacing up and down the theatre dressing room. He couldn't bear lateness at the best of times, but on a first night, when tensions ran so high, it was unforgivable.

'I'm sure he'll be here soon,' Cat replied, getting into her first costume, a wonderfully pauperish creation Jewel had fashioned from bin-liners and old sacking. 'He and Pablo were having their birthday dinner really early. There's no way he wouldn't be here for your big night.'

Danny nodded. Cat was right. Of course she was. His first-night nerves were kicking in and he had to be really careful not to show it. As the director as well as one of the stars, he had to maintain a calm centre for the rest of the cast.

'Oh, sweetheart, I haven't been this excited since Jimi and I French-kissed at Woodstock,' Lil exclaimed, bustling into the room.

'Oh, for God's sake!' Danny muttered. Unfortunately, his first-night nerves had left little tolerance for Lil and her trippy tales.

'What?' Lil sat down in front of one of the mirrors.

'You and your flights of fancy, darling.'

'They're not flights of fancy I ...'

'Did you remember to bring your potpourri, Lil?' Cat interrupted, clearly trying to keep the peace. 'The one with the soothing lavender?'

'Sorry, darling,' Danny said, giving Lil's arm a squeeze. 'It's just that so much is riding on tonight, and the cock-up with the lights in the tech rehearsal has got me all on edge.' At the tech the night before, the strobes had failed during the alternative ball rave scene. The lighting engineer had sworn that the problem was fixed, but Danny couldn't help thinking it was some kind of omen.

'Here we go,' Lil said, producing a Tupperware box of her home-made potpourri from her bag. She took off the lid and wafted the box under Danny's nose. 'Take a sniff of that, sweetheart. I put some sandalwood in there, too. It's great for calming the nerves.'

Danny inhaled deeply. Much as he hated to admit it, it did smell good. He needed to get a grip. It was really bad form to show fear in front of his cast members. That was the kind of thing Johannes did.

'Thank you so much for all of your hard work,' he said. 'You're both going to be fabulous.' Oh, how he hoped this would be true.

'Thank you. And you are, too,' Cat said, giving him a hug.

Danny had ended up casting himself as one of the ugly sisters. It had been years since he'd dressed in drag, and rehearsals had been a lot of fun. But now he was wondering whether casting himself had been the greatest idea. It was giving him double reasons for getting nervous.

Just then Maureen, the make-up woman, came into the room on a waft of perfume, pulling her wheeled case of make-up behind her.

'Hello, lovelies,' she said. 'Are you ready to put your faces on?'

Danny nodded and sat down. Everything was going to be OK, he told himself. If only he could shake his horrible sense of foreboding.

'That was the best birthday meal I have ever eaten in all of my life!' Pablo said, as they got up to leave the restaurant.

'That's great.' As Jewel stood up and turned to the door he finally saw the men sitting at the table behind them. Just as he'd imagined, they were shaven-headed and barrel-chested like pitbulls. The larger man, who had prison-style tattoos all over his hands, glared up at him.

Jewel quickly looked away.

'Thank you very much, have a good evening,' one of the waiters said, hurrying over to show them to the door.

'We had a wonderful evening,' Pablo said loudly – far too loudly as far as Jewel was concerned. All he wanted was to slink out of there completely unnoticed.

'Poof,' the large man muttered as they drew level with the men's table.

Just get to the door and get out of here, Jewel said to himself. But Pablo was now standing dead still.

'What did you say?' he asked.

'I said poof,' the man snarled. His mate laughed. An inane simpleton's laugh.

'Come on,' Jewel said, tugging on Pablo's arm.

'Ah, look! Your boyfriend wants you,' the other man sniggered.

'So what if he is my boyfriend?' Pablo flicked back his fringe, his green eyes sparking with anger. 'It is none of your business.'

Jewel internally groaned. What was Pablo doing?

'Oh, it is my business, mate, especially when you lot shove it in my face.'

'What do I shove in your face?' Pablo asked indignantly. His back was ruler-straight, his shoulders back, in full flamenco stance.

'Come on, let's go,' Jewel tried again.

'Your perversions,' the large man said.

'Yeah, pervert,' the other man added. Originality was clearly not his strong suit.

'I am no pervert,' Pablo said, his accent growing stronger. Then he yelled something at the men in Spanish.

'Can we please go?' Jewel pleaded.

'Yes, everyone, please, calm down,' the waiter said, looking as panic-stricken as Jewel felt.

'Go on, you heard what he said, do one!' the man growled.

Pablo sighed, then to Jewel's relief, he stormed over to the door. Jewel followed, almost tripping over his own feet in his haste.

Night had fallen now, and all along Brick Lane waiters stood outside their curry houses, trying to tempt people in. Jewel felt his dinner churning inside of him.

'Wow, that was pretty scary,' he said, running to keep up as Pablo strode off along Brick Lane.

'Why did you not stand up for yourself?' Pablo turned to him, glaring.

'What?'

'Just then. Why did you let them talk to us in that way?'

Er, because I didn't want to die, Jewel wanted to say. Instead, he shrugged. 'I didn't want to cause any trouble.'

'They were the ones causing the trouble. We did nothing wrong.'

'I know but …' Shame flooded through Jewel, burning hot in his cheeks. He'd seemed pitiful in front of Pablo – timid and weak.

'I'm sorry. I just didn't want us to get hurt.'

'Well, I am hurt,' Pablo said. 'I'm hurt that you didn't stand with me.' He stopped walking. He looked so hurt and angry that Jewel had to look away.

'I have to get to work,' Pablo added.

'OK. Will I see you after? Will you be coming to Danny's after-party?'

Pablo frowned. 'I don't know. I'm tired.' He brushed his fringe from his eyes. Jewel noticed that the stone in the mood ring had turned jet black. 'I'll see how I feel, OK?'

'OK.' Jewel felt as if the foundation of his world had been pulled out from under him, and it took his breath away how quickly it had happened. One minute he and Pablo couldn't have been happier, the next, this. And all because of someone else's bigotry. It seemed so unfair.

'See you,' Pablo muttered, before turning and heading across the street.

Jewel stood rooted to the spot. He wanted to yell after Pablo to stop, afraid that if he didn't he might never see Pablo again. But what could he say? How could he make things different? He looked at his watch. Crap! Now he was going to be late for Danny. He'd have to hope that Pablo would calm down and that they'd have a chance to sort things out later.

Jewel turned down a side street to take a shortcut to the station. As he left the lights and smells and chatter of Brick Lane, he remembered that it was the street where Jack the Ripper had killed one of his victims. When he and Pablo had come to Brick Lane on their first date they'd ended up tagging along on the back of a guided Jack the Ripper tour. In the heady buzz of a first date it had seemed like a fun thing to do, but tonight the street was empty, the old-fashioned streetlights pooling their dim glow upon the pavement, and Jewel shivered as he thought of what had happened here all those years ago. He heard the sound of footsteps behind him and breathed a sigh of relief.

'Oi, poof, I want a word with you.'

The voice caused a chill of dread to surge through Jewel. Without looking back he began to run.

The footsteps behind him became faster, louder. Jewel felt a hand grab his dungarees and wrench him backwards.

He turned to see the men from the restaurant. The larger one was holding him. The other one, the one with the voice of pure, cold aggression, came so close that Jewel could see the blackheads on his nose. 'I think it's time we taught you a lesson,' the man sneered, his breath hot and beery in Jewel's face.

Thirty-four

Cat waited in the wings, breathless and excited, as Danny and Lil performed their slapstick comedy ugly sisters' routine. It was the moment in the panto where the sisters realized that the hapless Prince Charming – played oh-so convincingly by Darius – was an idiotic waste of space. Judging by the roars of laughter and cheers ringing around the theatre, the crowd was loving it.

As Cat waited for her cue to go on and dance to 'Sisters Are Doin' It for Themselves', she allowed the magic of the moment to sink in. Barring any last-minute disaster, the first night was a huge success, in spite of Jewel being a no-show. Cat couldn't believe Jewel hadn't turned up, or hadn't even thought to call the theatre from a pay phone to let them know that he was staying out with Pablo. Danny had tried to brush it off, but she could tell he'd been hurt. Still, they'd all managed to dress themselves, and there'd been a real spirit of camaraderie in the dressing room. Everyone was really fired up to help Danny and save the White Lion Theatre from closure. It had been a momentous occasion for Cat, too – the first professional performance of her life where she'd found the courage to really let go and dance from the heart, as Danny called it. Performing with Danny and Lil had been a blast, too.

Hearing her cue, she strode out on to the stage in her alternative Cinderella attire of gold hot pants and neon green boob tube.

'Let the fun and games begin!' Danny cried as he led the other cast members into the Lemon Tree.

Stelios had very kindly let him have the restaurant for free for the first-night after-party. All of the tables had been pushed back to the sides, and the bar was crammed with a dazzling array of finger food. Danny's mouth instantly started to water at the smell of the mini kebabs, stuffed mushrooms and dolmades. He'd been so full of adrenalin all day he'd barely been able to eat a thing. Now his appetite was back with a vengeance.

'Tuck in, everyone,' he called, leading the charge on the food.

He was so happy and relieved that even the sight of Achilles smirking at him from behind the bar couldn't put him off. It was the first time he'd seen Achilles since cider-bath-gate, as Jewel called it. Thinking of Jewel, Danny frowned. He couldn't help feeling hurt that Jewel hadn't shown up for the first night. He got that the young man was head over heels in love with Pablo, but still, he was meant to be Danny's wardrobe manager. And if it hadn't been for Danny, Jewel wouldn't have even met Pablo. Danny pushed this thought from his mind and helped himself to a chicken kebab.

'Good evening, madam, can I get you a drink?' Achilles grinned from behind the bar, no doubt thinking this was a hilarious reference to the fact that Danny was still in drag.

'Evening,' Danny replied coolly. There was no way Achilles was going to embarrass him. 'Can I have glass of red, please?'

'Of course. So, how was the show?' Achilles reached for a bottle of red, the broad outline of his shoulders visible beneath his crisp white shirt.

Damn him and his broad shoulders! Danny looked away.

'The show was magnificent!' came a voice from behind him.

Danny turned to see Johnny beaming at him. 'Thank you, darling.'

'I had a feeling it would be,' Achilles said, passing Danny his drink. As Danny took the glass their fingers brushed, and he felt a sharp bolt of energy pass between them. He glanced at Achilles, who was staring at him intently. Danny's gaydar bleeped. What the hell? He had to be imagining things. He was probably so weak from hunger he was starting to hallucinate. Danny shoved a stuffed mushroom into his mouth.

'I must come to this show of yours,' Achilles said, still staring at him intently.

'You really must,' Johnny said, oblivious to the undercurrent passing between Danny and Achilles. 'It's a *Cinderella* like no other. You're a genius, darling.'

'Thank you.' Danny felt a huge wave of relief. Johnny wasn't one for false praise. That's one of the things he liked most about him, both as a manager and a friend. There was never any bullshit.

'I'm telling you, if you get the right people to come along and see it, this could do wonders for your career. For Cinderella's, too. She was amazing.'

Danny nodded. Cat really had done herself proud. He couldn't help feeling a slight hint of pride, too, at the thought that he'd helped coax her inner warrior princess out of her shell. He scanned the room for Cat and saw her laughing her head off with Lil. Even Darius had done brilliantly, which went some way towards compensating for the fact that he'd now been crashing on their sofa for two whole months.

'Maybe I'll go and have a word with Cat,' Johnny said. 'See if she'd be interested in Zoom Talent representing her.'

Danny nodded. 'I bet she'd love that.'

'It is weird to see you in your clothes,' Achilles said, as he poured a beer.

What the hell? Danny frowned. Was Achilles flirting with him? He'd shown no interest before. Maybe he liked a guy in drag or something.

'Yes, well, I apologize for any trauma my bath might have caused.'

'Oh no, it didn't cause any trauma.' Achilles grinned. 'It was the opposite.'

Danny frowned. What was the opposite of trauma? Bliss? Whatever, he wasn't in the mood for playing games, so he decided to throw down the gauntlet. 'Yeah, well, maybe you could join me next time.'

'There will be a next time?' Achilles looked so interested at this prospect, he forgot about the beer he was pouring and it flowed over the glass.

'Of course,' Danny replied. Now he knew he wasn't imagining things. The air between them crackled with tension.

Just then, the phone behind the bar began to ring. *Damn it,* Danny thought. Just when things were getting interesting. He watched Achilles turn to take the call, and checked out the contour of the barman's butt in his figure-hugging black trousers. What had seemed so off limits for so long was suddenly a tantalizing possibility, making the whole thing even more exciting.

'It is for you,' Achilles said, turning back and holding out the receiver.

'For me?' Danny frowned. Why would anyone be calling him at the Lemon Tree? Then he realized it had to be Jewel, no doubt calling to apologize for being a no-show. He slipped round the side of the bar and Achilles handed him the phone. Once again, their fingers brushed and, once again, Danny felt a charge course through him. They stared at each other for a second. A look of pure desire. Danny took a deep breath and tried to compose himself.

'Hello?' he said into the phone.

'Danny?' The voice was deeper than Jewel's, with an Australian accent.

'Lachlan?' Later Danny would remember this moment. The split second in which he thought Lachlan was calling from work to see how the show had gone. The split second before his joy morphed into horror.

'I'm calling about Jewel, mate.'

'Oh, why?' Danny frowned.

'He was brought into A&E earlier. He's been beaten up. He's in a really bad way.'

Danny gulped, his mouth suddenly dry. He gripped the receiver, pressed it closer to his ear. 'We're on our way.'

Cat squeezed into the back of the cab next to Lil and Danny. She felt so sick she could barely breathe.

'Did … did Lachlan say anything about Jewel's injuries?' she stammered. 'How bad is it?'

'It's bad,' Danny replied grimly. 'Apparently he'd lost consciousness when they brought him in.'

'Oh, that poor, sweet boy!' Lil sighed. 'What do you think happened?'

'He was attacked,' Danny replied.

'I know, but why?'

Cat's heart sank as she thought back to the time earlier in the year when Jewel had been so shaken up by the homophobic guys who'd hassled him when he'd gone to buy a paper. Could this attack have had a similar motive? Or maybe he'd been mugged for his wallet. Either way, it was horrible.

'Don't worry, sweethearts, he'll be OK.' Lil, who was sitting in the middle of the back seat, took hold of Cat and Danny's hands and clasped them in hers. Despite looking slightly bizarre in her ugly sister wig and make-up, Lil gave Cat an unexpected feeling of comfort.

'I can't believe I was feeling pissed off at him for not turning up,' Danny said. 'I thought he was out having a good time with Pablo. Oh my God! Pablo! I wonder if he was with Jewel, if he was attacked, too.'

Cat stared blankly out of the cab window. Normally the sight of London at night made her feel so happy, but not tonight. Now the darkened streets seemed to be teeming with hidden menace. *Please, please, let Jewel be OK*, she silently prayed as they headed deeper into the city.

Although the Accident and Emergency unit was as busy as always, Lachlan felt numb to the chaos. Ever since he'd seen Jewel lying battered and bloody on that trolley, it was all he could think of.

He checked his notes and went out into the waiting area to call his next patient. 'Reg Hollingsworth?'

An old man in a fraying dressing gown and worn leather slippers slowly got to his feet. The sight of such frailty in the middle of the pandemonium made Lachlan's heart hurt. 'Are you OK to walk, sir?' he asked, hurrying over. 'Do you need a chair?'

'I'm OK. I had a bit of a fall, that's all. Tripped on my kitchen lino.'

There was a nasty gash on the old man's forehead. Lachlan dreaded to think how long he'd been waiting there patiently in the middle of the mayhem. Sometimes he felt that a trip to A&E could actually be worse for a patient's health than staying away would be. He pushed his negative thoughts from his head and prepared to adopt the usual cheery, matey tone he used with patients.

'You *have* been in the wars,' he said, taking hold of the old man's arm. 'Never mind, we'll soon have you patched up.'

'I fought in the war, you know.' The old man chuckled. 'And Hitler didn't trouble me half as much as that bleedin' kitchen lino!'

'Is that so?' Lachlan loved talking to old soldiers. They always seemed to have such a sage perspective on things. He was about to usher him into one of the cubicles when he heard someone calling his name – *Cat* calling his name.

He spun round to see her clad in some kind of Day-Glo rave outfit, accompanied by two bizarre-looking women in cartoon-style make-up and huge wigs.

'Blinkin' Nora!' Reg exclaimed. 'I need me specs. I think I might be seeing things.'

'Well, that makes two of us,' Lachlan muttered.

'Lachlan, sweetheart!' one of the cartoon women cried and he realized it was Lil.

'Strewth, it's my housemates.'

'Don't suppose you've got a room going spare?' Reg chuckled.

'Trust me, mate, you might have seen off Hitler but I wouldn't fancy your chances against these guys.'

Cat and the others came racing over. 'Where is he?' Cat asked. Beneath her brightly coloured make-up she looked terrified. Lachlan fought the instinctive urge to hug her. Everything had changed between them since that night in the kitchen with Justin. It was as if a wall had gone up between them.

'How is he? Is there any news?' Danny asked, looking equally scared. 'Was he with Pablo? Has he been hurt, too?'

'No, he was on his own. They've taken him up to surgery,' Lachlan said.

'Surgery?' Cat exclaimed.

'What's wrong with him?' Danny asked.

'He's suffered a serious trauma to the head and bleeding on the brain.'

'Oh no!' Beneath her huge false eyelashes, Lil's eyes filled with tears. 'That poor boy.'

'Is there somewhere we can go and wait for him?' Danny asked.

'Yes, you need to go to the second floor, the Critical Care unit. Tell them you're his friends.'

'We'll tell them we're his family,' Lil said firmly.

As Danny took a sip of the insipid hospital coffee, his mind flicked back through a montage of memories of Jewel. He remembered how he'd initially been so dismissive of the nervous young man who'd appeared on the doorstep of 27 Diamond Street wanting to rent the box room. He'd had no idea back then how much Jewel would come to mean to him. It had been so exciting to see him grow into the person he always should have been, and such an honour to feel that he, Danny, might have helped in some small way to encourage Jewel's metamorphosis. But at what cost? What if Jewel had been the victim of a homophobic attack? What if he'd have been safer if Danny hadn't encouraged him to dress so flamboyantly? Danny's stomach churned with dread.

Cat started pacing up and down the small waiting room. Lil was sitting cross-legged in her chair, with her eyes closed and her hands in the prayer position – a weird hybrid of ugly sister and devout nun. Danny didn't care. Right now Jewel needed all the help he could get. A nurse had come out to see them about an hour ago to tell them that Jewel was still unconscious following surgery. She'd said they should go home and get some rest, but they'd all refused.

'You'll have to carry me out in a casket first,' Lil had said, which had struck Danny as a tad melodramatic, but the nurse had been lovely about it.

'I hate this,' Cat said. 'I just wish we could see him.'

'I'm trying to tune into his energy, sweetheart,' Lil said, her eyes still closed. 'So I can get a message to him cosmically.'

'Really, how do you do that?' Cat asked.

Oh God, don't encourage her, Danny thought with a sigh, although he couldn't help slipping his own message to Jewel into the ether, just in case: *Come on, darling, please pull through.*

'I've summoned his aura into my consciousness,' Lil said, 'and I'm requesting that the source of the highest truth and wisdom opens a portal of communication. I'm asking them to tell him, "Come on sweetheart, wake the fuck up!"'

Just at that moment, a nurse appeared in the doorway. She stared at Lil for a second, then cleared her throat. 'Are you here for Jewel Brown?'

'Yes.' Danny's voice came out dry and raspy.

'Would you like to come and see him?'

'Has he woken up?' Cat asked, her voice trembling.

The nurse shook her head. 'But sometimes it helps for the patient to hear the voices of loved ones.'

Danny put down his coffee and got to his feet, unsure if he'd ever felt so frightened.

It seemed as if every thought in Cat's mind had been compressed down into one little word, being repeated over and over again. *Please, please, please, please*, she begged any higher power that might be out there and listening. *Please make my friend better. Please, please, please, please.*

As they followed the nurse into a dimly lit room and she saw Jewel lying in a bed wired up to bleeping, flashing machines, the enormity of what had happened hit her like a juggernaut. The top of Jewel's head was wrapped in a snowy white dressing, and the skin around his right eye had swollen to the size and colour of a damson.

'Oh, Jewel, oh, sweetheart.' Lil went over to the bed and gently stroked his hand. 'Jewel, can you hear us? Come, come.' She beckoned Cat and Danny over. 'Cat and Danny are here, too, sweetheart. We're all here for you.'

Cat looked at one of the machines beside the bed. With its bright green line pulsing across the screen, it was something she'd seen in countless hospital shows and films – all too often in death scenes. She pushed the thought from her mind and looked back at Jewel.

'Come on, sweetheart, you can do this,' Lil continued, her voice soft and soothing. She turned to Danny. 'Maybe he could do with one of your pep talks,' she whispered.

'Oh, er, yes, OK.' Danny moved to the other side of the bed. 'Well, darling, you certainly know how to miss a first night in style!' He gently took hold of Jewel's other hand. 'Your costumes went down a storm, darling. Everyone loved them. So you'd better wake up. The theatre world needs you. One of the journos who was there has asked if they can feature you in an article.'

'Seriously?' Cat whispered.

Danny nodded. 'Yes, *Time Out* are doing a piece about up-and-coming designers in London.'

The room began to swim as Cat's eyes filled with tears. 'Come on, Jewel,' she said, fighting to keep her voice level. 'You're about to get your big break. We need to go out dancing again to celebrate, paint the town red.'

'Paint it red sequins,' Danny said with a laugh, but it sounded forced. 'Come on, Jewel, you're far too fabulous for this hospital bed.'

'My spirit guide is coming through,' Lil muttered. 'He wants us to pray for Jewel.' She held her hand out to Cat.

As Lil clasped her hand, Cat felt a strange sensation of peace come over her. She closed her eyes and, even though she wasn't exactly sure who or what they were praying to, she began to pray with every molecule in her body.

It was as if Jewel was suspended in murky seawater, heavy with salt. His body was drifting, sinking. Down, down, deep into a darker place. He wasn't sure if it was a safe place. He wasn't sure of anything. He couldn't feel anything other than this strange, dead-limbed weightlessness. He couldn't open his eyes, he couldn't speak. Was he asleep? He knew there was light, somewhere far above him, above the surface of this strange sea he'd found himself adrift in. But he was sinking. Deeper and deeper into the velvety darkness and the beautiful silence. There was nothing to fear in this place. No need to worry. All he had to do was give in. And then –

'Fabulous ...' a voice cut through. A man's voice. Deep.

'Dancing ... red ...' a different voice, drifting down, like notes of music on the water.

But the voices were so far above him. Too far above him. He let his body sink further and the voices grew quieter.

And then a strange noise, a louder noise. What kind of noise? A rhythmic, low chanting. There was something hypnotic about it. Magnetic. Pulling him up by his mind. Back up through the darkness, towards the light. And now he could feel the light, like sunshine upon his face. And now his entire being was craving it. He willed himself up, higher and higher. He felt something twitch. Was it part of him? It twitched again. And then there was a voice. A woman's voice, deep and gravelly.

'That's it, sweetheart, you can do it.' He knew the voice. He loved the voice. He wanted to be with the voice. He kept willing himself up, higher and higher. And there was the twitch again. And the sensation of being held. Being squeezed, so gently. It was coming from a part of him. A distant part of him. Somewhere at the very limits of his body. He had a body. He was in a body. It was his hand. Awareness began trickling back. Someone was squeezing his hand. Tighter and tighter. Pulling him back and up. Higher and higher and –

'He's opened his eyes!' The musical voice exclaimed.

'Oh, thank God!' The man's voice.

'Oh, sweetheart, welcome back.' The gravelly woman's voice. The woman who had saved him.

Thirty-five

'Happy Christmas, everyone!' Danny cried, raising his glass of 'Christmas Cheer' – a cocktail Lil had created especially for the occasion. He didn't know what was in it, and he felt certain he was better off not knowing, but it tasted delicious, despite its rather off-putting shade of canary yellow.

'Happy Christmas!' the others replied, raising their glasses.

Danny looked around the table at his housemates with the pride of a loving father admiring his brood. At least, this was how he imagined a loving father might feel. Cat was to his left, resplendent in a vintage, emerald-green velvet dress, her hair cascading over her shoulders in long curls, glowing amber in the flickering light of the candles on the table. Lachlan was sitting opposite her, to Danny's right, looking happy and relaxed and clean-shaven. Pete was next to Lachlan, in his trademark black trousers and polo neck, jotting something in his notebook. Clearly the poetry muse didn't stop for anything, not even Christmas.

Across the table from Pete, and next to Cat, sat Jewel, looking delicate and elfin, with his dark hair newly cropped. Although it had been a month since Jewel had been attacked, he still hadn't put back on all of the weight he'd lost while in hospital, and his cheekbones were more prominent than ever. Danny allowed his gaze to linger on Jewel for a moment, full of gratitude that Jewel was almost back to a full recovery. He was still too frail to be able to work, but he was alive and getting stronger by the day, and that was all that mattered. Pablo moved his chair closer to Jewel's, his long fringe falling forwards as he looked down and took hold of Jewel's hand. They'd been inseparable since Jewel came home from hospital. Danny was glad. Jewel needed all the love and support he could get in order to recuperate.

At the very end of the table, opposite Danny, sat Darius, clad in a Santa hat with a flashing bauble on the tip. Danny couldn't help giving a wry grin. He wasn't sure if it was the effect of Lil's Christmas Cheer or the Christmas spirit generally, but he'd definitely warmed to Darius over the past few months. The fact that he'd been going down a storm in the panto as the comical Prince Charming definitely helped.

'How's the goat doing? I'm starving,' Darius called over to Lil, who was standing by the stove, stirring a huge pot.

'It's almost ready, sweetheart,' Lil replied.

Having curried goat for Christmas dinner had been Lil's idea. 'Turkey is so passé,' she'd told them all the week before, 'and besides, we've been there, done that back in the summer.' She'd then offered to cook them a curry that one of Bob Marley's cousins had allegedly taught her how to make when she'd allegedly spent a summer in Jamaica. As with all of Lil's tales, Danny was inclined to take it with a huge pinch of salt, but there was no denying the curry smelled delicious. He grinned as he took in Lil's outfit. She'd really pulled out all the stops for Christmas, rocking a ruby-coloured ball gown, complete with a crown of mistletoe woven into her silver hair.

'Danny, could you give me a hand dishing up?' she asked.

'Of course, darling.' Danny took a swig of his drink and went over to join her.

Lachlan glanced around the kitchen, trying really hard not to let his gaze linger on Cat, who was looking all kinds of sexy in a figure-hugging green velvet dress. She looked like a princess, which was not the kind of thought Lachlan would ever normally have. He hoped Lil hadn't spiked the Christmas cocktail with anything dodgy. But the truth was, he was already high on the fact that he'd now started three weeks of annual leave and would be flying to Australia in the morning. Ever since he'd had his breakthrough about not blaming himself for Michelle's death, he'd felt the urge to go back home and see his folks. As Cat laughed at something Jewel said he glanced back at her and felt a twinge of disappointment. It was because of Cat that he'd had his breakthrough. She'd got him to see the error of his ways, but because of his stupidity that night with Justin, and boasting about kissing her like he was in some kind of dick-waving contest, he'd blown it. Cat had been perfectly polite to him ever since, but all of the warmth, all of the banter they used to share was gone. He sighed. It was the one cloud obscuring what had become the relatively sunny landscape of his life.

'I can't believe we're having curried goat for Christmas dinner,' Cat giggled.

'Yeah, well, as Lil said, we have already had roast turkey this year,' Jewel said.

Lachlan's disappointment over Cat faded as he watched Jewel grinning. He'd found out from colleagues who'd treated Jewel at the hospital that they'd feared losing him at one point. He obviously hadn't shared this with any of his housemates, but it had given him a reason to feel grateful every single day since. Jewel had told him that he and Pablo had had an argument and Pablo had stormed off right before Jewel got attacked. Seeing how Jewel hadn't held this against Pablo had also helped Lachlan. He couldn't help drawing parallels with the argument he'd had with Michelle right before her death. Seeing Jewel bear no bitterness towards Pablo helped reaffirm that Michelle wouldn't have blamed Lachlan, either.

'Our summer Christmas dinner was so much fun,' Cat said. 'That was our first night together. The night the Rough Diamonds met.'

'Rough Diamonds?' Lachlan asked.

'It's the name Jewel and I have for us housemates,' Cat replied, but without making eye contact with him.

Lachlan felt a twinge of hurt.

'Less of the rough, darling,' Danny said, raising an eyebrow before taking a pile of plates from the cupboard.

'I think it's the perfect name!' Lil stopped stirring her curry and clasped her hands together like an excited kid. 'We're all precious and dazzling like diamonds, but a little rough around the edges.'

'Speak for yourself!' Danny retorted.

'I can't believe how much has happened since we moved in together,' Cat said before taking a sip of her cocktail. God, her hair looked amazing in the candlelight. Lachlan forced himself to look away.

'Yes, life at 27 Diamond Street certainly hasn't been boring,' Jewel said. 'Although I wouldn't mind 1995 being a little bit quieter, to be honest.'

'I somehow doubt you're going to have a quiet year, darling, after that article in *Time Out*,' Danny said, as he began ladling steaming mounds of rice onto the plates.

'Yes, not now you're a "one to watch in the fashion world",' Cat added.

'I still can't believe they said that about me.' The tips of Jewel's cheeks flushed.

'I think we're all in for a bonzer year,' Lachlan said, taking another drink of his cocktail, which he had to say was going down a treat.

'Well, you certainly are, sweetheart,' Lil called over from the stove. 'Going back Down Under.'

'You … you're going back to Australia?' Cat stammered.

Lachlan nodded. He'd only booked his flight a few days ago and so far Lil was the only one he'd told.

'Awesome!' Jewel exclaimed. 'How long for?'

Lachlan shrugged. 'I'm not sure.'

'What? You might go back for good?' Cat was looking at him now, but it was impossible to read the expression in her eyes. Judging by her recent coldness towards him, he guessed she was probably relieved.

'I'm going to see how it goes.'

'I bet once you get back on the beach soaking up all that sunshine you're not going to want to come back,' Danny said.

Lachlan laughed. 'Yeah, you could have a point.' He looked back at Cat. She was staring down into her lap. Was it his imagination, or did she look disappointed?

'You're so lucky,' Jewel sighed. 'I wish I could afford to go somewhere hot.'

'We will go to Barcelona on holiday next year,' Pablo said, kissing him gently on the cheek.

'That's if I ever have enough money to go anywhere.' Jewel's smile faded. 'Right now, I don't even have enough for next month's rent.'

Lachlan's heart really went out to Jewel. While he'd been off sick, the show he'd been working on had come to a close and Jewel hadn't been strong enough yet to hit the job-hunting circuit.

'Don't you worry about that, sweetheart,' Lil said, ladling curry on top of the rice.

'Yeah, I'm sure if we all chip in something we can cover it for you,' Danny said.

'I don't mind paying a bit more for sleeping on the sofa,' Darius offered.

'There'll be no need for that,' Lil said.

'But I have to pay it,' Jewel said, looking stressed. 'We were so lucky getting away with that house inspection after the party. The landlord will definitely have a sense of humour failure if the rent's short next month.'

'Land*lady*,' Lil said, bringing the first of the dinners over to the table and placing it in front of Lachlan. It looked and smelled so delicious it took every sinew in his body not to grab his knife and fork and dive straight in.

'What do you mean, landlady?' Danny said. 'Denise isn't the owner of the house, darling, she just works for the letting agents.'

'I know.' Lil brought another couple of dinners over.

'But I'm sure the owner of the house is a man,' Danny said. 'Denise told me his name the last time I was at the agent's. Sir Something or other.'

'Sir Alexander Huntingdon-Davies.' Lil brought two more plates over.

'You know who he is?' Danny asked.

'Oh yes, I know him very well.' Lil served the final dinners and sat down next to Pete. 'OK, everyone, tuck in.'

But no one tucked in, they were all too busy staring at Lil.

'Who is he?' Cat asked. 'He sounds like a member of the aristocracy!'

'He is,' Lil said, taking a sip of her drink. 'Or rather, he was. He was also my father.'

'What?' Cat and Jewel cried in stereo.

'Lil, is this another of your tales?' Danny said with a sigh.

'What do you mean, tales? I can assure you, sweetheart, nothing but the truth ever passes from these lips. Apart from the time I told Janis Joplin that the lampshade she was wearing as a hat looked good on her. But that was only because I was trying to spare her feelings.'

'So, hang on a minute, if Sir Alexander was a member of aristocracy does that mean that you are, too?' Cat asked, wide-eyed.

'I'm afraid so, for my sins,' Lil replied, before taking a mouthful of curry. 'Oh my, this is divine. Do tuck in.'

Lachlan wasn't entirely sure what to make of Lil's revelation. And judging by the frown on Danny's face, he wasn't the only one.

'But, hang on,' Jewel said, eyes wide. 'If you're a member of the aristocracy what are you doing living in the attic room of a shared house – a house that your father owns.'

'Owned,' Lil said. 'I inherited it when he passed away.' She gestured at her curry with her fork. 'Enough of this boring logistical stuff. Let's have our Christmas goat!'

'You own this place?' Danny asked, staring at her incredulously.

Lil gave a dramatic sigh. 'I really don't see why we have to make such a big deal of it. I just wanted Jewel to know that he didn't have to worry if he couldn't pay the rent next month.'

'But why would you rent it out and live in the attic room?' Cat asked. 'It doesn't make sense.'

'Oh, it makes plenty of sense, sweetheart. Come on, don't let your curries get cold.'

Lachlan picked up his knife and fork, ready to dive in, but then Danny started speaking. Strewth! At this rate he was going to die of starvation!

'I don't suppose you have any way of proving all this?' Danny said. 'I don't mean to be rude, darling, but you can see why we might be struggling to believe this. It is a bit of a bombshell!'

Lil shook her head, looking seriously disappointed. 'I had been hoping that my word would be my bond, but if you insist.' She stood up and headed for the door. 'Back in a minute.'

Lachlan glanced around the table at the others, hoping they might now, finally, start eating, but they all sat motionless, looking gobsmacked. Apart from Pete, who was still scribbling away in his notebook.

'Do you think it is true?' Pablo whispered.

'I don't know,' Jewel replied. 'I mean, I really want it to be true because if it's not …'

'If it's not it means Lil is suffering from some kind of major delusion,' Cat murmured.

'I told you before, she took way too much acid back in the sixties,' Danny hissed. 'It's messed with her brain.'

'OK, ye of little faith,' Lil said, sweeping back into the room and placing an old scrapbook on the table in front of Danny.

Everyone stared at him in silent expectation. The silence only broken by a loud growl of hunger from Lachlan's stomach.

'Holy cow!' Danny exclaimed, as he opened the book.

Thirty-six

Jewel watched, spellbound, as Danny turned the pages of the old scrapbook Lil had given him. *What does it say?* he wanted to scream. Even by Diamond Street standards, the bombshells that had been dropped at this meal were earth-shattering, and they hadn't even begun eating! His glance moved from Danny to Lachlan, the only person at the table not staring at Danny, gazing longingly at his dinner instead. He couldn't believe that Lachlan might go back to Australia for good. From the way Cat's face had fallen when he broke the news, she couldn't believe it either. Just like Lil's revelation that she owned the house, this was a development Jewel never would have seen coming.

'Is this you with Mick Jagger?' Danny asked Lil, pointing to a yellowing newspaper clipping stuck inside the scrapbook.

'Yes, and there I am with dear, sweet David and his Spiders from Mars.' Lil pointed to a clipping on the opposite page.

'So you're the socialite Elizabeth Huntingdon-Davies?' Danny asked, reading from one of the clippings.

'I am indeed. Or I was, before I renounced the evils of the landed gentry.'

'Oh my God, let me see!' Unable to contain his curiosity a second longer, Jewel got up and went over to look at the picture.

Standing next to a whip-thin and extremely youthful David Bowie was a young woman with long hair, prominent cheekbones and cat-like eyes. Although the picture was black and white and faded, there was no denying that the woman looked a lot like a younger version of Lil.

'Wow, it really is you,' Jewel murmured.

'But I still don't understand,' Cat said. 'Why do you rent out all the rooms in this house if you own it? And why do you live in the attic?'

'There's nothing wrong with living in an attic,' Pete mumbled. 'Some of the world's foremost creative people did their greatest work in garrets.'

'Bloody hell, darling!' Danny exclaimed, looking at Lil. 'You really are a dark horse.'

Lil looked down into her lap. 'I just wanted to know what it felt like to have a family,' she said quietly.

'But you have a family,' Jewel said. 'The Huntingdon-Davieses.'

'Yes, and they were a bunch of cold and unfeeling arseholes.' Lil stabbed a piece of goat meat with her fork. 'They packed me off to boarding school at the age of eight, and let me tell you, it isn't all tuck boxes and high jinks à la Malory Towers in those places. It was brutal. And even when I got myself expelled when I was fifteen, they didn't want to know. My father was too busy building his empire and my mother had relocated to the Caribbean, along with her penchant for toy boy lovers and booze. They gave me a trust fund to live off and let me get on with it.'

'But I still don't get how you ended up here,' Cat said.

'Yes, why aren't you living in a fabulous riverside apartment in Chelsea?' Danny asked.

'Because I disowned my family and disinherited myself back when I turned thirty. And anyway, I wanted to live in Camden. Chelsea's full of yuppie idiots. I had more than enough of them in my childhood.'

'But …' Jewel broke off. He had so many questions he wasn't sure where to begin.

'My father gave me this house two years ago, right before he passed away. It was the only thing he left to me. The rest of his estate went to my step-siblings. The ones who didn't bring shame upon the family. The ones who are devoid of all personality. I was going to live here on my own, but it became lonely. And I needed a source of income. So I decided to rent out the rooms, and I realized that if I got the right tenants, maybe we could be our own little family.'

'Wow!' Jewel went back to his seat. He needed to sit down. Processing this shock development was using all of his energy.

'There were a couple of false starts,' Lil said. 'Like that pretentious man with the walking cane.'

'Oh God, Brendan,' Danny groaned.

'Yes, exactly. That's why I put you in charge of interviewing the others,' Lil said. 'I thought you might be a better judge of character.'

'So that's why Denise told me I was in charge,' Danny said.

Lil chuckled. 'Yes, I phoned her pretending to be my father's PA and told her to tell you.'

'And that's why we never got into trouble after the house inspection,' Jewel said.

Lil laughed. 'Oh yes, that was so funny. When Denise sent me the report I laughed my head off. Those photos!'

'But how did you get her report?' Cat asked.

'She sends all correspondence to a PO Box number – *my* PO Box number. When I got the inspection report I wrote back to her, as my father's PA of course, telling her that a little high jinks never hurt anybody.' Lil hooted with laughter. 'The looks on your faces when you thought you were all going to be evicted!'

'But you could have saved us all that stress!' Danny exclaimed. 'You could have told us then that you owned the place.'

Lil sighed. 'I didn't want things to change. I wanted you to see us as family. I wanted you to keep thinking of me as the batty old woman up in the eaves.'

'We still think that, darling, don't worry,' Danny grinned and shook his head. 'I need another drink.'

'Things won't change, we *are* family,' Jewel said, leaning across the table to give Lil's hand a squeeze. The truth was, ever since he'd heard Lil's voice pulling him back to consciousness that night in the hospital he'd felt a deep sense of connection to her that he'd never felt to any of his actual family members.

'Really?' Lil looked at him hopefully. 'You won't resent me for being a bourgeois property owner? You won't rise up and try to overthrow me?'

'You're our landlady, darling, not Marie Antoinette,' Danny replied.

'Strewth!' Lachlan said, grinning and shaking his head. 'This is definitely a Christmas to remember!'

'And it ain't over yet,' Darius said. 'God, I love living here. There's never a dull moment.'

'Strictly speaking, you don't actually live here,' Danny said. 'You're sleeping on our sofa.'

'Yeah, well, if Lachlan decides to stay in Australia I could always move into his room,' Darius said hopefully.

'Cheers, mate. Would you jump in my grave that fast?' Lachlan chuckled.

'I don't want you to stay in Australia,' Jewel said.

'He won't,' Lil said sagely.

'Oh, yeah?' Lachlan looked at her.

'Yes,' she replied firmly.

Jewel glanced at Cat to try to see what she was making of Lachlan's possible departure. She was pushing her fork around her plate but not eating, and it was safe to say she didn't look happy. Jewel sighed. He knew from their many heart-to-hearts that Cat was trying to teach Lachlan some kind of lesson, but surely now it was time for her to quit. It was clear to him that they both still really liked each other. It would be a tragedy of epic proportions if they lost each other because of their pigheadedness.

'Right, can we please eat our dinner?' Lil said.

'Yes!' Lachlan exclaimed.

'That depends,' Danny replied. 'Do you have any more bombshell revelations?'

'Not for today.' Lil smiled at him.

Cat played with her dinner listlessly. Although it looked and smelled amazing, ever since Lachlan had revealed that he was going to Australia and might never be coming back she'd completely lost her appetite. Not even the news that Lil was in fact some kind of society heiress and owned 27 Diamond Street could shake her from her gloom. She'd been distant with Lachlan since the altercation with Justin in the kitchen, but the truth was, in recent weeks, her anger at Lachlan had faded. All she'd needed was some time on her own, to focus on her dancing dreams and figure out who she was and what she wanted. Starring in *Cinderella*, and signing with Danny's agent, who'd already got her a role in a West End show starting in January, had all helped her regain her sense of identity. She'd been waiting for the opportunity to try to clear the air with Lachlan. Now it seemed as if she might never get that chance, and she was shocked at how devastating this prospect felt.

Just then, the doorbell rang.

'I think that might be dessert,' Danny said, getting to his feet.

'But we haven't even finished dinner yet,' Darius said.

'Yeah, and whose fault is that?' Danny grinned and shook his head at Lil then went out into the hall.

A few seconds later, he returned with Achilles, who was holding a large tray covered with a cloth.

'Oh, I'm sorry, did I come too soon?' Achilles asked, looking round the table at everyone's still full dinner plates.

'Very good of you to apologize,' Danny chuckled.

In spite of her gloom, Cat couldn't help smiling. Ever since Danny and Achilles had finally got it together, there'd been a new lightness about Danny, and she couldn't be happier for him.

'Would you like some curry, Achilles, sweetheart? There's loads left,' Lil asked.

'Yes, please.'

Cat shifted closer to Jewel so Achilles could sit between her and Danny.

'I brought some crackers,' Achilles said, producing a box of crackers from a carrier bag.

'Yes!' Pete yelled, causing everyone to jump. 'I love crackers,' he muttered, before looking back at his notebook.

'Me too!' Jewel exclaimed. 'Let's pull them.'

Once Achilles had handed out the crackers Cat turned to the people sitting on either side of her, but Jewel was pulling his with Pablo and Danny was pulling his with Achilles. Great. She glanced across the table at Lachlan. He was tentatively holding his cracker out to her, as if extending an olive branch. She gave him a weak smile and took the end of the cracker and pulled. There was a loud crack as she rebounded back in her chair and saw that she'd won.

'What did you get?' Lachlan asked.

She tipped the contents of the cracker into her hand. A paper crown, a joke and a fish made from clear red film. 'A Fortune Teller Miracle Fish apparently,' she said, reading the slip of paper it came with.

'Oh, I love them!' Jewel exclaimed. 'Put it in your hand, let it tell your fortune.'

Cat placed the fish in the palm of her hand. Instantly, the head and the tail started moving.

'What does that mean?' Lachlan asked.

Cat shrugged and looked at the instructions on the paper. Her cheeks flushed.

'What does it mean?' Jewel asked.

'Apparently, I'm in love,' she muttered, hurriedly placing the fish on the table.

'I knew it!' Lil exclaimed.

Cat shot her a daggers look. Now was not the time for one of Lil's psychic interventions.

'I thought you and Justin were history,' Darius boomed at her from the end of the table.

'We are,' Cat replied firmly.

For some annoying reason the others had all stopped talking and were looking at her, especially Lachlan, who was staring at her intently. She wasn't sure why he was interested. After all, he was leaving tomorrow. Clearly he didn't care a thing about her anymore. Her embarrassment grew, causing her face to flush even brighter. The thought of Lachlan noticing this was too much to bear.

'I … I think I might just go and get a breath of fresh air,' she stammered. 'The curry's making me overheat.'

'Sure it isn't the menopause?' Darius chortled.

'I can categorically confirm it isn't the menopause,' she muttered. Great, now everyone was probably imagining her on her period. She hurried through the living room and into the backyard, taking a welcome gasp of the cool, crisp air. Maybe she was suffering from PMT, though. Why else would she be so overemotional?

'Are you OK?' A voice, *Lachlan's* voice, said quietly from behind her.

She turned to see him standing in the doorway.

'So, you're going away?' was all she could manage to say.

He nodded.

'And you might not come back?'

'I haven't decided anything yet. It kind of depends.'

'On what?'

He shifted uncomfortably. 'On whether I have anything to come back to.'

'You mean your job?'

He shook his head. 'I still have my job.'

'What do you mean, then?' She could barely breathe as she waited for his response.

'Look, Cat, I'm so sorry for what happened that night with Justin, for what I said. I was an idiot.'

She couldn't help nodding.

'But he was winding me up so much, the way he was speaking to you.'

Some residual anger prickled at her skin. 'I didn't need you to defend me. And I certainly didn't need you to tell him you'd kissed me.'

'I know. I know. And I'm sorry.'

She nodded. 'I'm sorry, too.'

He cleared his throat and looked down at the floor. 'I know this sounds

343

weird, given that we live together but … I miss you.'

Relief bubbled up inside of her. 'You do?'

He nodded. 'I miss our chats and I miss making you laugh. I even miss that camo-vile tea.'

'Camomile!' she corrected.

'Easy mistake.' He looked at her and grinned.

'You gave me my life back,' he said softly.

'How do you mean?'

'The things you said, that day on Primrose Hill. You got me to stop blaming myself over Michelle.'

'You should never have been blaming yourself.'

He came closer and her breath caught in the back of her throat. 'Have I blown it?' he asked softly.

'Blown what?'

'Things with you. I need to know before I go.'

Everything seemed so silent and still all of a sudden. Even the constant soundtrack from the surrounding Camden streets seemed to have faded to nothing.

'No,' she whispered.

'I haven't?' His face lit up and his joy was infectious. She felt it fizzing through the air into her.

'You almost blew it,' she said, not wanting him to get off too lightly. 'But no, you haven't blown it and I don't want you to go. Well, I want you to see your family and friends obviously …' *DON'T START RAMBLING!* she warned herself inside her head. 'I want you to have fun. But not too much fun. Not so much fun you never want to come back …' *STOP RAMBLING!* 'I want you to want to come back.' Finally she stopped and drew breath.

'Is that so?' He grinned at her.

She nodded.

'And you're not just interested in me for my arm hair?'

'Oh no!' she groaned at the memory.

'I mean, I'm more than an object, you know. I do have a personality beneath these arm hairs.'

'Really?' She attempted to give him a pointed stare but couldn't help grinning.

'Well, this is an interesting development,' he said.

'Isn't it?' She was enjoying this now. Slipping back into their verbal sparring felt like the most natural thing in the world.

'So, are you going to come here, or do I have to come there?' he asked, looking at the short distance between them.

'Oh, you have to come here,' she replied.

In a second, he was standing right in front of her.

'I was wondering if it would be OK if …' he murmured, getting closer and closer.

'If?' she whispered.

'If I kissed you.'

'I think that would be very OK,' she replied.

As his lips touched hers she heard a cheer ring out from inside the house.

'What the hell?' she broke away to see Lil and the others crowded around the door.

Cat shook her head and burst out laughing.

'The Fortune Teller Miracle Fish never lies,' Lil said with a wink.

'Now that you two have finally sorted yourselves out, can we please go back inside? It's freezing,' Danny said.

'I'll warm you up,' Achilles said, putting an arm round his shoulders.

'You two are so cute,' Jewel said.

'Talking of kissing, did I ever tell you about the time I kissed Andrew Lloyd Webber?' Darius asked.

'Yes!' they all cried in unison.

As they followed the others into the house, Lachlan took hold of Cat's hand. 'I don't want this to just be a kissing or an arm hair thing,' he whispered.

'Can you please stop mentioning the arm hair? I was high!' Cat giggled.

'Whatever.' He stopped and pulled her close. 'Look, I'm not very good at talking about stuff like this, but I really like you. I want this to be the real deal.'

'I want that, too,' she said, holding him tighter.

As Achilles arranged the desserts on the table, Danny filled everyone's glasses with fizz. He smiled as Cat and Lachlan came back in, their cheeks flushed. It was great to see them back on again. He only hoped it lasted this time!

'Here you go, Lil, I didn't even need it,' Lachlan said, handing Lil back her sprig of mistletoe.

'I had a feeling you wouldn't, sweetheart, not with your natural charm,' she replied with a wink.

'Not to mention my arms,' Lachlan muttered.

'Shut up!' Cat nudged him playfully.

'Happy Christmas, everyone,' Danny said, passing out the glasses. 'Here's to the Rough Diamonds – and their special guests,' he added, raising his glass to Achilles and Pablo.

'To the Rough Diamonds,' everyone echoed, raising their glasses. All apart from Pete, who raised his notebook.

'Would anyone like to hear my acrostic poem titled *Santa is Dead*? An acrostic poem is where the first letter of each line spells out the title,' he explained.

There was a moment's silence and then everyone started laughing.

'Good grief, darling! Scrooge just called, he wants his poem back,' Danny quipped. But the truth was, he felt so completely and utterly happy in that moment, he even felt an abundance of love for Eeyore Pete and his poetry. Danny's choreography career was on track, he was enjoying the first buds of what could hopefully be a special something instead of just a fling and, thanks to not-so-trippy Lil, he'd acquired a surrogate family. Yes, life was good. As he brought his glass to his lips, he drank to many more dances and dreams on Diamond Street.

Acknowledgements

W hat a great joy it was to finally have the opportunity to write my very first novel. Fiction is such a great way of expressing yourself with no holds barred and being able to use life experience and beyond to create fantastic characters and bring them to life so they are free to jump from the page was a true joy.

I must thank the following people, without whom, this book would simply not have come to fruition. My manager Gavin Barker for being such fun and believing in me all those years ago when he poached me from another agent. The oh-so-extremely talented and irrepressible Siobhan Curham for making a huge contribution in construction and advice. Louise Dixon at Michael O'Mara Books for encouraging me and giving me the confidence to believe in myself. My fiancé Jonathan for putting up with me over the years, picking me up when I was down, always smiling and bringing enormous joy into my life. My sister Sue for being honest, a true inspiration to me all my life and a talented writer in her own right. Clifford Leo Harris 'Clifftops' one of the original 'Heartbreakers' for being such a true, good friend and for sticking out in 'The Heartbreak Hotel' until the very end.